I0606711

The last think Frank saw before everything faded to black was his partner. Michelle wasn't moving.

It all went down in a flash, yet played out in slow motion. A horn honked at a strutting prostitute. A woman walking a poodle was jaywalking. A homeless man was looking through a garbage can. A street performer was banging on small containers. Innocent pedestrians were crossing at the corner. Elijah reached into the backseat.

Frank felt the heat before hearing the thunderous detonation. The ground rocked beneath him. No chance to react, to comprehend, he found himself airborne, propelled over the top of the Nissan, arms instinctively flailing about, his hands reaching out desperately but grabbing nothing.

Frank was flung like a small bird in a twister tearing across the plains. Slammed headfirst into a brick wall, his brain felt like it'd been repositioned within his skull.

Unlike his partner who served two tours, Frank had no military background. He'd heard the expression *war zone* but never grasped it. Until now. The explosion destroyed everything in sight.

Relieved to be on solid ground, Frank intuitively sat up while getting his bearings. His stomach undulated. Reflexively, he reached for his sidearm but his muscles were nonresponsive. The message from his brain blocked. He again saw Johnny in his mind. The entire right side of Frank's body was numb.

He found himself unconcerned with the Leaches' twenty. Frank was cold, losing sensation in his arms and legs. His vision constricted, the periphery closing around him. He felt his upper body weaken…weaken and found himself flat against the concrete sidewalk.

Peacefulness came over him as his weighty eyelids lowered. Abby, Jake, and Ashley appeared in a fog but, as the hazy image of his family dissipated, his head lobbed right.

Michelle was twisted abnormally. He tried to call to her but he couldn't get air into his lungs.

A bomb rocks West Hollywood. And with that, LA joins the brotherhood of American cities hammered by the harsh fist of terrorism—a dozen murdered and numerous injured, including Frank Grace, a cop with a checkered past, who once again is at the wrong place at the wrong time.

While recuperating, Detective Grace is handpicked by the police chief to do whatever necessary, legal or not, to swiftly apprehend the perpetrators. Chief Kent refuses to stand by while his city burns and his legacy is tarnished amidst the growing rage and prejudicial violence spreading across Los Angeles.

Along with his principled partner, Michelle Santana, Frank begins to unravel a perilous network of deceit, dishonesty, and distrust. A fellow officer with a shady history, a judge with a dubious past, and a high-class prostitute are abducted. A homeless man is murdered. All are seemingly unrelated to the terrorist attack. Or are they? Frank Grace doesn't think so.

With the feds breathing down his neck, the chief pressuring him, the knowledge that even longtime allies can't be trusted, and another attack looming, Frank realizes time is running out. Exposing the truth may further damage his already-tainted reputation, end his career, and cost him his life. Is he just a pawn in someone else's game?

KUDOS for *Sacrificing the Pawn*

In *Sacrificing the Pawn* by Rob Silverman, Frank Grace is a LAPD homicide detective, unjustly disgraced for his handling of a restaurant hostage situation four years ago. Now he just tries to get through day without drawing attention. Unfortunately, that is not to be. He and his partner Michelle Santana are at ground zero when a terrorist bomb goes off in Hollywood. Already in trouble again for "harassing" a couple of low lifes, at least according to the men's lawyer, Frank is surprised when the chief of police calls him personally and asks him to take the terrorist case. Frank and Michelle are also working on a rash of kidnappings and murder, which Frank fears may be related somehow to the terrorist attack, but he has no proof. Now Frank's family is being threatened and his career is on the line. He needs to find the perpetrators and fast. The story is a well-written, fast-paced, police-procedural mystery/thriller that will keep you on the edge of your seat from beginning to end. A great read. ~ *Taylor Jones, Reviewer*

Sacrificing the Pawn, A Frank Grace Mystery, by Rob Silverman is the story of a homicide detective in LA who has a penchant for being in the wrong place at the wrong time. Frank Grace is still hounded by the press for his "mishandling" of a hostage situation in a restaurant four years ago, which resulted in a blood bath. Now Frank and his partner, Michelle Santána, are questioning a couple of thugs in West Hollywood when a terrorist bomb goes off, practically in their laps. Frank believes the two losers he was questioning have something to do with the bomb, as well as a series of abductions and murders. A female cop, a judge, and a high-priced hooker have been kidnapped, a successful business executive and a homeless man murdered. The FBI has been called in, so Frank is stunned when the police chief tasks him to solve the case, "whatever it takes." As Frank closes in on the truth, he and his family are threatened, along with his partner, making him even more determined to solve the case and put an end to it all. *Sacrificing the Pawn* is a gritty, down-to-earth, mystery-thriller, giving us a glimpse of the hard, unrelenting, and often unfair, job of a big city cop and the scum they have to deal with. A hard-hitting, poignant, and thought-provoking story, with plenty of twists and turns, this one is hard to put down. *~ Regan Murphy, Reviewer*

ACKNOWLEDGEMENTS

Sitting down at the outset of creating a work of fiction is thrilling, exhilarating, challenging, daunting, and over-whelming—all at the same time. Writing is a solitary journey, where you travel to the deepest corners of your mind, limited only by your own imagination. However, it *is* necessary to have assistance along the way. I'm deeply indebted to several people who encouraged me, kept me grounded, and *sacrificed* a little of their own time.

Thanks to: Brian Wright, Denice Duffin, Barb Blutt, Bruce Banks, Lisa Trachtman-Silverman, Kristy Micak, Amy Feiner, Rex Richardson, Alethea Lawson, Tonya Royston, Bonnie Vaughan, Katie Compton, Kristina Cavener, and Terece LaBruce.

It's not a good sign for an author to be at a loss for words but I am when it comes to a select few who went above and beyond what I could've asked for. Extra special thanks to Heather Craft, Georgia Stephens, Brad Lapitan, and Lori Edens. Hope you enjoy seeing your name in a novel.

I'd also like to thank Vince Flynn (1966-2013) who revealed to me how magical and captivating writing could be, who demonstrated how words on a page could make my heart beat faster in my chest, a man who *sacrificed* what he knew to pursue his lifelong dream, and who overcame personal obstacles far greater than his protagonist Mitch Rapp ever could.

What you're about to read would not have happened if it wasn't for the great team at Black Opal Books. Thanks to Faith, the best and most patient editor an author can hope to have, Jack for the artwork, Arwen, Lauri, and everyone else. You guys rock!

Sacrificing the Pawn

A Frank Grace Mystery

Rob Silverman

A Black Opal Books Publication

GENRE: THRILLER/SUSPENSE/MYSTERY-DETECTIVE

First Publication: JANUARY 2017

Published by Black Opal Books **http://www.blackopalbooks.com**

DEDICATION

My dad always told me, "If you want to write, you have to read." It took a couple of decades, but I finally listened. No one could tell a story like he could and, hopefully, I inherited some of that from him.

My mom never stopped believing in me and encouraging me through all the typical self-doubt writers battle with.

This novel is dedicated to them.

"Revolutions, our own included, require a certain amount of rationing, a certain amount of calluses, a certain amount of sacrifice." ~ *Lee Harvey Oswald*

Preface

Abby Grace retreated from the corpse and stared at her blood-soaked hands.

She evaluated the situation, scrutinizing the crushed expressions and million-mile stares of her defeated colleagues. Forlornly, they looked at the individual who would make the call.

Three words.

From her vantage point, the one in charge appeared detached, hesitant. And dangerously young. Without raising his head, his vacant eyes swept the room, seeking affirmation, seeking guidance, seeking *something*. What he received were empty glares. This was completely on him.

Abby bowed her head, glimpsed the crimson patches dotting her scrubs like strawberries sprouting in a field. The lone sound reverberating within the frosty operating room was the incessant droning of a steady beep. She'd heard it plenty, yet never became accustomed to it.

One of her coworkers, a grandmotherly type affectionately dubbed NeeNee, stepped right, flipped the switch on the heart monitor, and thrust the room into tomb-like stillness. "Doctor?"

Three words.

He shifted his glance from his nursing team and anesthesiologist to the silent machines and stagnant devices that now taunted him. His staff was stock-still, awaiting his next directive. UCLA, M-CATS, a three year clinical rotation, three more specializing in cardiovascular surgery and a fellowship back east at New York-Presbyterian didn't mean a thing. Cardiothoracic surgeon Cody Ladd was well trained, well educated, and damn well talented. Still, he was unable to speak three words.

Abby noticed a young nurse roll her eyes and begin tapping the floor with the heel of her hospital-issued booties while impatiently eying the wall-mounted clock.

Dr. Ladd yanked the surgical mask away from his face. A deep inhalation and through quivering lips he grumbled, "One-seventeen," followed by three words: "Time of death."

His best efforts thwarted, Ladd indignantly stormed from the OR. Before the door closed behind him, the toe-tapper remarked, "One seventeen already? No wonder my stomach's growling. What's for lunch?"

A handful of RN's began debating the pros and cons of the cafeteria versus eateries within walking distance of St. Bartholomew. Taking the lead, NeeNee dabbed the pallid lifeless face with a baby wipe and began prepping the patient for transport. "Call the boys in the basement. Let 'em know we've got one."

"Right away," replied an overly eager pre-med student.

Abby stood beside the inert form while a colleague withdrew the now unnecessary endotracheal tube from the decedent's mouth. "Sweetie," NeeNee said from across the table. "My back's killin' me somethin' fierce. If you wouldn't mind, unlock the wheels for me."

Abby dutifully nodded but did not immediately react. Instead, she sympathetically held the being's shoulder with one hand, closed her eyes, and, while clutching the crucifix draped from her neck, prayed for his soul.

Minutes later, Abby trailed her colleagues from the enervated room. To her right, three nurses bounced their way toward the lunchroom, discussing BLT's and Tuna Melts. To her left, two others headed for the smoking patio.

Cody Ladd stood alone. Shoulders slouched, he leaned, deflated, against the wall.

"Dr. Ladd?" Abby murmured. He'd been on staff almost one year but conversations between them were sparse.

It took the gifted surgeon a beat to return from his contemplative state. Upon raising his head, Abby was surprised to see reddened eyes.

Ladd was a good-looking fellow with fetching bone structure who carried himself with the confidence of his own handsomeness. Abby found him to be somewhat arrogant, bordering on conceit at times. But she knew swagger was a job requirement for professionals who played God.

"I've never been good at telling the family."

Fearful of sounding trite, Abby replied, "Sometimes it's out of our hands, Doctor." As soon as she finished, she realized her words came off...well, trite.

Ladd pulled on his chin and noticed Abby's crucifix. "Out of our hands," he mirrored. His eyes traveled from Abby's unblemished skin and supple neck to a stunning face, high cheekbones, and penetrating cobalt eyes. He felt less manly, displaying emotion in the presence of such beauty. "Thanks," he sighed meekly, gazing at the endless corridor that led to other ORs, radiology, recovery, and a bank of express elevators to ICU. And the waiting room. "Will you come with me?"

"Where, Dr. Ladd?"

"Cody, please." He cocked his head. "To inform the family. I've never...felt comfortable doing that."

Abby's throat tightened and she shot a look at the foreboding hallway, hesitated.

His eyes were weak, his voice pleading. When she felt his soft hand clasping her forearm, she swallowed.

"Your husband's a police officer, right?" Ladd said.

Abby furrowed a brow, wondering where this was going. "Homicide detective, yes."

"I'm sure you're more familiar with this, with...you know, dealing with death, than I am."

Abby smirked. Ladd was doing a piss-poor job of persuading her. "It's not like Frank brings home victims and stretches them across the kitchen table during dinner."

Ladd laughed, louder than necessary. "I'd truly appreciate your support."

Abby exhaled. "Give me a moment to change. I don't want the family seeing his blood."

Dr. Ladd was first through the airtight doors, Abby at his heels. They were met by dozens of concerned eyes laced with fear and uncertainty, hope and terror.

Ladd turned to Abby who scanned the crowd searching for a familiar face. "Mendelheim family," she called questioningly.

From the center of the room an elderly female was assisted to her feet by a young couple, the twenty-something woman clutching a newborn. The aged lady creaked to an upright position—as upright as she could manage. Her back was humped by the weight of her years. Relying on a cane, she threaded her way between strangers and inched nearer to Abby and Dr. Ladd, her ashen expression obvious as she tottered closer.

"I'm Sara Mendelheim," the frail woman declared in a surprisingly firm tone. "This is my son, David, his wife Katie, and my granddaughter, Chaya."

Ladd stalled. "Chaya?"

"Yes." She beamed proudly. "Chaya is Hebrew for life."

Life. He gulped, delayed another moment, then stated, "I'm Dr. Ladd. This is my assistant, Abigail Grace."

Sara angled her head and looked down the hallway behind them. "Can I see my Lenny now?"

Lenny. Lenny Mendelheim. The patient had a name.

Ladd opened his mouth, closed it. Opened it again but no words came out. He peeked at the newborn, drew his eyes away, stole a glance at Abby for help.

"Is Dad okay?" David asked apprehensively.

Ladd swallowed. "Mrs. Mendelheim."

"Yes?"

A pause, this one longer. "Mrs. Leonard Mendelheim?"

The woman chuckled nervously. "Yes?"

Abby noticed that David seized his mother's elbow, as the family instinctively huddled closer. As if on cue, the infant began crying. Then Abby frowned when Dr. Ladd unexpectedly pulled his phone from his pocket and pretended to read a text that wasn't there. The phone was off. "I'm very sorry, but I need to take this call," he said. "Nurse Grace, would you mind?"

Before Abby could react, Ladd scurried away to an area off-limits to family. Wide-eyed and abandoned, she pivoted and was greeted with inquisitive countenances.

"Miss," Sara Mendelheim said. "I'd like to see my husband now. St. Bart's is one of the finest hospitals in Los Angeles. But I want Lenny to come home. He needs to finish working on our tomato garden."

Abby reached out for the frail woman's papery hands. "I'm very sorry."

Three words.

⋐⋑⋐⋑

"Bastard!" Abby yelled while pacing. "That chicken-shit little bastard!"

"Take a breath, relax."

"Relax?" she clipped. "Amita, he left me there. It was *his* patient, *his* surgery. And he just walks away and leaves *me* to tell the family? That…that…"

"Bastard?" Amita smiled, took a drag on her Marlboro.

Unsure if she wanted to laugh or scream, Abby looked longingly at Amita's hand. Forty years old but, for the first time since adolescence, she craved nicotine. She needed to hit something, be it a cigarette vending machine, a bottle of whiskey, or better yet, Dr. Ladd.

"Ladd's a pompous ass," Amita pointed out unnecessarily." Everyone knows that."

"I agree," Abby countered in a quieter tone. "But so what? Just 'cause he doesn't like giving bad news, he shouldn't dump it on me. It wasn't my operation."

"You going to answer that?"

"Huh?"

Amita indicated Abby's pocket.

Only now hearing her chirping phone, Abby checked the display but didn't recognize the number. She returned the phone to her scrubs. "Do you think I should go to the head of nursing or the chief surgeon on staff? Ladd's actions are just…inexcusable."

"Not to mention unprofessional."

"Yes, unprofessional *and* inexcusable."

"Bastard," Amita said and winked.

Abby smiled, her rage temporarily dissipating.

"Just be careful."

Abby frowned.

Her friend hesitated before continuing. "You're good. You've been a good nurse for almost ten years. But…" Her words trailed off.

"But what?"

"You and I? We're just nurses. When push comes to shove, we're easily replaceable. Cardiothoracic surgeons are not."

Abby began to respond but instead cried, "*What?*" She jerked her cell from the pouch of her scrubs and answered in a clipped tone. "Hello?"

Amita took an extended drag, flicked the butt toward the ashcan, missed, and watched the color drain from Abby's face.

"Yes…Hi, Lieutenant Gallardo." With the phone pressed against her ear, she looked at Amita with helpless frightened eyes.

Amita said a silent Hosanna, grateful she'd ended it with that cop she'd been dating. He was great with her kids, mature, funny, and freaky between the sheets. But she wasn't the type to live in fear of receiving a dreaded call.

"Wha—what do you mean?" Abby stammered. "How? Where?" She recalled Sara Mendelheim's innocuous comment. *My husband needs to finish working on our tomato garden.* Now she made her own. "I didn't say good bye to him this morning."

Her husband's commanding officer somberly uttered three words. "I'm very sorry."

Chapter 1

Earlier That Morning:

Kendra Nichols woke from a deep sleep by a peculiar sound slicing through the darkness.

She lay in bed, staring into shadowy patterns enveloping her in an unfamiliar setting. With tentacles of streetlight slithering closer, reaching for her, she perked her ears while suppressing her breathing. The house seemed alive.

A remnant from sleep?

Beyond the drawn curtains, she identified a train whistle piercing the early morning. Kendra knew it was too distant. Whatever roused her was here. In the house.

The second time she heard the scraping sound, she sprang upright. Fingernails on a chalkboard. Grating. The disturbance sent chills tapping her spine and ended with skin crawling on the nape of her neck. No, not fingernails on a chalkboard, Kendra now deduced. A chair sliding across a floor.

Kitchen tile? Downstairs?

Summer had yet to dig its claws into southern California, but Kendra wiped a bead of sweat from her brow anyway.

To her right, she heard the far off howl of a coyote. To her left, she perceived footsteps coming up the creaking stairs. Closer…closer.

She placed her suddenly clammy fingers on a taut stomach and whispered, "Phil, I think I heard something."

His eyelids marginally fluttered, but he remained asleep. Kendra peered across the dark bedroom toward the invasive disturbance. She then watched her hand rise and sink on Phil's belly in conjunction with his breathing. A splinter of light from outside stretched across his upper body and seemed to highlight gray chest hairs.

Calmness returned. No screeching train, no howling coyote, no scraping. Tranquility encircled the home. Kendra continued utilizing her well-tuned senses. She'd been trained for this exact situation but, as seconds passed and the rustling ceased, she found herself both relieved and disappointed: Relieved there was no danger, disappointed her skillset failed her.

An interminable few moments slipped away, and Kendra snickered at the absurdity of her own paranoia. Here she was, a professional woman in her mid-thirties, afraid of the boogeyman in the dark like a frightened child. She shifted her position and nuzzled Phil's ear. Instinctively, his arm reached through the dimness and draped her bare shoulders. Kendra lowered her head onto his chest, closed her eyes.

The scraping returned.

"Wake up, Phil," she whispered loudly, frantically shaking him.

He shook off the cobwebs of sleep, blinked repeatedly, and did a double take at the woman by his side. He tried to speak but his words were silenced by her hand covering his mouth.

"I heard something. On the stairs." She pointed, as if Phil had forgotten where the stairs were located.

He grinned. A thin beam of ambient streetlight illuminated Kendra's shoulder length blonde hair and green eyes in an angelic glow. Recalling last evening, Phil kissed her fingertips and tousled her hair. "Amazing. You look amazing."

Phil had been a sweet-talker since day one. Charming, educated, and good looking. But now wasn't the time for compliments. Kendra glared at him. "I'm not joking. I heard something."

Sitting up, Phil studied his overly distrustful girlfriend and kissed her lips affectionately.

Kendra snaked away, shot a wary look toward the sinister doorway. "I know what I heard."

"What *did* you hear?" His tone was placating.

"I'm—not sure."

"Mm hmm." He added a moment later, "I don't hear a thing." Both sitting up in bed, Phil drew her closer. "But since we're both awake—"

Kendra wiggled free again. "You don't think it's your wife, do you?"

Phil's growing flames were instantly doused as the image of his family raced across his mind. "Lori won't be back with the kids until the weekend."

"Unless they came home early."

Phil grimaced but conceded her point. Months earlier, his wife nearly found a hotel receipt. What happened that weekend in Vegas almost didn't stay in Vegas.

He waited a few moments, heard nothing. But he knew unless he investigated the noise himself, Kendra would keep him awake until sunrise. She rocked his world like no one else ever had, but her paranoia was beginning to strain their trysts. "I'll check it out."

"Don't you think I should," she replied. "After all—"

He shushed her. "My house, my wife, my problem. Chivalry is not dead, my dear." He kissed her on the lips once, a second time, got out of bed, and adjusted his boxers. Phil attributed his weak-knees to last night's passion and not from potential danger lurking beyond the bedroom.

"Be careful," she cautioned.

Pulling a Louisville slugger from behind an armoire, Phil mockingly walked toward the door like a cartoon character imitating a cat burglar. "Round three when I come back? Or is it round four?"

"Two." Kendra winked. "But who's counting?"

Phil took one step over the threshold. Suddenly his body lunged backward. His torso fell against the armoire. A pained expression of shock and agony appeared on his face. The bat fell from his grip as he clutched his stomach.

Kendra choked down the scream rising in her throat. Horror filled her soul, her bones instantly chilled. Paralyzed by fear, she couldn't move.

His hands moved away from his abdomen, exposing…nothing. He righted himself, laughter replacing a tormented expression. "Gotya!"

Furious but grinning, Kendra flung a pillow at him. "Asshole."

"Ah, yes, but a rather well-hung asshole."

"Keep dreamin'."

Phil scooped up the bat, blew her a kiss, and chuckled at his shenanigans. He departed the bedroom, promptly becoming cloaked in the obscurity.

Kendra focused her auditory skills and tracked Phil's location in the home. His footsteps became gentler by distance as he padded the hallway and descended the stairs. Soon, she heard nothing more.

Placing one foot on the floor, she surveyed her environs. Her jeans, bra, sequin top, and one shoe had been discarded haphazardly around the room in the throes of hunger. Instead of gathering her clothes, she lifted Phil's Hugo Boss shirt from a reading chair and slipped into it. Getting back into bed, she buttoned his shirt halfway and pulled a throw blanket over her shoulders. She was surprised at the gooseflesh that coated her arms, her legs, her entire body. Shivering, she now remembered her purse had been left on the dining room table and in it was her Beretta.

More time, more silence. Her head told her to go down and have a look-see. She was trained for this, Phil was not. But her heart reminded her Phil was the homeowner, Phil was the man of the house and all that male ego crap. Kendra weighed her options and decided to stay put. For now. If, in fact, Mrs. Edens had returned home early, Kendra didn't want to put herself in the middle of a family squabble. Being a mistress sucked.

The stubborn peacefulness was shattered by the belching sound of a large garbage truck meandering the small housing tract. Three-forty-five a.m. A tad early for their rounds, Kendra thought, looking at the curtained window. She listened to the grumbling engine and began reflecting.

She'd met Phil in, of all places, a car dealership. Her vehicle was there for routine maintenance. Phil was, ironically, buying a $35,000 anniversary gift for his wife. Numbers were exchanged. Voicemails, late night phone calls, texting, sexting, and finally dinner. Their relationship consummated three weeks to the day after their lives intersected standing in front of Delco batteries. Next Thursday they'd be celebrating five months.

Their arrangement suited their needs perfectly. Phil got a little extra on the side—and with a woman nine years his junior, a fact Kendra was sure he shared with the guys at the ad agency. For her, Phil satisfied her desires—to a point. He was far from a good lover, definitely had his share of annoying quirks, and, despite what he said, he was anything but well hung. However, Kendra didn't have the time needed to develop a meaningful relationship, nor did she have the desire for something permanent. Biological clock ticking or not, Kendra Nichols was not mini-van-white-picket-fence-PTA material.

The emergence of a figure in the doorway snapped her back from introspection. She twitched at first then flashed a cautious smile at Phil. "So?"

He said nothing and edged into the bedroom. Kendra noticed the same painful expression on his face. Once again his hands were fisted against his gut.

She shook her head. His silly pranks were getting tiresome. "You really expect me to fall for that again?"

It was Phil who did the falling. As he collapsed to the floor, Kendra saw the handle of a large butcher knife sticking out of his abdomen.

She screamed.

As Phil crumbled, a shadow exploded from the blackness. Kendra couldn't discern much. The figure was in head-to-toe black. All she observed in the onrushing silhouette were soulless distant eyes and a ski-mask cutout that displayed a crooked almost goofy smile. Trying to ascertain any important details such as body type, height, weight or ethnicity was moot. No time to react. With blinding quickness, the entity was on her. Knocked onto her back, she thrashed about in a futile attempt to dislodge the attacker-burglar-rapist-*whatever*. All her training was worthless. A hand over her mouth, a cloth in the palm.

Then she became one with the darkness that engulfed the room.

Chapter 2

"Detective Grace, get down!"

Frank pivoted in time to see his colleague driven backward from the impact. He dove forward, pulling over a table in the process for protection. Gunfire whizzed overhead. He could actually feel the heat of bullets rocketing inches from his face. Looking left he saw his friend was hurt. Bad. Some customers screamed, others simply whimpering in agony. One woman prayed, a grown man sobbed. Smoke and the smell of cordite filled the air. Frank checked his Beretta, then lifted his head an inch and surveilled the scene. He was outgunned, outmanned and out of time.

Frank bolted up in bed. Light was limited, the darkness overwhelming. He suppressed his breathing and listened. All he heard was his own heartbeat.

Green hue from his alarm clock displayed the time: 3:57 a.m. Turning, he was relieved his herky-jerky motion hadn't woken his wife. Abby was resting peacefully in a fetal position facing away. Her blue lace teddy had risen to mid-thigh. Fifteen years of marriage and he still gawked at her shapely legs. Her hourglass figure and flawless features earned her a pass on snoring that reached five-point-nine on the Richter scale. He massaged his neck, surprised at the beads of sweat coating his skin. The collar of his frayed *Giants* T-shirt was also damp.

He didn't bother shaking off the bloody carnage-filled dream. He couldn't. He'd never be able to. It wasn't a nightmare but rather a memory.

Frank lowered his head but sleep did not return. He seldom had difficulty shutting off the stress of his job, the harsh realities he witnessed daily. Many of his comrades in the LAPD battled insomnia, some unable to find sleep without first downing a few shots of bourbon. Frank, however, was the exception. For the most part, he compartmentalized his work life from his home life. For the most part.

Tonight was an exception.

He'd never bought into that psychobabble mumbo jumbo new age doubletalk. Premonitions, schmemonitions. Sleeplessness was rare in Frank's world. But the few instances when he'd been struck by it, the day ahead always brought trouble.

That day, the day that haunted him and periodically morphed his dreams to nightmares, was one of those days he lost a battle to insomnia. It was a turning point in his life and the lives of many others.

For twenty minutes Frank listened to the purring of a slowly rotating ceiling fan. Reaching over, he angled the alarm clock.

It read four-oh-two a.m. Twenty minutes was only five. While staring at the display he recalled the date and now understood why the memory returned. Tomorrow would be the four-year anniversary. "Screw it," he griped and got out of bed.

By the bottom of the hour, Frank had shaved and showered. He switched on the light in their walk-in, closed the door so he wouldn't disturb Abby, and dressed. Wearing a rust-colored button down, blue Khaki's, dress shoes that had long ago passed their life expectancy—but *were* comfortable—the last thing he strapped on was his over-the-shoulder holster. He removed the department-issued 92f Beretta from his gun safe and checked the magazine.

Bedside, he took a prolonged gaze at his wife, his presence going undetected. Squatting, Frank lovingly brushed aside blonde strands that shielded her face and gently kissed her cheek.

Abby's eyelids fluttered, her hand waving away the disturbance. Frank whispered, "I'm heading out."

Her eyes remained closed but her brows knitted. "Now?" she mumbled sleepily. "What time is it?"

"About four-thirty. Just can't sleep."

Instinctively, her hand rose and found her husband's face. She patted his cheek twice.

"I love you, Abby."

Moving across the bed, Abby found comfort on her husband's pillow and promptly fell back asleep. She didn't say good-bye.

Frank ambled through the hallway and found the light switch. He originally wanted hardwood floors upstairs but Abby pushed for carpeting with thick padding. Frank knew extra cushioning would mute footsteps of a potential home invader but he reneged. After all, Abby relented on his storing a gun in a home where children resided, but he insisted on *that*. Win some, lose some.

The first bedroom he came to was his son's. Jake had recently turned eight and insisted he no longer needed a nightlight. *Not too grownup, though.* He wasn't ready to sleep with the door closed. Frank stood in the threshold and studied his son longer than usual. Only Jake's blond bed-hair and face was exposed from a dinosaur-laden blanket. The walls were adorned with ten million posters. The only one Frank recognized was Spider-Man. He detected a frown cross his son's face. Either a bad dream or the hall light disturbed the boy. *Bad dreams? Nightmares?*

"He's too much like me," Frank whispered to himself.

Next stop on the farewell tour: his daughter's room. Unlike her younger brother, pre-teen Ashley insisted on a closed door, relishing her privacy. Frank furtively eased it open, peeked in. His first-born lay in a fetal position, just like her mom. She'd look like the spitting image of a young

Abby if it wasn't for the brown hair she inherited from her father. Luckily, Frank thought, that's the only physical attribute she inherited from him. Her sleeping hand clutched a pink case containing her iPod, iPad, iThingy, or whatever it was called. Gone from the walls were Princess Leia, Dora the Explorer, and The Lion King. Her youth was replaced by cutouts from teen magazines, a rap star Frank didn't know, a hulking TV character from a show he never watched, and a poster of a shirtless well-chiseled teenage boy resembling a prepubescent Fabio. *I need to talk to Abby about that.*

He walked outside clutching his briefcase. Sunup was still an hour away, the darkness unwilling to yield to the light. Frank decided to return for a jacket. The Santa Ana winds whipped through the valley and carried with them the singed aroma of a fire up in the hills. He slipped into the navy windbreaker, slid behind the wheel of his conservative four-door sedan, and idled a moment before shifting gears. Reversing from the driveway, Frank took an atypical prolonged final look at his home before driving away into the uncertainty of the coming day.

Cruising down the street, his cop gut kicked in. He glanced over his shoulder, for some reason wondering if he'd return. Then, he discarded it.

Premonition, schmemonition.

Midway in the commute from Toluca Lake to the West Bureau-Hollywood station on Wilcox, Frank elected to detour.

Homicides and violent crime dipped slightly in early April but after thirteen years on the force, he knew this was the calm before the storm. The warming temperatures and leftover debt from Christmas would soon combine to bring out the crazies.

Yes, a detour. There was no reason to go in early. He and his partner had no pending investigations that required burning the midnight oil. And there was also Detective Wadkins.

Wadkins was routinely the first detective arriving in the

bullpen. He was a one-man welcoming committee when his colleagues started their day, greeting everyone with dough-nuts and bagels he'd pick up faithfully.

Frank knew if he looked up *ostentatious* in the dictionary it would say: *see Troy Wadkins.*

Wadkins had been bestowed some bogus award from a community leader, was hailed as a hero for closing a murder that Frank's eight year old could have solved, and wore too much cologne. Wadkins's oldest was recently accepted to an Ivy League school somewhere back east, his second child had been voted homecoming queen, and his wife, a former Laker girl, was recently promoted to a more prestig-ious position in the mayor's office. Sleep-deprived, Frank was not up for dealing with Wadkins's holier-than-thou awesomeness. He exited the freeway at Franklin.

∽∾∽

Seated on a tree stump on the slope of Mount Lee, Frank glanced up at the iconic Hollywood sign a hundred yards above and then regarded the city below him. Dark and light were one. Streetlights glittered like diamonds as far as the eye could see, flickering in the charcoal pre-dawn glow. From his viewpoint, the city appeared almost serene, almost beautiful, almost peaceful.

Almost.

The city of broken dreams and shattered lives.

Most Angelenos were snug in their beds, others just ris-ing to face a new day. Teenage girls from small towns in Kansas or Nebraska or someplace would step off a Grey-hound downtown, determined to see their name in lights. Young musicians would strum guitars until blisters would bleed, hoping for one single gig at *The Whiskey.* Tourists would escape for a day and submerge themselves into a make-believe world at one of many theme parks.

But after being a cop for so long, Frank dealt in reality, not fantasy. The naïve teen from the Midwest would lose her innocence and end up parading beneath the neon lights on Sunset Blvd. The struggling musician would forego his dream, blisters on his fingers replaced by needle marks on his arm. The tourists would return to their ho-hum lives where bills, mortgage payments, and pressure awaited them. Escape is a temporary thing.

His wife, his partner, and countless others had no qualms telling Frank he was a cynic. Rather than dissuading them, he wore the label like a badge of honor.

Still, despite the violence, the murders, the wasted lives and utter ugliness, Frank cherished the City of Angels. Randy Newman wasn't the only one who loved LA.

Occasionally he and Abby discussed getting out, but it was nothing more than idle banter. He had thirteen years in with the LAPD. His wife earned a nice paycheck at St. Bartholomew. Their children were born here and were being raised here. Frank knew when roots were planted, they needed time to grow.

The city was a living breathing organism. It wasn't just a bunch of steel and concrete and asphalt ribbons stretching from the desert to the ocean. It was a mesmerizing woman who, from a distance, looked undamaged and unblemished. But upon closer inspection was imperfect and flawed. A seductress, a temptress, that lured you in and, once in her grip, there was no escape. Frank knew he should take his family and get the hell out. But there was something about this god-awful metropolis that kept him here. Vacating the city he both loved and hated would be tantamount to throwing in the towel, to giving up, to admitting defeat.

And Frank Grace didn't like to lose.

The rustling brought his musing to a dead stop. Frank perked his ears and squinted west into the thicket. He heard it again. The most photographed hillside in southern California—the Hollywood sign—was also the location of many homeless encampments as well as paparazzi who liked to lie in wait with high-powered cameras to catch a glimpse of a celebrity and sell the photo for thousands to some rag sheet.

Frank was in no mood to deal with Detective Wadkins, but he also wasn't in the mood to confront some deranged vagrant.

When he heard muffled laughter, however, his instincts took over. The chortling didn't sound like it belonged to some crazy individual living on the streets. He followed the sound through the foreboding shrubbery and approached.

The hills were pockmarked with makeshift trails, both by tourists looking for the perfect photo op and local kids seeking romantic solitude. After a moment of silence, Frank again picked up the origin of the cackling and lumbered up an incline. Coming closer, he detected a second voice, also laughing. Through the shadows, he observed a beam of light. Several beams.

He accidentally stepped on a beer can that had probably been here since Reagan was governor. The crushing sound echoed through the canyons.

"Shhh."

Peering toward the sound, Frank moved his right arm across his body and thumbed off the safety but kept his weapon holstered. Brushing aside low hanging branches, he advanced into the clearing. "What's going on?"

The blond-haired, blue-eyed surfer dude spun around but didn't seem surprised at the interruption. Wearing a wife beater T-shirt, a backward ball cap, and bling that outweighed him, he made no effort to hoist up his pants. "Who you, dawg?"

"Fort Knox called. They want their gold back."

Over surfer's shoulder, Frank detected a young girl leaning against a tree. She moved left and came into view. Wearing only a black bra and panties, she gave a skeptical scowl to the old guy who emerged through the woods.

"LAPD," Frank declared. He elected not to present his badge, knowing sudden movement would not be wise, especially when spotting a second young man in his periphery using the light from one of those I-thingies Ashley always held for dear life. Frank tensed, knowing he was outmanned. "Don't make me ask a third time. What's going on?"

Surfer scratched his balls. "You know how it is, dawg. Ho wants a little and who am I to turn down a woman in need?"

"Very magnanimous of you."

Surfer took a step forward. "Very *what*?"

Frank eased aside his windbreaker to offer a view of his weapon. "Stay where you are." He turned. "You, flashlight, stand next to your buddy."

Flashlight sought approval from Surfer, as if he was Vito Corleone. Surfer nodded and, as Flashlight sidled up to him, he pleaded, "Dude, we ain't lookin' for no trouble."

"Miss, are you okay?" Frank inquired.

A strange expression crossed her face. Not shame, not embarrassment. "Can I cover up?"

Frank nodded *yes* and instructed Surfer to pull up his pants. It was at that moment when Frank detected something hovering in mid-air, just a few feet over the lone female. He squinted at the oblong object, realizing what it was. A boom mike. His eyes traced the pole where it fed into trembling hands extending from behind the tree.

"You! Come out slowly."

Outnumbered three to one, Frank drew his weapon.

"Easy there, Stacey," Surfer warned.

As the newest male appeared, his arms were bent and his fingers already interlaced behind his head. No stranger to the positon. The fear in his eyes along with the defeated body language of Flashlight, indicated Surfer was the only potential threat. "Stacey?"

"Stacey Koon, man. No baton this time, no Taser?"

Frank arched a brow at the reference to the police officer indicted in the beating of Rodney King. "Ouch."

"I know how it is."

Frank played along. "How exactly is it, Einstein?"

"Cops, man, you all the same." He theatrically raised his arms. "Hands up, don't shoot." He smiled at his cohorts who smiled back before continuing. "Shoot first, ask questions later. Violatin' my rights. We just gettin' some, dawg. You were young once. Didn't you like bustin' a nut?"

Ignoring the taunt, Frank asked, "Miss, do you wish to press charges."

"The only thing she wants to press is her lips to my dick."

The three boys snickered, two of them fist-bumped.

"I wasn't talking to you," Frank replied. "Miss?"

She guffawed. "*No*, I don't want to press charges."

Frank was relieved. Having three individuals taken in and booked as well as obtaining a witness statement would be time consuming, especially when no real crime had been committed, thanks to his intervention. Plus, with the four-year anniversary nearing, he knew he'd be scrutinized more than usual. He waved his arm dismissively. "Take your crap and beat it. Don't let me catch you around here."

Surfer waited a beat, making a show of leaving on his own volition, rather than being ordered to. "Whatever."

The quartet began shuffling away when Frank extended his arm. "Not you, miss."

Her shoulders dropped as she grunted her irritation.

"Hey, Stacey!" Surfer shouted.

Frank turned.

Surfer made a gun with his hand and snapped his thumb signifying firing a weapon. "Fuck you, man." For good measure, he added to the supposed intimidation by grabbing his crotch before guiding his posse through the brush where they were swallowed up by the breaking dawn.

"Nice guys," Frank commented.

"They are," the girl countered.

"Yes, they seem like fine upstanding citizens. What's your name?"

"What's yours?"

"Detective Grace, Hollywood Homicide."

"What's a homicide cop doing up here?"

"Long story. Want to tell me your name?"

"Josefina." She paused, exhaled. "Josefina Mendes." She moved right and lifted her purse from some overgrown weeds. "Just getting my ID. Don't shoot me."

"Mind telling me what was going on, Josefina Mendes," he asked while taking her ID.

"For a cop, you ain't too bright."

"My lieutenant tells me the same thing." He removed a penlight from his pocket, shone it on the license. "Is this your current address, Ms. Mendes?"

"Yes, *sir*," she replied sardonically.

"You're pretty far from La Puente." Frank did a double take at both her and her ID. "Fourteen?"

"Huh?"

He held the laminated item in his fingertips. "You're fourteen years old."

Unsure if it was a question or statement, Josefina bristled. "So?"

Frank would've guessed eighteen. Maybe nineteen. But *fourteen*? In the woodlands, about to engage in a sex act with at least one twentysomething, Frank's throat became parched.

"This was my chance."

"Chance for what?"

She leered. "You don't get it, do you?"

"Enlighten me."

Josefina turned and searched for the proper words in the waking city below. The fingers of the night releasing their hold. "Guys don't want me. Girls at school hate me. Teachers, they don't give a shit." Disappointment on her face became pride. "But after this? After this, they'd all notice me. The guys would all want me."

The flashlight, the boom-mike, the phone to film it. "You think recording yourself having sex will make you popular?"

Josefina snickered. "Pam Anderson, Kim Kardashian, Paris Hilton. Any of those names ring a bell? Hell, yes, it'll make me popular."

"What about your parents?" The instant the words left his lips, he knew he sounded old.

She snorted. "What about 'em?" Frank said nothing, allowing her to fill the silence. "Dad's never home and if he is he's nursing a hangover. Mom left when I was seven. I got a brother in…Afghanistan or some place and a sister in Miami trying to find herself a sugar daddy. Any more questions, *Detective*?"

Frank pursed his lips, hoping the right words would come to him. He fretted coming off like some social worker, priest, or an out-of-touch old fart. "Trust me, Josefina. Being unpopular in school doesn't mean a thing. When you get a little older and look back, you'll see—"

Josefina laughed in his face. She tossed her ID into her *Coach* knockoff. "A little older? Shit, man, I won't live to see eighteen."

"You don't know that. No one can predict what tomorrow will bring."

Josefina emitted a bemused laugh and waggled her head flippantly.

"I'm just saying…"

"Can I leave now?"

Frank wanted to say something prophetic, something life changing, but his mind was blank. He knew of two teen shelters who housed runaways but they'd been filled since Thanksgiving. Any advice would be mocked. "You need a ride?" he offered solemnly.

She waved away the offer and began walking the trail that led back to civilization. "I'll make it," she claimed.

"I hope so," Frank muttered. Fourteen, just a touch older than Ashley. He found himself wondering if his daughter was unpopular in school. "You sure you don't need a lift?" he called out.

"Leave me the fuck alone, cop." With that, Josefina was gone.

Frank sighed. "So much for my good deed of the day."

Chapter 3

With hands folded atop her closed menu, Michelle Santana ordered, "I'll have an egg and cheese sandwich, hash browns, white toast and a refill when you have a moment." She raised the coffee cup.

"And for you, sir?"

Frank clucked his tongue, rolled his lips. He flipped two pages forward, one page back. He looked at the back of the menu where desserts greeted him.

"Bear with him," Michelle stated. "He doesn't get out much."

Frank gave his partner the evil eye and tossed the menu some more.

"Sir?"

Finally, Frank nodded. "Let me just have an order of toast, if you wouldn't mind."

"Would I mind? Heavens no, it's my job. White, wheat, sourdough, pumpernickel, or rye?"

Frank dithered. The waitress masticated her gum louder.

"He'll have white," Michelle interjected.

"No, wheat."

The server snatched both menus before the indecisive guy could reconsider.

"You always get white."

Frank lifted his coffee cup to indicate he'd also like a refill but the waitress had already vanished into thin air. He leaned forward and spoke softly. "Didn't she look like that chick from those insurance commercials?"

Michelle nodded. "Frank Grace, super sleuth."

"My doc said my cholesterol was a bit high and wants me to watch it. And wheat is healthier…*supposedly*."

"That's what they say," Michelle replied, brushing away crumbs from the previous customers.

The waitress materialized and began pouring from the carafe. Michelle shielded her face and mouthed to Frank, "Yep, Flo."

Frank smiled. "I'd like some more also, please."

"Flo" made a production of unscrewing the lid and peering inside. "Just the grounds. I'll make a fresh pot. Give me, say, twenty minutes." She winked before walking away.

"She clearly has the hots for you."

Frank tilted his head right and left. "It's the touch of gray. Distinguished, isn't it?"

"On *some* men."

Frank feigned hurt. "You know what I don't get? How come there are no *B* batteries?"

"You know what *I* don't get? Those signs that read 'Keep off the Grass'? How do they get there?"

Frank countered. "If we arrest a mime, do we still tell him he has the right to remain silent?"

"If Chief Kent has his way, yes."

"Agreed. The guy's a total brasshole."

Michelle grinned upon hearing the slang for cops who climbed the chain of command and promptly became ass-kissers. After a short silence she narrowed her eyes at her partner and moved her hands around in front of his face like a psychic.

"What're you doing?" he asked, leaning back.

"I'm going to say last night it was…Humphrey Bogart."

He smiled. "John Wayne."

"Ah. Rio Lobo?"

"The Searchers."

Michelle chuckled. "You and your old movies."

"I like old movies," Frank said defensively. "The lines weren't blurred."

"The lines?"

"Between what's right and what's wrong. There's good, there's bad. Simple. No gray areas. No blurred lines."

"Life's not black and white, Frank."

He nodded miserably and fiddled with sugar packets as he related the story from this morning. "I just don't get kids today," he said when finishing."

"You're forty-one, not eighty-one."

"I know, but still…" His eyes lowered. In fifteen months, his Ashley would be the same age as Josefina Mendes.

"Kids have longed to fit in as long as there've been kids. That's just the new way."

Frank scoffed. "Filmed having sex?"

"It's a new world, my dear partner."

"I prefer the old world."

Michelle squinted, noticing for the first time crow's feet around Frank's eyes. "Didn't you play Baseball in high school to meet girls? Being all jock-like?"

"That was my father's idea actually." He paused. "I made the team. First baseman. But I never could master the footwork so I joined the Chess Club."

Michelle feigned arousal. "Ooh, baby. The cheerleaders must've been climbing over each other to get at you, oh great chess master."

"No, but it pissed off my old man. 'Jocks get the girls,' he told me. 'Chess players get pimples on their ass.'" With the image of his preteen daughter now replaced with one of his overbearing father, Frank needed to redirect his thoughts elsewhere. And quickly. "Being popular is one thing, but filming yourself having sex?"

"I was on my school volleyball team," Michelle blurted out matter-of-factly.

"You were?"

"Are you implying I'm short? I happen to be almost five six—in heels. I was a damn good weak side hitter."

"Did you join to attract boys?"

Michelle winked devilishly. "Didn't need to." She leaned back as breakfast arrived. Flo gingerly lowered the plate in front of Michelle, presenting the meal as if it had been personally prepared by Emeril himself. The plate with Frank's toast was slid across the table, nearly ending up in his lap.

"Excuse me. I ordered wheat." Frank stated but Flo had already disappeared.

While dousing her hash browns in salt, Michelle asked, "You hear the news this morning?"

"Yeah. Didn't you know Detective Nichols?"

Michelle nodded. "Kendra and I went through the academy together way back when. She's a couple years younger than me. Just crazy, though. She didn't report in."

"Family, kids?"

Michelle smiled as a cheerful memory flitted across her mind. "Nope. She and I threw down a few once in a while but that was it. She was a big-time partier, even after graduation. It amazed me she could party all night and be sharp as a tack the next morning." Michelle paused. "She was cool, just…reckless, promiscuous."

Distrusting by nature, Frank considered the possibility Kendra was dirty. Perhaps being on the take finally caught up with her. The fact that a *reckless promiscuous* detective had gone missing and the married man she'd spent the night with was now on a steel slab in the morgue made him speculate. "I'm sure Internal Affairs will probably want to speak with you."

"It's gonna be one of those days," Michelle claimed casually.

Frank said nothing.

Shit. Bad choice of words. Aware of the significance of tomorrow's date, Michelle was happy to see Frank in surprisingly good spirits. Then again, she knew full well men kept everything internalized.

She hoped her *one of those days* comment wouldn't change that.

Twenty two months ago, Michelle had wondered who she'd pissed off. It was the two-year anniversary of what the media sensationalized as *The Azusa Bloodbath.* At the time, Michelle fervently voiced her unwillingness to be partnered with the guy at the center of it. Twenty-first century or not, police work was a man's world. She worked twice as hard to receive half the recognition. She thrived, she excelled, and was building a name for herself.

Then her upward trajectory was knocked off kilter when she learned she'd be working alongside this burn out. The worst thing that could possibly happen to her rising star was being teamed with Frank Grace of all people. The guy had more baggage than LAX at Thanksgiving. Lieutenant Gallardo did not relent. "Frank's a good cop," he maintained. "He's got the instincts, the know-how. He just lost the fire in the belly."

Still, Michelle complained, even considered filing a complaint with the Police Union. Gallardo compromised. "Give it four weeks. If you're not happy, I'll reassign you."

Four weeks was now almost two years—and counting. She couldn't imagine working with anyone else.

Frank removed some jelly packets from the stainless-steel contraption until it was empty. Nineteen packets, no strawberry. He peeled one open and spread jam he didn't want on toast he hadn't ordered.

By the front door the agitated voice of a customer filled the diner. Frank pointed his chin and Michelle turned for a better view. A bulky man with a petite Filipina at his side was screaming about something. "Probably brought him the wrong toast, too," Frank whispered.

The timid cashier begged him to lower his voice then shuffled away to get the manager. Patrons tensely watched the scene unfold. A few parents drew their children closer. The manager, an older man with a pleasing smile and bad toupee, diffused the situation. The irate customer stormed out and, in spite of getting a free meal, shouted, "Fuck this place!"

"Another day in paradise," Frank commented then made a face when biting into the blueberry covered cardboard.

Trying to keep her partner's mind off tomorrow's anniversary, Michelle averted shoptalk. "I heard from my sister, by the way."

Frank smiled appreciatively and examined Michelle's cocoa-colored eyes. His stare resulted in her slipping some strands of chestnut hair behind her left ear. It was obvious she was steering the conversation away from the anniversary. He allowed himself to be driven.

There'd always been an unspoken understanding between them. Michelle never admitted her reluctance to be teamed with him but Frank knew it. Two years ago, no sane individual would come anywhere close to the department's number one pariah. He was no super-cop. He closed his share of cases and mostly flew under the radar, just one of ten thousand in the LAPD.

Then, Azusa. And overnight Frank Grace became the poster boy for everything wrong in the department, the city, and, to a point, society in general. Thrust unwillingly into the local and national spotlight, he spiraled into darkness. Depression, a brief bout with alcoholism, self-doubt, self-loathing, he began questioning his career choice, his marriage, his life. Abby saved lives but Michelle saved his soul.

Eleven years on the force before he had the *misfortune* of a female partner. He had no problem working with a woman. But as he questioned everything, especially his actions in Azusa, he also wondered if he could trust himself to be in close quarters with a member of the opposite sex during an all-night stakeout. Frank wasn't thrilled, but he had no leverage. He was lucky to have a job. He was lucky to be a free man. Like his female partner, he had to work twice as hard to get half the recognition.

Over the twenty-two months, he developed respect for Michelle, both personally and professionally. He'd gladly take her over anyone in the boys club. She was driven, motivated, focused, and, although his male ego hated to admit it, she always kicked his ass on the firing range. There was something to be said for serving in the military.

He even admired her naiveté. Whereas Frank viewed each day returning home as a victory and inched him closer to retirement, Michelle actually bought the company line and believed they were making a difference. He viewed the job as Band-Aids on bullet wounds, preventing the discontent of an inherently violent society from boiling over. His partner viewed every arrest and closed case as one step closer to a Utopian civilization. He thought her outlook was childish and privately hoped his negativity wasn't contagious. However, he yearned to be more like his partner.

"Hello? You go to the Bahamas for a moment?"

The snapping of her fingers at the tip of his nose nearly caused him to sneeze. "So, yeah, your sister? How is she?"

"Bianca's thinking of going back into Rehab."

Bianca. Frank always found that name sexy. He'd met Michelle's sister a couple times and her name fit. "Didn't she just get out?"

"Five months ago. I've researched things online and there *is* some connection between alcoholism and family history, but no one in my family had a drinking problem." Michelle hiked her shoulders, took a bite, and continued. "Then again, I don't know a thing about my father or his side of the family."

"What about Sophia? Your mom gonna watch her again?"

Michelle shook her head. "Mom's getting too old to take care of a nine year old. Last time it took too much out of her."

"So if Bianca readmits herself," Frank asked, "who'll watch Sophia?"

Michelle gave him a knowing look.

"You?"

She shrugged. "She's my niece, Frank. What can I do? And she's a great kid. Plus—there's no one else."

Frank chose his words carefully. "You're a detective, Detective. Hard to babysit an energetic rambunctious nine-year-old."

"I don't have to *babysit* her. I've got some time accrued. I can put in a white paper and take off a coupla weeks while Bianca's getting clean. It *can* work. And if my sister really straightens herself out, it's worth it."

"Kids can be a handful, especially at that age. Take it from someone who knows."

Michelle downed the last few mouthfuls of coffee. "She's a year older than Jake, and he's a great little boy."

"Thanks to Abby, not me."

Michelle stared through the window and lost herself in the gridlock on Los Feliz. "B's my sister. Sophia's my niece. And—well, kids at that age are full of life. It'll be nice having her around."

Frank decided to hold his tongue for once. Michelle's profile was illuminated by the rising sun. He quickly intuited the deeper meaning. His partner was single, thirty-seven years old, and attached only to her job. It was now he who lifted his partner from melancholy and redirected the conversation. "Let's go," he said, patting Michelle's hand twice.

Michelle smiled her appreciation. Her goal was to keep Frank occupied and get him through the next forty-eight hours. For Frank, the sleepless night that usually foreshadowed a hellish day was jabbing into his psyche. He just wanted to survive today and tomorrow and simply return home to his family.

Instantly, that objective became challenging.

"Of all the gin joints in all the towns in all the world, you're at the same diner as me."

The man extended a hand. Frank didn't take it.

"Blake Finch, KLAG News."

"I know who you are, Finch. Everyone does."

"You've done wonders for my career, Detective Grace." The reporter reached across the table, lifted a spoon, and simulated a microphone while searching his pocket for an audio recorder. "Tomorrow's the four-year anniversary of the Azusa Bloodbath. Any comment?"

Michelle glowered at the *journalist*. "Been counting down since the *three*-year anniversary, Finch?"

Whereas Frank had the misfortune of being at the wrong place at the wrong time, Finch had the good fortune of being at the right place at the right time. A small time reporter from some shithole town in Idaho no one ever heard of, Finch and his family happened to be vacationing in Disneyland. When all hell broke loose after Azusa, Finch replaced his suitcase with a microphone. He was the station's eyes and ears on the ground in the exploding chaos of Los Angeles. It earned him his shot at the big time and three months later a top slot on one on Southern California's most coveted news teams.

As Frank's career derailed, Finch's took off like a high-speed bullet train.

Attempting to ease himself from the suddenly restrictive booth, Frank grumbled, "No comment."

"Nothing at all?" Finch pried, refusing to step aside. "Surely, you must have something to say. The good citizens of our fair city would love to hear your side."

"There is no side. There are facts, facts that came out in the trial, facts that have been analyzed, dissected, and picked apart. Now, move out of my way."

"We both know, Detective, the LAPD has a reputation of being less-than-forthcoming with accuracy. It doesn't take a gifted investigative journalist such as me to recognize that."

Blocked by the reporter, Frank moaned. "What do you want?"

"An exclusive."

Frank laughed. "You should know as a *gifted journalist* I can't do that. It's old news. However, I'd be happy to put you in touch with my CO, Lieutenant Antonio Gallardo or with the department's public relations division. Now, step aside."

"Off the record, Detective, just us. Two guys shooting the shit. We can go for a drink."

"I don't really drink."

"You drank heavily after the Azusa Bloodbath."

Before Finch could get an answer, he wailed like a little girl in response to the finger shoved between his ribs. He turned and was met by a death-stare.

"Let it go," Michelle threatened.

Frank looked up from his seated position, not recalling until now that at five-five Blake Finch was short for a man, an inch taller than his partner. Frank wondered if the guy sat on a phonebook behind the news desk. With Finch distracted by Michelle, Frank slid from the booth.

"Detective Santana, isn't it?"

"That's right. S-A-N-T-A-N-A."

"I realize you did not have the tribulation of being Detective Grace's partner at that critical juncture in time, but do you have any comment after working with said Frank Grace?"

"Back off, Finch."

"I take that as a no comment?"

"No comment."

Frank had made his way to the register, whispers and finger-pointing tracking his every step when Finch's voice carried across the restaurant. "Do you think Officer Glenn Duckworth would be willing to comment?"

Frank felt his stomach drop.

Michelle was in Finch's face. The reporter looked around hoping someone was capturing this brazen act of police brutality that would surely result in his landing the coveted anchor spot.

"Leave Glenn Duckworth out of this."

"Is that a threat, Detective Santana?"

Michelle sneered. "Do you have any outstanding warrants?"

"I most certainly do not."

"Would you like one?"

Finch stood open-mouthed as Michelle about-faced and exited.

"Don't let that guy get to you," Michelle said once outside. "He's a prick."

"Four years. Four years and people don't forget."

"They don't 'cause guys like that keep fanning the flames."

As they walked toward their vehicles, Michelle observed a press placard hanging from the mirror of a spotless white sedan. Glancing back at the restaurant, she saw Finch on his cell, facing away from the lot. "Wait here."

Frank watched his partner disappear around the far side of Finch's Infiniti. A moment later, she returned. "See you back at the barn."

"What'd you do?"

Reaching into her purse, she removed a small switchblade. "Wonder if Finch has roadside assistance."

"You punctured his tire?" Frank laughed. "The department would be so proud."

"To serve and to deflate."

"See you at the barn. And Michelle? Thanks."

"We're partners. Partners look out for each other."

Chapter 4

By the time Frank arrived at Division at 1358 Wilcox, Michelle was engrossed in a call with a robbery detective in Van Nuys discussing their mutual colleague.

Although Frank was unacquainted with Detective Nichols, a pall hung over the station here in Hollywood and likely every precinct across Los Angeles. Nichols was one of their own and, with the probability of foul play lingering ominously, it preyed on everyone's mind.

Guilt filled Frank's soul. He hoped—as did his comrades—that Kendra would be found safe. His guilt, however, stemmed from timing. Perhaps the disappearance of Detective Nichols would divert attention from tomorrow's anniversary.

The Barn had been recently modernized. Walls painted, computers updated, newfangled ergonomic chairs purchased. Desks had been replaced with shared workstations. *Work stations.* Frank thought the new digs resembled a call center, not a Homicide unit. Sauntering from the bullpen, exchanging good mornings on the way, he entered the break room and immediately scowled.

The vending machine had also been modernized—greasy chips, salty pretzels, and candy bars replaced by nutri-this and soy-that. He noticed an open box of doughnuts and almost took one before remembering they were undoubtedly supplied by Wadkins. Frank decided, instead, to indulge in a tasteless but supposedly beneficial mango smoothie something or other. Thankfully the coffee maker hadn't been replaced with some French Roast Latte Frappuccino blend or whatever the hell people substituted nowadays for a good ol' cup of Joe. He raised the pot, sniffed once, and then poured what resembled motor oil into his porcelain mug.

"Frank, my man. How's it hangin'?"

Frank turned then lowered his eyes. "Hey, Johnny,"

Johnny, whose real name was Glenn Duckworth, slipped his hand from a leather glove and engaged Frank in a complicated handshake. "Step aside. I'll brew up a fresh pot."

Frank extracted the filter tray. "I got it."

Johnny repositioned his wheelchair and nudged Frank away. "Nothing personal, dude, but your coffee sucks."

One day shy of the anniversary that changed everything, Johnny served as a vivid reminder. It was Frank's action that had relegated his friend to life in a chair.

During his academy days, Glenn Duckworth was labeled *the chosen one*. Instincts that many officers spend a career searching for came naturally to Duckworth. Respected by fellow cadets, admired by training officers, and blessed with good looks, he appeared destined to single-handedly restore the negative light that shone upon the LAPD for decades.

In addition to his innate aptitude and skills, he was also quite the ladies' man. *Johnny*, due to the slight resemblance to Johnny Depp.

All of that came thunderously crashing down: the promising career, the throngs of women, the limitless opportunities. If only Johnny hadn't agreed to have dinner with Frank one night in Azusa.

Through the ceaseless uproar and witch-hunt that followed, Johnny was Frank's most ardent supporter. Irony of all ironies: the man paralyzed for life, the individual with a bullet lodged in his lower spine, was the sole voice of reason, calling for calm and restraint. Frank was grateful his friend harbored no ill will. He carried enough for both of them. Johnny, who now worked as the computer geek and IT wizard for the station, helped save Frank's career.

Johnny wheeled himself to a Formica table, pushed aside a seat, and lifted a Rubik's Cube that had baffled the detectives for a generation. He tousled his mustache and adjusted his eyeglasses while studying the toy. "I just finished reading a book about the Battle of Tayacoba."

"Oh?" Frank glanced at the Braun, the first drops beginning to leisurely trickle. Deciding he had time, he sat down. "Sure, the Battle of Tayacoba."

Johnny arched a brow. "Duh, the Spanish-American War?"

"Of course." *That was what, late-nineteenth century?*

While rotating the Rubik's Cube this way and turning it that way, he imparted his newfound wisdom about the famous battle.

Frank was no history buff like Johnny. Few were. Nor did he have any real interest, but he listened, anyway. He owed Johnny more than just a few minutes.

"It was 30 June, 1898."

"Late-nineteenth century. I knew that!"

Johnny smiled and continued. Moments later with the historical recount concluded, Johnny pointed at the Braun. "Coffee's done." He tossed the Rubik's Cube onto Frank's lap, each side displaying one uniformed color. "And so is this."

Back in the squad room, Frank lowered himself into his chair and moaned. He glanced at his partner with whom he shared the workstation.

"Don't look at me. I didn't touch it."

Frank reached below the seat and fiddled with levers, knobs, buttons, dials, and handles. Johnny mastered a Rubik's Cube but Frank Grace was befuddled by the intricate workings of a piece of furniture. He leaned back, sat forward, bobbed in his seat a few times, and finally emitted an agreeable outbreath when finding comfort. Then the voice of God carried across the expanse.

"Grantana! My office!"

Frank and Michelle exchanged a questioning look and stood simultaneously in response to their nickname that was derived from their last names: *Grace* and *Santana.* Meandering the cubicle-maze, Michelle whispered, "What does Lieutenant Gallardo want?" She picked up the pace, adding, "And I hate when he calls us Grantana."

"I'm senior detective. You're just mad I get first billing."

Antonio Gallardo—Tony to his friends—appeared more suited to dole out drinks with little umbrellas on a beach in the Caribbean. Today, as usual, he wore a loud partially unbuttoned Hawaiian shirt, white shorts, and sandals. His girth matched his booming voice. Six five and close to three hundred pounds, he came to America as a teenager in the summer of 1980, part of the mass emigration of Cubans in the Mariel boatlift. On the corner of his desk was a framed photo of his younger sister who fell overboard ten miles off the coast of Miami. Olive-skinned, a pompadour, and a vein-laced bulbous nose, Frank never understood how Gallardo was a reputed chick magnet. More importantly, however, he'd earned Frank's respect.

The lieutenant skillfully balanced the wants of the higher-ups while preserving loyalty to his squad. In recent months, however, Frank noticed Gallardo was ever-so-slowly becoming a by-the-book type, on his way to *brasshole* status

Gallardo heaved himself up, closed the door to his office, and rolled his chair as close to his desk as his belly would permit. He shuffled a few papers, pointed a beefy finger at Michelle. "Santana, you knew Detective Nichols from Rampart Division, right?"

"To a point, Lou. We went through the academy together but that was a while back. We haven't really kept in touch."

"From your limited interaction with her, did she strike you as the type to associate with undesirables?"

Undesirables? Michelle vacillated. Gallardo was her superior, Kendra was a colleague. "She *could* be…reckless, as

I mentioned to my partner this morning. She had a wild streak but that was on her own time. I never had reason to question her integrity or work ethic."

Gallardo took a gargantuan bite of a Wadkins doughnut and, while chewing, continued. "And this—" He rearranged papers, lifted one. "—Phil Edens character? You've never heard the name before?"

"No, sir."

"He was married, coupla' kids."

"Yes, sir."

"Cady and Millington are leading the investigation," Gallardo announced. "They've got a couple leads and I want you working in a support role."

"Lieutenant!"

Gallardo bore his eyes into Michelle, *through* Michelle—the chastised schoolgirl called to the principal's office. Her shoulders slouched.

"As I was saying, this—disappearance, kidnapping, whatever it turns out to be—has shit storm written all over it. The media will dig and dig until they find something even remotely questionable in Nichols's past. The fact that she was doing the horizontal bop with a married guy, a big ad exec who's about to be sliced and diced by the ME, won't bode well for the LAPD."

"But, Lieutenant."

The principal look. "The higher-ups want this closed," Gallardo continued. "Quickly."

"With all due respect, Lou, this is a crap assignment."

"With all due respect, Santana, I don't recall asking for your input."

Michelle turned to Frank for an assist, but he simply tightened his jaw and remained silent. To Gallardo, going with a gentler tone, Michelle pled her case. "I realize Detective Grace and I currently have nothing urgent, but playing second fiddle to Cady and Millington?" Michelle recalled the breakfast conversation. "We don't need to babysit them."

"If I wanted your opinion, Detective, I'd give it to you."

Frank watched the ensuing power struggle, knowing full well Gallardo would prevail. He was initially perplexed by Michelle's vociferous refusal, before remembering something. Last fall during a charity softball game between members of the LAPD and the LAFD, Millington was touchy-feely with Michelle, a fact more distasteful since Millington's wife was days away from delivering their third child.

Michelle bellyached. "This is a waste of our time."

"There's no *'our'* on this one. Detective Grace will be handling something else."

Michelle arched a brow at her lieutenant then her partner. Frank opened his palms. *I don't know either.*

"That's all, Detective."

"But, Lou—"

"That's *all,* Detective."

Michelle's departure left Frank and his superior alone in what everyone referred to as Gallardo's Cone of Silence. "You get a doughnut?" the lieutenant asked.

"No."

"Wadkins brought them in."

"Of course, he did."

"They're delicious."

"Of course, they are."

Before Gallardo could inquire what Frank had against doughnuts, he was asked, "What's up, Tony?"

The corpulent lieutenant rearranged files and reports that perpetually covered his desk. He found what he was looking for, slid it closer. "Elijah and Xavier Leach."

Frank leaned in, eying the arrest record. "Yes?"

"This was Monday, Frank. Tell me what happened. *Exactly.*"

Frank shifted a guarded glimpse between the narrative he'd written and his boss. Gallardo's demeanor left no doubt something was brewing. Frank had given testimony on more witness stands in more trials than he could recall.

Now, that same sensation came over him in his lieutenant's office. He proceeded vigilantly, not wanting to perjure himself in the Cone of Silence. "Monday night into Tuesday morning, Michelle—Detective Santana—and I were supporting a stakeout on Virgil Truck's residence over in Pasadena. It was the Larrimore homicide, and a tip came in about Truck's proximity to the murder scene that evening. A surveillance camera from a 7-Eleven put him in the vicinity of the crime scene at what forensics determined to be time of death."

"Go on," prodded Gallardo.

"We arrived at 23:45 Monday evening. Over the course of the next three plus hours, I observed an unusual amount of foot traffic into a neighboring property." In all actuality it was his partner who initially noticed the abundance of late night visitors but if something was coming back to bite him in the ass, he'd be the one falling on the sword for Michelle. Her future was bright, his was in the shitter. "The address was 2355 North Mar Vista, just off the Ventura Freeway."

"Continue, Detective."

Detective, not Frank. "Leaving my partner in the vehicle, I approached the residence in question. Crossing the front lawn, I detected something in the air. I overheard a TV. I knocked several times before the door was opened."

"You had not set foot in the home, correct?" Gallardo said evenly.

It was a leading question, but Frank took it. "No, sir. The party who answered the door refused to ID himself. I subsequently discovered this was Elijah Leach, the resident. As I stood there, the odor I first detected at the perimeter became more defined."

"Did you ID yourself as LAPD?"

Offended, Frank said, "Of course."

"It appeared to be what, in your estimation? The odor, that is."

"Homicide's my specialty, Tony, but to me it had the smell of a Meth lab." Frank paused and studied his lieutenant for a reaction, *any* reaction. There wasn't one.

Gallardo leaned back, the armless chair groaning under his weight. Drumming his fingers on his stomach, he said, "You asked for ID?"

Frank nodded his confirmation.

"His response?"

Frank released a slight snicker. "He claimed he didn't recognize my authority. I found Mr. Leach's eyes to be bloodshot, glossy. He was fidgety and nervous. As he spoke, he continually looked beyond me as if waiting for more customers. He tried to hurry me off the property."

"Was he fidgety or was that your assumption?"

"He was acting in a suspicious manner," Frank responded quickly. *Maybe too quickly.* "And that's when I heard the scream."

"Continue."

Frank did. "I entered the residence—"

"And although there were two other teams on the stake-out you didn't call for back-up."

Frank's gut roiled. Still unsure why Gallardo was riding his ass about a routine bust, he picked up where he left off. He repeated, "I entered the residence—"

"Without a search warrant."

Frank inhaled and fought to maintain a level voice. "Correct, without a search warrant. But I believed, based on the screaming, a life was in danger. There were exigent circumstances. I had probable cause."

Gallardo rolled his wrist. *Keep going.*

Frank tried to become personal. "Tony?"

"Continue, Detective."

"Upon entering the property, I realized the screaming was coming from a willing participant engaged in consensual sex. The two brothers, Elijah and Xavier, had purchased services from a pair of prostitutes."

"So no one was in danger?"

"No, sir."

"And the Meth you *thought* you smelled?"

Frank lowered his head. "It was from an adjacent home behind the residence in question. At 2365 North Michigan, one street over."

"And the foot traffic?"

"From our surveillance position the front door to the home was obscured by trees. Buyers were simply crossing through the Mar Vista backyard en route to the Meth lab one block north."

Gallardo's glass enclosed office became cemetery quiet. Frank felt the eyes of his fellow detectives penetrating his back, wondering what the hell Frank Grace had screwed up this time.

Gallardo broke the stillness with a shake of his head. "In case you forgot, the Fourth Amendment to the Constitution of the United States protects American citizens from illegal search and seizure." He let that hang in the air.

"I had probable cause."

"Did you?"

"Yes!" Frank snapped, immediately regretting his tone.

"Screaming? But it was consensual sex. A Meth lab? But it was from another residence. Your probable cause went out the window and right up my colon!"

Not liking where this was heading, Frank grasped at straws. "The prostitutes were arrested. The Narc guys made a bust." Frank halted, narrowed his eyes, and tried to ascertain if Tony Gallardo was his friend or his boss. "What's going on here?"

"What's going on is last night I have my face between breasts the size of grapefruits when Chief Kent calls me. Already today I've gotten two calls from the ACLU, three from the media, and a crapload from the brass. I won't be able to sit on a toilet ever again 'cause everyone's taking a slice outta my butt." Gallardo shook his head disgustedly. "Frank Grace. Again."

"It was clean, Lieutenant."

Gallardo ignored Frank. "And if that's not enough, I've been contacted by Colby Ferrell."

Frank's stomach tossed. "*The* Colby Ferrell?"

"The one and only."

Frank closed his eyes. *Shit.*

In his mid-fifties, Ferrell spent as much time in front of a judge as he did in front of the cameras. He was the city's best-known high-profile attorney. Ferrell was a media darling, a cutthroat lawyer, and the LAPD's biggest pain in the ass. For two decades, his clients tallied up north of one hundred seventy million stemming from frivolous lawsuits. He'd cast enough aspersions and stir public outcry to a point where the department settled out of court in order to quell public dissent. *The People's Lawyer*, a moniker he created for himself, was anything but. Cops dubbed him Colby *Ferret*.

Gallardo resumed. "And with Kendra Nichols missing, the last thing—the very last thing—this department needs is Ferrell crawling up our collective asses all the way to our ears. When he heard your name mentioned in an illegal search, the guy nearly creamed in his pants, especially with tomorrow's anniversary."

Frank held his lieutenant's gaze before replying in defeat. "What do you want me to do?"

"Get outta town a couple weeks. Take the wife and kids and go…wherever the hell families go. The best thing for all of us is for *you* to disappear a while."

With Michelle temporarily supporting Cady and Millington and nothing time sensitive pending, Frank weighed his options. There weren't any. Jake was struggling academically, Ashley had a big part in her school's production of *Arsenic and Old Lace* and the checking account wouldn't allow for any extended vacation.

If things would blow up again, he couldn't stay home. His address had become common knowledge after *The Azusa Bloodbath.* "I didn't do anything wrong, Tony, and you know that."

"You didn't do anything wrong four years ago," Gallardo answered, "and look what happened."

ᘯᘓᘯᘓ

When Frank returned to his desk, Michelle was taking out her frustration on a defenseless stress ball. "Cady and Millington," she moaned.

"I can top that. Colby Ferrell."

"*What*?"

Frank updated her on what transpired in Gallardo's office. Upon completion, his partner confirmed what he already knew. "The Leach collar was by the book."

"Guilty until proven innocent nowadays. Any small hint of any possible impropriety brings the lawyers out from under their rocks."

"Still, though. Colby Ferret?"

"You know me, Detective," Frank said with self-deprecating humor. "When I screw up, I royally screw up."

Grace and Santana sat in silence, independently grappling with their new *assignments*.

Frank lost his battle with insomnia and, although he never bought into premonitions, so far the hunch that today would be a shit day had come to fruition. The incident in the Hollywood hills with an underage girl agreeing to be filmed fornicating, the altercation with Blake Finch one day prior to the anniversary of the Azusa Bloodbath, and now his judgment was being called into question by his lieutenant.

Just when he believed things couldn't get worse, they did.

Chapter 5

No blaring trumpets heralded his arrival. No red carpet rolled out before him. No subservient cretins dutifully following in his wake or lowering grapes into his mouth. Detective Troy Wadkins simply appeared. "Grantana, you get doughnuts?"

Michelle rolled her eyes. Hearing *Grantana* from the lieutenant was irksome enough. Coming from Wadkins, it was repugnant. "Yes, I did." She paused for effect. "Tasted a bit stale, though."

Wadkins seemed genuinely wounded. Wearing a form fitting royal blue shirt half-unbuttoned under an open suit jacket and new jeans that were snug in the appropriate places, Wadkins sidled between *Grantana,* though he positioned himself somewhat closer to Michelle. Placing a hand on each of their shoulders, he asked, "I was hoping you'd do me a favor."

"What'd you need?" Frank asked as he reflexively pulled in his slight paunch.

Wadkins stood silent for a beat, allowing those nearby to become awash in his self-importance. He stood six three and was a chiseled one ninety-two. At forty-one he was Frank's age but looked a good ten years younger and healthier. A perpetual smirk—though some called it confidence—on his face, well-defined chin, broad shoulders, jet-black hair, and deep-set brown eyes. Frank had overheard females in the squad extol his bedroom eyes—whatever the hell *bedroom eyes* were.

Wadkins popped an Altoid into his mouth. "My wife, Melina—you know she used to a Laker Girl, right?"

"The photos and magazine covers all over your desk make it hard to forget," Frank said.

Wadkins hooted. "Such a jokester. Anywho, Melina dropped me off this morning on her way to the gym 'cause I had to bring my Beemer in and didn't have a ride. No, just routine maintenance." He laughed. "I was wondering if I could hitch a ride over to Westwood to pick up my baby."

"Which baby?" Michelle questioned.

Since a woman made the comment, Wadkins laughed louder. "*Two* jokesters. My Beemer baby."

Michelle chewed her lip and faced Frank. "My sister called while you were in with the lieutenant. She wants to meet for lunch and discuss Sophia."

Wadkins's face brightened. "How is Bianca anyway?"

Frank knitted his brows, wondering how Wadkins knew Michelle's sexy-named sister, then wondered why he felt perturbed about Doughnut-boy's reaction to his fantasy girl.

"Bianca's fine," Michelle replied. To Frank, she claimed, "I'm meeting her in Culver City so—we could drop Troy off first, then take the 405 down."

Frank inhaled and blew out slowly. "Why not? I've got nothing else to do."

"You're a good man, Grace. And a better chauffeur."

ↄ◦ↄ

"Just stay on Sunset," Wadkins instructed from the rear. "I'll tell you where to go."

I'll tell you *where to go.* Frank's agitation increased with each mile.

"Not much room back here but a decent ride. What is it anyway?"

"Chevy Malibu." Frank heard a snicker and for some reason felt a need to justify his choice of automobile. "Gets me from Point A to Point B. That's what a car's supposed to do."

Leaning forward, Wadkins studied the console. "My Beemer's pushing four years. Time for a new one but Melina—you know she used to be a Laker girl, right? Anywho, she wants a new Benz and you know what they say, Grace: Happy wife, happy life."

"Uh huh."

"Speaking of wives how's Gabby?"

"Abby. She's fine."

Emitting a wicked laugh, Wadkins claimed "She sure is" and squeezed Frank's shoulder firmly. "Just guy talk, Santana. No offense."

Peering into the rearview mirror, Frank thought of that scene in *Goldfinger* when James Bond pushes a button and ejects his captor. Frank wished his Chevy had that same feature as Bond's Aston Martin.

"Something chappin' your ass, Frank?"

Needing to vent about his *suspension,* he shared details of the meeting with Gallardo, then immediately kicked himself for opening up to Wadkins. Doughnut-boy would hear about it anyway. At least this way Wadkins would get it firsthand rather than via squad room gossip.

When Frank concluded whining about the Leaches and Colby Ferrell, Wadkins threw himself against the backseat. "Whoo, boy. What is it with you always being at the wrong place at the wrong time?"

Michelle defended her partner. "The Leach collar was clean."

Wadkins extended his palms like a traffic cop. "Hey, I'm just telling you what I see. Pull over."

"Huh?"

"Pull over, right here!"

Frank pulled to the curb. "What is it?"

"My mechanic loves Sam Adams. I always bring him a

twelve pack as a way of saying thanks." Opening the door, he pointed at both Frank and Michelle. "Do you guys want anything?"

Michelle sighed. "Just get your beer."

As Wadkins entered the derelict mom-and-pop liquor store on Sunset, Michelle commented, "That guy's so slimy I feel like I need a shower."

Wrapped up in his own thoughts and knowing Wadkins's arrogance was a given, Frank added nothing. Body temperature rising in conjunction with his anger, he powered down the window and gazed around. A young couple shared a *Map to the Stars' Homes*, oblivious to the homeless man lying a few feet away. Three prostitutes sashayed along the sidewalk, a bleached-blonde strutted over to an idle car. A city bus hiccupped. A cab nearly rear-ended a slow moving Ford as it swerved to pick up a fare.

The city earmarked several million dollars to refurbish this section of West Hollywood for gentrification but Frank had yet to see one iota of improvement. The only change he noted was a former two-story motel, now boarded up and abandoned, on its way to becoming a medical center. Many local establishments, including the one Wadkins entered, had filed a lawsuit. City planners proposed razing a three square block area and replacing the longtime family-owned businesses with high-rise condos carrying a seven figure price tag.

Unsure what to say but wanting to soothe her partner's anger, Michelle simply muttered the name again. "Colby Ferrell. He's a smug bastard also. I never understand how he has time to represent anyone with all those interviews he does."

Frank arched a brow at his partner. "What'd you say?"

Frowning, she repeated herself.

"The car."

"Hmm?"

Frank's mind began reeling. "Riddle me this, Detective."

"Riddle away."

Frank began enumerating on his fingers. "The house on Mar Vista where the brothers lived, Elijah and Xavier Leach, was a dump. Hardly a stick of furniture and what they had was second-hand, thrift store stuff."

Michelle drew out an "Ohh-kay."

"Elijah's twenty-two, twenty three. Not working because he's waiting for his *rap career* to blossom. The older brother, Xavier, is late twenties and works as a stock boy. They want to get laid but they don't go to some bar or splurge for a couple high-class call girls. Instead, they pick up two hookers and bring them home, rather than getting a room. And the car in the driveway is a fifteen-year-old beat-to-hell Maxima. Safe to say they're not exactly rolling in dough, correct?"

Michelle stated, "As my *abuela* used to say 'They ain't got a pot to piss in.'"

Staring forward, Frank asked, "Then explain to me how two losers like that can afford to retain Colby Ferrell."

"Pro bono, probably. Publicity for him, not that he needs it. He undoubtedly believes it's a slam dunk. Easy money for him and his clients."

"I'm going to ask them."

Michelle chuckled. "We don't exactly travel in the same circle as the Leach brothers, Detective."

Frank angled forward, repeated his earlier statement. "The car."

Michelle looked through the windshield. Parked in front of them was a fifteen-year-old Maxima.

"Be right back."

"Frank!"

But he was already out of the car.

With traffic crawling by, Frank came upon the open window, and said to the driver, "Will Smith and LL Cool J live up in those hills but even they realized most rap careers are short-lived."

Wearing blue overalls, Elijah peered up. Sunlight was not in his eyes but he made a visor with his hands as if it was. A frown gave way to an insidious almost goofy smile. "Grace, isn't it?"

"*Detective* Grace," Frank proclaimed, knowing Lieutenant Gallardo would be proud for identifying himself. "License, registration, and proof of insurance."

Elijah Leach was scrawny. Shoulder-length curly brown hair and brown eyes, his five-eight, one-sixty-pound frame looked even punier behind the wheel. "You already know who I am. Why you need ID?"

Frank pointed to the sidewalk. "Fire hydrant."

Elijah overtly laughed in his face, the silly smile more befitting a mischievous child. "They bust you outta Homicide down to traffic Nazi?"

"License, registration, and proof of insurance," Frank repeated. And as distasteful as it was, he added, "Sir."

"I'm not parked, *Herr Grace*. I'm waiting for someone."

Observing a black cloth of some kind strewn across the rear seat, he claimed, "Your engine is off and you're parked illegally. License and—"

The eye visor gone, Elijah snapped. "Fuck you, man! I don't accept your bullshit authority. You're violating my rights. Again! Make it easy on yourself. Turn around, walk your bony ass back to your car, and I won't tell my attorney about this latest infringement on my civil liberties."

"Speaking of your attorney, how did—"

Frank was interrupted by an impact between his shoulders that slammed him against the vehicle. He swiftly pivoted.

"What the hell is going on here?" barked Xavier Leach. "You bustin' my brother?" His voice was stern, his shoulders squared, his eyes enraged.

"Calm down, Xavier!" yelled Michelle, taking up position on the street at Xavier's two o'clock. Her windbreaker was pushed aside for quick access to her Glock.

Motorists slowed. Some looked for camera crews while others began recording the event on their phone.

Xavier, the older brother, had a trace of Eskimo somewhere in his gene pool. A pronounced Adam's apple, close-cropped black hair, soulless black eyes, and a strapping physique on a six-two broad-shouldered frame, he only marginally resembled his younger brother. He was the more physically imposing of the two, despite also wearing blue overalls as if he was some hayseed.

"You okay, Eli?" Xavier asked.

Elijah nodded.

Frank's lower back was vulnerable against the open window where Elijah was seated. The at-risk position conjured up images of Johnny and his wheelchair.

Xavier stepped closer, invading Frank's personal space. To right himself, Frank would need to come in physical contact with the elder brother. The image of Johnny was replaced with one of Colby Ferrell, Esquire.

Xavier narrowed his eyes at Michelle, shouting loud enough for passers-by to hear. "You gonna to shoot an unarmed man in broad daylight, bitch?"

Michelle inched her hand closer to her weapon. "Stand down, Leach!"

The unexpected always led to dangerous situations. Dealing with drugged up perps on who-knew-what or desperate crazies brandishing weaponry was perilous. But it was the less extreme situations like routine traffic stops that rapidly turned bloody. And sometimes deadly.

"You just assaulted a police officer," Frank claimed.

As he straightened up, Xavier refused to step back, each big dog staking claim to their turf. They could feel each other's breath.

"Police officer, my ass. You think that bogus badge gives you power over me? You're *dead* wrong."

"You and your brother some kind of anarchists?"

Xavier snickered. He jammed his finger into Frank's chest but spoke in a hushed defiant tone. "When Colby Ferrell is through with you, Grace, I'll have you licking dog shit from my shoes. I'll own your ass."

"Hands off!" Michelle commanded, assuming a combat

stance, her Glock aimed on Xavier's upper body.

"Tell me how two scumbags like you hooked up with a guy like Ferrell."

The two combatants eyed each other in silence. On the sidewalk, Michelle cocked the hammer and tightened the grip on her semi-automatic. She threw a quick glance toward the liquor store, willing Wadkins's assistance. She was getting a bad feeling.

Xavier blinked first. Snorting satirically, he said, "Growing up I was told to pick my battles. You win this one, Grace, but we'll meet again one day." He promenaded around the front of the car, his steps traced by the barrel of Michelle's Glock.

"Slow, Xavier. Nice and slow," she cautioned while Frank remained alongside the driver's door, vehicles passing behind.

As Xavier lowered himself into the vehicle, he blew Michelle a kiss. Once inside he opened the glove box, handed a small packet to his brother to pass through the window, and claimed, "Here's the license, here's the registration." He lifted his phone. "And here's me calling my attorney."

Frank took hold of the proffered documents. A passing glance at his partner indicated she had the situation under control if Xavier tried something.

It went down in a flash, yet played out in slow motion. A horn honked at a strutting prostitute. A woman was jaywalking with a poodle. A homeless man was looking through a garbage can. A street performer was banging on small containers. Innocent pedestrians were crossing at the corner. Elijah reached into the backseat.

Frank felt the heat before hearing the thunderous detonation. The ground rocked beneath him. No chance to react, to comprehend, he found himself airborne, propelled over the top of the Nissan, arms instinctively flailing about, his hands reaching out desperately but grabbing nothing.

Frank was flung like a small bird in a twister tearing across the plains. Slammed headfirst into a brick wall, his brain felt like it'd been repositioned within his skull.

Shrill car alarms perforated the morning. A steel gray debris cloud blanketed the street. Dazed cries penetrated the macabre scene. Soot and shards of broken glass littered the sidewalk.

Unlike his partner who'd served two tours, Frank had no military background. He'd heard the expression *war zone* but never grasped it. Until now. The explosion destroyed everything in sight.

Relieved to be on solid ground, Frank intuitively sat up while getting his bearings. His stomach undulated. Reflexively, he reached for his sidearm but his muscles were non-responsive. The message from his brain blocked. He again saw Johnny in his mind. The entire right side of Frank's body was numb.

He found himself unconcerned with the Leaches' twenty. Frank was cold, losing sensation in his arms and legs. His vision constricted, the periphery closing around him. He felt his upper body weaken…weaken and found himself flat against the concrete sidewalk.

Peacefulness came over him as his weighty eyelids lowered. Abby, Jake, and Ashley appeared in a fog but, as the hazy image of his family dissipated, his head lobbed right.

Michelle was twisted abnormally. He tried to call to her but couldn't get air into his lungs. The last thing Frank saw before everything faded to black was his partner. She wasn't moving.

Chapter 6

The spectral vision erupted from Frank's subconscious with the impact of a sledgehammer.

To his right, his frail mom was dressed in black, tears hidden behind a veil as she clutched a balled-up tissue. To his left, Abby, pregnant with their first child, held Frank's hand. In front of him, a coffin with his father inside. Circle of life indeed.

The priest talked in an imperious baritone, but his words carried no substance. He was merely going through the motions. Only six people attended the funeral for Ernest Christopher Grace. And that included the man of the cloth and two groundskeepers simply waiting to lower the casket into the earth. Ernest pushed everyone away his entire life, so it was apropos that no one was here at the end. Friends—of whom there'd been few—had other commitments. Siblings were too busy.

Frank spent over twenty years trying to live up to his father's unrealistic expectations. And always fell short. Nothing was ever good enough for the overbearing tyrant. Wrong career, wrong college, wrong sport in high school, wrong wife. Even the wrong name. Nothing Frank did was acceptable in that son of a bitch's mind. Now, even in death, the elder Grace was reaching from the great beyond to give his son one departing blow.

Frank's life was finally taking shape. Just days earlier,

he'd graduated from the police academy. His father didn't attend. "I got other obligations," he stated. Frank had recently married the intelligent, funny, and stunning Abigail McKenzie. Together, they'd present Ernest with his first grandchild, but even that was met with cynicism. "A daughter?" his father scoffed after hearing about the ultrasound. Frank couldn't even do *that* right.

When he was six or seven, Frank heard from a cousin that it was Uncle Jack and not his father who drove Mom to the hospital. Frank asked her about it. His mom, as always, defended her husband. "He had a lodge meeting."

Frank?

And since Ernest wasn't around at his birth, Mom, a Sinatra fan, named her son after Ol' Blue Eyes. That, too, added fuel to Ernest's constantly raging fire. "Francis Albert Grace? FAG? You named our son Fag?"

"Get me another beer, Fag," followed by a slap to the side of the head.

"Turn down your music, Fag," followed by a slap to the side of the head.

"You broke your arm playing basketball?" followed by a slap to the side of the head.

Dinner on the table at six-fifteen instead of six? Frank's fault. Whiskey cabinet empty? Frank's fault. Phone company raising their rates? Frank's fault. "Goddamn you, Fag!"

No wonder no one showed up to the funeral.

A wave of gunfire redirected Frank's psyche to a different suppressed memory. Carnage everywhere. Crimson splatter. Cordite hanging in the air. Desperate wails of victims in the throes of death. Blood of the executioners mingled with blood of the innocents. Frank's eyes met them all. Some pleaded for help, others staring into a void of eternal nothingness. In his hand he gripped a .92F Beretta, his shoulder still pulsating from squeezing off endless rounds.

Frank.

The painfully excruciating recollections, both physical and emotional, morphed together in one gray mosaic. Memories became visions. Remembrances became grisly night-mares. Azusa. The patrons of Il Vittorio's, their skin ashen and their eyes a lifeless void, reaching for him, reaching *at* him. It was as if Frank had been inserted into some cheesy B-movie horror flick. But he couldn't pull himself out.

Frank?

The dead were alive, surrounding him in some ghoulish episode. Fearfully, he backpedaled, backpedaled, until he could backpedal no more. He stumbled against a casket. He looked over his shoulder to see his dead father sitting up.

"A daughter?"

Frank tried to run but his feet sank deeper into a viscous substance. Quicksand. And Frank was being pulled down. He saw them. Strange pale forms, nondescript and lacking in detail. Stephanie Hagen, a girl he dated in high school who was killed in a car accident senior year. Andy Moore, a college buddy who never woke after snorting too much blow in his dorm room. Ty Kendall, the first person Frank shot and killed just months after hitting the streets. The dead walled him in, coming closer. Then, another person from his past entered the morbid experience. He stammered her name. "M—Michelle?"

Frank.

The apparition of his partner transformed into one of an angel. Ghastly illusions meticulously peeled away layer by layer. The morose scene replaced by bright, warm sensations. And pain.

His head weighed a ton, his skull a block of cement. His neck was immobilized by a contraption of some sort. His mouth sandpaper dry. He was horizontal. *A hospital bed?* The familiar scent was comforting, soothing like the melodic tune a mother sings to a newborn clutched to her breast.

"Frank? Frank? Oh, God, you're awake."

The angel took form. Abby's blonde hair pulled back tight against her pale face. Her cobalt eyes exhibiting sadness and relief. Her knuckles white on the crucifix hanging at her throat. She appeared striking, flawless. Angelic.

Where am I? What happened? Where are the kids? However, the queries were only heard in his own mind. The lone sound in the room was Abby sobbing his name repeatedly, convincing herself he was really alive.

After fifteen years of marriage, words weren't necessary. Abby answered his silent questions.

"It's okay, *you're* okay. You're at Cedars Sinai. The kids are fine."

Frank frowned. Even his eyebrows hurt.

Abby addressed his confusion. "Cedar's has a better trauma center than St. Bart's." She sniffled once, steadied her breathing, looked at the sunlight streaming through the verticals, and said a thankful prayer before wiping away more tears. "My sister's watching Ash and Jake. But you're okay, sweetie, you're okay." She leaned over and nuzzled her face against his neck. "You're okay," she repeated, more for herself than him.

He instinctively tried to hold her but his right arm didn't move, couldn't move. Frank swallowed. Or tried to. His throat was on fire. He parted his lips and tried to speak but only an unintelligible grumble came out.

"An explosion. They're saying it was a terrorist attack. Eleven killed, a few more still critical."

Terrorist attack? In LA?

"I got here as soon as I could. Lieutenant Gallardo called me at the hospital. I've been here since."

Frank felt his brows furrow. *Been here since? How long have I been out for? And who's Lieutenant Gallardo?* His lips trembled.

"Water? You want water?" Abby scanned the room.

Frank shut his eyes tightly, shook his head in annoyance, tried to speak.

"You can't drink anything but I can probably get you some ice chips. Is that was you want?"

After so many years, he and Abby were always on the same page—except now. He grew agitated with his inability to verbalize his worst fear.

Helplessness crossed Abby's face, frustrated she couldn't read her husband's mind. "Ice chips? Is that it? A nurse? You want the nurse, Frank?"

He said something but it sounded like the croaking of a frog. *Michelle? Is she...*

The curtain of drowsiness drew closed and enveloped Frank's weakened weary body. The fleeting encounter left him drained and depleted. His eyes closed and he drifted away before knowing his partner's fate. He battled against the overwhelming tug of exhaustion but lost. Drifting to sleep, he hoped the dead would not be waiting to haunt him again.

☙❧

The terrorist attack on Hollywood was the best thing to happen to Eddie Evanovich in years. Maybe his luck was finally changing. He'd collected more at highway off-ramps in the last two days than he had in two weeks. Nothing made Americans more charitable than a good old attack on US soil. One good thing about those towelheads attacking America, it put more coinage in his pocket.

And not just the usual spare change motorists gingerly handed to him—they always extended their arm through the window and let the dimes and quarters fall into his hands, clearly avoiding physical contact—but actual paper. Real dollar bills, sometimes even a five! There was that one woman with Jesus hanging from her rear view. She not only handed over a twenty, but also gave him a large fries from In-N-Out. "God Bless you," she said before driving away.

Yeah, whatever. A couple more profitable days and he could afford one night in that motel on skid row.

As night covered Southern California, Eddie Evanovich shuffled north on San Pedro Street. He was glad he chose to leave his cart and all his worldly possessions at the underpass where he now slept. He hoped Demi—he doubted that was her real name—would live up to her word. After yesterday's big haul, he thanked her with a pack of cigarettes in exchange for watching his belongings.

His pace slowed, he began hobbling. He'd cut away the front of the Reeboks so his size eleven foot could fit into a size eight shoe. Nine hours standing and holding a sign sapped him, and he was grateful he didn't need to push his cart.

Lumbering along he took note of school busses parked beyond a barbed-wire fence. He halted for a moment. The lot was faintly lit, undoubtedly void of security. Perhaps he'd spend a few hours sleeping inside a bus before continuing to his underpass/home. Considering it, he stared at the school bus, then thought of his children. How old were they now?

He laughed so hard at what his life had become he began hacking. He winced, put a dirty finger in his mouth and slid it across his diseased gums. Evanovich had not always been invisible. In fact, he'd been a ruthless ballbuster.

He used to drive a Lexus, not push a shopping cart. He used to wear imported Italian shoes, not ratty footwear he pilfered out of a Dumpster. He had a closet overflowing with suits from the finest tailors in Beverly Hills, not a reek-covered trench coat and torn trousers he kept up with shoelaces.

Always Ready Eddie, or simply *Double E* to his colleagues, Edward Evanovich was once one of the top real estate agents in Southern California. He earned six figures with nary an effort. One time, he pulled in so much from one single sale he took a leave of absence from his job and lived on his yacht for seven months, sailing up and down the west coast. One-hundred-seventy-five Gs from selling a mansion in Malibu to that snot-nosed pop star. When he advised the teen heartthrob the estate had once been owned by Spencer Tracy the little punk just frowned. *Who?* As if that wasn't sacrilegious enough, the little bastard ripped out the movie theatre and replaced it with a video arcade.

Irony, indeed. The man who made millions putting affluent people into luxurious homes no longer had a home of his own.

The economy turned to crap, the housing bubble burst. The money, the wardrobe, and the car all went away, as did his trophy wife and her thirty-six double Ds. Last he heard, she took the children—*his children, however old they were*—to her sister's in Tucson.

Evanovich was yanked back from happier times when a car nosed in to the curb and honked twice. An arm extended through the rolled down window. The passenger rotated his hand in a *c'mere* manner.

Evanovich's ankles burned and his knees throbbed but he shuffled over to the Good Samaritan as quickly as he could, an old dog seeking table scraps. The lighting on San Pedro was weak. As he drew closer, he couldn't help but notice extensive damage to the Nissan.

"Hey, old timer," said the passenger.

Evanovich smiled, a smile displaying missing teeth. "G' evening."

The passenger's hand was fisted. Evanovich opened his palm, preparing to receive the charitable donation. Recalling that motorist with dangling Jesus, Evanovich said, "God Bless you."

The passenger extended his fingers and let a few nickels fall into the homeless guy's calloused filthy palm. "God Bless *you*," he replied.

A foolish almost goofy smile appeared on the man's face. After depositing the change, he grabbed Eddie's wrist and jerked him closer. With extraordinary speed, he whipped his left arm around and thrust the blade into the bum's gut. He twisted it once to insure a job well done.

Eddie gazed down, watched the knife being pulled from his belly. He frowned at the generous man and clutched the red patch that widened across his abdomen. His body shivered, despite the warm piss that trickled down his leg. He crumbled to his knees then toppled over along the sidewalk.

He heard laughter as the damaged Maxima drove away into the gloomy night. With his torso lying cockeyed on the pavement, Eddie saw the school buses sheathed in an amber vaporous glow. He thought of his children. Thirteen and nine he now remembered. A fleeting smile of happier times soothed his final seconds.

Chapter 7

"I can walk on my own," Frank protested as he was wheeled through the hallway by a nurse seemingly his daughter's age.

"Sorry, Mr. Grace, hospital rules."

From behind, he heard, "You know what I don't get? If we really have freedom of speech, why do we get a phone bill each month?" Frank looked back, and finally exhaled. "I'll take him the rest of the way," Michelle said, moving behind Frank's wheelchair.

The nurse hesitated before relinquishing control.

Frank smiled at his partner, his friend. Michelle was not in a hospital gown but rather a jeans skirt, a nondescript T-shirt, and her hair in a clip. She also had bandages on her chin and a contusion under her right eye.

"How are you feeling?" he asked.

"Just minor lacerations. Glass mostly, other crap." Michelle grinned. "When I tell you to stay in the car, stay in the car."

Huh? It took Frank a moment to comprehend. Then he remembered she tried to stop him from confronting the Leaches. "You'd think after being married for…a while…I'd know to listen to women."

Michelle leaned against the wall and studied him. "How 'bout you?"

"Just coming back from a CT Scan of my head."

She winked. "I'm sure they didn't find anything up there."

They locked eyes, the brief silence speaking volumes. They were thankful to see each other and grateful it wasn't worse. "I heard eleven people," Frank remarked somberly.

"Twelve. Twenty-nine-year-old dude from Cerritos didn't make it through the night."

Frank curled his lips. "The Leaches?"

"Nope. Elijah got stitched up at the scene, Xavier walked away."

"And Wadkins, he okay?"

Michelle brayed. "Troy Wadkins, golden boy of the department? Of course he is. I think a few hairs were mussed but that's it."

Frank lowered his head. "I'm—sorry."

Michelle waved it away. "So, what's the prognosis?"

Frank breathed deep, winced due to a pain in his ribcage, and explained slowly. "Concussion. Apparently a pretty bad one since I lost consciousness. They just wanted to run some tests, make sure there wasn't bleeding in my brain."

Michelle paled, touched his shoulder. "But you're okay?"

He nodded. "Okay as I was before—which isn't saying much. I've got a throbbing headache I can't shake. And I've thrown up twice."

"They kept me overnight for observation, and after eating their breakfast I can't blame you for upchucking."

Frank held his head. "I don't even remember much of it. Just flashes really. I remember standing next to the car. I remember hearing the explosion. I remember you lying on the ground. Then I woke up here."

"Self-preservation. They say the brain blocks out traumatic events like a bad car accident or a beating—or that date I had last month with Foster from Robbery."

For the first time in a while, Frank laughed. "You talk to Abby?"

Michelle was distracted as a bald-headed child in a

gown, precariously pushing a walker, ambled by. One of two nurses said encouragingly, "You're doing wonderful, Brianna."

The child beamed from ear to ear as if accomplishing a major triumph, then continued focusing all of her attention on the simple act of walking, watching her shuffling feet. Trailing behind were parents, clinging to each other, hoping for the best but fearing the worst.

Michelle shook it off. "Uh…yeah. Abby and I grabbed a bite to eat yesterday. She's doing well. Scared, but she's tough."

"And the kids?" Frank queried as the nine-year-old cancer patient disappeared around the bend and out of sight.

"Jake just wants Daddy home. Ashley's having a rough go of it. When will you be home, anyway?"

"Tomorrow, unless they find something in my head." Frank stuck up his hand. "Don't even go there."

Michelle feigned shock. "*Moi*?"

A lull, then he sighed. "A terrorist attack, here?"

"It was only a matter of time. Why not here?"

"True. No pun intended but it hits close to home when it's actually close to your home."

"No one's claiming responsibility. The FBI, Homeland, and NCTC are all over the place."

"NCTC?"

"National Counterterrorism Center. The Fed's bringing out all the alphabet agencies. Of course, the conspiracy nuts are accusing the LAPD of being behind it."

"The LAPD?" Frank made a face. "Why?"

"You were cooped up here and yesterday marked the four-year anniversary of Azusa. The crackpot bloggers are claiming the Hollywood bombing was designed to divert attention away from it. And with you being involved in *both,* it's fanning the flames."

"Like Wadkins said, wrong place, wrong time."

Michelle nodded, pleased Frank remembered that. "You should get some rest. Want me to wheel you in?"

"I got it." Frank engaged the brake on his wheelchair, wrapped his hands firmly on the arms, and lifted himself warily, gingerly. His knees buckled, but he slowly straightened. He expected a wave of nausea to wash over him but there wasn't any. He was making progress.

Following behind, Michelle watched closely as Frank took baby steps, figuratively and literally. She knew it'd be a while until he was one hundred percent but both of them were lucky, damn lucky. "Cute butt," she commented at his open gown.

"Control yourself, Detective."

❧❧❧

It'd been a living hell for…two days? Three? Less, more? She'd lost track of time. Of her surroundings. Of her sanity. Despite being blindfolded since her abduction, Detective Kendra Nichols could still *see* the haunting images in her mind: Phil Edens collapsing to the ground with his intestines spilling out, the sinister shadow leaping from the darkness, pouncing on her before she could react. And worst of all were those unfeeling eyes and the stupid crooked smile peering down hatefully as she was drugged.

She'd undergone unending sensory deprivation. Music blared intermittently, the cold concrete beneath her bare feet reverberated. Lights randomly flickered on and off. The temperature in the chamber was drastically manipulated to extremes. Kendra went from perspiration on her neck to chills on her spine. She'd been fed basic sustenance—soup, energy bars, water, one ham sandwich. But the blindfold had yet to be removed since being kidnapped.

Taken, but why? She had no fortune, no wealthy relatives who could come up with a hefty ransom. She had a brother up in one of the Dakotas, a cousin down south somewhere, a mom who succumbed to leukemia six months ago, and her father, sadly wasn't Liam Neeson but rather some guy who abandoned his family when Kendra was a teenager. *So why?* Did these kidnappers know she was a detective? Perhaps *that* was the reason? Would they care? She'd had her share of lovers, but it seemed doubtful any of them would go to these extremes. Nope, not an ex. The voices she'd heard over the last however many days were not recognizable.

If she somehow survived this ordeal, this nightmare, Kendra would have very little to go on.

Based on the limited conversation she'd heard when she was brought food, she estimated her captors to be in their twenties, possibly early thirties. The one with a gruffer tone came from a higher position, indicating he was taller. She put him around six one or six two. *Gruffy,* as she dubbed him, spoke in an authoritative tone. But Kendra became unnerved when in the presence of the other kidnapper who she nicknamed *Short One.* His voice was weedier, less boisterous. But he carried fury in his words. Suppressed anger.

Gruffy worried her, Short One terrified her.

Kendra was filthy. She could smell herself. Her hair was tangled and wildly unkempt. Her clothes—whatever they put her in—felt grungy and soiled. They'd obviously seen her naked, feelings of being violated adding to her contempt. She craved a hot shower but was not desperate enough to ask.

Gruffy scored favor with her when binding her to a chair. It was a welcome departure to being hogtied on a stony cement slab. Still, she was resolute not to bow to Stockholm Syndrome and empathize with these bastards.

"Well, well, well."

Shit. Short one. Kendra said nothing.

"I got a Snickers bar. Want some candy, little girl?"

He snorted. Even his insidious laugh made her skin crawl. She heard a wrapper tear. When she was told to open her mouth, she clenched her lips and turned away.

Fingers clamped her head like a claw. "Open your mouth."

Although her mouth watered, she refused to obey the command.

"This'll be over soon. Make it easy on yourself and you'll get out alive."

She resisted. When she felt the candy bar—*chocolate*—gliding across her lips in pseudo-phallic style, she momentarily considered surrendering. *No.*

Short one pressed it harder against her lips. "Either take this or I'll shove something else in your mouth."

Vulnerable and helpless, Kendra was reviled, knowing they'd seen her naked, but she was grateful she'd not been sexually assaulted—yet.

"I said open your mouth, bitch!"

She tried to angle away as much as possible.

The vicious blow to her stomach pushed air from her lungs. She doubled-over, felt the ham sandwich from earlier rising in her throat.

"Think you're tough? Just 'cause you're a cop, that makes you a bad ass?" The backhand to the side of her face nearly sent her and the chair she was bound to toppling over. Kendra was righted by a hand that yanked her head back and exposed her throat. "I'll fuck you up so much there won't be nothin' left."

Here it comes. Her luck had run out, the kidnapper becoming the rapist. When she heard a zipper undone, she readied herself. And her jaw. A beefy paw on the back of her head shoved her face forward.

"What the fuck?" shrieked Short One.

"What's your problem?"

Gruffy saved me.

"This whore needs to be taught a lesson."

"No," asserted Gruffy, the one calling the shots, his voice more imposing than ever. "Help me untie her. It's time."

Chapter 8

Frank was home, standing at the kitchen counter making himself a turkey sandwich and couldn't help but laugh. A bomb exploded, sending him sailing over a vehicle and pirouetting through the air where he did a face plant against a brick wall resulting in a concussion. In the hospital he was poked and prodded and probed with more tubes in more orifices he cared to count. Yet, here he was, having his sandwich on wheat rather than white because his cholesterol was a tad high.

The doctor who treated him at Cedars Sinai, a woman with seventeen consonants and not one vowel in her name, wrote a prescription for painkillers and to *take as needed*. Frank wasn't big on the medical community that doled out meds like candy to kids at Halloween. He promptly stored the bottle in the rear of a cabinet.

He made his way to the living room and sat when realizing he'd forgotten something. Returning to the kitchen, he removed an ice pack from the freezer. Wrapping a rag around the pack, he held it to his head, pausing once to verify he hadn't forgotten anything else. Dr. Consonant had instructed him to apply pressure to the hematoma, a common result from a severe concussion. The swelling would go down—eventually.

As expected, the cable news stations provided wall-to-wall coverage about the attack in West Hollywood less than ten miles where Frank lived with his family. Each network had their share of pundits and talking heads, dissecting and analyzing every minutia of the terrorist attack. Everyone pointing fingers, everyone blaming someone else. Teachers who failed to properly educate their children, parents who failed to properly educate their children, Americans who were falling away from religion, the NRA, movie studios whose films glamorized violence, TV stations whose programs glamorized violence, musicians whose lyrics glamorized violence. The President who wasn't keeping American's safe, Congress, the FBI. Anyone and everyone was impugned. Everyone was to blame, everyone that was except those who committed the brazen violence.

A vibrant graphic with scary sound effects filled the screen: *Real Life Horror Comes to Hollywood.* Frank snickered. "Who thinks up this stuff?"

He had just finished his sandwich when the phone rang. "Yes, Abby, I'm fine," he said to himself while reaching for it. His wife wanted to use a personal day and make sure Frank was okay his first day home. He insisted he'd be fine and, reluctantly, she went to work. She departed three hours and five calls ago. He answered the cell and jokingly said, "Hey, baby, I bet you're wearing that sexy little nurse's outfit."

"Grace?"

Oops. "Yes?"

Frank turned beet red after the caller identified himself and a conversation ensued. Cradling the phone Frank jotted down the address on a napkin. He threw on pressed slacks, an open collared mauve dress shirt, a pair of Rockports, decided to forego a much-needed shave, and was out the door in under ten minutes, wondering why he'd been summoned with such urgency.

৩৩৩

The red brick Georgian in chic Calabasas was set far

from the street, shielded behind a sentry of towering olive trees, a wall wrapping the estate and a top-notch security system. After being granted access by the gatehouse guard, Frank felt underdressed and overwhelmed. His Malibu was in the shop, likely on its way to being deemed a total by the insurance company after the bomb blast. He parked his rental, a Chrysler-something, alongside luxury vehicles that cost more than he made in a year.

Brick chimneys were situated on opposite ends of the gabled two-story home. Frank slid his hand down his shirt, used his fingers as a makeshift comb, strolled between pure white pillars, apprehensively rang the doorbell, and took a deep breath.

Before he exhaled the door opened with a flurry. "You must be Frank Grace."

He knew it was a rhetorical question. Unless you'd been living under a rock for four years everyone knew the name Frank Grace, especially the wife of the police chief. "Afternoon, Mrs. Kent."

"Please, Charlotte," she advised with an airy wave of her hand.

In her early fifties, a touch younger than her husband, Charlotte Kent maintained her shapely form. Wearing stilettos, a powder-blue top with plunging neckline, and jeans tight enough to cut off circulation, she stood eye to eye with Frank's six-one frame. Brown eyes, big black hair that went out of style when MTV stopped playing videos, she was doing a commendable job of holding back time. He'd heard she'd worked as a choreographer and dance instructor, first on Broadway and later for movie studios, when her husband anointed her wife number three. She still retained the angular frame of a dancer. A welcoming smile crossed her high cheekbones.

Frank extended his hand but found himself embraced. With her full breasts pressed against him, she said, "Right in the middle of that God-awful blast. I'm glad you're alive."

"Yes, ma'am."

Charlotte broke the embrace and laughed. "*Ma'am*? Dispense with the ma'am stuff. Charlotte."

Frank murmured her name. It sounded too familiar.

"Weldon's out back." She moved onto the portico, threw her hair back with a flourish, and sashayed away.

Assuming that was his cue to follow, Frank fell in step behind. She referenced the new garden, the Hispanic landscapers not doing their job, and the impeccable weather that settled over Southern California. A few times she peeked back to see if Frank was gawking her backside. He almost got caught.

Frank's cell began chirping the iconic opening notes to *The Good, the Bad, and the Ugly*. Charlotte wasted no time. "Is there a stirring in your pants?"

"It's my wife." Embarrassedly, he slid the cell from his pocket and silenced it.

Reaching the rear of the manor, Frank first noticed an Olympic-sized pool centered on a pristine well-maintained lawn that rivaled the outfield at Dodger Stadium. The aroma of fresh cut grass extending to the tree line of neighboring properties filled his senses. Chief Kent appeared peaceful in a lounger, taking in the sun, eyes closed, deep in thought.

"Weldon? Weldon, honey?"

Frank suppressed a chuckle. His brothers in blue referred to the chief with a variety of epithets, most not flattering. Hearing him called Weldon *sounded* funny but Charlotte let it ooze from her lips with bewitching sexuality.

It took a moment for him to respond, either deep in a trance or having dozed off. Charlotte presented Frank as if she was one of those models from *The Price is Right*.

Chief Kent sprang from the chair and firmly pumped Frank's hand. He gave his wife a peck on the lips followed by a smack on that impeccable ass.

Frank realized that some couples just naturally looked good together. Weldon and Charlotte Kent did not.

In his mid-fifties, Military-cut close-cropped brown hair, rugged features, and a ruddy complexion, Kent had more lines on his face than a roadmap of Indiana. His tan was more pronounced than Frank expected, his bright yellow shorts with pineapples and other fruits were not befitting the man who commanded the third largest police force in the country. He stood a good six inches shorter than his stiletto-clad leggy wife. *Bizarre.*

As Charlotte moseyed away, she peered back, as if hoping someone—anyone—was watching.

"Mmm hmm," Kent remarked through a shit-eating grin. "Pull up a chair, Detective. Make yourself comfortable."

Frank dutifully followed the order. Kent was his superior and it felt awkward to sit in a chair placing him higher than his boss so he sat and purposely slouched.

Kent withdrew a Heineken from a cooler and handed one to Frank. Unsure if he was permitted to drink alcohol after the head trauma, Frank thanked him and fake swigged. As Kent repositioned himself on the lounger and his flamboyant shorts twisted irregularly, Frank unfortunately discovered that the police chief went commando.

Weldon Kent was a medical mystery. He downed red meat like it was going out of style, had a dangerously short fuse and no patience. Quick to anger and highly strung, he smoked three packs a day, a fact evidenced by a croaky voice. A heart attack waiting to happen.

Shortly after hitting the streets decades ago, *Patrolman* Kent walked away unscathed after being thrown from a third story fire escape by a crack addict. Another time, he'd been shot twice in the stomach but was back on patrol before the month ended. He once took down a guy twice his size with the attacker's switchblade still imbedded in his forearm. Kent reminded Frank of Tom Berenger in *Platoon:* The only one who could kill Barnes was Barnes. Weldon Kent was too tough to die.

The LAPD had a love-hate relationship with the top cop. He was an autocrat, hard on the department, and had no qualms throwing one of his own under the bus. On the flip side, however, he was good at his job and excelled playing politics. Despite the financial woes that strapped California, Kent always found a way to get what his people needed.

"How's Abby holding up?" Kent huskily inquired.

Frank was surprised the police chief knew the name of one of his detective's spouses. Then again, Frank's reputation preceded him. "Shaken but holding up. She's thankful I'm okay."

"To the wives," Kent toasted, looking off and hoping to get a glimpse of his curvaceous spouse.

Frank clinked bottles and took a small sip this time.

"Jake and Ashley, how're they managing?"

Either Kent knew more about Frank's family than he realized, or he'd been perusing his personnel file. "They're fine—"

"*Fuck*!" Kent twisted his face into a strange almost comical expression, as if he inadvertently swallowed a Jalapeno. He lowered the bottle, removed a piece of Nicorette from his mouth, tossed it away, and lit up a cigarette. All business, all the time, Kent stated, "Let's cut right to the chase."

"Yes, sir," Frank replied heartily. His curiosity had been piqued since receiving the call.

"This is my yard," Kent started, blowing smoke in Frank's face. "And I'm the big dog in my yard. I don't appreciate these tight-assed bureaucrats from DC crawling up my rectum with a microscope. The mayors across Southern California, the higher ups, even the governor, are not happy about being second guessed. There was no way we could have prevented what happened. It's called *national* security for a reason. Yet, those jackoffs are faulting *us*." Kent angrily threw his thumb over his shoulder. Frank realized he pointed west to Canoga Park, not east toward Washington DC. He let it go.

"No group of camel jockeys is going to cause my city to come apart at the seams or screw up the reputation I've built for myself. After Nine/Eleven all the federal agencies planned to work in synch. That sure hasn't happened. You hear the news this morning, Grace?"

Frank confirmed he had. Kent continued as if he hadn't. "A Mosque in Lancaster was torched overnight, another one over in Hemet this morning. Two men and one woman were yanked out of their car while sitting at a red light in Irvine 'cause they *looked* Middle Eastern." Kent's voice grew more agitated by the moment. "I got a call just before you showed up that a rabbi was assaulted outside a kosher deli in Simi Valley. Idiots don't even know the difference between a Jew and a Muslim. A local imam, Abdullah Mohammed Al-Abdullah or whatever his name is, is insisting on extra police presence at his home." Kent took a final puff, stubbed it out into the overflowing ashtray, and immediately piggybacked another. "This will *not* happen on my watch. I'm not Nero. I won't fiddle while my city burns."

Kent rose and began pacing, the cigarette dancing between his lips. "No surveillance cameras in the area caught anyone suspicious planting any incendiary device. I've had my people go back twenty-four hours, more if local merchants recorded farther. No shit bag is seen loitering. Four bystanders, including one still in the hospital, claim they heard someone shout 'Allahu Akbar.' God is great."

"Regrettably, sir, I'm unable to shine any light. My partner, Detective Santana and I made a routine traffic stop and—"

Kent cut him off. "Yes, yes, I read the statement you gave from Cedars Sinai." It was clear Frank was summoned here to listen, not speak. "Their God may be *great* but he can be great in someone else's city. Two of the victims blown to smithereens were tourists. Now I've got the Chamber of Commerce and tourism muckety-mucks raising hell. Of course, they fail to realize it could've been more catastrophic."

Frank leaned forward. "I heard it was a low-impact device."

"Yes. These *A-rabs* were more concerned with instilling fear and ripping away our sense of security than inflicting casualties."

Frank stared off in the distance. It did not go undetected by the police chief. "Something on your mind, Grace?"

Frank debated internally. He surely hadn't been beckoned here to merely chitchat. Perhaps Kent wanted to hear directly from one who was smack dab in the middle. On the other hand, Frank's history with the LAPD left him little wiggle room.

"If something's on your mind," Kent pushed, "let's hear it. Don't pussyfoot."

Frank decided at the last minute to switch gears. "I realize everyone from here to DC wants to grab the brass ring and close this quickly." He paused, choosing his words thoughtfully. "You definitely don't need *me* to tell *you* how to play politics, but I wonder if possibly Mrs. Kent could be of assistance."

Kent became stock-still, hands on his hips like Superman deflecting bullets. "Explain."

"Everyone knows your wife's daughter from her first marriage is an aide to Congressman Brower. And her older child is becoming an influential lobbyist on Capitol Hill."

"And *my* daughter's enrolled at Whittier Law. What's your point?"

Frank lifted the Heineken, this time taking a real swig. "Again, I'm not telling you what to do but have you considered pulling some strings? With the influence of Mrs. Kent's children, you have eyes and ears in Washington." Frank noticed a shift in his boss's body language. He concluded with, "If you can throw your influence around and successfully unite the local investigation with the feds, it would reflect positively on you, sir."

Kent pulled his chin, smiled. He lowered himself into a chair opposite his detective. Frank looked the chief in the eyes, determined not to see the Kent family jewels again. The chief puffed once and pointed the cigarette at Frank. "That's why I like you, Grace. No matter what others say, I like the way you think."

Frank forced a smile. "Thanks…I think."

"I don't need help from Congressman Brower. Nor do I want to drag Charlotte's kids into this. I already have a secret weapon. You."

It took a moment. Frank gulped and pointed to himself. "Me?"

"Yes, you. Let's cut through the crap, Grace, shall we? Your reputation is questionable. The public distrust of the LAPD grew in large part from Azusa four years ago. Am I correct?"

Frank's stomach knotted, his shoulders lowered a bit. "Sir, I—"

"I get it. Trust me, I do. You and Glenn Duckworth go out for a routine dinner. Six punks come in with stocking masks and shotguns, start brandishing AR-15s. A routine holdup turns into the OK-fucking-Corral. Customers get pistol whipped. One scumbag starts pulling a woman toward the stockroom to rape her. The owner, Joe Frattiane, tries unsuccessfully to defend his business. All hell breaks loose. No matter what the media says, no matter how many lawsuits the city got slapped with, no matter how many millions it cost in restitution and settlements to *emotionally scarred* customers who forgot you saved their lives, no matter the outcry of community leaders and the riots that followed, you did the right thing. You and Officer Duckworth may have been off the clock, but members of law enforcement are never off duty. It was your heroic actions that prevented a deadly situation from becoming deadlier. Thanks to your bravery, only a handful of customers suffered superficial wounds and five of the six assholes are dead." Kent paused before adding, "If that'd been me, I'd have taken down all six."

"And Officer Duckworth?"

"Collateral damage. Sad fact of life, but shit happens."

The police chief once again proving political correctness is not his strong suit: Shit happens? Still, Frank's insides churned. He didn't need to be vividly reminded of that horrific evening. He'd set foot in too many damned crime scenes where walls were doused with blood splatter, linens soaked in crimson, and corpses whose insides were on the outside. But in thirteen years on the force, the most carnage he ever witnessed was that night in Il Vittorio's, carnage he helped create.

He also pondered why Kent, who now spoke proudly about Frank's *heroic actions* like a father boasting of his son's game-winning home run in Little League, hadn't been a more vocal supporter years ago. At the time, Kent played to the media, giving them sound bites they craved and distancing himself and the entire department from one of their own. "Detective Frank Grace may be a detective, but he's not one of our brothers." Kent's cutting indictment still stung. Frank accepted the chief had a role to play. He just wished he had played it differently.

"Grace, you with me?"

"Sorry sir." Frank refocused. "How can I help?"

Kent sat, leaned forward, made a triangle over his nose, and spoke systematically. "I want you personally handling this investigation. You will be working for me, reporting directly to me and no one else. Whatever you need to crack this case, you let me know. Full carte blanche."

Frank's head swelled. He longed for his icepack. "Why me?"

"Why not you? It's a win-win. Homeland Security, NSA, NCTC, and God knows who else are overrunning my city. I refuse to be treated like a guest at my own party. *You* can turn everything around. Cracking this one case can redirect your entire career and clear your name. Wouldn't it be nice not to be second guessed, Detective? Wouldn't it be a welcome change to not have your own colleagues snicker behind your back and talk shit about you? With a single arrest, you can go from goat to hero. You'd go from poster boy of everything wrong with the PD to everything right. And yes, it would reflect positively on me. I won't lie about that. The thought of flipping DC the proverbial bird would feel good." Kent extended his middle finger into the air, again toward Canoga Park. "Fuck you, Washington. It was one of mine who solved this."

Frank pursed his lips. What Kent lacked in political correctness he made up for in salesmanship. *One of mine* was nice to hear. Four years and four days had passed since his judgment was called into question. It would indeed be euphoric to have his career and his name reestablished. Still, he had reservations. "And if I don't succeed?"

"Then you don't." Kent shrugged. "You've got nothing to lose and everything to gain. And although I'd never admit this to the media, I respect you, Grace. You fly by the seat of your pants. You break the rules, hate the bullshit. But you close cases. I look at you and I see myself fifteen years ago."

"I appreciate your words, sir. I truly do."

"But?"

"But—this is an act of terrorism. A federal crime and I'm a local Homicide detective."

Kent leaned back in his lounger and blew a few smoke rings. "Is it?"

Frank remained silent. When Kent bore his eyes into him, Frank pried. "What are you saying, sir?"

"Don't pull punches. You've been a cop a long time. What do *you* think?"

Frank rubbed the back of his neck, surprised to find himself sweating. "I think there's more buried beneath the surface," he offered in a less-than-confident voice.

"Go on."

Frank vacillated. "I—I look at what happened here and I don't see New York and Washington. I see Boston and Oklahoma City."

Kent shifted. "Meaning?"

Frank put things together in his mind. The confidence had returned. "Meaning I'm just a local cop, not some superspy or well-connected spook." He pointed to his temple then his stomach. "My head confirms what I feel in my gut. These terror groups wear slaughter like a badge of honor.

They get a hard-on—pardon my language—for this. So, why has no one stepped forward and declared this as their handiwork? After Nine/Eleven, Bin Laden and Al-Qaeda were immediately in the crosshairs. Be it Mumbai or Paris or Berlin, they can't wait to attach their signature to murder. But Boston and Oklahoma City were different. No one claimed responsibility. McVeigh, Nichols, and the Tsarnaev brothers had to be hunted down. Four days removed from the explosion in Hollywood and still no one has taken credit."

"You're insinuating this was domestic terrorism?" Kent's words were sharp, accusatory.

Frank held steadfast to his belief. "Yes, sir, I am."

Kent scrutinized Frank, his craggy features and fiery eyes burning into the detective's soul. The stern expression morphed into something never displayed by Weldon Kent— a smile. He rotated a finger between them. "Great minds think alike. That's why, as I said, I like you. Can I take that as a yes?"

Frank stalled, bowed his head for a moment, and weighed the pros and cons. He doubted he could succeed but, as the chief pointed out, he had nothing to lose and everything to gain. "Yes, sir."

The men simultaneously stood, a firm handshake exchanged. Chief Kent concluded the meeting with a few housekeeping issues. "This stays under the radar. I'll pull some strings and give you the leeway. But, as they say in DC, this is a need-to-know basis and no one needs to know. Anything you need, you tell me. Anything. You report to me only. You're a one-person task force."

Frank stuck up two fingers. "Two-person task force. I want my partner working this with me."

Kent seemed tentative. "Isn't your partner assigned to the disappearance of Detective Nichols?"

Frank nodded his confirmation and reminded Chief Kent that Michelle, for what it was worth, had served two tours in Afghanistan while the image of an irate Tony Gallardo appeared in his mind. His lieutenant would go ballistic when learning Frank went over his head to have Michelle reassigned back with him.

"This is a black op, Detective," Kent declared. "No one—and I mean no one—can get wind of this. Do you trust Detective Santana?"

"With my life."

Kent chewed his lips, took one final long drag, and nodded. "Consider it done."

With a bounce in his step and excited nervousness in his gut about the opportunity to rid ghosts from his past, Frank promenaded out of Casa de Kent. Reaching the driveway, he remembered something. He checked his phone. Four voice mails, six missed calls—all from Abby. He smiled at his wife's overly worrisome nature. First day home from the hospital and she was panicking. But it warmed his heart to feel loved. Frank hit number one on speed dial and was instantly greeted by a frantic voice. "Where were you?"

"Sorry, sweetie. I was—I couldn't answer. I'm fine, no need to stress."

"No need to stress?" Abby cried. "It's Ashley. Something's happened."

Chapter 9

Even at eight years of age Jake Grace could sense the tension in the air. It was rare that Mommy, Daddy, his icky sister, and he ate dinner together but, when they did, there was lots of talking. Tonight, silence hung over the table like an ax about to come down on a zombie in one of those movies he loved. Looking at the slop on his plate, Jake twirled his fork and asked, "Why is all green food yucky?"

"It's not yucky," Abby replied, "It's healthy."

"Popeye eats spinach," Frank added.

Jake scrunched his face and looked across the table. "You didn't finish your spinits, daddy."

Abby smiled at her husband. "Yeah, Daddy, you didn't finish your *spinits*."

"I like spinits so much that I have it for dessert instead of ice cream."

Jake's mouth curled into an O. Daddy was being silly— or crazy. "Boogers are green. Are they healthy, too?"

"Everyone's except yours," Ashley piped in, glancing at her brother but avoiding eye contact with her parents.

"My boogers are not icky. Yours are."

"Are not."

"Are too!"

Ashley leaned over and pinched her brother's arm, which instigated a piercing scream that reached San Francisco.

When he saw his sister laugh, he followed suit. He then shoved his chair back, shouting to everyone within a six mile radius, "I'm done!" and began running out of the dining room.

"Come back here, young man."

Uh oh. The Mom voice. He pivoted, sulked, and pointed at his sister. "It's her turn to do the dishes. I did 'em last night."

"No," Abby said. "Your sister did. But actually I need you to help me with something upstairs. Your sister will be clearing the table tonight. And maybe for the rest of her life."

Jake clapped, jumped up and down in place, and stuck out his tongue at Ashley.

Abby took her son by the hand and led him away, an over the shoulder wink at Frank before leaving.

"So, what happened?" Frank asked seconds after he and his daughter were alone.

Ashley tilted back, lifting the chair onto two legs. "Didn't Mom tell you?"

His twelve year old was months shy of becoming a teenager. She was beginning to exhibit the attitude and backtalk Frank had dreaded for…well, since the first time he held his newborn daughter. "I want you to tell me."

"Why? You already know what happened." Slouched down, peering under the table, she began knocking the floor with her sandals.

"Look at me. Ash, I'm up here. Look at me."

"What?"

"I want to hear your side."

"No you don't!" she clipped. "You already decided I'm guilty and convicted me."

Ashley's dig was meant to cut deep. And it did.

Frank's job resulted in countless late nights, obtaining witness statements, stakeouts, crawling around crime scenes, and, as such, being a pseudo-absentee father. It shredded his soul. Instead of watching his children grow, he was dealing with human trash. While saving a city of strangers, he was losing his family.

There'd been numerous evenings, especially recently, when both he and Abby had to work late, thrusting Ashley into the role of makeshift mom to her younger brother. Were Frank and Abby's careers, their need to make a buck and provide for the family, indirectly robbing their daughter of her childhood? Frank wondered.

The toe tapping beneath the table caused a memory to be wrenched free from a chamber long since locked away in the recesses of Frank's mind.

Tapping.

Rhythmic pattering.

The drumming of a pewter butane lighter bashing a badly chipped kitchen table. His father would slam louder and louder, scolding young Frank for something trivial. It didn't matter what the indiscretion. Specifics never mattered to Ernest Grace. Frank's birth was guilt enough. The hammering got louder in conjunction with the disparaging comments mercilessly shouted at him through a cloud of alcoholic breath. Frank found himself grateful for the eventual smack across the head. It meant the verbal assault was over and his father was finished—at least until the next night.

"I'm going upstairs."

It took Frank a beat to return from the troubling memory. He did a double take at Ashley, thankful she'd never met her grandfather. "I'm not letting you leave until you give me your side."

"Don't I have the right to remain silent?"

A second stab, equally penetrating. Frank glared at his daughter, hoping he didn't resemble his own father.

Ashley sighed, slammed her shoe harder, and started twirling her brown hair. "Fine!" She relayed the details Frank heard from Abby, the same ones Abby heard from the principal, two teachers, and a security guard. Four girls, including his daughter, were taunting another girl in the schoolyard. The student was backed against a wall. A finger jabbed into her face caused her to swipe the hand away. The quartet viewed that as a provocation and began beating the girl. The daughter of Detective Grace was one of the assailants.

Glimpsing the bruises on her knuckles, he asked "Why'd you hit her?"

Ashley shrugged.

"*Why?*"

"I don't like her. No one does. She's a bitch." Ashley defensively added, "Even *you* wouldn't like her."

Frank furrowed his brows. "How could I not like someone I don't know?"

"Trust me, Dad, you wouldn't. Plus, anyone whose name is Sabiha Mansoor deserves to get their ass kicked." She cackled. "Man Sore."

Frank saw the open door and walked through. "Is that why you and your friends attacked her? 'Cause she's Muslim?"

Ashley's instantaneous response floored him. "Hell, yes."

Frank inhaled and gazed down the vacant hall, willing his wife to return so she could take over. He collected his thoughts and started positively. "You're almost thirteen, Ash. That means you're practically an adult so I'm going to talk to you like an adult—"

"I already *am* an adult!"

Frank's heart skipped a beat. He tried to recall seeing her in the company of boys. "Wha—what?"

"I got my period months ago." As it sank in that his little girl was, in fact, becoming a woman, she added, "Maybe you should work less and talk to Mom more."

Insert knife, twist for maximum pain. "That's—" Frank gulped and shook his head as if a fly was buzzing his ears. "That's not what I want to talk about. So you and these others attacked this girl 'cause of her religion?"

"Yeah, she's a towel head." Ashley seemed delighted. "I thought you'd be proud."

"*Proud*?" Frank howled. "Why would you ever think that?"

Ashley resumed the tap-dancing beneath the table and twirled her hair with more fury.

"Talk to me, Ash."

She initially held back, then burst like a dam. "They almost killed you, Dad. I saw you in that hospital bed. I saw what they did to you. I saw what that did to Mom. While you were unconscious and Mom was by your side, it was me who had to listen to Jake crying himself to sleep at night. He even asked me what happens when people die and if he could visit you in Heaven. I lived it. I saw it!" By the time she concluded, tears ran down her face. She wiped her flushed cheeks with a napkin. "I'm going to my room."

Frank reached across the table and clutched his daughter's trembling wrist. "You can't judge an entire group of people based on the actions of a few."

Ashley leaned forward and locked eyes with her father. "And what if it'd been Mom lying in a hospital bed? What if some bomb went off, and Mom was the one almost killed? Tell me *you* wouldn't want revenge against someone?"

The image of Abby immobilized and catatonic was not a picture Frank liked imagining. He rapidly pushed that from his mind. "Revenge, sure. But revenge against the people responsible, not just the first person I could take it out on." He folded his arms across his chest and studied his daughter before continuing. "People are always blaming someone else for their problems. The big guy is always picking on the little guy. There's always some scapegoat, sweetheart. Romans threw Christians to the lions. Nazi's killed six million Jews 'cause they viewed them as the root of all their problems. You know about slavery and, when you get a little older, you'll learn that our own government locked up American citizens in something called internment camps just 'cause they were Japanese." Since his little girl was becoming an adult, he spoke to her like one. "Assholes come in every shape and color and yes, religion. So, if your friends want to pick on someone just 'cause they're weaker or have different beliefs, walk away next time. Be the bigger person. Your mom and I raised you to think for yourself and be independent, not to follow what someone else says."

Ashley pursed her lips. "You don't get it, do you?"

"Get what?"

"It was me. Kicking Sabiha's ass was *my* idea."

Chapter 10

"Did they find anything in your head?"

"We knew you were hard-headed, Frank, and this proves it."

His colleagues at West Bureau-Hollywood Homicide gave him the expected ribbing when he returned to work. There was plenty of backslapping and smiles. But after Chief Kent's remark yesterday about fellow detectives talking behind his back, Frank wondered about their sincerity. Golden Boy Troy Wadkins commemorated the momentous occasion by supplying extra doughnuts. Everyone seemed genuinely happy to see Frank but Detective Craft's reaction seemed a bit over the top.

Red hair and brown eyes, the detective in her early-thirties held Frank's bicep with an easygoing manner. "It's so great having you back, Frank. I've been worried sick. I mean, we all were but especially…you know, you're a nice guy and a good, no, a great detective, and things always seem gloomier when you're not around." She gripped his other bicep and smiled. "Really, really good seeing you again."

"It's good seeing…everyone, Heather."

Frank closed cases, investigated homicides and arrested murderers. But sometimes the biggest mystery of all was understanding women. He got to his workstation, surprised his partner was not there. He was about to call her when

Lieutenant Gallardo tapped Frank's shoulder and motioned for him to follow.

In Gallardo's glass-enclosed Cone of Silence, the door was slammed shut, but it made little difference. He screamed, *"Chief Kent?"*

"Tony, let me explain—"

Gallardo cut him off, his eyes enraged, his bulbous nose flaring. "How many times have I pulled your ass out of the fire? Ten, twenty, fifty? How many times have I covered for you? Ten, twenty, fifty? And this is how you repay me? You go over my head to get Santana pulled off Kendra Nichols's disappearance. Not cool, Grace. Not cool at all."

"The chief called you directly?"

"One of his minions did. All I know is that he's got you working some other angle of the attack and that you insisted on Santana. Why didn't you just ask me, dammit?"

"It was spur of the moment. The chief wanted me and, if I was going to get Michelle, I needed to strike while the iron was hot."

"So you break protocol to get what you want. That's what you're saying?"

Frank explained his reasoning while keeping the assignment's finer points secretive. He got nowhere. He understood Gallardo's anger and regretted having played it the way he had.

"How's your head?" Gallardo inquired after a protracted silence.

Frank wondered if the question was idle banter or stemmed from genuine concern. "Getting better. Still get some killer headaches, and I forget things some time. But I'll be back to a hundred percent soon."

"I hope so, for your sake. If Kent personally chose you, you better be two hundred percent." Gallardo leaned forward. "I don't know why I'm telling you this, especially now and especially since you already know. But look, you have a volatile past and a dubious future. Kent plays politics and I'm sure he offered to wipe the slate clean, let bygones be bygones, and all that hogwash. But think it through. You succeed, all well and good. You screw up and it's a one-way ticket out of the LAPD and the end of your career." He allowed a moment for that to register with Frank's concussed mind. Then he threw his chin toward the door. *Meeting over.*

Frank had just exited when Detective Craft's voice carried across the squad room. "Break room, everyone. Hurry!"

Frank and a couple dozen others hustled over. Tables and chairs hastily shoved aside so detectives and support staff could huddle close to the wall-mounted HDTV. Craft aimed the remote like a gun and arrowed up the volume. Several parted, allowing Johnny to wheel himself to the front. Murmurs of "shh" filled the room.

The twenty-something Latino reporter nervously fiddled with papers at the anchor desk and shot glances between someone off-camera and millions of viewers watching. His customary plastic grin and polished white teeth were nowhere to be found, replaced with a countenance of doubt and angst. KABC's morning *gabfest*, as Frank referred to it, always focused on human interest pieces, recipes, and stories about health. Programming was geared to single parents and retirees. Breaking news was not in the job description of the neophyte anchor.

A collective gasp pervaded the break room when the grainy video began rolling. The woman was blindfolded and on her knees, trembling, defeated, and clearly fearing for her life. Her blonde hair was matted, her chin quivered in fear, and she'd been beaten—badly. Pressed against her left temple was the barrel of a Glock. She was topless, adding to the humiliation and dishonor. Her breasts were indistinct due to improvised circles the graphic arts people quickly created. There was nothing noticeable in the background other than a dangling black curtain.

An automated voice, clearly altered with the use of an electronic voice changer, was heard. To Frank it sounded tinny, robotic, like someone who'd undergone a laryngectomy and now communicated through a device held to their neck.

"What is your name?"

Her head lowered.

The off-camera voice shouted furiously, "What is your name?"

"K—Kendra. Nich—ols."

The captor mocked her. "What is it you do, K—Kendra Nich—ols."

She couldn't lift her eyes. "I'm a de—de—detective with the LAPD."

"This woman is a police officer. She is also a cancer. She is one of many cancers in your city. The only way to defeat a cancer is to kill it." The click of a bullet chambered was heard off screen. Her head shoved right as the barrel pressed harder against her head, nearly toppling the helpless detective.

"Oh, God, no," someone gasped behind Frank.

The voice continued. "She is a whore, a scourge on society. Yet, your country commends her for something she is not. War is being waged. Innocent children and women are being killed all over the world by you, burned by your cowardly drones that rein fire from the sky.

"Now we bring war to your shores, to your homes. We will bring it to your schools where your children are brainwashed. We will bring it to your sporting events where thousands gather. We will bring it to your shopping malls, and to your darkened movie theaters where you escape the reality of your lives and remain oblivious to the murders your government causes.

"This whore is a detective, a police officer, highly trained in protecting herself. Yet, here she is, cowering like a beaten dog. If we got to her, we can get to you. Sleep tight, infidels. For tomorrow, this may be your wife, your mother, your child. Allahu Akbar."

The Latino reappeared on the screen, ashen and gaunt.

He heard instructions in his ear and stammered, "We're—going to t—take a commercial break."

Half the break room cleared quickly while others stared vacantly, the troubling video replaced by a commercial for erectile dysfunction. "Fucking bastards," someone lamented while Frank watched an elderly couple dancing in the sunset.

His gut was in knots, his head pounding. Yesterday, he felt invigorated to be handpicked by Chief Kent. Now he wondered what he was up against. And, as usual, what the hell he'd gotten himself into.

Appreciating that local and federal agencies from sea to shining sea were analyzing, scrutinizing, examining and studying every possible lead from the forty-five-second clip, Frank relied on his own expert.

He wrapped his knuckles on Johnny's door, affectionately dubbed *Cyberopolis*. Technically challenged, Frank tried to avoid this high-tech geek cave at all costs. He always felt as if he stepped through a time machine and stumbled into the twenty-fifth century. "What's your take on the video?"

Johnny's head was going back and forth, as if he was watching Center Court at Wimbledon. He wheeled himself between three separate monitors, a pair of printers, and other instruments Frank was clueless about.

Frazzled, Johnny pushed his eyeglasses back up but waved Frank away.

"Did you notice anything that can help?" Frank pried.

"Not yet." Johnny paused then added confidently, "But if it's there, I'll find it."

Frank second guessed himself. He insisted on Michelle's assistance, why hadn't he requested Johnny's as well? He now weighed the pros and cons of bringing the IT guru into his inner circle. However, his friend was currently too engrossed in the video. Maybe later. He turned and departed Cyberopolis.

So deep in thought, he didn't initially respond when hearing his name. "Detective Grace?"

Snapped back, he blinked twice and stared at the desk sergeant whose name had slipped his mind. "Hey…"

"This guy was asking to speak with you."

Frank cocked his head as a man got up from a wooden bench and approached. Frank presented his professional smile. "Detective Grace, how can I help you?"

The man pulled Frank's right hand forward and sandwiched it with a warm friendly handshake. "Santiago Mendes. But please call me Sandy. All my friends do."

Sandy Mendes enunciated every syllable. Clearly English was not his first language but he spoke it proudly. Standing a few inches shorter than Frank, the man wore frayed jeans and a light blue workman's shirt over a trim one-seventy-pound frame. Close-cropped white hair made Frank guestimate him to be late forties. His hands were heavily calloused, and Frank felt as if he was shaking hands with a bag of walnuts.

"How can I help you, sir?"

"It's my daughter."

"Your daughter?"

"Josefina. She told me what almost happened with those young men by the Hollywood sign several mornings back." He shook his head and added solemnly, "It's so hard nowadays to raise children the right way."

Frank waved it away. "It was nothing, Mr. Mendes. Just happened to be at the right place at the right time." *Something new for me.* "I do have to disagree with you. Young *men* don't do what they tried. How is Josefina?"

"Oh, you know…" His words trailed off. "I just wanted to thank you for saving her. Do you have children, Detective Grace?"

"One of each, twelve and eight."

Mendes noticed the wedding ring. "It's easier with two parents but still an uphill battle. We can only do so much before sending our children off and pray for the best. I'm a single parent myself."

"Mm, hmm," Frank replied, hoping his boredom was not

obvious. He glanced beyond Mendes's shoulder, craving to see Michelle enter the Barn.

"Again, I just wanted to thank you for helping my girl." Mendes removed his wallet and handed over a tattered business card. "If there's anything you need, give me a call."

Frank took the card. "Sandy's Tree Trimming?" He despised yard work, avoiding it completely until Mount St. Abby was close to erupting. He longed for Jake to be a few years older and pawn it off, giving him the ol' *hard work never killed anyone* speech. "I'll hang onto this."

"I do good work. My padre raised me to have a strong work ethic. I just sort of fell into landscaping. It's not like anyone grows up dreaming of mowing other people's lawns."

Frank nodded but remained silent. Perhaps a non-verbal response would give Mendes the hint. With everything going on, he didn't have time to discuss flora.

"Believe it or not, Detective Grace, I wanted to be a cop. Sorry, police officer."

"Oh?" Frank overtly glanced at his wristwatch.

"My dream was to get into the DEA. When I was *poquito*…um…little, I saw what those cartels did to my village in Culiacan. I promised myself that when I grew taller and stronger, I'd do whatever necessary to bring them down. If I could arrest even one kingpin or save one child's life, I'd feel content."

"What happened?"

"Pard'n?"

"Why didn't you?" Frank asked, now interested.

"Life happened. I passed all the tests and applied to the LAPD just after turning *dieciocho*…eighteen. But I was rejected. When I was *poquito*, I had a few bouts of epilepsy. That disqualified me." Sandy smiled woefully. "Funny how things from our past always have a bearing on our future."

Don't I know it? "Sorry to hear."

"Met a wonderful lady, fell in love, was blessed with

Josefina. Then the wonderful lady took off and left me alone with my little angel. Josefina's all I have, Detective. That's why I wanted to personally thank you. If I lost her, I'd lose myself."

Frank felt a lump in his throat. Santiago Mendes was doing everything right—or at least trying. He sacrificed for his daughter, tried to remain a positive light in her life. Yet, in spite of his brave efforts, she longed to fit in and agreed to be filmed engaging in a sex act. He listened about Josefina, but thought of Ashley.

Frank felt his hand warmly sandwiched a second time and, with that, Santiago Mendes exited into the Los Angeles morning. Mendes, like Frank and countless others, fought the good fight against overwhelming odds, hoping that tomorrow would be better than today.

෧෧෧

"Hey."

Frank turned to see his partner fall into her chair on her side of their cubicle. Michelle's usual enthusiasm at the start of their watch was missing. "You okay?"

She absentmindedly brought her computer to life. "Rough morning."

"You see the video?"

"Heard it on the radio but haven't seen the footage." She faced Frank. "Did it look as bad as it sounded?"

"Worse."

Michelle shook her head once, turned to her computer. "Damn shame." She seemed preoccupied.

To get her mind off whatever was troubling her, Frank prophesized. "You know what I don't get?"

"Why Noah just didn't swat those two mosquitos?"

Frank pondered for a moment. "That, too. But the video? Whoever's holding Detective Nichols didn't make any demands. No calls to open the gate at Gitmo and let everyone out, no telling us to pull troops out of the Middle East. Nothing."

"This isn't some half-cocked kidnapping, Frank."

"Are you positive about that?"

Michelle's hands froze on her keyboard. "You sure this isn't the concussion talking?"

Frank rolled his chair close enough to where he couldn't be overheard. Speaking in a whisper and changing topics when someone strolled by he told her about yesterday's meeting with the chief of police and the subsequent proposal. When he finished, Michelle seemed perplexed.

"I can't. Did you forget? I'm supporting Cady and Millington on Kendra's dissapp—well, kidnapping now."

"Kent did me a favor. Plus, after that video, the feds will take over. I already spoke to Tony."

"How'd Gallardo take it?"

Frank gave her a look. *How do you think?* "And if I'm right, Kendra's abduction and the bombing in West Hollywood *are* related."

"Okay," Michelle said, thinking out loud. "Maybe they are. But if both acts were carried out by the same extremists, it's still terrorism. And therefore, a national security problem. Not our jurisdiction."

"Or domestic terrorism?"

"Even so," Michelle countered, "Domestic terrorism still falls into the lap of Uncle Sam. Oklahoma City, Boston, San Bernardino. Remember?"

Frank was taken aback by his partner's reluctance to join forces. He'd gone out on a limb with Chief Kent, burned yet another bridge with Lieutenant Gallardo. Michelle's unwillingness left him flatfooted. Taking a page out of Kent's playbook, Frank reasoned. "Look. We've got nothing to lose and everything to gain. If the feds nab these guys first, great. But if we somehow pull it off, it'll help rebuild my rep and categorically will reflect positively for you. My career's in the crapper but your future is still bright. It'll help me, but do wonders for you." Frank grinned. "And tell me you wouldn't rather work with me than Colby and Millington."

"Cady."

Frank frowned.

"You said Colby. It's Cady. Cady and Millington."

"Oh," Frank murmured as his hand reflexively went to the spot on his head that slammed against a brick wall.

Michelle studied her partner for a beat as if he was a perp in the interrogation room. She changed topics. "I had breakfast with Bianca. That's why I was late."

"How's your sister doing?"

"She wants me to take Sophia for a while. Maybe for a long while."

Frank remained tightlipped and waited for more.

"She seems determined to get herself straight this time. I really think she's serious about it. She even started talking about opening that B and B in Oregon she always wanted and thinks now would be a good time. Ya know, after she sobers up."

Frank didn't recall ever hearing about a Bed and Breakfast in Oregon. Maybe he'd forgotten.

"She thinks getting out of town and away from the temptation of drugs and alcohol is the only way she'll save her own life."

Frank knew Bianca had a drinking problem. Drug addiction was news to him. "I thought she was readmitting herself to rehab."

"She thinks that after she cleans herself up, she's going to leave the city altogether. Too much temptation here. Maybe that's why she always goes back to her old life." Michelle sighed and looked off at nothing. "We talked about legal guardianship of Sophia. Maybe even permanent custody. I love my sis but Bianca's not mom material. Everyone realizes that, even her own daughter."

Frank's eyes widened. "You're going to adopt Sophia?"

Michelle waggled her head. "Sophia's my niece. There's no one else."

"Sophia's nine. Eighteen is a long way off."

"Don't you think I know that?" she replied and took a deep breath.

Frank clucked his tongue. If memory served, the longest relationship Michelle ever had was four years. Raising a child for nine? He had his doubts. "I think it's great what you're doing, but what does that have to do with what I'm proposing?"

"If I have Sophia, it has everything to do with it. I can't be a single *parent* and put my life on the line every day. If Bianca's out of the picture and something happens to me, who cares for my niece?"

"I've got two kids," Frank said weakly.

"That's you. Plus, you have Abby. And you're accustomed to children. I'm not."

"Doesn't adoption take a while?"

"It's not an adoption, it's a legal guardianship. And it's not like my sister is going to fight me. This was her idea. Well, ours really. It could take as few as thirty days."

"Wow," said Frank. "I can loan Ashley to you for a few weeks. That'll change your mind."

"Ash's a great girl. I love her like she's my own." When Frank twisted his lips, Michelle noticed it. "Problems?"

"Just…stuff. How about this? Let's start working some leads, pounding some doors, and see what happens. If at any time you want off, let me know."

Michelle smiled. "Detective Grace, you know I would never back away once I commit."

"Is that a yes?"

"A temporary yes."

"The offer to walk away is there if you're so inclined."

"Need I remind you, we're partners?"

Frank raised his arm, made a fist. "Grantana?"

Michelle chuckled. "I want first billing. Sant-ace."

"Sant-ace it is, though Grantana sounds better."

Grace and Santana fist-bumped. Frank thanked her and then pivoted to his computer. Moments later, after opening an email, Frank asked, "Does the name Eddie Evanovich ring a bell?"

Chapter 11

After being exhibited like an animal, Kendra was belligerently manhandled. The ropes were sadistically cut away, her left ankle getting gouged in the process. She was thrown back in the same filthy clothes she'd been wearing since her abduction. Jerked to her feet by a handful of hair, Kendra screamed when a hood was placed over her head. She recalled seeing those gory beheadings on TV and feared she'd meet the same fate. Still, she managed to focus. Warm sunlight on her shoulders. Marched precisely thirty nine paces across what felt like wet grass beneath her bare feet. Manure and something else in the air. Ammonia? One, two, three locks disengaged. What sounded like a barn door creaking open on a rusty track. She heard a chain pulled followed by the sound of fluorescent bulbs whirring to life.

A palm between her shoulders thrust her forward. She stumbled and collapsed onto the same fetid mattress where she'd spent the bulk of her captivity. Hostilely, she was manipulated and twisted like a rag doll. Arms extended overhead, secured by handcuffs. *Are those my handcuffs?*

The hood was aggressively ripped from her head, the blindfold yanked off. She blinked several times to adjust her eyes to the murky lighting. She cringed as Short One leaned over, his hot breath tantalizing her ear. "How's it feel to have the most famous tits in history?"

Kendra said nothing.

The powerful slap to her face stung, her eyes watered. But she wouldn't give this bastard the satisfaction.

"You think you're tough?"

Silence.

Another slap, this one harder.

"I asked you a question, bitch."

Kendra met his soulless eyes. "How 'bout you untie me and see for yourself."

The smile was a mixture of amusement and malevolence. "I've got good news and good news. If everything goes according to plan, this'll be over in a couple days." He paused theatrically. "It also gives us plenty of time to become better acquainted."

"And your partner?" Kendra said with confidence she lacked. "He's clearly the brains of your little faction. How do you think he'd react?"

"Few more bruises? He wouldn't even notice."

Before she could reply, Short One drove his knee into her belly. Again. And again. Her lungs emptied. She tried to cry out. She began to weep. A strong hand gripped her neck and began to close like a vise. She couldn't breathe. Her eyes bulged. She lost control of her bladder. She flailed as much as possible, wriggling about under the weight of her kidnapper.

Slowly, her energy slipped away, and Kendra's world went dark.

⌘

Frank knew that solving a case, any case, required dogged determination, drive, and dedication. But this was not just any case. He'd been personally chosen by the chief of police and given carte blanche to be his own one-man task force. In a way, he felt as if the safety of all Los Angeles was in hands. *Sure, no pressure.*

In nearly two years, his partner not only matched but frequently surpassed his tenacity and resolve. Now, regrettably, when he and Michelle needed to be at their best, she appeared to be half-assing it. He wondered if she'd agreed out of the desire to bring those responsible to justice or simply out of loyalty to him.

For Frank, it was second-nature to balance his job with his career. But with Michelle caring for her niece, being responsible for someone else, he agonized about her ability to balance Detective Santana with Aunt Michelle.

Her career and her life had always been one in the same. Sure, she dated from time to time but for one reason or another, relationships never lasted. Abby was old-fashioned, believing everyone should be happily married. But even she eventually grew tired of playing matchmaker for Michelle.

Now, facing the biggest case in either of their careers, Michelle had to successfully walk a tightrope without a net. Frank hoped she'd be able to perform the balancing act. Their careers, and innocent lives, hung in the balance.

Michelle had announced she'd be questioning Lori Edens, the widow of Phil Edens, on her own. Perhaps Lori had been aware of her husband's infidelity and could offer some insight to Kendra's kidnapping. To Frank, her choice to interrogate the Edens woman solo, indicated Michelle's willingness to work the case with him, just not too closely.

The footage of Detective Nichols being held against her will, vulnerable, and cowering in fear, was not an image Frank or anyone in the LAPD would soon forget. The meeting with Police Chief Kent was fresh in his mind, along with his partner's lack of enthusiasm and his daughter instigating an attack on a Muslim girl. Frank needed to get the hell out of the stifling squad room. And quick.

On his way out, he detoured to Cyberopolis. Johnny's head rotated like Linda Blair in *The Exorcist*. Frank handed him a piece of paper with *Eddie Evanovich* scribbled on it. "When you have a chance, thanks."

Johnny grunted without lifting his eyes.

Frank hurried from the suffocating building, the bright California sunshine ineffective against his gloom.

Sixteen miles but an hour later, Frank exited his loaner and was promptly overcome with the pungent aroma of jet fuel. He watched a United flight climb west over the ocean before banking and heading to parts unknown. As the plane became a gray pinprick against the cerulean blue backdrop, he recalled being woken by his frantic wife on the morning of Tuesday, September 11, 2001.

And he thought of West Hollywood a week ago.

Around the rear of the squat building he waved to his contact and approached.

"As I live and breathe, Frank Grace. How's it hangin'?"

First Johnny, now Brad Lapitan. "Was there a department memo I didn't catch."

Lapitan stroked a black Lab with his left hand and pumped Frank's with his right. If anyone was to make a movie of his life, Bradley Cooper would get the lead. The physical resemblances and mannerisms were uncanny. Three years earlier, Frank and Abby had dinner with Lapitan and his girlfriend, ironically the spitting image of Jennifer Lawrence.

During the drive home, Abby appeared smitten with Lapitan's good looks. Since then, Frank kept his wife far away.

Lapitan was one of two dozen officers assigned to the Bomb Detection K9 unit. The elite group worked jointly with TSA just across the tarmac at LAX sniffing out shells, missiles, explosives, and other combustible materials. They were one of many growing organizations enlisted to fight terror. They chatted, caught up on mutual acquaintances, and discussed baseball. Brad, like many others, chastised Frank about his loyalty to the hated Giants rather than the Dodgers.

"I grew up in the Bay Area," Frank reminded him.

"That's your problem, not mine."

When Brad asked about Abby, Frank claimed, "She's

put on about ninety pounds, came down with some rare skin disease, and lost a lot of teeth."

"You're bullshitting me."

"That's nothing compared to her flatulence problem."

Lapitan laughed and patted his shoulder. "Always good seeing you, my man. But what's so important that you didn't want to discuss on the phone?"

"I can't just stop by and see your smilin' mug?"

Lapitan cocked back his arm and tossed a red ball to the far end of the enclosed yard. The bomb-sniffing dog remained motionless until the object stopped rolling. His eyes were enlarged, his ears pricked. But he remained stationary.

"Go get it, boy," Frank commanded. The dog didn't budge.

Then Lapitan ordered, "Cagney. Go!" The Lab scampered across the expanse with blinding speed and exquisite refinement.

"Your dog listens to me about as well as my kids," Frank remarked. "So, West Hollywood?"

"Why do you want to know?"

"Just working on something."

Lapitan held his gaze before beginning. "Coupla' suits from DC interrogated us the other day. Ripped apart our security procedures and demanded we refine techniques and protocol for LAX."

"Can you tell me anything about the bomb itself?"

"Yes. It went off." Cagney materialized at Lapitan's side and sat on his haunches, not even panting.

"I was there," Frank said "The destruction would've been much worse had I not blocked it with my head."

Lapitan arched a brow and spoke professionally, the jocularity gone. He prefaced his talk with a disclaimer, stating his group wasn't involved in the investigation and what he'd heard was circumstantial. "It appears to have been low-grade explosives. Amateurish, really. A poor man's IED. IEDs were first used, albeit on a limited nature, during Viet Nam but became the weapon of choice by the IRA in the

1970s. They normally consist of semtex and simple fertilizer. Think roadside bombs used to stop a military convoy."

"How about against buildings?"

Lapitan nodded. "That's not their general purpose, but yes. A bomb is a bomb, Frank. They can be designed for any type of destruction. All you need is patience and the right mindset." As Frank listened, he realized he was just a visitor in Brad Lapitan's world.

As Lapitan continued, the deference he held for explosives and their delivery methods was unmistakable. "There are five main parts: activator, initiator, the container—which is the source of the bomb's contents—a battery or other power source, and, of course, the charge itself. Depending what the intended target is, they can be constructed for numerous types of devastation."

"Meaning?"

"Meaning they can be loaded with ball-bearings, nails, fragmentary objects, or even, in rudimentary cases, rocks. The choice of what to use is minor when compared to the source of delivery, the impact. Blast radius to use lay terms. Even something seemingly insignificant as rocks can be deadly if the blow-out force is powerful enough."

"I always imagined IEDs being…activated, I guess, by pressure of a passing vehicle. Roadside bombs like we hear about on the news."

"That's merely one of many possibilities. Dirty bombs and even chemical or biological weapons can be delivered through an IED."

"Simple to construct?"

"Fifteen minutes of online research, a basic understanding, and a novice can bring an entire platoon to their knees. Very basic, very cheap, and very deadly."

"Does someone just…I don't know…light a fuse?"

Lapitan cringed at the neophyte statement. "No, Frank. It's not like they're black and round with a fuse that Wile E. Coyote gets from Acme bombs. They can be engaged by remote control, cell phones, trip wires, even infra-red laser sight from a rifle."

Frank craned his neck and glanced at the statuesque black Lab. "Cagney, you deserve a biscuit." A moment later, he added, "Overall, do you consider them to be effective?"

Lapitan waggled his head in a yes-no fashion. "There are as many variables to bombs as there are stars in the sky. Like anything else, it comes down to desire, effort, will, and intended impact." Sensing the homicide detective was overwhelmed, Lapitan let that sink in and said, "Let's take a walk."

As the two men trooped the perimeter of the field, Cagney remained behind until Lapitan tapped his left hip once. "The IEDs we hear about in Sand Land are extremely rudimentary in design. They—be it the Taliban, Al-Qaeda, ISIS, or whomever we're fighting this week—don't have time to produce high tech devices. They're concerned with volume, not range. On the other side of the bomb ledger is Oklahoma City. *They* were concerned with maximum impact. Those whack jobs brought down half an office building in seconds, damaged more than three hundred others over a sixteen block radius, and tallied up more than half a trillion in damage in 1995 dollars. And worst of all, one-hundred-sixty-eight lost souls. They executed their operation with five thousand pounds of nitromethane, nitrate fertilizer, and a fuel mixture." Lapitan paused, adding, "It actually registered on the Richter scale. Converse is Boston, which was, by all logic, slipshod."

Frank strolled alongside Lapitan a bit longer, absorbing the information. "Tell me, Brad," he said after some reflection, "what's your gut tell you about West Hollywood."

"West Hollywood could have been much worse. Whoever planned it was more concerned with shock value, no pun intended, than bloodshed. Chaos, not causalities. And that's not good."

"Because?"

"Like roadside bombs, there are undoubtedly lots more out there that we don't know about."

Chapter 12

Ferrari, Maybach, Porsche, Lamborghini. And one Honda.

Michelle eased her Accord curbside, purposely parking inches from the rear of a gold Bentley, making it challenging for the *one-percenter* to leave. She entered the high-end jewelry store on Rodeo Drive and immediately felt like Julia Roberts in *Pretty Woman*. Salesgirls busied themselves. One smirked after eying Michelle. Surely this peasant girl would get her no commission.

After speaking with the manager, a middle-aged woman whose Botox made her resemble a mannequin, Michelle learned Lori Edens hadn't returned to work since Phil's murder. Michelle thanked the plastic woman and left. *Can I help you find anything?* was never spoken. Back in her car, Michelle accessed the DMV records, plugged the Edens' address into her GPS, and, just for her own amusement, tapped the Bentley's fender before heading to affluent Brentwood.

A short time later, Michelle strolled along the sinewy flagstone walkway, passing a pair of matching Corvette's in the driveway, and rang the doorbell of the Spanish Colonial. Surprised to hear exuberant children inside, she rang a second time.

When the door was hastily opened, Michelle did a double take. Phil Edens' widow, with her blonde hair and green eyes, was a perfect double for an older version of Kendra Nichols, the woman he was having an affair with. Unnecessarily, Michelle asked, "Lori Edens?"

Holding a glass of champagne in one hand, the woman pressed the Bluetooth against her ear. "Hold on, I'll be with you in a minute." Unlike her curmudgeon partner, Michelle welcomed technology. Nevertheless, she despised Bluetooths…or was it Blueteeth? She remained in the doorway, listening as Lori concluded booking a flight to Maui. "Can I help you?"

Assuming it was now her turn to speak, Michelle again asked, "Lori Edens?"

"Yes," she responded irritably.

She presented her badge-wallet. "Detective Santana, West Bureau Hollywood Homicide."

The woman gave it a passing glance. Wearing a form-fitting leather skirt and sparkly black top, Edens was doing everything conceivable to hold back time. Michelle noticed expensive-looking earrings and a French manicure—at least what she thought a French manicure was.

"Hollywood? Aren't you out of your jurisdiction?"

"I'm assisting with the investigation into your husband's murder, Mrs. Edens. May I come in?"

"Haven't you people traipsed through my home enough? I've been rather accommodating but my patience is wearing thin."

Michelle apologized for the intrusion and assured the woman she'd only need a few moments of her valuable time.

Lori relented and stepped aside with a flurry. "Fine! Let's get this over with."

Inside, among the ascetically pleasing furnishings, Michelle noticed three children between ages six and ten. One stared at the TV while two sat on the floor, independently playing a game on their phones. They paid no attention to each other. "Perhaps we can talk somewhere more private?"

"Not necessary. My children are well aware of their father's adultery."

Michelle tried to throw the woman off-balance. "Going somewhere?"

"Hawaii. Not that it's any of your business. I need to get away from your intrusions into my life and this media circus for a few days."

"Have you left a contact number where we can reach you?"

Lori avoided the question. "My children will be staying with a friend. Now that Phil is out of the picture, I'm entitled to some me time."

"I see," Michelle remarked, deciding how to play this.

"I don't think you do," Lori hissed. "Phil and I got married young. I was naïve and thought I was in love. I wanted to be one of the few couples whose marriage actually worked. *He* had other intentions. *He* liked the *idea* of being married more than actually being married. *He* relished in the thrill of being caught. Six weeks after we exchanged our vows he was fucking one of my bridesmaids."

Fucking. Michelle glanced at the Edens children, two of them doing a poor job of pretending not to listen. Trying to empathize and gain the woman's trust, Michelle forced a smile. "Men."

Lori noticed Michelle's barren ring finger. "I see you're one of the smart ones."

"There were other women?"

The non-grieving widow released a loud laugh and sipped the bubbly. "Other women? Six that I know of." She narrowed her eyes at Michelle. "Did you happen to know this Nichols floozy?"

"No, ma'am," Michelle lied. "I'm assuming you were unaware of their relationship until after your husband's murder and Ms. Nichols's abduction."

"Phil—God, I always hated that name—*Phil* and I had our own don't-ask-don't-tell policy. I ceased caring years ago. Now that he's finally gone, I can have time for me. It was all worth it. The years of lies, deception, and adultery paid off."

Michelle arched a brow.

"Three, maybe four years ago, I insisted we get life insurance. I figured eventually he'd screw the wrong woman and some jilted husband would blow his balls off. I'm not sorry for what happened. The cheating bastard had it coming to him. And now I've got four hundred fifty thousand coming to *me*."

There was no doubt the Edens lacked affection. Michelle had been cheated on by past boyfriends, but never a husband. However, as sleazy as Phil Edens unmistakably was, he was still their children's father. "Do you happen to know anything about the other women your husband was involved with?"

"Yes, you can say that."

Michelle waited, allowing Lori to fill the silence. "Come with me." She set her champagne glass on a bureau and trekked upstairs. Michelle followed.

Smudge marks and fingerprint dust remained, leftover from forensics. Seeing that Lori had yet to tidy up made Michelle wonder if she planned to ever return from the Aloha State.

Michelle stood in the doorway, studying the bedroom, the lay out of the furniture, and tried to recreate the murder/kidnapping in her mind. Lori backpedaled from the closet, holding two shoeboxes. "I just found these this morning and didn't have a chance to tell those other detectives about it."

The boxes were lowered onto the bed. Michelle stepped closer. "Old-fashioned VHS tapes?"

"I've only had a chance to check a couple of them but I'm sure they're all the same. It's one thing to fuck other women in our bed, but to record it for posterity? Twisted bastard."

"May I take these as evidence? There could be valuable information on here."

Lori waved it away. "Help yourself. I've seen enough."

"Thank you."

Michelle exited the residence and deposited the shoe boxes in the trunk. She was about to get behind the wheel when Lori summoned her back. Michelle met her half way. "Something else, Mrs. Edens?'

"Think you'll find the person who did this?"

Michelle nodded confidently. "We'll do our best. The LAPD is above the national average of solving homicides." She had no idea if that was true but it sounded good.

"I'm sorry about that Nichols woman. I do hope she's okay. But can you do me a favor?"

"Yes?"

"If you find the man who killed my husband, tell him I said thanks."

Man? How did she know for sure it was a man? Michelle filed away the passing remark and handed over her card. "If you remember anything that could be beneficial, please call me. My partner's number is on the back as well. Detective Grace."

Michelle again thanked the woman and chose not to express her condolences, since they'd be unappreciated. She brought her Honda to life and headed back to West Bureau Homicide, oblivious to the tail she'd picked up back on Rodeo Drive.

ↄﾟↄ

"Anything?" Frank asked when she entered their shared cubicle.

Michelle left the tapes of Edens's sexual romps in her car. Since she and Frank were working independently of local and federal agencies, she decided to keep them—for now. The squad room was surprisingly sparse of activity, considering all that was happening. Despite the emptiness, she updated Frank in a hushed voice.

As Frank listened, Michelle noticed he'd held his head a couple times and grimaced once. Either the strain of this case and the pressure of being handpicked by Chief Kent were weighing him down or the concussion lingered.

Frank released a long drawn out sigh. "We should check out Lori's whereabouts the night of the murder. Life insurance policy, huh?"

Michelle titled her head. "She was at her family's place in Aspen. That's already been substantiated."

"Oh, that's right."

"You okay?"

Frank dismissed it. "Just a rough day." He paused, leaned back, and crossed his ankles. "At least you got something. My day was useless."

"No leads?"

"I wasted time with this Eddie Evanovich thing. Thought maybe it would lead somewhere. It didn't." Frank relayed what he uncovered about Evanovich which, while being tragic, was irrelevant. He'd been a top real estate broker in the area for ten plus years, pulled in high six figures annually. Then the economy tanked and Evanovich lost everything. Frank contacted his wife, now living in Tucson and, while the woman seemed saddened, she didn't sound surprised. "My sister offered to let him stay here with us while he got back on his feet," Frank was told by Kim Evanovich. "But last I heard he was living in some shelter in LA." She didn't know which one, hadn't had communication with her ex-husband in eighteen months.

Subsequent calls to the city's abundant shelters provided little information. Father McCabe from the Salvation Army advised Frank that Evanovich spent three months residing at their facility on East Fifth Street downtown but left the previous November. Frank grimaced. "And in the midst of this entire circle jerk, Kent called me twice."

"And?"

"He's not pleased I've made no progress."

"*We've* made no progress. What does he expect? It's

been twenty-four hours since he commissioned you."

"You know how he is," Frank moaned. He mindlessly lifted and dropped papers on his desk.

"Grantana!" Wadkins bellowed.

The pain in Frank's head now became secondary to the pain in his ass.

"It's Sant-ace now," Michelle said.

Detective Wadkins entered their cubicle uninvited. He curled his lips and studied Michelle before pivoting and doing the same to Frank. Grinning he announced, "She looks better than you, Frank. She *should* get first billing."

The swelling on Michelle's cheek was barely noticeable now. Unlike Frank, she was recuperating nicely from the explosion. "Frank, you got a minute?" Wadkins pointed his chin toward the hallway.

"Michelle's my partner. Whatever you need to say you can say in front of her."

"It's guy talk."

Michelle rolled her eyes, turned to face her monitor, and waved them away. "Go, go."

In the corridor, Wadkins appeared uneasy. He glanced right, looked left, stared at his feet. Frank had never seen Golden Boy insecure and unconfident. "What is it, Detective?"

Wadkins inhaled. "This is not easy—especially for me." He faked a smile. "I just want to apologize." He even gripped Frank's shoulder for effect.

"Call Mr. Ripley, I don't believe it. Apologize for what?"

"You were kind enough to take me to pick my car up. Had I not asked in the first place, none of us would've been in West Hollywood when the bomb detonated. It's…well, crap…it's my fault you were hurt."

Frank was moved by Wadkins's sincerity. Making a joke of it, he said, "That must've killed you to apologize."

"You know it." Wadkins laughed. "Are we cool?"

"We're cool. It's not your fault, Troy." *Did I really call him Troy?*

"Anything you need just let me know."

Frank clucked his tongue. "Actually there is." He led Wadkins to the sergeant's desk, jotted something on a piece of paper, and handed it over. "Just for shits and giggles, when you're not busy, see what you uncover about this guy."

Wadkins took the note. "Eddie Evanovich? Consider it done." He walked away, pleased to repay his debt.

Frank watched Wadkins stride away and realized he hadn't eaten all day. The thought of munching on a Wadkins doughnut suddenly seemed less repulsive. Upon entering the break room, he nearly tripped over Johnny who was wheeling himself out.

"How's it hangin? I was just about to come see you." Johnny wiped his mouth with the back of his hand and slipped a bag of ranch flavored *Bugles* into a pocket on the side of his chair.

"Saved you the trouble. What's up?"

Johnny updated him about the two-word email: Eddie Evanovich. Within seconds Frank's head was about to explode as the department's IT wizard and resident hacker spoke in tongues. Frank nodded when he thought it was appropriate and threw in the occasional "Oh, okay."

Seeing Frank's deer-in-the-headlights gaze, Johnny smiled. "I forgot. You're still waiting for vinyl records to make a comeback."

Frank smiled meekly. "In English."

Johnny ran his fingers through his brown hair. It was taxing to dumb down the conversation but he needed to in order for tenderfoot Frank Grace to fathom. "Basically, it's a digital cul-de-sac. ISPs and especially email addresses are a piece of cake. But this one? I'm not sure where the email with Evanovich's name originated from. I'm good. But they're better."

Frank had wasted his own time and now Johnny's as well. "Thanks, anyway."

"I'll take another crack at it when I have a chance. I've got so much on my plate right now."

Frank shrugged. "If you find anything, forward it to Wadkins."

"Golden Boy?"

"Yup. He felt like he owed me and I threw him a bone."

The two men parted ways.

Back in his cubicle, Frank announced a short time later that he was taking off.

Surprised he was leaving just after four, Michelle said, "Now?"

"I need to be home for dinner. Abby and I are having a serious talk with Ashley."

Watching her partner slip into his windbreaker, Michelle noticed his pained expression. After hearing Lori Edens hatefully recount her husband's numerous affairs and now seeing the strain of raising children etched deeply into Frank's lined face, Michelle thanked her lucky stars that she was single. "I'll stay a little longer. See if I come up with anything."

Frank wished her a good evening.

He mechanically walked to the employee lot before re-membering his parking permit had been left in his Chevy. He pivoted and traipsed toward the street where he'd parked his loaner. Frank was second guessing himself about accept-ing Chief Kent's proposal. It'd only been a day but he'd turned up no leads. He was fighting against other agencies with better resources and more manpower. The warning Lieutenant Gallardo expressed also burdened him. If Frank should fail to solve this case, a case he'd personally been handpicked for, would he be writing his own ticket out of the LAPD? And there was the disturbing knowledge that his daughter—his very own daughter—instigated an assault on a fellow student.

Abby had advised him that school authorities were considering treating this as a hate-crime. So wrapped up, he was oblivious to the hurried footsteps.

"Frank Grace?"

"Yes?"

The twenty-something shoved an envelope into Frank's hand, stepped back, and took a picture with his phone. "Frank Grace. You've been served."

Chapter 13

Earl Sherman enjoyed women. He enjoyed women with raven hair. He enjoyed women under five two. He particularly enjoyed the ones barely legal, slightly older than his granddaughter. And two years ago when vacationing across the Pacific, he confirmed what he once heard: Asian women will do *anything* to satisfy their man. He became hooked.

On her hands and knees, Hiromi apathetically viewed the bedside clock and continued thinking what she needed at the grocery store. As an afterthought, she remembered why she was here and cried out, "You're *so* big!"

"Say it," puffed Sherman as he thrust.

Skimmed milk, gluten-free frozen vegetables, Gatorade. Oh, and those double-stuff Oreos, my guilty pleasure.

Hiromi was twenty-three but her immaculate skin, guiltless face, and diminutive figure got her carded regularly. She first became acquainted with him seven weeks prior at an upscale art gallery. She didn't know the name Earl Sherman or recognize him, a fact that left him flabbergasted yet intrigued.

"Let me hear it. Say it." His panting grew labored, his hips jackhammered faster. His grip tightened on her supple waist as he continued driving into her.

He was close, thank goodness. She'd been with many men. Women, too. But rarely anyone as ancient as this geezer. In his mind, he viewed himself an energetic strapping nineteen-year-old stallion. His withered body said otherwise. *Oh, that's right.* "You're *so* hard." Just for the hell of it, she added, "Not so deep. You're hurting me."

Hiromi smiled to herself. She knew from experience everyone had their fetishes, sexual secrets they shared with her and not their spouse. But Sherman's obsession was comical. When he insisted on calling her *Mabel* for some reason, she burst out laughing. Nevertheless, for two thousand an hour, he could call her whatever he wanted. After all, she had groceries to buy.

"Say it," he howled. "Hurry, Mabel, hurry!"

Hiromi managed not to laugh. "Fuck me, Your Honor. Fuck me with that long hard gavel." *That'll do it.*

Sure enough, it did.

Earl Sherman withdrew a moment later, and his face twisted into a vile look of disgust, as it always did after he finished.

"You were amazing," she cooed, flopping onto her back and feigning exhaustion.

Sherman stared at her naked body and his own flaccidity with disdain. "You little whore," he spat.

"*Your* little whore. And you love it." Just to entice him for their next rendezvous Hiromi erotically tugged her left nipple.

"Dirty little whore," he scowled. But she was right. He did love it.

"See you next week."

Sherman nodded, already anticipating their next tryst seven long days away. He slipped off the condom and lowered it into a baggie to be discarded later. *Mabel* was sexy, wild, and submissive. But he wouldn't take any risks when it came to DNA, his reputation, or his frigid wife. "Next week."

"Tootles," she pouted and for good measure erotically slid her finger between her lips. That last little act did the trick. Sherman threw down an extra five hundred. As he swiftly dressed and departed, Hiromi flung her naked body onto the bills and giggled uproariously. "Long hard gavel."

Earl Sherman guardedly exited the room and verified there was no snooping media or snot-nosed kid with a camera. After determining the coast was clear and his pristine reputation was intact, he marched down the exterior corridor of the shoddy Tarzana motel en route to his vehicle. The air had a bite to it. Sherman withdrew keys from his pocket, beeped his car unlocked twenty yards away.

He never made it.

༄༅

"It's Jake's turn!" Ashley shouted.

"Don't take that tone with me, young lady," Abby replied louder.

"I've done the dishes every night. This is bullshit!"

"Watch your mouth, Ashley Jacqueline Grace!"

Jake's eyes widened as his mommy and his sister screamed. And used bad words, too.

Frank looked at his son across the table, shook his head no.

Naturally, Jake wasted no time. "Bullshit." He giggled.

"Jake, c'mon now," Frank lamented.

"See what you did?" Abby yelled at Ashley.

"Like he hasn't heard it before!" Ashley countered.

"That's not the point."

Frank slid his chair back. "C'mon, kiddo. Let's go outside."

Jake was beet red from laughing. "Bullshit, bullshit, bullshit."

Frank quelled his desire to smile. His son *was* cute, mimicking his older sister. Nonetheless, sharing in the merriment would only further infuriate a raging Abby.

As he led his son away, Jake continued in a singsong way. "Bullshit, bullshit, bullshit…"

Once outside, screams filtering to the front yard, Jake remarked, "I don't like seeing Mommy mad."

"Me neither."

"Is Ashley in trouble?"

Frank nodded.

Seeing his sister in trouble was kinda cool. "What'd she do?"

"Don't worry about it. Mommy and I will handle it." *Not sure how but we will.*

The yelling grew louder, resonating through the serene Toluca Lake community. Jake looked up at Daddy and said with a shake of his head, "Women. I don't get 'em."

Now Frank did burst out laughing. "Join the club, kiddo."

⌘

Frank and Abby lowered themselves in two chairs side-by-side. Opposite them a third one remained unoccupied. Holding a bottle of *Guinness,* Abby made mention of the abundant weeds pushing up. She glanced at Frank, waiting for an offer. Frank reacted by looking at the sky and downed a mouthful of Bud. "Nice night."

"Frank!"

"I know, I know," he sighed. "But I'm waiting for Jake to do it."

"He's eight!"

"Three years, four tops."

Abby swigged. "Never mind."

"Actually two of the blades on the mower need to be replaced," Frank declared, perhaps too enthusiastically.

"You need a Weed Wacker, my dear."

"Oh." *Crap.*

"Don't worry about it."

"I'll get to it, sweetie. Promise."

Abby waited a beat. "You know who I ran into at the gym a few days ago? Connor Harbaugh."

"The little kid from down the street?" he replied after a thoughtful pause.

Abby grinned. "Not so little anymore. He's nineteen already. Can you believe it? Time goes fast."

"Too fast. What's he up to?" Frank asked, making conversation.

"He's doing well. I almost didn't recognize him at first. So tanned and chiseled. Tight abs, too."

"Uh huh."

"He's been working out in preparation of becoming a lifeguard this summer. He's turned into such a handsome young man. And fit, too."

"Uh huh."

"He's looking to pick up a few extra bucks on the side. I wonder how he is with yard work."

"Uh huh."

"He looked really good."

"Uh huh."

"Did I mention he's nineteen?"

"Yes, you did."

Abby took another gulp, stared into the distance, and started humming *Mrs. Robinson*.

"Okay, point taken."

Ashley stormed over, plopped herself into the unoccupied chair facing her parents. "How long will this take? I have homework." She lowered the Red Bull on the ground next to her and reached into a bag of M&M's.

Frank and Abby exchanged a look. They couldn't recall the last time Ashley was eager to do homework. Since last night proved futile, they decided Abby would try her hand at it. His wife pulled no punches. She reached over and, in a blur, snatched the can from the ground, ripped the bag from her daughter's hand, rose, and deposited the items in a nearby trashcan.

"Hey! I was eating that."

"You don't need that."

Ashley was stunned. "Huh?"

Frank, equally stunned, remained silent.

Abby glared. "You're putting on a few too many pounds, my darling daughter."

"No, I'm not!" Ashley objected.

Abby leaned forward, puffed out her cheeks, and extended her arms.

Ashley contorted her face. "Are you drunk, Mom?"

"I'm totally sober. You, on the other hand, are getting plump."

"Mom?"

"You don't need that candy bar. Or that drink. You should eat peanuts, like all the other elephants."

Frank's insides churned, already regretting their decision to let Abby handle the situation regarding their daughter's assault on Sabiha Mansoor. "Abby—"

"Shut the hell up, Frank," Abby roared while continuing to bore her eyes into their daughter.

"Mom?" Ashley's voice was softer. A lump developed in her throat.

"Picking on someone 'cause they're different? What makes you so damned perfect, Ashley Jacqueline Grace?"

"I'm not…perfect. But she's a bitch. They almost killed Dad." Ashley sought affirmation from her father, but Frank was too astounded to utter a sound.

"Sabiha tried to kill your father?"

"No…of course not."

"Oh, I see now. So, her family planted the bomb then?" Abby turned. "Hear that, sweetie? Our daughter knows the Mansoor family planted that bomb. You should go arrest them. And, if you can, pick up some milk on the way home too."

"Don't make fun of me," Ashley said. "Not her personally. But her…people."

"At least she's not *fat*."

Silence encased them before Ashley stood with such force the chair toppled backward. "I don't need to listen to this. I'm outta here!"

"Getting more chocolate, tubby?"

Ashley halted, fisted tears from her eyes.

Abby rose, hustled over, and stood in front of her daughter. Ashley attempted to slither out but couldn't break away.

"I was fourteen, just a couple years older than you," Abby explained, speaking gently. "I was bullied, made fun of. Fatso. Lard ass. Dumbo. Blimp. Flabby Abby. I heard it all, Ash. In gym, I was always the last one picked for every game. Recess? I sat along the fence and watched everyone else run around and have fun. But not me, not Flabby Abby."

Ashley lifted her gaze slowly, her cheeks bright red, her eyes puffy. "Why?"

"'Cause it was less humiliating to watch others have fun than to be teased about the way I ran. I mean *waddled*. I couldn't sit with friends in the cafeteria 'cause…well, no one wanted to be seen with the fat girl. Almost daily, someone would come over and throw my lunch into the garbage. 'You don't need to eat anything. You might explode.' I heard it all. So, you know what I did?"

Ashley gave her mom a sideways look, unable to speak through her constricted throat.

"I ate in the girl's bathroom. Yep. I spread out my little sandwich your grandma made, my chips, and my juice across paper towels on the counter ten feet away from toilets. How'd you like eating lunch while smelling urine and crap? I was excluded. I was teased, humiliated, and yes, beaten up. Why? 'Cause I was different."

Ashley wiped her nose and fell into her mom's comforting embrace. Sobbing uncontrollably, shoulders rising and sinking, she apologized profusely. "I just—just wanted to be popular. I just wanted to fit in. Everyone'd been making fun of Sabiha, and so I thought it would—make everyone like me. I'm sorry, Mom. I'm sorry." She extended her arm, pleading for forgiveness. "I'm sorry, Dad."

"It's okay, Ash." Frank stood, took his daughter's trembling hand in his own. *I just wanted to be popular.* He'd heard the same comment from Josefina Mendes in the Hollywood hills.

Ashley uncoiled from her mom's loving grip a moment later. "I'm going to friend Sabiha on Facebook and apologize."

Abby smiled. "Good."

"Proud of you, Ash," Frank added, amazed how his wife's atypical approach somehow morphed into something out of *The Brady Bunch.*

With their daughter inside, they lowered themselves into their chairs and simultaneously took a much needed swig of alcohol. Frank toasted Abby's unusual method. "Good job. Unorthodox and unconventional, but it worked."

"I got my point across."

Frank took another sip. "I never knew you were heavy in school."

Abby winked. "I wasn't."

☙❦❧

The salvoes of gunfire erupted in his ears. The fading eyes of the dying, bloodied, and mangled, stared at him. *Azusa.* Then an ear-splitting explosion from behind. An inferno against his back. Frank was again airborne, flailing over an inert Michelle Santana. His head thundered against the brick wall, resulting in him bolting upright and gasping for air.

Abby hadn't stirred. Clearly, she was growing accustomed to the nightmares that haunted his sleep. He rubbed the back of his clammy neck and the sweat-drenched collar of his T-shirt. The glow of the clock read three-twenty-seven. Familiar with the pattern, he knew more sleep was pointless. Normally, when this occurred he'd get a jump on the day. However, the last time he did, he ended up encountering Josefina Mendes and a band of wanna-be porn stars and later found himself smack dab in the center of a terrorist bombing. As hard as it was for this creature of habit to break with tradition, Frank decided to do some work from home.

In the kitchen, he began brewing a fresh pot of coffee. He powered up Abby's laptop, loaded *Revolver* by The Beatles into the portable CD player, keeping the volume low.

Although he pawned off Eddie Evanovich on Wadkins, Frank decided to do some digging on his own. After a Google search revealed nothing relevant he switched gears and read updates on the bombing in West Hollywood. The FBI detained a man and questioned him as a person of interest late last evening. The article on the *Times* website claimed the man had been released but the fed was continuing to pursue all possible leads.

"Hey."

Frank's heart skipped a beat. "Sorry I woke you."

"You didn't," Abby murmured. Half asleep, she removed a bottle of water from the fridge and took a small drink.

Frank leaned back and took in his wife. She was wearing a gray Pepperdine T-shirt and loose fitting blue shorts that hung mid-thigh. Hair ruffled, eyes half-mast, one side of her face showing sleep lines from her pillow, she looked amazing. That line about men aging better than women didn't apply. He'd seen her transform from a cute twenty-four-year-old girl into a remarkable woman. More enamored with her today than a decade and a half ago. The physical attraction, the friendship, the laughter, the lovemaking, the maternal instincts all tied together. In a life filled with bad decisions, putting a ring on Abigail McKenzie's finger was a rare good decision. He'd married the right one.

"All these years and you still amaze me." She yawned.

"Just couldn't sleep—again. Figured I'd see if I could uncover anything."

"Not that," Abby said. "I can't believe *you're* using a laptop."

Frank smiled and, as hard as it was, looked away from eyes that glistened like the Pacific on a dazzling summer day. He handed her an envelope. "I got served on the way out of the Barn yesterday."

Abby removed the contents, studied the document for a moment, and then looked at Frank questioningly.

"That'll be my first stop in the morning. Trust me."

Abby lowered the summons on the table and gently whispered, "It's late. Come back to bed."

"I'll be up in in a few."

Abby bent at the waist, placed her soft fingertips tenderly under Frank's stubble, and kissed him on the lips. She then shimmied into the tight space between the chair and the table, and lowered herself onto his lap. She tantalizingly glided the tip of her tongue across his lips and effortlessly swayed her hips. "I think you're already up."

The hell with Eddie what's-his-name. He held her hips and returned the passion with equal fervor. "You're so bad," he whispered, glimpsing the stairs leading to the kids' rooms.

"Maybe you should frisk me, Detective."

"Maybe I will."

Frank slid the chair back and stood. With Abby's ankles locked behind his lower back, he began carrying her from the kitchen. As he did, he noticed a red mark, a blemish, on her otherwise flawless face. Even with a smudge of some sort, she was stunning. He kissed the smear. It remained. A second peck also did nothing.

Frank narrowed his eyes at the irremovable smudge.

The front window exploded. Shards of glass like fine crystals flew halfway across the room. Frank pulled Abby to the ground and shielded her with his own body. She trembled beneath him. He cradled her head. Through the torrent of gunfire and the bullets shredding the kitchen cabinets behind him, Frank detected the sound of footsteps padding down the stairs.

"What was that, Dad?"

"Ash, back in your room!" Frank shouted. "Abby, Abby, you okay?"

Too stunned to speak, she warily nodded once.

"Stay here and don't move!" Frank sprang to his feet and raced to the front door, again yelling, "Back in your room, Ash! Now!"

By the time he reached the front lawn, squealing tires ripped through the night. Taillights vanished around the corner. "Son of a bitch."

"What—what was that?" Abby stuttered.

"I told you to stay inside," Frank clipped, then embraced his wife and tried to soothe her. "It's okay, sweetie. I've got you. You're safe." As porch lights began flicking on and neighbors tentatively peered through curtains, Frank glared down the darkened street. A theory he'd been contemplating was now confirmed.

Abby clutched her husband tightly, her body shuddering against his. "Is—is it over?"

"No, it's just beginning."

Chapter 14

Colby Ferrell hadn't even reached the punch line and already his captive audience was cackling like a clan of hyenas. For extra effect, he held them at bay as he raised his wine glass and sipped the vintage Dom Perignon Oenotheque Rose before delivering the final line. "And then the Scotsman said 'At least I don't have scented hand soap named after me.'"

Colby Ferrell, Esquire angled back at the head of the table and sized up his adoring lunch guests. He knew full well the joke was not *that* hilarious. But when you're the one picking up the tab and treating nine guests to a thirteen hundred dollar French import, they damn well better find him humorous.

Early sixties, bald, and a perpetual aura of haughtiness surrounding him, he noticed a disturbance at the entrance of the exclusive Beverly Hills bistro. The tuxedo-clad maître d was joined by the restaurant manager as they attempted to stop the interloper. The intruder broke free and stormed over to the table where he was immobilized by a block of granite.

"We have a problem here?" Granite asked.

"It's okay, let him through," Ferrell ordered. "Do we know each other?"

"You damn well know who I am."

Ferrell rubbed his chin and feigned thoughtfulness.

"Frank Grace, isn't it? Why yes it is, Frank Grace." Ferrell addressed his guests. "Ladies, gentlemen, it looks like it's our lucky day. We are, pardon the pun, graced by the presence of Detective Grace."

Fake boisterous laughter emanated.

"You may not recognize the infamous homicide gumshoe," Ferrell broadcast to his cohorts, "But I'm sure you're well aware of his name. This fine individual has quite the reputation for insubordination which, as I'm sure you all know, culminated just over four years ago in Azusa. Five young men gunned down, several wounded, and one of his fellow officers paralyzed." Ferrell shook his head. "How's that jittery trigger finger, Detective Grace?"

Unmindful to the murmurs of Ferrell's cronies—they weren't his concern—Frank tossed the envelope onto the gold leafed plate where the attorney just finished Lobster *something*. "You had me served?"

Ferrell contemptuously clapped and faced his guests. "Bravo. And apparently, Detective Grace has also mastered the ability to read." He repositioned his gaze as sardonic laughter burst forth again. "I most certainly did as even you deduced with your limited education."

Frank's hands fisted, an action noticed by Granite. "Someone took a shot at my wife last night."

"And—you think I had something to do with that? Please, Mr. Grace, don't flatter yourself with your fact-finding abilities." A trace of Ferrell's Texas twang entered his words. He'd mastered subduing his southern roots, knowing an accent from the Deep South made him sound *slower,* less influential in California. The slip was unintentional. Frank was making headway.

"I saw a Maxima speeding away from my house."

"There are over ten million residents of our fair city, young man. I think the odds are astronomical there'd be only one Maxima." More laughter from his fans.

"Was it Elijah or Xavier?"

"Ah, yes, the Leach boys you detained and harassed

without due process. The Leach boys, who, by your illegal and unwarranted traffic stop, were nearly killed in that horrific explosion. The Leach boys, whose home *you* trespassed without a search warrant and violated their fourth amendment rights. Those are the Leach boys you're referring to?"

"How does scum like that afford a lawyer with your retainer, Ferrell?"

"That's *Mr.* Ferrell to you. Was your wife injured?"

"That's not the point."

"Are you sure about the Maxima? Perhaps, you and the little woman got into a spat and you overreacted? Let's be forthright. You do have…oh, how can I word this delicately?…a tendency to react recklessly and ask questions later."

"And now you served me 'cause I pulled them over and, once again, allegedly violated their rights?"

Ferrell laughed in his face. "Your inexcusable action and unwarranted harassing of two young men almost resulted in their demise. I am only countering the latest in a long history of failing to uphold laws that you ostensibly swore to defend. Someone will pay for such brash indiscretions. The department, the city. Maybe you, personally."

"Where are they?" Frank asked through gritted teeth.

Ferrell's response was to sip his wine.

"Where are they?" he asked, louder this time. When he felt his arm seized by Granite, Frank locked eyes on the behemoth. "Get your hands off me, shithead."

"You have their address, Mr. Grace. Why do you ask me, other than to come down here and make a spectacle of yourself?"

"I went by the Mar Vista house this morning."

"I hope you remembered a warrant this time."

"It's empty, cleaned out as if they never lived there."

"Good day, Mr. Grace."

"Where the hell are they?"

"Good *day*, Mr. Grace. You may leave now."

"You're the son of a bitch who made this personal by sending your punks to my home."

"And you're accusing me of what, exactly?"

"Conspiracy to commit murder for starters."

Ferrell dismissed it. "In front of my guests? Thank you kindly. I can now add slander to your growing litany of infractions. You'd need to find an excellent attorney to prove your accusation. Oh, I forgot. I'm the best attorney in the city."

Unrestrained laughter fanned the raging fire in Frank's gut. Granite pawed Frank's shoulder but he broke free, grabbed Ferrell by his shirt collar, and brought their faces closer. "I'll find the connection between you and those punks. And after I arrest their sorry asses, I'll spend every waking moment watching you. You'll regret the day you met them. And the day your clients tried to murder my wife."

Ferrell arched a brow. "Take your hands off me, Mr. Grace. This suit costs more than you make in a year."

❧❦❧

Michelle ended her conversation with Wadkins's partner Jimmy Stoner and hurriedly met Frank halfway across the parking lot. "Abby and the kids okay?"

Word traveled fast across the LAPD, especially when it was one of their own. "Yup. Hell of a night. Hell of a morning, too."

When Frank apprised her of his confrontation earlier with Colby Ferrell, the reaction on Michelle's face left no doubt; she disagreed with his antagonizing the high profile attorney. But she kept her concerns to herself. After two years, she knew Frank marched to the beat of his own drum, especially when a case hit close to home. Literally.

"I'd been kicking around something and, after last night, I think I'm right." Frank mused.

He adjusted the collar on his windbreaker. It was a rare cloudy day in Los Angeles and thunderheads were rolling in from the ocean. A storm was coming.

"Let's hear it."

"I don't remember some minor details of the blast. I guess that's common after a concussion. But I spoke with Brad Lapitan yesterday."

Michelle contorted her face.

"Bradley Cooper."

"Ah, okay"

"Lapitan's outside the investigation but he said something that triggered my memory. Apparently incendiary devices can be engaged by cell phones."

"Of course."

Frank halted. His partner understood what was news to him. *I really need to brush up on technology.* "Anyway, when Xavier handed me the license and registration he took out his phone and threatened to call his attorney, Colby Ferrell."

Michelle drew out her response. "Ohh-kay."

"Maybe he wasn't calling Ferrell. Maybe he was calling in the code to arm the bomb."

Michelle creased her brows. "Xavier and Elijah were right there, too. Why would they set it off when they themselves were in harm's way? They could've just as easily been killed." Michelle paused before gently shooting down her partner's theory. "Look, the Leaches were in the wrong place at the wrong time. Just like us."

"This is still a work in process," Frank confessed.

"And if you're thinking the brothers are suicide bombers, then that flies in the face what you said the other day when you hypothesized these terror attacks could be domestic. The bombers in Boston and Oklahoma City were home-grown and too chicken shit to sacrifice themselves for their cause, whatever the hell their cause was. Nine-Eleven, on the other hand, they willingly did to get their fifty-three virgins or whatever they believe."

"You're correct," Frank warily admitted a moment later. "But I still don't know how they are tied to Colby *Ferret*."

Rather than responding, Michelle asked, "Why do you think the Leaches would take a shot at your house?"

"Revenge? Retribution? I intruded into their home and they want to show they can intrude into mine. I just wonder—What?"

Michelle's face clearly displayed she saw no validity in Frank's allegation. "I understand you're pissed. I sure as hell would be, and I'd want someone to—never mind."

"Talk to me, detective."

She inhaled deeply, exhaled slowly. "You're carrying a huge weight right now. You're under a lot of pressure. Being personally handpicked by the chief of police would stress out anyone. But *that's* what should take priority. You and I are fighting an uphill battle, trying to solve a case that's over our pay grade. I say we focus on who's behind the bombing. And *then* we can take down the Leaches, assuming they're not involved with the bombing." Michelle had no qualms about helping Frank dig deeper into the background of the brothers. What pained her—and concerned her—was their affiliation with Colby Ferrell. The shyster had destroyed more people than the plague. And Michelle was not eager to put her career in the crosshairs.

In the past, she'd never wavered when going to the mat for Frank. He was her partner. But more importantly, he was her friend. Jeopardizing her livelihood was trivial when compared to doing what was *right*. However, she'd have custody of her niece shortly and, for once, she needed to think long-term.

Frank chewed his lip. "I guess you're right."

Stepping into the station, Frank announced he'd go get some coffee but when Michelle walked away, he went nowhere near the breakroom

Instead, he trekked to Cyberopolis. Johnny appeared frazzled but completely in his element. He relished dissecting the Kendra Nichols's video, knowing the better-equipped and better-trained FBI, NSA, and whoever else was doing the same thing. It was a cyber-race and Johnny hadn't become Master of Cyberopolis for nothing.

Knowing he'd need to butter up his pal, Frank nearly choked when he heard himself utter, "Hey, how's it hangin'?"

Johnny's brows skyrocketed. *Must be the concussion.* "Umm—Hi, Frank," he stammered.

Frank crossed the threshold, closed the door behind him and whispered, "Can you hack into cell phone records?"

"Can I? Yes. Will I? I don't know. The real question is why?"

Frank sat opposite Johnny, leaning away from the imposing high-tech gadgetry that far exceeded his mental capacity. "I'd like you to hack into databases for all local cell providers, tower relays, and call logs for both an Elijah and Xavier Leach. I'm hoping to find a number dialed at the exact moment of last week's bombing."

Johnny's face twisted into suspicion. "Like I just asked, why?"

"I'm asking as a favor. Please."

Johnny vacillated, his reluctance obvious. "I don't know, Frank. That's illegal. I don't mind breaking down firewalls and breaking code. But with the feds crawling all over this, I'm sure a flag will go up. I want to help. But—"

Frank pushed. "I'm fairly confident the Leaches are somehow linked to the attack. And I'm extremely confident they were the ones who paid me a visit last night."

Johnny bowed his head. "I heard."

"They tried to kill my wife, Johnny. They tried to kill Abby."

Johnny pinched the bridge of his nose. "Give me twenty-four hours."

Frank warmed at his friend's willingness to put his ass on the line. "Thank you."

"Just remember to write me when I'm locked up for treason."

⁓⁓⁓

Frank had nearly made it back to his workstation when he felt his arm grabbed. Heather Craft appeared shaken. "Frank, I'm *so* sorry. I heard about it. Shooting up your home? Appalling. But you're okay, right? No injuries? You're not hurt, are you?"

"I'm fine, Detective Craft. Thanks for worrying."

The woman with a schoolgirl crush on Frank moved closer, almost whispering in his ear. "If your house is damaged or being repaired, I have a spare bedroom you're welcomed to."

"Appreciate it, Detective, but me, my kids, and my *wife* would be pretty cramped in one room."

The hopeful smile dipped for an instant. "How are your children?"

"They're fine. Abby is, too."

Her hand slinked higher up Frank's bicep. "If you need someone to talk to or a shoulder to lean on, I'm here for you. Day. Night. Whenever."

"I'll keep that in mind."

Frank managed the last few steps without more impediments. "She totally wants you, Detective Grace," Michelle snickered.

"Say what you will about her, the woman's got good taste."

"Or cataracts."

Frank's comeback was interrupted by his ringing phone. "Hollywood Homicide, Detective Grace."

The call was under a minute. When concluded, Frank held his head in his hand.

"Who was that?"

It took a moment to gather his thoughts. "Malikowski from ballistics. They discovered polytetrafluoroethylene on the bullets taken from my home."

"Polytetrafluoroethylene? Oh, hell."

"Yep." Frank corroborated. "Cop killers."

Fifteen minutes later Frank was browsing the assessor's website while Michelle was on the phone discussing Sophia with her sister—Bianca—when Heather Craft's voice echoed across the squad room. "Break room. Hurry."

"B, I gotta go." Michelle ended the call and followed the throng.

The video was nearly identical to that of Kendra Nichols. Earl Sherman was cuffed, blindfolded, shirtless, cowering. The barrel of a Glock pushed against his left temple. He gently wept. The mechanical voice again spouted anti-American, anti-establishment, pro-anarchy rhetoric. Frank hadn't heard such trash since the Leaches mouthed off those same bullshit talking points.

One codicil added to this clip, however, sent Frank's stomach churning. "Like Detective Nichols, the *Honorable* Earl Sherman is a symbol, a tool of justice. Yet, who mourns for Eddie Evanovich?"

Frank and Michelle looked at each other wide-eyed, shocked. Wadkins, who unbeknownst to Frank was standing a few feet behind him, clutched his shoulder. "I'm on it!" Golden Boy hustled out of the break room.

The reaction was vastly different than Kendra's. Detective Nichols was one of their own. Judge Sherman was no friend of the police. He consistently admonished the LAPD for wandering into gray areas, foregoing protocol and procedures to make a bust. Someone in the rear grumbled, "Fuck 'em. I hope they *do* shoot him."

The room emptied, leaving Frank and Michelle alone. "Evanovich? But—"

Frank stuck up his hand. "No idea, Detective." He'd first come across the name when it arrived from an email address deemed untraceable by the department's cyber master. After Frank wasted a day looking into Evanovich, he pawned it off on Wadkins. Now—somehow, someway—Evanovich was tied to these abductions. Frank considered a possible connection between the kidnappings and the West Hollywood bombing, the latter being his personal mission via Chief Kent. Had he inadvertently handed off a key component of the investigation to Wadkins? If Golden Boy ended up breaking this case open—

"Shit."

Frank jogged to Wadkins's cubicle. The detective was already working the phones, reenergized by the carrot Frank unwittingly dangled before him. Helping Grace would be nice, but one-upping him would be, like those commercials say, priceless.

Frank contemplated asking for the file back but between the personal request made by Chief Kent and his thirst to payback the Leaches, he already had too much on his plate. And ultimately, as bitter a pill as it was to swallow, nabbing bad guys was his job.

If enlisting Wadkins's help accomplished that, so be it. "Come see me when you're done," Frank stated. "I've got a number for the ex-wife in Arizona."

Wadkins vacantly nodded and continued his call.

Frank detoured to Cyberopolis. The IT Jedi was enthusiastically doing…whatever it was an IT Jedi did. Frank relayed the information. Johnny hadn't seen the footage. He signed onto *KABC's* website. He leaned back in his chair and cracked his neck, something that always made Frank cringe. "Evanovich. That's the indecipherable email address you gave me."

Frank nodded. "I know."

"Give me an hour."

Back at his desk, Frank had two voicemails, each from one of his bosses.

Chief Kent had offered to assist Frank with anything he needed. He originally doubted the man's sincerity. But now he'd come through in a big way by procuring round-the-clock protection for Frank's family.

A black and white would be stationed outside the home as well as uniformed officers in his children's classrooms. Jake would relish the attention, Ashley would be mortified.

"St. Bartholomew's is a secure facility," Kent stated, "So your wife is protected anyway. And manpower is limited. Good luck, keep me posted."

It's good having friends in high places, Frank told himself. For the first time in his career, he valued Weldon Kent. And for the first time in his career, he wondered if he himself was becoming a *brasshole.*

The second voicemail was from his other boss. Abby reminded him Jake was sleeping over at a friend's tonight. She'd be working late and Frank needed to be chauffeur. He glanced at his wristwatch and tried to figure out how to co-ordinate the heating-up investigation with playing Dad. He peeked over his shoulder at Michelle. "You sure you want custody of Sophia?"

"Huh?"

"Never mind."

Most of his colleagues had generic screensavers. Michelle's consisted of soothing mountain scenes scrolling across her monitor. Detective Wadkins had an image-shrine to his former cheerleader wife. Frank's consisted of crime scene photos of victims whose murderers had yet to be ap-prehended, a reminder of why he showed up every morning. As he moved the mouse, the image of an eighteen year old farm girl, who came west to become a movie star and in-stead wound up dead in an alley, faded. The assessor's web-site reappeared and Frank frowned, momentarily forgetting what he'd been searching for.

Waiting for news from both Johnny and Wadkins, Frank perused the property records.

Moments later, he muttered in astonishment, "Detective Santana, take a look at this."

Michelle scooted over. "What am I looking at?"

Frank pointed. "Roscoe Woods."

"I think I once dated a guy who had a cabin up in Roscoe Woods."

Frank smiled. "Woods owns several properties around town including, get this, commercial space in an office building under construction right across the street from the blast."

"All right?"

Frank slid his finger down a few inches. "He also owns the residence at 2355 N. Mar Vista in Pasadena where the Leaches lived. Son. Of. A. Bitch. Roscoe Woods is the connection between the Leaches and the explosion. I think we need to pay Woods a visit."

"*We*? What about Jake?"

Frank blinked. In passing, he'd mentioned his son's sleepover to Michelle. She remembered. He forgot. Maybe she'd be better at balancing life and work than he thought.

"I have to pick up some of Sophia's things from my sister," Michelle said. "I can run out to the Woods place." She paused. "The Woods Place? Sounds like a cartoon I watched when I was little."

"I don't know what this guy is capable of. I don't want you going alone."

"Frank, in case you haven't noticed, well, I'm kinda not too bad with this cop stuff, ya know."

Frank had asked Johnny to work two different angles. He'd handed off Evanovich to Wadkins. It was his case but it felt like everyone else was carrying the load for him. "I know, but—"

"Someone shot up your home. Be with your family tonight," Michelle insisted.

Chapter 15

Ventura was sheathed in an orange hue as carroty veins of sunset snaked across the landscape. It was just after eight that evening when Michelle trudged closer to the surprisingly meager bungalow. The man owned seven properties in and around LA and she expected more from the residence. "Roscoe Woods?" she called out.

A dozen motorcycles packed the garage and brought to mind a Harley Davidson showroom. A large figure uncoiled from behind one. Mid-sixties, he sported a gray goatee and a ponytail. Wearing biker boots, Levis, and a T-shirt that read *Ever Ride a Fat Boy?*, he stepped forward and examined her well-toned body and winked. "If you're looking for a ride, then yes, I'm Roscoe Woods."

Ignoring the double entendre, she identified herself.

"The LAPD is lookin' better every day."

"I'm wondering if you can help me."

"Little lady, I can help you in ways you never imagined. As long as you ain't a Yamaha girl."

"No, Schwinn." Michelle was born and raised in East LA. She worked in the male-dominated world of law enforcement. Woods might be double her girth and triple her size, but she'd have no problem rearranging his teeth if need be. "I'd like to discuss a couple of your properties. You own one that was damaged in the West Hollywood explosion—"

"Fuckin' camel jockeys," Woods barked. "Let me and

some of my buddies go over there, and we'll solve this war on terror bullshit in three weeks."

"You also own property in Pasadena."

Woods's face hardened. He pulled on his chin and sauntered nearer to Michelle who stood her ground. "Yeah, 2355 Mar Vista," he confirmed, wandering around to gander the detective's backside. "Get you a beer?"

Michelle declined.

"Pity you don't like to ride."

"I ride, but not like anything you've experienced before. What can you tell me about the property?"

"What's it worth to you, little lady? I've always had a thing for *poquito* Latinas."

"And I've always had a thing for George Clooney but that's not happenin' either."

"People tell me I kinda look like George."

"Clooney or Curious?"

The chase was half the fun but this little spitfire seemed beyond even his irresistible charm. He took a deep breath. "About four months back, just before Christmas, fella named Vernon Wayne contacts me about renting the Mar Vista place. I'd only had it listed a few days and, in this market, it was a blessing."

Michelle removed a pad and pen, jotted down the name. "What can you tell me about him?"

"Within five minutes, he said he'd take it. Guy didn't even look around or anything. Struck me as strange."

"How so?"

"Single dude, no kids. Why'd he need a three bedroom?"

"Did you ask?"

Woods shook his head. "Dude said he was only in town a few months. Something about his sisters' will in probate, whatever that means. I wanted a twelve month lease but he said he didn't need it that long. We settled on six."

"In town a few months? Did he say where he was from?"

"No, ma'am."

"Anything strange come up in a background check?"

"Don't know, didn't look. You *sure* you don't ride? The Laughlin River Run is coming up soon."

Keeping him focused, Michelle claimed, "One person, three bedroom house, only gave your property a brief onceover, insisted on six months instead of twelve. And you didn't check him out?"

"Santana, right?"

Michelle nodded.

"Miss Santana, in this economy you don't ask, especially when someone writes you a check on the spot for all six months, including deposits. Man gives you almost twelve thousand bucks, you don't question him."

"The check cleared?" Michelle immediately regretted the wasted question.

"Yup. But the more I thought about it, it didn't sit right. I liked having it all upfront, but I still don't need the place trashed. I rode out to Pasadena a few times to see what's what. People sneak in pets or make changes they ain't supposed to. It was…mid-February when my gut proved correct."

"What happened?"

"Wanna come inside for a beer?"

"I'm on duty. Thanks, anyway. What happened when you arrived, Mr. Woods?"

Woods smiled briefly. A *poquito* Latina and a hard-ass? *Sweet.* "There were two kids livin', there but no Vernon Wayne."

Michelle tried to trick him. "Squatters?"

"No. They said Wayne was their uncle."

Michelle's enthusiasm spiked. There were certain moments during an investigation where critical information broke free. This was one of them. Keeping her hope in check, she asked, "You recall their names?"

"Strange names. Leach. The older was Xavier, the young one with the stupid grin? Shit, I can't recall. Ellis or something."

"Elijah?"

"Yeah, yeah, that's right. Ooh, you *are* good." When the sassy cop didn't throw herself on the ground spread eagle for the taking, he continued. "I wasn't happy this Wayne fella rented out my house that I was renting to him. He's prohibited from doing that. Says so right in the rental agreement. But since the rent was paid in advance, it wasn't worth contactin' a lawyer."

When Michelle advised him the property had been vacated, Woods wasn't surprised. "Why's any of this matter to the fuzz?"

The fuzz? "We think the Leach brothers may be involved in drug smuggling," Michelle lied. "Thanks for your time." She extended her hand which was taken and kissed. Michelle shuddered when she felt the warm tip of a tongue.

"It's a damn shame what's happening to our country."

⁊⁊⁊

Michelle was eastbound on the one-oh-one, contemplating burning the midnight oil back at the barn. As she drove, she rolled things around in her mind. Vernon Wayne apparently felt close enough to his nephews, Elijah and Xavier Leach, that he re-rented the property to them. But now the three of them were MIA. Somehow, based on her partner's instinct, the *domestic* terror attack in West Hollywood, the abductions of Detective Kendra Nichols and Judge Earl Sherman, and even the shooting at Frank's home were intertwined. Although the Leaches knew enough to contact Colby Ferrell, Michelle believed they lacked financial resources and the know-how to coordinate all of this. Elijah was recklessly spontaneous, Xavier the brains of their clan. But Michelle sensed someone else was pulling the strings.

Vernon Wayne?

Traffic on the freeway dictated a change of plans. She returned to her Sherman Oaks duplex, choosing instead to turn in early and arrive at the Barn by sunrise. Hopefully,

Wadkins would remember the doughnuts. Waiting for her TV dinner, she rearranged items in the spare bedroom in preparation of her niece moving in. Michelle knew as much about nine-year-old girls as she did about Einstein's theory of relativity. Or why black olives came in cans and green olives came in jars. *I'll have to ask Frank about that one tomorrow.* It would be a learning experience for both she and Sophia. Michelle was anxious, but in a good way. Although she was doing it primarily to allow her sister to defeat her inner demons, the reasoning was deeper. It would be gratifying having her niece under the same roof. As much as Michelle was helping her sister, Sophia was indirectly helping her aunt. Michelle wouldn't feel so alone, so lonely.

After making the room feel *homey,* she slid the processed Salisbury steak, corn, and a red glob of something from the oven. While she consumed the pseudo-meal, she called Frank and updated him on the meeting with Woods. Frank, like her, agreed they needed to jump on finding Vernon Wayne's whereabouts tomorrow. Frank sighed. "Shit."

"What is it?"

"I got another call coming in," Frank groaned. "I hate call waiting."

"Put me on hold. I'll wait."

Silence. Then, "I'm not sure how to switch over."

Michelle grinned. "Okay, Bill Gates. That's everything, anyway." Michelle wished her partner a good evening, hearing him lament, "Oh, crap, what happened? Hello? Hello?" as she ended the call.

Tomorrow they'd hopefully make some headway. Knowing she needed to bring her A-game but also knowing her head was spinning, she downed an Ambien and turned in early.

↷↶

Although she didn't open her eyes, a smile crossed Michelle's face realizing it was still dark. More sleep. She turned over and draped her arm across the unoccupied side of the bed. Patting the empty void, her smile faded. Her next day off she'd buy a smaller bed. The emptiness she slept with night after night was draining, a painful reminder of her loneliness.

With eyes closed, she turned right and mechanically reached for the Evian on her nightstand. Instead of locating the plastic bottle, her hand came in contact with something different, something cold. Michelle had been in law enforcement eleven years, nine as a detective. She knew what the barrel of a gun felt like.

Her eyes popped open. Even in the inadequate light, the silhouette of the black-clad shadow standing over her seemed menacing.

The entity leaned forward and slammed his hand over her mouth. Figuring it was an attempt to silence her, she bit down hard. She came in contact not with skin but with a cloth. The sweet aroma of chloroform filled her nostrils.

The hand was big, strong. *Male.* She flailed about, arms and legs kicking wildly. Her training went out the window. This was primal instinct, fighting for survival. The image of Kendra Nichols restrained and blindfolded flashed in her mind.

Her abductor made a critical miscalculation. He got onto the bed and straddled Michelle, using his leverage to apply more force. The mistake was that it afforded Michelle an opportunity. She brought her leg up, driving her knee into his testicles. He screeched, his grip weakened but he still had the upper hand. Michelle tried again but mostly connected with his thigh.

"Bitch!"

The voice somewhat familiar.

Michelle cocked her arm back, pummeled him in the head. A second blow knocked him from the bed to the floor. With her attacker crouched, whimpering, and clutching his crotch, Michelle went for the Glock she kept in her bureau. Oddly, as she yanked open the drawer, she realized she'd need to purchase a gun safe before Sophia moved in. *Funny how the mind works.* She had just gotten her hand on the grip when her assailant charged from behind. The two combatants tumbled into the hallway.

Michelle was thrown onto her back. Staring down at her were icy soulless eyes and an evil goofy grin through slits in a charcoal ski mask. The attacker pressed his forearm against her neck, pushing down on her windpipe. She couldn't breathe. A gurgling sound emitted from her lips.

Again the chloroform-laden rag was placed over her mouth. Again, the man had no luck.

Gasping for air, battling to stay conscious before the drug incapacitated her, she attempted to yank the mask from her attacker's face. He turned away, trying to keep his identity secret but in the process, his throat became exposed. If she couldn't breathe, she wouldn't let this bastard breathe either. Michelle slammed her palm into his Adam's apple. His hands instinctively went to his neck as he emitted a gagging-choking sound.

Michelle dislodged him and kicked aside the cloth, taking that out of play. Both detective and invader simultaneously rose to their feet.

He launched a roundhouse that caught nothing but air. For his weak effort, he received a powerful kick in his stomach. He doubled over.

Michelle had kicked him in the belly, palmed in the throat, and rearranged his balls. She'd gained the physical advantage. Now it was time to gain a psychological one. Going on Frank's intuition, she shouted, "Elijah Leach, you're under arrest!" She yanked the ski mask from his head. Her partner's theory was confirmed.

Winded, Elijah stared at this cop, this *woman* cop. This bitch was a hell of a lot tougher than Kendra Nichols. Failing to execute his assignment would be bad enough. Having his older brother Xavier riding his ass about not being able to take down a woman was not appealing.

Elijah, enraged, released a guttural scream, summoning strength from deep within. He drove his shoulder into Michelle's abdomen and, like a battering ram, barreled her down the hall toward the staircase that led to the first floor of her duplex.

Michelle glanced frightfully over her left shoulder. Just when she expected to be bulldozed down the stairs, pain filled her entire body. Lightning bolts raced up her spine as her lower back was violently slammed into a credenza.

Elijah ran away, but not before planting a vicious kick into the side of her head that stretched her out. The hurrying footsteps toward the front door were a welcome relief. Elijah was hurt but Michelle was weaker. Had he wanted to kidnap her the way he likely had Kendra, she'd be unable to mount a defense.

She thought of her partner. And Azusa. As much as Frank was maligned, the ultimate bone of contention in the public was that he had exited Il Vittorio's and given chase to one of the gunmen who fled the scene. Above and beyond securing the restaurant, Frank acted out of the need for revenge. Adrenalin coursed through his veins.

She, too, often second guessed Frank's extreme reaction—although she kept those thoughts internalized. Perhaps Frank *had* gone too far. Perhaps he *did* overreact. The gunmen had already escaped. Yet Frank pursued him into the street, down an alley and discharged his weapon. One bullet severed an artery. The bad guy bled out on his way to the hospital.

Now, four years later, Michelle found herself overcome with that same age-old thirst for vengeance. She struggled to her feet, hobbled down the hallway, retrieved her weapon, and seconds later lumbered into the street.

Elijah was gone, having become one with the night. Michelle straightened and breathed deeply to fill her lungs with much needed oxygen. It was a good thing for Leach he'd gotten away. Had she caught him, she would've killed the son-of-a-bitch, been disciplined, suspended, possibly fired. And then who would care for Sophia?

Chapter 16

"Hollywoodhomicidedetectivegrace."

"Huh?"

"Hollywood Homicide, Detective Grace."

"Oh." An older but influential voice resounded through the earpiece. "Detective Grace, this is Father McCabe."

Who? "Yes? Oh, from the Salvation Army. How are you, Father?"

"Blessed. I'm glad I was able to get hold of you."

Frank couldn't immediately remember why he reached out to the priest. On the other hand, any divine intervention would be welcomed. Rather than using the line that was sweeping across the LAPD, he chose not to ask the servant of God, 'How's it hangin'?' and went with a traditional, "How can I help you?"

"Demi procured a bed in our shelter the other evening."

"Demi?" Frank stole a glance at his partner.

"How's the rest of the Brat Pack doing?" Michelle whispered.

"Demi befriended the man you contacted me about, Eddie Evanovich," McCabe expounded. "The two of them left our facility months ago and took up shelter in an encampment a few blocks away. They looked out for each other but now, according to Demi, Mr. Evanovich never returned."

Although he handed this off to Wadkins, the reference to Evanovich in the latest video had thrown the name into the spotlight. The search for the vagrant, both by Frank, Wadkins, and undoubtedly the feds, had turned up nil. Upwards of nearly sixty thousand dispirited souls lived in the streets, alleys, and underpasses of Los Angeles. Finding one was unfeasible. "You wouldn't happen to have a description of Mr. Evanovich, would you?"

"I have more than that. For identification purposes, we photograph everyone who stays with us. Would a picture be beneficial?"

Frank straightened. "Most definitely. Let me give you my email address and—"

"Unfortunately, Detective, our computers have been down since late last evening. I can send you the photo tomorrow."

The Lord works in mysterious ways. "This really can't wait, Father. I can be there in an hour."

Father McCabe said he'd pencil it in and ended the call with "Godspeed, Detective Grace,"

Frank was unsure how to reply. "Um, yes. Godspeed, yourself."

As Frank updated his partner he tried not to look at the shiner on her cheek, courtesy of Elijah's boot. "You all right?"

"I'm better than Leach's balls." Michelle shared details about the pre-dawn altercation in her home. She finished up with, "I still don't see the connection between all of this, but I'm starting to think you're right."

Frank snickered. "Actually, I'm starting to think I'm wrong. What happened to you actually *disproves* something I'd been formulating."

"Let's hear it."

Whenever Frank was putting things together, he habitually rubbed his hands as if he was cold. With elbows on his knees, he slid closer to Michelle and began the same mannerism. "We both know Elijah and Xavier are anarchists. Anti-government, wanna-be revolutionaries, or whatever you want to call it—"

"Yet, they retain Colby Ferrell," Michelle interrupted. "They're anti-establishment until they want legal representation from the very system they condemn."

"True. They spouted the same BS in Pasadena when I entered the Mar Vista home. They repeated the same baloney when I stopped them in West Hollywood. Two guys, hell-bent on bringing down society just happen upon the exact location where a bomb goes off? I work Homicide. No such thing as coincidences. Putting that aside for a moment, look at the two people kidnapped. Kendra Nichols, a detective, and Earl Sherman, a judge. Both are symbols representing order and justice. However, and I know you and Kendra had been friends, she was not exactly…untainted."

Michelle scoffed. "You think she was on the take?"

Frank extended his palms. "No, no, I'm not saying that." He resumed scrubbing his hands. "She partied, she slept around. By the same token, Judge Sherman, even though he was no friend of the LAPD, has skeletons in his closet. Remember that sweetheart deal he was accused of a few years back? And the rumors of sexual escapades? Sherman, like Nichols, has a questionable history. Both are pillars of society during the day but less than reputable afterhours."

Michelle nodded.

Frank pressed on. "One of the Leaches, be it Xavier or Elijah, took a shot at me. And well—my reputation isn't exactly untarnished either. *Three* people entrusted with the public good, but all with checkered pasts. But what happened to you flies in the face of my theory. You have no skeletons."

"I'm no choir girl, Frank."

"No one is. But nothing in your background equates to Nichols's, Sherman's, or mine."

Michelle pondered. "So they're after anyone with a shadowy past? If that's true, Frank, why did they not try to kidnap *you*? And then, how does Evanovich fit into your theory?"

"As for the former, Nichols is a woman, no offense. Easy

to kidnap. Sherman's an older guy. As for the latter, Eva-novich is collateral damage, a sideshow. I'd bet you any-thing we never find him." He added as an afterthought, "Or he'll turn up dead. The outcry about a detective and a judge being kidnapped is troubling to the public. A homeless guy, who cares? He's the exclamation point on their mission."

"For a guy who suffered a head injury you may be right. We need to find them—quickly."

"Before your niece moves in," Frank inserted. "And the best way of locating them may be through their uncle. There's a BOLO for Elijah and Xavier but we *have to* find Vernon Wayne. He might lead us right to his nephews."

"How's it hangin, Grantana?" Johnny asked, joining their discussion.

"Oh, hell no!" Frank bemoaned. "You, too?"

"It's actually Sant-ace," Michelle clarified.

"I stand corrected," Johnny said. "Scratch that. I sit cor-rected." He laughed. His self-deprecating humor about his disability always left Frank feeling awkward. Still, Johnny's positive outlook on life and the fact that he didn't see him-self as a victim was marginally soothing to Frank's guilt-riddled spirit.

Johnny made sure Detective Santana was okay, asked how Abby and the kids were holding up, and then scratched his head pensively. "I heard you mention Vernon Wayne."

Grantana/Sant-ace both leaned forward. "Ring a bell?"

Johnny fisted his chin, cracked his neck with a violent jerk to the left. Frank and Michelle winced, waiting for an answer. "Vernon Wayne, huh? I'll have to do some digging. Anyway, I've got bad news and more bad news. There's no cells registered to either Leach brother so they must've used burner phones. I took a second crack at the origin of that email address which mentioned Eddie Evanovich, but again hit a wall. Nada."

"That's what I feared," Frank said, then added in a whis-per, "I know I handed off Evanovich to Wadkins but thanks for coming to me instead."

"I looked for Wadkins but he didn't make it in today."

Michelle sighed. "Crap. The one day I could really use a doughnut."

"You didn't hear?" Johnny shifted a glance between them. "Wadkins's got shot at last night."

"*What*?" Frank and Michelle cried in unison.

"Yeah. He was sitting in his car outside his home when someone pumped a few rounds at him. He wasn't hurt, though."

Frank considered this latest development. He, Nichols, and Sherman were targeted. If his notion was correct—and he felt confident it was—they all shared dubious pasts. Michelle, on the other hand, had an unblemished track record. *Which side of the ledger does Wadkins belong on?*

"Gang related?" Michelle asked.

Frank disagreed. "Wadkins lives in Simi, no gangbangers up there. What time was it?"

"A little after one," Johnny claimed.

Michelle reasoned Elijah could've paid Wadkins a visit in Simi Valley and easily made it to her Sherman Oaks duplex. However, she didn't recall a trace of gunpowder on his gloved hands. "So Wadkins took the day off?"

"He'll probably be in later."

"Hey, I got attacked and still managed to get in on time," Michelle boasted.

"And that's why I've got the best partner in the department," Frank said graciously.

"Wish I could say the same thing," Michelle said with a wink.

Johnny departed. Frank was about to do the same when his phone rang again. After identifying himself, he straightened in his chair. "Chief Kent, good morning."

The call was under five minutes. Michelle overheard the gravelly Police Chief barking at Frank. Between the penetrating volume and Frank's gradually slumping shoulders, it was obvious Kent was fuming. Frank mostly gave one word answers but was finally able to get in a full sentence. "The matter we discussed…yes, sir, yes, sir, thank you, sir." Frank hung up and massaged his temples. The burden of being the anointed one by LA's Police Chief was draining.

"You've got protection."

Michelle's chin dropped.

"I called in a favor. You'll have a cruiser posted outside your home starting tonight."

"*You* asked Kent for a favor?"

"Not bad for a guy you don't like being teamed up with, eh?"

"Thanks, Frank. I appreciate it."

"Don't flatter yourself. I just don't want to have to break in a new partner." He reciprocated the earlier wink.

Frank trudged out of the Barn, concerned about his partner. Michelle claimed it'd be better use of their time to divide and conquer. She'd stay behind to work angles from the safety of West Bureau. Normally, she'd accompany him but today seemed unenthused. He feared last night's home invasion/botched kidnapping may have left her shell-shocked. He then quickly discarded that preposterous notion. Detective Santana was tough, focused, and driven. At least on the surface.

The trip into the bowels of the city made Frank grateful his patrolman days were over. He seldom ventured into the concrete jungle of Skid Row anymore but each time he did, the homeless population had swelled.

Beds were scarce, shelters bursting at the seams, and there was no money to improve conditions. For a time, city officials thought they'd found a cheap way to combat the homeless problem: a one-way bus ticket across the desert to Las Vegas. It worked for a while until the powers-that-be in Nevada caught on and shipped *their* displaced to LA. A never-ending cycle.

The ramshackle yellow and white paneled shelter was losing its battle against the elements. The pockmarked lot resembled a lunar landscape.

A line of thirty or so people stood, waiting to secure a

bed for the evening, although cots would not be available for seven more hours.

The waiting room was equally depressing. After signing in with a rent-a-cop behind bulletproof glass, Frank's senses were overwhelmed with the stench of rancid body odor. The smell of whatever they were preparing in the kitchen only fueled his queasiness. Forty folding chairs in the lobby were all occupied. Another dozen lost souls languished in the hallway.

Frank took it all in but tried not to be obvious. He studied his shoes, busied himself with his phone. Anything to not have to face what surrounded him. They waited for vouchers to the food bank, referrals for day labor, shoes. Mostly men, some women, a few children—all shells of what they once had been. The drooped shoulders, reeking clothes, matted hair, sullen faces, and expressions of defeat and shattered dreams were everywhere. Some murmured softly, holding conversations with invisible friends. In one corner, a woman, who looked about fifty but clearly was not, sat with a breast exposed, a newborn suckling. *There but for the Grace of God go I,* thought Frank Grace.

Moments later, he was beckoned by Father McCabe. The office was quaint. Paintings of Jesus, crucifixes, and scriptures adorned the goldenrod walls. The desk was one of the old-fashioned metal jobs the PD cast off when the outdated Parker Center was renovated. Frank remembered hearing much of the older office furniture had been donated. He wondered if this piece was one.

McCabe was a large man in his late-fifties. Dressed in traditional priest garb, he lowered his torso into a cozy chair and took a bite of a partially eaten breakfast burrito. Whereas Frank was reeling from the heartbreaking scene and stench outside McCabe's office, the priest appeared in good spirits, jovial. And detached.

The two men engaged in idle chitchat. With the eyes of Jesus bearing down upon him, Frank recalled he'd not stepped into a church since Jake's christening. And even that had been Abby's idea. The tête-à-tête ended when Father McCabe presented the detective with a five-by-seven-inch black and white photo. Eddie Evanovich resembled a clichéd homeless man. The blond hair was greasy and disheveled, but he'd attempted to comb it neatly. His skin was leathery, his complexion ruddy. His smile displayed rotting teeth, but Frank saw something else. Behind the brooding expression and faraway eyes, he could see a trace of confidence and purpose. Eddie Evanovich had once been a *somebody*.

Frank felt guilt rise up. An hour ago, he'd referred to Eddie Evanovich as nothing more than an *exclamation point*. The main players were a detective and a judge. Yet, Evanovich, like Nichols and Sherman, was also a human being, a living person. By giving lower priority to this destitute individual, Frank played right into the hand of the kidnappers, most likely the Leaches.

Who mourns for Eddie Evanovich?

Frank thanked Father McCabe for his time and assistance. On the way out of the office, he gave a parting glance to Jesus as the priest chucked the half-uneaten burrito into the garbage while dozens sat famished beyond his door.

Stepping clear of the stifling facility, Frank inhaled deeply. By comparison to the putrid shelter, the smog of LA was actually refreshing. He needed to move quickly and try to somehow find Evanovich, though he was confident the man was dead. He wanted to get back to West Bureau and see if Michelle or Johnny had come up with any leads. Time was short but there was something he needed to do first.

Frank got into his loaner, drove to a corner convenience store he'd passed on the way. When he put a fifty and a cluster of items on the counter, the young Asian gave him a curious glance, shrugged, and bagged the purchase. Frank returned to the shelter and, armed with bags in hand, reentered the stink-filled waiting area. He spent the next ten minutes handing out fifty-dollars' worth of candy bars.

Back in his car, Frank tried reaching his partner but Detective Santana was neither answering her direct line nor her cell. He was in the midst of leaving a voicemail when a beep indicated an incoming call. "Oh, shit." Frank pantomimed, looking at the display of his cell, lifting it to his ear, placing it to his lips, wailing, "Hello, hello?"

Call lost.

He'd been cherry-picked by the Police Chief of Los Angeles to get to the bottom of a terrorist attack and return a city of millions to safety. Yet, he couldn't grasp call waiting. He located the *missed calls* log, saw it had been Michelle, and pressed *send*.

"Call waiting is your friend," Michelle said by way of greeting and laughed.

"With friends like that, I don't need enemies. I need a favor."

"Want me to teach you how to use speed dial?"

"Cute." After considering the offer, Frank admitted, "Maybe later. I'd like you to look up any John Doe's found within a ten mile radius of Skid Row in the last week."

"Arrests?"

"No, check with the coroner."

Silence. "Give me fifteen minutes."

"Thanks."

Fifteen minutes was closer to ten. Luckily, Frank was not engrossed in another conversation when she called back. "Whaddya got?"

There'd been three: One African-American female, one male with prosthetic legs, and one matching the description of Evanovich. "Thanks." Frank was about to hit *end* when Michelle stated, "Abby called."

He unwittingly fretted that Ashley had gotten in trouble again. His stomach tightened. "I'll call her in a few."

"It's not always about you, Frank." Michelle said. "She invited me over for dinner."

"Oh. Okay, great." He frowned. "Hey, weren't you going for pizza with your niece tonight?"

As soon as he recalled the passing comment Michelle

made earlier, he smiled. The effects of the concussion were wearing off. Frank Grace was on his way back.

"Oh, you *do* listen? Abby insisted. I think, because of what happened last night, she didn't want me to be alone tonight. That's very sweet of her."

"Yeah, she's not too bad," Frank replied with a smile. More confirmation he'd chosen the right one.

"I tried to get out of it. Last minute and all but she *can* be persuasive."

"Of course. Why do you think we got married?"

"*Sure*. Later 'gator."

En route to Mission Road, Frank found himself reflecting. Obviously it was brought about by what he witnessed at the shelter and he started thinking about his own path in life.

Every person who entered law enforcement did so for different reasons. Frank had always kicked around the idea but never seriously. By his late twenties the window of opportunity was closing. He had a fairly new bride and a baby. He applied, made it through the academy in the middle of the class. A job became a career, a career became a purpose, a paycheck became a calling. Frank found himself speaking for those who couldn't, for those whose voices had been silenced forever.

Frank had observed more murder scenes, more blood, and more corpses than he wanted to remember. But each one remained separate, compartmentalized. Every ruined life occupied one small niche in his mind. Crime scenes were lumped together but the victims never would be.

Michelle's reason for becoming a cop was based on unbridled optimism. She grew up in an unsafe neighborhood where she witnessed daily the savagery and ugliness of people. She joined the LAPD in her own little attempt to make the city cleaner and nontoxic, one case at a time, so that other young children wouldn't bear the scars she did.

Frank enjoyed his work with three exceptions. One was the unending bureaucracy that paralyzed the department. The second, he'd now confront head-on. Frank's reflective period ended as he climbed from the vehicle and entered the Los Angeles County Morgue.

When investigating crime scenes, examining slashed torsos and bullet riddled bodies in the precise location of their deaths, Frank was able to disconnect. However, here at the morgue, he had a difficult time. This was the end. This was final.

The facility was, as always, taciturn and icy. Worst of all for Frank was the unique sounds. The bone saw cutting through a skull, the electric Stryker slicing through the cranium, the suction slurping of a brain being disconnected.

Frank threw on a gown, mask, and booties. He matched the image from Father McCabe to the unmoving pale form of Eddie Evanovich. The *Y* incision on his upper body was blatant.

"You made it just in time," the ME announced as he slid Evanovich back into the storage chamber. "He's slated for Evergreen tomorrow."

"Potter's Field?"

The ME nodded. "Mass grave, name on a stone with forty nine others. No one claimed the body. No family, no friends, no funeral, no money."

Frank slid free from the mandatory attire, deposited it into the receptacle, thanked the man for his time, and stepped outside. Now he'd have to bookend the visit to the morgue with the other aspect of his job he equally detested: contacting the family.

Chapter 17

The United States was often referred to as a melting pot. And perhaps Los Angeles more than any other city typified that. But now, in the face of prejudicial violence, the very diversity that unified us was now dividing us. The City of Angels was being ripped apart. People scrutinized neighbors with a wary eye. Those of Middle Eastern origin—even those that *looked* a certain way—were yanked from vehicles and beaten. Innocent law-abiding citizens were becoming victims of a mob mentality. The innate thirst for revenge was overriding common sense and decency. More than a week had passed since Angelenos had their innocence ripped away, and still no one was in custody. The melting pot was boiling over, and Frank Grace was designated to keep the lid on.

The discontent rose to the highest levels of government. The LAPD, always first to be criticized, was being disparaged by a media that fueled the fires of discontent. The future of Chief Weldon Kent was on the line. Mayors across Southern California were bombarded with accusatory grills by the press. Governor McMasters delivered a prepared statement at West Hollywood's Ground Zero where a memorial would be built, claiming the worst was over. The FBI, DNI, JTTF, and NCTC held joint press conferences seeking the public's help while vowing those responsible would be brought to justice. Just an hour ago, the president appeared from the Oval Office urging restraint, pledging no attack would bring down this great country and no act of terrorism could destroy the American dream.

But life *was* becoming altered.

A surfing competition in Malibu was cancelled, due to security concerns. The San Dimas Festival of the Arts and The Monterey Park Cherry Blossom Festival had been negated as well. The start of the Renaissance Pleasure Faire, the largest of its kind in Southern California, was pushed back two weeks. The Toyota Grand Prix of Long Beach was rescheduled for the fall. Major League Baseball was ruminating over moving the Dodgers' home opener to San Diego. The port of Los Angeles was backlogged as shipments from the Pacific were inspected with a critical eye. Passengers departing LAX and John Wayne Airport were told to arrive three hours prior to departure. Estimates put the city's losses at eleven million dollars per day.

Yet, for a few hours this particular evening, the normalcy and familiarity of routine was uplifting. It felt good to spend time with friends. And to laugh. Although the troubled outside world was never far from Frank or Michelle's mind, they kept it repressed. No shoptalk tonight.

The adults worked together preparing Chicken Marsala while Jake and Ashley frolicked with Michelle's niece, Sophia. Frank grew uneasy when seeing his daughter was initially a bit standoffish. He couldn't help but recall her instigating the beating of Sabiha Mansoor, a girl who like Sophia, was of different heritage. However, after some time, his daughter came around. Ashley would soon be a teenager and cavorting with a little kid of nine years old was beneath her.

Nevertheless, the Grace children and Michelle's niece soon bonded. The giddy laughter of youthful innocence filled the home.

Kids said the darndest things and Jake Grace was no exception. He'd been gawking at Daddy's partner throughout dinner, then quickly turning away when caught. Unable to subdue the curiosity any longer he pointed to the contusion on Michelle's face. "What happened to *you?*"

"Jake!" Abby sighed, red faced. "I'm sorry, Michelle."

Michelle dismissed Abby's concern. "I was just moving some boxes around, Jake, and one hit me in the head. I'm kinda klutzy."

"But I thought—" Ashley felt Mom's foot against her shin, followed by a shaking head and a nod toward Jake. At eight, he was too young to be told of Michelle's home invasion. Ashley beamed, feeling like an adult. She then leaned over and whispered into Michelle's ear, "Some guy punched you, huh?"

Michelle returned the whisper and, for only Ashley to hear said softly, "He did. But I kicked him squarely in the balls."

Ashley laughed. Being a grown-up was pretty cool.

"What?" Frank breathed.

"Just girl talk."

"Yeah, Dad. Just girl talk," Ashley mirrored.

After dinner, Frank moved his portable CD player to the front steps, dropped in a Beatles CD, and pressed Shuffle. Fittingly on this pleasant spring evening, the upbeat *Here Comes the Sun* floated across the yard.

"Can you at least put on something from the second half of the twentieth century?" Michelle protested.

"This is. 1969, Abbey Road."

She fondly patted Frank's face. "Don't ever change."

Abby ganged up on her husband. "Hey, you work with him. I have to live with him."

"It's *only* The Beatles. I'm sure they'll never amount to much."

After the assault on Frank's taste in music finished, they began shooting hoops in the driveway. Girls versus guys: Abby, Ashley, Michelle, and Sophia against Frank, Jake, and Officer Newsted, the patrolman assigned to watch over Frank's house, who Frank invited to join them. The guys got trounced, twenty-five to thirteen. When the shellacking concluded and Newsted returned to his cruiser, the adults headed back in, but the kids insisted on staying outside. Before Frank or Abby could say it, Michelle beat them to the punch. "Stay in the driveway. Don't go into the street."

Frank smiled. Perhaps his partner would be okay caring for a child, after all.

As the table was cleared and the dishwasher was loaded, Jake came running inside and pulled on Frank's shirt. His face exhibited excitement, his words jumbled together. "Daddy, Daddy, guess what?"

"What, Jake?"

"Guess."

Abby and Michelle pivoted to hear.

Jake stared at Mommy and the lady with the bruise, then said, "Come down here." Frank dropped to his haunches, listened, smiled, and turned to his animated son. "Are you sure?"

Jake shot an apprehensive glance at the two women before saying "Yeah, but you can't tell Mommy."

Frank put his hand to his mouth, turned his fingers. "My lips are sealed."

Jake clapped twice, raced out of the kitchen, but quickly returned. He had another secret. Frank squatted again, listened, bowed his head. "I guess I'll have to raise your allowance."

"Thanks, Daddy!" Jake excitedly scampered outside.

As Frank stood, his knees creaked.

"What was that all about?" Abby inquired.

Frank looked at his partner and his wife. "Looks like Jake and Sophia have decided to get married."

The evening progressed. Sophia, Frank's nine-year-old soon-to-be daughter-in-law, showed him a game on her phone. He tried to play but had worse luck than on the makeshift basketball court. Abby offered to help Michelle get her duplex ready for her niece.

Before anyone realized it, it was midnight. Michelle, clutching a slumbering Sophia to her, was heading home.

Jake had conked out watching TV. Ashley, though fatigued, struggled to stay awake with the grownups.

Frank and Abby escorted Michelle to the door. They exchanged pleasantries and all insisted they needed to do this more often. For real.

"I had fun," Frank declared.

"Me too." Michelle lovingly patted the back of her niece's head. She held Sophia extra tight as she looked at the Graces. Frank and Abby stood in the anteroom, side by side, arms hooking each other's waist. One didn't need to be a detective to see the love they still shared after fifteen years. Under normal circumstances, Michelle would dread leaving. The vitality of their home was a parallel universe to Michelle's solitary life and sparsely furnished duplex. However, with her niece pressed to her heart, going home seemed less dismal.

Frank's phone chirped as he started closing the door. He checked the display, curled his lips, and answered, "Hey."

Abby and Michelle watched him pace in a circle.

"Okay, see you in twenty." He looked regretfully at his wife. "Sorry, sweetie." To his partner, "It's Johnny. He may have just found the break we need."

Michelle grinned miserably. "It was nice to forget—for a few hours, anyway."

ℯジℯジ

Time had stopped. Morning, evening, day of the week, he had no idea. Each second was a minute, each minute an hour.

Judge Sherman's wrists and ankles were chaffed. He'd been stripped to his boxers and placed spread eagle on the four-poster bed. He had no idea how much time had passed since being kidnapped outside the tawdry Tarzana motel. He was unaware of his whereabouts, but the strong reek of manure and something unidentifiable made him believe he was beyond the city limits. Far away. Isolated.

He'd been blindfolded. A gag of some sort was only removed when he was fed. The meals brought to him—if you could call them meals—were basic sandwiches. He was only permitted to drink well water. He'd heard about the kidnapping of that detective. Nichols, wasn't it? Something inside told him that the same party was involved with his own abduction.

Prior to each meal, Sherman heard what sounded like rusty hinges turning, footsteps, and muffled conversation to his right. If he was correct in his assessment, he considered the irony of a district court judge and a female detective both imprisoned. But why? Where? And for how long? Dammit, how long?

The one saving grace was if Detective Nichols was still alive, perhaps he'd survive as well.

He'd spent the time in captivity trying to grunt a conversation with the prisoner in the adjacent chamber, hoping to ascertain it was, in fact, that detective. They conversed through exchanges of snorting and grumbling. Although attempted dialogue proved fruitless, as expected, it led Sherman to believe their abductors were not posted nearby. The exchanges between inmates would have been overheard and promptly stopped.

It was common knowledge the Honorable Earl Sherman was one of the LAPD's biggest detractors. He probably shared the top spot on the department's Most Hated with Colby Ferrell. But Sherman was doing his job. If the LAPD and Police Chief Kent would do their jobs, his would be much easier and he wouldn't need to bring down the hammer time and again. It wasn't his fault they operated in that gray area.

Still, he knew that if he somehow was rescued, he'd cut them more slack in the future. As of this moment, the judge didn't give a damn about legal precedence or justice. He wanted his ass saved by any means.

The first four sandwiches brought to him...or was it

five?…were delivered by an individual who enjoyed taunting. He remarked once, "You should've seen the mold on that bread you just ate," immediately after Sherman had downed the last bite. Knowing his questions would go unanswered, Sherman still quizzed the man. All he got were ominous statements and menacing responses. Even an occasional chuckle.

Once, Sherman endeavored to turn the tables. If Detective Nichols was still alive, he felt reasonably confident they were being held for ransom. Pawns in a game. The kidnappers *needed* them—for some reason. Sherman therefore elected to go on a hunger strike until being told what the hell was going on. All he got for his effort was a savage beating.

He wasn't sure how long it'd been when he first heard the voice of a second kidnapper. This man sounded all business. He spoke slow, methodical. Although he didn't share any valuable information, he advised Sherman eating was essential. There were no threatening remarks. Instead, he pointed out that the judge needed to keep his strength up and that this would all be over shortly. He pled his case as if he was an attorney in Sherman's court.

"Hey, dickwad."

Shit. It was the reckless one.

Sherman tightened his stomach in preparation of another blow. Instead, relief flooded his spirit as his wrists were freed. Methodical one had promised him this would soon end. Was his captivity over?

Sherman's shoulders burned from the abnormal position he'd been placed in. He managed to rub his raw wrists. His ankles were unrestrained. *It's over. I'm being released.* The blindfold remained in place but the gag was ripped away. "Thank you," Sherman murmured. "Thank you."

The captor who always tittered did it again. "Don't thank me…yet."

Sherman was pulled to an upright position, hoisted to his feet. He winced as his arms were viciously wrenched behind his back, the handcuffs now replaced with Flexi-cuffs. His ankles were re-shackled. He was belligerently prodded forward like a steer on its way to slaughter.

"Where are we going?"

"To have some fun."

Sherman's bound wrists were used like a rudder as he was directed through darkness. Twice he was purposely navigated into a wall, resulting in hilarious laughter from his captor. The third instance caused his eyes to water and blood to trickle from his nose.

After marched in what seemed like a circular journey, Sherman was flung onto a chair. "Sit!" The chair nearly toppled, taking the judge with it. More laughter from his crazed tormentor.

Sherman's blindfolded was removed. He blinked several times as his eyes adjusted to light. He couldn't see his jailer lurking behind. But what he saw before him caused him to blink again. Was this real or a mirage?

She sat bound on a cot, helpless, wearing nothing but an expression of fear. Like Sherman, she too did a double take. He muttered "How," but through the rag it sounded more like the whine of a dying animal. What was she doing here? How did they find her? More importantly, how did they know about her?

He and the woman stared into each other's panicked and confused eyes. He remembered her real name. *Hiromi.*

Depraved glee resonated from behind. Sherman waggled his head as the blindfold was reattached. He'd only been granted a glimpse. For the next torturous twenty minutes, hearing was far worse than seeing. His subconscious filled in the gaps he could not view.

Finally a shout of release from the male followed by the incessant sobbing of a broken female.

Chapter 18

The Santa Ana winds had intensified. Garbage danced across the pavement. Papers pirouetted in a dust devil in the corner of the lot. The temperature was unseasonably cool for mid-April, the air possessing a strange chill.

Frank entered the hushed building and headed to *Cyberopolis* while Michelle searched for a place to lay down Sophia.

With the exception of gale-force winds beyond the walls West Bureau-Hollywood was cemetery silent. Frank's rubber soles squeaked like he was Kobe Bryant driving down the lane. At the outset of his detective days, he took pleasure in arriving early. It was invigorating to come in before sunup. The solitude, tranquility, and lack of interruption afforded him the opportunity to make progress on whatever case he caught. After Azusa, however, that stopped. As he greeted Johnny, he wondered why the change.

Johnny had been here going on sixteen hours. And despite rumpled clothes, mussed hair, and stubble, his bloodshot eyes were alert. He apologized for calling Frank so late, adding, "This couldn't wait."

Frank waved it off and advised him that Michelle was right behind him.

As if on cue, Santana appeared and pulled a chair alongside her partner. She sat closer to Johnny's desk than Frank, visibly less intimidated by the abundance of high-tech gadgetry.

Johnny thanked them both for coming and put his fist to his chin.

"Oh, God, please don't," begged Michelle but she was too slow.

Johnny cracked his neck, first left, then right. Noticing Michelle cringe, he did it again and grinned.

She smiled. "Asshole."

"Where to start, where to start?" Johnny shuffled papers. "So, Vernon Wayne?"

The detectives simultaneously angled forward. Frank asked eagerly, "You found him?"

"Yes and no."

Whenever the department's tech guru and resident hacker discovered something, he habitually savored his findings, bringing it out slowly for max drama. It was a pet peeve and, with time short, Frank wanted him to skip the dramatics. However, he held his tongue. This was Johnny's performance. He and Michelle were his audience.

"Gordon Whitefield owned a construction company down in Texas, San Antonio to be exact."

"Who's Gordon Whitefield?"

Frank clutched Michelle's arm, shook his head.

"Go on," she said apologetically.

Johnny started over. "Gordon Whitefield owned a construction company down in Texas, San Antonio to be exact. Small potatoes, really. Barely turning a profit. Divorced, no kids. Guy was pretty much a loner and kept to himself. One of those married to their job." Johnny had been alternating glances between the detectives but on this point he inadvertently gazed at Michelle a bit longer. "So…um…in the early '90's Whitefield Construction and Rigging bids on a contract for an oil company drilling out in the Gulf of Mexico. He hits the mother lode and gets awarded the very lucrative seven-year contract that runs through the end of the century. We're talking big bucks here. Then the craziest thing happens." Johnny looked at his rapt spectators, his eyebrows danced. "Care to venture a guess what happened next?"

"He disappeared?"

Johnny stared at Frank wide-eyed, appearing wounded, his big climax ruined. "Yeah, he did," Johnny grumbled and took a moment to regroup. "Dude was wealthy and about to get even wealthier. Then, poof, he's gone."

Johnny took a long pull of his Red Bull and dropped it into a garbage pail, where it clanked against other empty cans. "San Antonio PD looks into Whitefield's disappearance but comes up empty. Nothing suspicious in his house or office. No clues, no leads. Coworkers and family are interrogated. Still nothing. Not only was Whitefield missing but so was his sixty-five-foot class-forty yacht docked in Corpus Christi. Police close the case, determining the millionaire was lost at sea. Body was never found." In a conspiratorial tone, he added, "Mighty convenient, wouldn't you agree."

"Agreed."

"Meanwhile in another part of Gotham City, or more specifically Paso Robles, an entrepreneur named Casey Dillon buries his wife of forty-two years. Dillon is distraught. He starts questioning things. What's the meaning of life and all that? He puts his winery on the market after working the same fields his family operated since the early twentieth century. He's not looking to make money, he just wants out. He's got one son, but the kid's making a name for himself in Silicon Valley. Enter our buddy, Vernon Wayne."

Frank and Michelle gave each other a look.

Johnny continued. "VW finds out about the auction and steps in. He procures the land and everything included. And at anywhere from twenty to thirty thousand per acre, do the math. We're talking in the neighborhood of five or six million."

"Whew," Michelle breathed. "Pretty expensive neighborhood."

"Wayne insists that Dillon's son run the winery, basically doing the grunt work. This way it stays in the family."

"Nice gesture but why?" Frank asked. As an afterthought, "And why would the kid say yes? If he's working in Silicon he doesn't need the dough."

"Wayne offers to put him on the payroll. Annual salary of four hundred thousand plus ten percent of the profits. The son—" Johnny rearranged some papers. "—Justin Dillon assumes control. He knows nothing about the business but quickly learns everything he can."

"Why would Wayne buy the winery for millions then immediately turn it over to a novice?" Michelle asked. "On the surface, it seems foolhardy."

Johnny did his dancing eyebrow thing. "On the surface, yes. Frank, any ideas?"

Frank inhaled and stared at nothing. "'Cause Vernon Wayne didn't want to get personally involved."

Johnny pushed an imaginary button. "Ta-dah, we have a winner. There's nothing in Wayne's background to indicate he knew a damn thing about wineries or vineyards. Yet, he forks over millions to invest in something completely foreign to him. That'd be like me buying a Stairmaster. Or you, Frank, splurging for an Android." Johnny clucked his tongue proudly.

Michelle nodded. "It was a simple business deal for Wayne, an investment. Most entrepreneurs and CEOs are so far removed, they don't even know how to perform menial work. I read somewhere Bill Gates doesn't even know how to attach a Jpeg picture to an e-mail."

"Is that true?" Frank asked.

"No idea, but it sounds good."

Frank eased his chair back, and started to wring his hands. "So, Vernon Wayne buys a business he knows nothing about. You sure there's nothing in his background?"

"The closest Vernon Wayne ever got to a winery is when he bought grapes at the neighborhood Ralph's. Actually, there's nothing *at all* in Wayne's past."

"Never owned a winery?"

"No, Detective Santana. Nothing, zilch, the big nada." Johnny made a circle with his fingers. "The guy just materialized out of thin air with millions at his disposal. Then promptly hands over millions to a complete stranger to operate a business he knows squat about."

"It's a business investment, nothing more," Michelle claimed, not yet on-board with Johnny's take.

Frank squinted. "So, you're implying that Gordon Whitefield, our missing construction guy from Texas, became Vernon Wayne?"

"That's *exactly* what I'm implying." Johnny swiveled, typed a few keystrokes, and turned back to the detectives. "Vernon Wayne appeared on the grid shortly after Whitefield dropped off. The guy—Wayne I'm talking about—has no digital footprints anywhere in cyber space. No credit cards, never purchased a car, hasn't even filed a tax return."

"With that much money, he probably pays cash," Michelle stated.

"Oh, ye of little faith." Johnny smiled. "Trust me, the guy is a ghost."

Frank mused for a moment. "Question. Let's say, for the sake of argument, Whitefield is indeed Wayne—"

"No doubt about it," Johnny proclaimed.

"Did Whitefield reap the benefits of that contract, vanish, and *then* use that money to reappear as Wayne?"

"No," Johnny replied. "He vanished before he signed the contract for the job in the Gulf. Never saw a nickel."

"It's an old worn-out cliché," Michelle said. "But follow the money. Where'd Wayne get his fortune?"

Johnny leaned back, clasped his hands behind his neck. "You tell me." He thrived on having details ahead of others and watching them come around to what he'd already uncovered.

"Why does someone change their identity?" Frank asked rhetorically. "To hide, to start over. But what was Whitefield hiding from? Johnny, is there anything questionable in *Whitefield's* past?"

Johnny shook his head. "Guy's cleaner than Caesar's wife."

Frank arched a brow at Michelle then back at Johnny. "Does that mean he is clean or he isn't?"

Johnny snickered. "Yes, Frank. Cleaner than Mother Theresa's hard drive."

Frank stopped kneading his hands and pursed his lips. "When was Whitefield reported missing?"

Johnny beamed like a proud parent. Finally, someone was seeing the light. "Nineteen-ninety-five."

"And Wayne materialized around that same time I'm guessing."

"You learn well, grasshoppa."

"Whitefield's from Texas?"

"Yup."

"Shit."

"What is it, Frank?" Michelle asked.

"Colby Ferrell's from Texas."

Michelle locked on her partner's profile. "*The* Colby Ferrell, aka Colby Ferret?"

"That's the one."

Frank thought out loud, as much for Michelle and Johnny as for himself. "Gordon Whitefield, aka Vernon Wayne, comes from Texas, same state where Colby Ferrell started practicing law. Wayne rents a home in Pasadena and then has Elijah and Xavier Leach, his nephews, move in. The same nephews who now retain Colby Ferrell in a lawsuit against me and the city. They're all connected."

"Colby Ferret's an attorney," Michelle pointed out. "Earl Sherman, a judge, gets kidnapped."

"Name of Vernon Wayne still not setting off your Spidey senses, Detective Grace?" Johnny asked.

Before Frank could respond, Michelle shifted in her seat. "None of this explains where Wayne/Whitefield earned his millions from."

"He didn't *earn* it," Johnny announced. "He won it. In a settlement."

"Musta been a hefty chunk of change," Michelle claimed.

"You could say that, Detective Santana. Think Texas, early nineties."

"Waco," Frank blurted.

Johnny put one finger on his nose and pointed at Frank. "You got it. In the winter of 1993 the ATF presented a search warrant and attempted to enter the Mount Carmel Center, a religious compound inhabited by a group calling themselves Branch Davidians, an homage to their founder, David Koresh. The group was suspected of storing an enormous cache of weapons. A gun battle ensued and when the smoke cleared, four government agents and six Branch Davidians lay dead. A standoff began and after nearly two months, the FBI raided the compound. During the assault, the facility became engulfed in flames. The result was the death of the group's founder along with seventy-six of his followers. Exactly two years later, April 19, 1995, the Alfred P. Murrah Federal building in downtown Oklahoma City was leveled. One hundred sixty-eight dead. The men responsible for the domestic terror attack claimed it was in response to the blood spilled at Waco."

"How's this tie together?" Michelle asked.

Johnny shot a glance at both detectives. "Not sounding familiar yet? Vernon Wayne?"

Frank scratched his head. "If memory serves, several families sued everyone from the federal government down to the governor and Texas National Guard. It was a class action suit, but I can't recall who the court sided with."

"The plaintiffs lost," Johnny reminded them. "The judge ruled that Uncle Sam acted within their constitutional rights. No negligence on the part of the government. Basically, the Branch Davidians fired the first shot, no pun intended, and the ATF acted accordingly and abided by the rules of engagement. Families and relatives never saw a dime." Johnny raised and lowered his brows. "Or did they?"

Frank sensed where this was headed. "Go on."

Johnny enlightened them. "The class action suit went nowhere. However—and here's the kicker—a handful of civil suits were filed individually. The fed didn't want to push their luck. From coast to coast, people were torn. Some argued the federal agents were defending themselves against a fanatical cult. Others argued the strike on Mount Carmel Center—better known as the Branch Davidian compound—was an overzealous government encroaching on law abiding citizens. Illegal and unconstitutional. The court decided Washington acted within reason and without neglect. Close the book. Let's move forward as one happy nation and all hold hands. Reopening wounds through ongoing legal battles with a new president in office would prolong the healing of the country. So Uncle Sam settled with many families out of court."

"Hush money," Michelle commented,

"Definitely," Frank stated. "Easier to settle out of court silently, placate grieving families with a few million, and shovel Waco under the rug." He drew out a lengthy stare at Michelle before eying Johnny. "And Whitefield/Wayne's involvement in this?"

"Sister and brother-in-law were killed in the raid."

"I bet I know the answer," Frank said slowly. "But I'll ask anyway. Their names?"

"Sharon and Chad. Leach."

Frank lowered his head. "Parents of Elijah and Xavier." His conclusion hung in the air like a guillotine about to fall.

Michelle ultimately broke the silence, summing up. "Mom and Dad killed by the government, brothers raised by their uncle, Gordon Whitefield. Whitefield becomes Vernon Wayne. Brothers grow up hating the government, become anarchists, seek revenge on the nation that murdered their parents, plant a bomb in West Hollywood, maiming and killing innocent people. Then kidnap a police detective and a judge. You were correct, Frank. It *is* domestic terrorism."

"Wish I felt happier about being right."

"Ghosts from the past have reappeared," she remarked.

Frank pointed at Johnny. "Do we know for sure Colby Ferrell was hired by Gordon Whitefield in the lawsuit against Uncle Sam?"

Johnny shrugged. "The records are sealed."

"I'm sure he was. The timing all coincides. So, Gordon Whitefield gets a settlement from the government, establishes a new identity for himself under the alias Vernon Wayne, raises his sister's children. And Colby Ferrell uses his percentage of the disbursement to move to California and establish himself as a top notch attorney."

"Not sure if that's a statement or a question, Frank, but yes."

"Colby Ferrell built his reputation from blood money," Michelle noted.

Johnny spoke cryptically while pivoting his monitor. "David Koresh was born seventeen August nineteen fifty-nine in Houston. His birth name? *Vernon Wayne* Howell. Whitefield's taking the name Vernon Wayne is his little way of giving the finger to the government. To the entire nation, really."

Frank shifted in his seat and looked at the calendar on the wall. "And the anniversary of Waco and Oklahoma City is coming up."

Chapter 19

"I s he in?"

"And you are?"

Frank displayed his badge wallet. "Detectives Grace and Santana. Is he in?"

"Mr. Ferrell is a busy man."

"Busy defending terrorists?"

The rosy-cheeked receptionist ignored the jab and remained professional. "Do you have an appointment?"

"I don't have an appointment, lady. What I *do* have is a short fuse, a long record of insubordination, and a loaded Beretta. Is he in?"

Frazzled that this detective was causing a scene in her waiting room, she said something about calling security. Before Frank could reply, Michelle peered down the corridor. "He just went into that room."

The offices of Colby Ferrell, Esquire occupied the top two stories of a high rise in Century City. It more resembled a conglomerate that cut million-dollar deals before lunch than it did a law firm. Ferrell was distinguished, celebrated, and big time wealthy, all of which was haughtily exhibited.

The thick padding beneath the indigo carpet created a floating sensation. Ficus trees and faux waterfalls lined the wide luxurious corridor. The walls were adorned with photographs of the high profile attorney rubbing shoulders with athletes, A-list movie stars, and influential politicians.

Reaching the end of the T-shaped corridor, the detectives came upon a fifteen-foot oak door, a pair of desks where personal secretaries sat nervously and a barrel chested thug with arms like tree trunks folded across his chest. "Where do you think you're going?"

"Four seconds," Frank claimed.

"Four seconds?"

"That's how long it will take you to hit the sidewalk when I throw your ass through the window."

Unfazed, the bald-headed Neanderthal eased aside his expensive suit jacket to display his holstered sidearm.

"You *really* don't want to make that move," Frank warned.

The oncoming footsteps behind indicated security had been summoned to subdue the rogue cops. Frank leaned nearer to the human blockade. "Step aside before someone gets hurt."

Neanderthal moved his right arm, reached for his weapon. He never made it. An elbow slammed against his nose. The snapping of cartilage caused the receptionists to shriek. Neanderthal's eyes watered as he collapsed to his knees.

Frank stepped over him.

Ferrell's office was the size of Michelle's entire duplex. As she followed her partner in, she couldn't help but feel riveted. A colossal mahogany desk was set in front of a window that pushed from wall to wall, ceiling to floor. All of Southern California seemingly east to Riverside stretched beyond. From up here, the city actually looked breathtaking. There was also a conference table, a bank of wall-mounted TVs, paintings better suited for the Louvre, and leather couches that befitted a New Orleans bordello. There were even three marble statues. *Statues.*

"Mind if I come in?" Frank asked after he came in.

The high-and-mighty attorney reclined in his winged backed chair. "It's okay," he said and, with a flippant wave of his hand, dismissed the security force that filtered in behind Frank. "You can leave us."

The door was closed, leaving the detectives alone with the attorney and a client who had the misfortune of being present. The man in the guest chair seemed uneasy, shooting nervous glances between Ferrell and the two intruders. He moved nervously in his seat.

"If I recall, the last time we met you seemed under-dressed for the ambiance of the restaurant." Ferrell made a show of regarding Frank's sport coat, rust colored dress shirt, and beige Khakis. "Apparently some things never change."

"Where are the Leach brothers?"

"Have we not had this discussion? Perhaps your concussion is affecting your memory. Asked and answered."

Frank fisted Ferrell's desk. "Where?"

Michelle had worked with her partner almost two years. Frank was professional, levelheaded, and a by-the-book type. However, when a case became personal as this one had, he had no qualms about dipping his foot in dangerous waters. Hell, he had no qualms about cannonballing into dangerous waters. Sternly, Michelle bristled, "Frank." Then again she too, had been victimized. In her home. Days before her niece would move in. She played good cop and sighed. "Just tell us where they are."

Ferrell gave Frank a pathetic look. "Do you make it a habit of acting so irresponsibly, Detective Grace? We have laws in this country. May I suggest you read up on something called the US Constitution? It could be quite beneficial in your career." Ferrell halted as if he had an epiphany. "That is, while you still have a career."

Frank looked to the fidgety guest. "If I were you, pal, I'd look into retaining another attorney. Mr. *Ferret* is more concerned about his reputation than what's good for his clients."

Ferrell scoffed. "I've heard it all now. Frank Grace telling *me* the law."

Glaring at Ferrell, Frank sneered. "If you're such a good lawyer, you'd have the Leaches turn themselves in, represent them, and let the courts decide. Or are you more worried about losing a case in the glare of the national spotlight? You'd be finished."

Unfettered, Ferrell said evenly, "And you could be finished with one call to Police Chief Kent."

Frank ripped the receiver from the cradle, his knuckles whitening. "Call him!"

In her mind's eye, Michelle envisioned Frank cracking Ferrell in the skull with the handset. She sidled around to Ferrell's side, eased her backside against the desk, and said in a placating voice, "Just do what's right."

Before Ferrell responded, Frank continued. "Harboring a pair of fugitives wanted for an act of domestic terror. Aiding and abetting. How about treason against the United States? Maybe *you* should read up on the Constitution." Frank let that hang in the air before swinging for the fences. "By the time I'm through with you, you'll be back chasing ambulances in east Texas." He extended his arm at the lavish surroundings. "You can kiss this goodbye."

Ferrell was playing it close to the vest. Michelle found it curious that he didn't distance himself from the Leaches.

"I've spent my entire adult life, *Detective*, believing in our justice system. I've seen it up close. I'll be the first to admit that, while it's far from perfect and greatly flawed, it is the fairest and finest in the history of mankind. That is, when someone *can* receive a fair trial. If my clients did turn themselves in, they will never be afforded such an opportunity. They probably won't even live to see a trial date."

"Mr. Ferrell," the potential client squeaked.

"Not now," Ferrell snapped, silencing his visitor.

"You're sounding more and more like your antigovernment clients you represent. You only trust the system when it's convenient."

"I trust the system entirely, *Mister* Grace. What I do not trust, however, is the ability of your law enforcement cronies to see to the safety of the Leach boys."

"Boys?" Frank barked. "They detonated a bomb in West

Hollywood. They murdered twelve innocent people in cold blood. Caskets filled with body parts, not bodies. They took a shot at my wife. They tried to kill my partner." Frank's voice grew louder. "They kidnapped a judge, a police officer, and they murdered a homeless man named Eddie Evanovich, just for shits and giggles. *Boys?* Really?"

Ferrell's pompous grin widened. "As my granddaughter would say, *puh-leeze.*"

"Save the melodrama for the courtroom."

"Mr. Ferrell—" the seated man interjected.

Frank cocked his head at Ferrell's visitor, did a double take.

Counsel and client stole a glance at each other, something Grace and Santana noticed. The attorney inhaled and blew out slowly. He emitted an unintentional whistle sound. "Hypothetically speaking, can you promise me my clients' safety? Can you unequivocally guarantee they will see the inside of a courtroom?"

Michelle took that one. "No matter if they wind up in a federal penitentiary or state facility, the severity of their crimes will guarantee they'll be held in solitary, not general population. Others arrested for domestic terror all lived to the trial."

Ferrell eyed her. "There's always a first time."

"Prick," Frank muttered.

Michelle threw her arm out, a futile attempt to prevent her partner from leaping over the desk and choking the daylights out of Ferrell. She went for a personal approach. "Look, this is going to end badly for Xavier and Elijah, no matter what. They'll eventually be captured, be it two hours or two months. The government doesn't take kindly to terrorism. If they can find you in a backyard on a boat in Boston or halfway around the world in Abbottabad, they can find you anywhere. With the growing rage people feel and the fact the LAPD is pissed one of our own was taken, it's likely your clients will go out in the proverbial blaze of glory. We both know that, unlike religious fundamentalists, they're not willing to die for their cause." Ferrell arched a brow but gave no telltale sign. Michelle continued. "Will they be given the death penalty? It's very likely. But perhaps not. The lightest sentence they'll get is life, probably with no chance of parole for at least a generation. And, sadly, Americans have a short attention span. However, if you leave them dangling in the wind, more innocents may be killed. That will only ramp up desire to find them. And by that point, they won't simply be taken into custody, if you get my meaning."

"Are you stating they'll be assassinated by your fellow officers, Detective…"

"Santana. I'm stating facts. You spend your days in court, Mr. Ferrell. I spend mine on the street. I know how the real world works."

Frank had calmed, albeit slightly. He still wanted to give into his primal rage and pummel Ferrell's face until he'd be on a liquid diet the rest of his life. However, he followed Michelle's levelheaded approach. "You're in a Catch-22."

"How do you figure?"

He's breaking. Frank made his closing argument. "No matter what, you're in a lose-lose situation. The media will be aware you represent the Leaches. That will have a long-lasting negative impact on your career. However, if you choose to drop them as clients, you will come off looking like a quitter, a typical shyster abandoning clients in their greatest time of need. The only way—the *only* way—you can come out of this with a shred of dignity is by having them come in of their own volition. That single act could mean the difference between life and old Sparky. And you'll gain a small bit of favor in the most important court of all: the court of public opinion. You'll at least be perceived as doing what's right."

"Until you can promise me my clients will survive their incarceration to stand trial," Ferrell said, "I will give you nothing. And that's not a promise you can make."

"You're right, I can't," Frank admitted. "But they have a

better chance once they're in the system than on the run. It's unlikely they'd be taken alive."

Ferrell's guest turned in his chair and faced the detectives. "You're saying they'll be shot down in cold blood?"

"And you are—" Frank asked.

"That's not important," Ferrell snapped. To his guest, he stated, "I advise you to remain silent."

The man's eyes swept from the cops to the lawyer and back. "Are you someone who keeps their word, Detective Grace?"

Frank nodded. "Yes. And my partner as well."

"Be still," Ferrell urged.

"Who are you?" Michelle asked.

The man lowered his head and spoke to the lavish carpet, unable to look anyone in the eyes. "Elijah and Xavier have done bad things, that much is obvious—" He cut himself off, finding it difficult to speak. "But they are family. And I do care about them."

"Vernon Wayne?"

He nodded, stood, and extended his hand. "Gordon Whitefield to be correct. My nephews have lost their way. I tried my best to raise them properly. But they—they've both had this hatred, this venomous anger brewing inside since they were young boys."

"'Cause of Waco?"

Whitefield seemed unfazed by Michelle's revelation. "Yes. I don't have children of my own. And considering how my nephews turned out, that's probably a good thing. I want you to know I did my best to teach them right from wrong. I honestly gave it my all."

The guilt was etched in the creases lining his face. Members of his family, people who shared his blood, were murderers, cold-blooded butchers. His very own nephews—domestic terrorists. He slumped into the chair, the weight he carried too heavy.

Michelle dropped to her haunches alongside the troubled uncle. She thought about taking his hands in a reassuring manner but chose not to. They were the hands of someone who cultivated a pair of killers. "Mr. Wayne?"

He said nothing.

Michelle resorted to his real name. "Mr. Whitefield, help us. Help us and you'll help your nephews. You could very well be their only hope at getting out of this alive."

"Gordon, I have to strongly object against—" Ferrell barked.

Frank threw a finger at the attorney. "Overruled! Now shut the fuck up."

Whitefield hyperventilated, his shoulders rising and sinking with each breath. He wiped a tear from his eye. "I tried my best. I truly did. Do you believe me, Detective?"

"I do," Michelle confirmed. And she did. Parents—or family—should never be held accountable for the sins of their children. She decided to take his hand this time. "You have my word. Give us their address and Detective Grace and I will bring them in. Unharmed." She looked up at Frank.

"Yes, unharmed." Frank agreed, knowing full well it was easier said than done.

The Leaches weren't religious fanatics. But they were fanatical. He never liked making a pledge he wasn't confident he could keep. This time, he had to give his word and hope it played out accordingly.

Whitefield signaled for pen and paper. Ferrell counseled against it. Frank again told Ferrell to shut the fuck up.

With a trembling hand, Gordon Whitefield scribbled something. Michelle watched him writing and gave Frank a fleeting smile. *We got 'em.*

Whitefield folded the paper excessively. He started to hand over the address then pulled his arm back. "Five, correct?"

Michelle frowned. "Five?"

"The reward the government is offering. Five million for information leading to the arrest of Elijah and Xavier Leach."

Frank snickered. "I thought you were concerned about the safety of your precious nephews."

"Oh, I am, Detective, very much so. But five million is five million."

In-fucking-credible.

"Do we have a deal?" Whitefield inquired.

"Yes," Michelle confirmed, reaching for the address.

"You'll bring them in alive?"

"Yes," Frank claimed, though his words carried less conviction than his partners.

Gordon Whitefield handed over the note. Michelle unfolded it, showed it to Frank. Detectives Grace and Santana now had the location for the two most wanted men in America.

Chapter 20

Love, honor, cherish. These were vows Frank made to his wife fifteen years earlier. Luckily, there was nothing about keeping secrets. He took pride in the fact that in a decade and a half he'd never lied to his wife, never had been deceitful. There were times, however, when he kept things from her. Yesterday was one of those times.

"We have a lead on the Leaches." That was true. Thankfully, Abby never asked if he'd be going alone so therefore Frank's track record of truthfulness remained intact. But after so many years together, he wasn't the only sleuth in the family. Abby didn't ask for details but she picked up on the clues, what those in law enforcement called *the tells*.

In the doorway, Abby held her husband longer and tighter than usual. Something in her gut told her this wouldn't be just another day at the office for him.

When Frank said "I love you," there was more emotion than the simple rote statement spouses exchange after years together. This time it carried substance, it carried sincerity. He broke the embrace and trudged away. Like some sappy Hollywood film Abby ran after him. At his vehicle, she held her husband's face, stubble prickling her soft hands. "Tomorrow, you'll be home."

"Yes."

"You will, won't you?"

He lost himself in her hopeful eyes and quivering chin,

nuzzled his face against hers and whispered, "I promise." *Like I promised Gordon Whitefield about bringing his nephews in alive.*

After obtaining the address, Frank felt he'd been dropped into the middle of a tornado. Things moved with whirlwind speed.

His request to confer with the police chief couldn't happen. There was too much on Kent's agenda, what with meetings and daily press briefings for the information-starved public. Behind the scenes, however, Kent operated capably. He contacted an acquaintance, a renowned Hollywood director, and secured a Gulfstream for Grace and Santana to fly north. He arranged for a hotel near where Whitefield claimed his nephews were holed up. He secured all weaponry needed to arrest the Leaches. "Whatever you do, Detective," Kent had insisted, "bring them in alive."

"Yes, sir."

"And whatever you do, don't fuck this up."

Frank swallowed. "Yes, sir."

As he now lay in bed in a Holiday Inn in Atascadero, CA, Frank was reassessing his opinion of the police chief. Never in his wildest dreams had he envisioned working hands-on with a *brasshole* like Weldon Kent. But he was thankful the chief had his back. The guy cut through the bureaucracy and did what was needed to get the job done. Worry about the consequences later. In that way, Frank realized, he and Kent were similar. The insight caused him to shudder.

Kent was putting his ass and career on the line, staking his legacy to the success of Grace and Santana's covert mission. He made it clear that if things went south, he'd deny knowledge of their charge. Frank understood where the chief was coming from. The feds would come down hard if some yokel mucked up their investigation. If things went well, however, the chief would be commended for his gutsy decision, extolled for nabbing two terrorists. Kent would reap the admiration. Frank would finally escape the onerous shadow of Azusa, a darkness that had enveloped him for four years. Apprehension of the Leaches would cause Michelle's shooting star to rise even faster.

It was a double-edged sword. Frank always harbored guilt, believing his past was an anchor to his partner's upward trajectory. Being teamed with Frank Grace was not something to brag about. Yet, he couldn't imagine working with anyone else. It's a cliché to say partners put their lives in each other hands but he returned home to his family every evening thanks to Michelle Santana.

But now, if things went well, his partner would conceivably move up within the PD, and Frank would lose her.

To keep his mind off tomorrow's mission, he turned on the TV. He channel surfed before settling on a rebroadcast of the newest reality show to sweep the nation. Frank avoided watching the idiot box at all costs. He never had anything to add when colleagues at West Bureau started discussing some TV program. After a few minutes of watching the mind-numbing show, he realized why.

At first, he thought it was part of the show but the knocking continued. He glanced at his watch wondering who'd be here at one in the morning. Reaching for his Beretta, Frank disengaged the safety and sidled up to the door.

"It's me, Frank," came Michelle's voice from the opposite side. "You can put the safety back on."

Frank smiled, unlatched the chain, and stepped back. The expression on his partner's face was not one he'd ever seen. "You okay?"

Michelle nodded weakly.

"Come in."

She hesitated then entered, hugging herself and studying the décor as if it was different from her room.

"You want a drink? I've got some Cokes in the little fridge."

She shook her head and sauntered over to the TV.

"Next week on...*The Nut House*." The screen showed men engaged in a tug-of-war, women beating each other with pillows while wearing provocative lingerie, and a Chippendale dancer grabbing a tennis player's ass. Michelle arched a brow at Frank.

"I was just flipping around and…uh, never mind." He sidestepped Michelle and turned it off. "What's up?"

"I spoke to Bianca before."

Frank said nothing.

"We decided Sophia's gonna move in next weekend," she said, her voice barely audible.

"That's good, right?"

Michelle resembled a fidgety child in trouble. She bowed her head, shoved her hands into her pockets.

Frank filled the silence. "Are you having second thoughts?"

"Oh, no, not at all," she replied with conviction.

"Then what's wrong?"

"Big day tomorrow. The Leaches. Terrorists."

"Yeah, I know." Frank picked up on his partner's doubt. He wondered if perhaps his tough-as-nails sidekick was having second thoughts. He'd offered her the opportunity to renege several times but she declined. Offering an *out* hours before the mission would indicate he was having doubts about her resolve. He remained quiet.

Still embracing herself as if chilled, Michelle mumbled to the floor, "We're going to be all right this time, aren't we?"

"Of course." *Too quick?*

"I have a bad…If something goes wrong…well, I mean…what would happen to Sophia?"

Frank stepped closer. He placed one hand on her shoulder, the other below her chin and tilted her face up so she could see the tenacity in his eyes. "Nothing will happen, Michelle. We'll be fine. Just a routine walk in the park."

Yet another promise.

Michelle sniffled once, twice, and dabbed at something in her eyes. She nodded, pursed her lips, and said, "Let's just nail these bastards so we can go home."

Chapter 21

The sky was ablaze with light of the coming day. Orange streaks fragmented the heavens, splintering into the blue-black of the west.

Sitting shotgun and dressed head to toe in black cammo, Frank welcomed the sunrise. He and Michelle had taken up reconnaissance under cover of darkness. That doomed Frank to use thermal imaging night vision goggles. After minutes of frustration, he tossed them into the back seat. *Technology.*

He was pleased, however, with the Kevlar vest. The predawn carried a crisp bite and the extra weight warmed him.

He took a Styrofoam cup from the dash, sipped his coffee, and glanced at Michelle. She, too, was sheathed in blackness. But despite the eye-black she wore, Frank still noticed lingering doubt from last night. Despite serving two tours in Afghanistan, Michelle appeared anxious, uneasy. Frank didn't know what to make of that.

Their rental car was parked in a clearing just off Route 46 several miles east of Paso Robles in wine country. Sixty yards, through the curtain of dense tree line that shielded them, was the residence Vernon Wayne/Gordon Whitefield purchased, where the Leaches now stayed. Michelle raised the Bushnell high-powered binoculars. "You want to take a look?"

"I've had enough with the twenty-first century for one morning."

Despite the vineyard stretching to the hills, the residence seemed out of place. The land was worth north of ten million. Yet, the two-story clapboard was weather-beaten and appeared derelict. The caretakers were more concerned about tending their profitable fields than extravagant living quarters. There was a pair of muddied pickups alongside a shack toward the rear but no sign of the Nissan Maxima.

A bank of fog skirted the ground, creating an eerie almost otherworldly setting. The dew covering the windows made surveilling the property troublesome. However, they couldn't turn on the wipers. A clean windshield would indicate the car had not simply been abandoned overnight. Their breathing added to the condensation.

Frank took another sip of coffee and remembered why he hated stakeouts. They were hours of interminable tedium interrupted by seconds of heart-thumping action. He savored being alert before a takedown. But, as always, the prolonged cycle of dullness blunted his senses.

"The last time we worked a stakeout also involved the Leaches," Frank remarked flatly. They'd been casing the home of Virgil Trucks in an unrelated investigation when they noticed unusual activity on Mar Vista, the home where Elijah and Xavier resided at the time. "We should just go now," Frank added impatiently.

"We have no warrant," she reminded him.

They'd previously decided the best way to approach. Frank wanting to change plans midstream didn't sit well with an already apprehensive Michelle.

The stillness, the calm before the storm, was broken when Michelle asked evenly, "You don't think we're being set up, do you?"

Frank arched a brow. "By Wayne slash Whitefield?"

Michelle nodded.

"Why?"

"Would he really turn in his own family?"

"The guy seemed genuinely hurt," Frank recalled. "I think part of it stems from guilt. He wonders if he did something wrong. Had he brought up his nephews differently, maybe none of this would've happened." Frank paused. "Then again five million dollars can go a long way in soothing any remorse."

Michelle hemmed and hawed while readjusting settings on the Bushnell. "I don't think I could turn in a family member. Right or wrong, family is blood."

Frank said nothing.

Michelle lowered the field glasses and fisted her eyes. She took a deep breath, let it out slowly, and then removed from her wallet a photo of herself with her niece from years earlier.

"No, no. Don't do that," Frank wailed.

"What?"

"The picture. Put it away."

Michelle snorted. "Why? Soph's adorable."

"It's bad luck. It's like the fighter pilot in those World War II movies who looks at a picture of his pregnant wife just before going into battle. You *know* he's gonna get shot down."

"Is someone a bit superstitious?"

"Hell, yes."

"You're silly," she said. But then again, why tempt fate. Michelle put the picture away and resumed surveillance. As Frank took another sip, she commented, "How many have you had?"

"This is my fourth."

"Your kidneys rock!"

Frank continued scrutinizing the property, trusting his own eyes more than newfangled high-tech binoculars. He extended his legs as much as possible, then fiddled with the lever to slide the seat back. Unsatisfied, he moaned, repositioned himself, and grumbled, "Ah, shit."

"What?" Michelle chuckled.

"You."

"What'd I do?"

"Power of suggestion. Now I gotta pee."

"You didn't bring a piss jar?"

"No, 'cause as you said, my kidneys rock." Frank got out of the car. "Be right back."

He sauntered a few feet away and, with his back to the vehicle, unzipped. As soon as he did, he heard the window power down behind him. "He's come out!" Michelle exclaimed.

Looking down, he did a double take, wondering how his partner could see, then muttered, "Oh."

Frank heard the door open and, as Michelle bolted from the vehicle, she called out, "Let's go, let's go."

"Umm, kinda busy right now," he replied, trying to pee faster. "I'm getting old, things slow down."

After the longest piss of his life, Frank zipped up and shadowed his partner. He dropped alongside Michelle behind a thick tree stump.

"Bogey exited and went into that shed on the north side."

Frank grinned. Michelle was amped up, adrenalin coursing through her body. The use of military lingo assuaged his earlier doubts. She was in the right mindset. "Who?"

"Elijah."

Frank studied the lay of the land. With no sight of the Nissan, he deliberated if Xavier was also on the premises. And he recalled Michelle's question: *Do you think we're being set up?*

Frank withdrew his Beretta, thumbed off the safety. Although he'd done it three times in the last ninety minutes, he again verified the magazine was fully loaded. Thirty-two rounds. Cocked and locked.

Michelle had her Glock tucked in the rear of her waistband but her more familiar weapon had been replaced for this attack. She clutched a Heckler and Koch G36 assault rifle, capable of carrying five thirty-round clips—normally, the weapon of choice for soldiers engaged in a fierce prolonged firefight. Frank had misgivings. The fluency of a weapon in his hand became part of him, an appendage. He liked the familiar feel of his Beretta. His partner preferred the reliability and quick reloading of her Glock. The fact that Michelle was going into battle with a weapon she was unaccustomed to did not sit well with Frank. He'd voiced his concerns earlier. Michelle dismissed it. He dropped it.

She surveilled the terrain, determining her safest and quickest approach. She winked at Frank. They fist bumped.

"Grantana."

"Sant-ace," she corrected. She took a few deep breaths, gave Frank a farewell semi-salute. "Let's finish this." And off she went.

Rifle held out before her like an infantryman taking a hill, Michelle dashed across the open field.

Frank repositioned himself for a better view and prepared to lay down cover fire if needed. On the second floor, he noticed an open window. *Was it open before?*

The sound of Michelle going down redirected his focus. Frank's stomach clenched. His partner was laid out.

Michelle grunted, furious with herself. The morning precipitation caused her to lose her footing. She went down hard. Luckily, the weapon hadn't discharged and alerted the Leaches of the coming assault. She gave Frank a thumbs up, belly crawled forward, scooped up the bulky rifle, and got to her feet. She stumbled for the first few steps but did not give in to the throbbing in her hip. Within seconds, Santana was in full sprint again, hopscotching the perimeter. She dashed around the south side of the home and took up position along the side of the shed.

Once again Frank checked his magazine and promptly charged forward. With his Beretta gripped tightly, he ran a more direct line, speed taking priority over chucking and jiving.

He was in the open, vulnerable, an easy target. Elijah Leach emerged from the shed.

Frank dove flat out, doing a swan dive, and crashing hard against the ground. Air was pushed from his lungs.

Michelle was to the right of the open door. Her arms extended, she'd discarded the unfamiliar H&K rifle for the cozier Glock semi-automatic.

Grace and Santana were at Elijah's nine and six. Behind him, the barn. He had nowhere to go.

The extremist exited the outbuilding boldly, arrogantly. And with a hostage.

Michelle looked at the blindfolded, bound victim with a gun pressed to her head. "Kendra."

"Give it up, Elijah!" Frank shouted.

Elijah stepped forward, not heeding Frank's warning. He was in the crosshairs. There was no escape. Yet, he displayed a goofy smile and half-waved to the woman cop. Either he was overly confident or just insane.

"Let her go!" Michelle screamed.

"Drop it!" Frank added.

There was a discernible change in Kendra's body language. A memory from her past, the voice of an old friend. "Michelle?"

Through the eerie stillness, the morning fog not yet vacating the valleys of central California, Elijah's evil chilling laugh seemed to resonate across the fields. With Kendra Nichols on his right between himself and Michelle, he knew she had no clear shot. He marched toward Frank, daring him, taunting him. "We meet again, Herr Grace."

Frank wished Nichols was on Leaches left, leaving his right side open. His partner, thanks to the US Army, was better with the hardware. If anyone could get off a perfect kill shot, it was Michelle.

Unable to see, Kendra tried to wiggle free. That only caused Leach to slam her cheek with his handgun. Her knees buckled, her cheek burned, she tasted blood in her mouth. Her tongue glided over a partially dislodged tooth.

Michelle tracked his steps, her arms following Leach, keeping him in her sights. She didn't like the way this was playing out. Not only was Elijah oozing coolness and poise, but by walking forward, he had brought Michelle out into the open. Both she and Frank were now easy targets. "Where's your brother?"

Without turning, Elijah stated, "Wouldn't you like to know?" and laughed.

"There's no way out," Frank said. "Let her go. There's been enough killing."

"Enough killing?" Elijah parodied. "The killing hasn't even begun." His arrogance was revolting. He even did a little two-step in an effort to provoke the detectives. "Herr Grace, check this out."

He rotated Kendra while keeping his weapon pointed at her head. She now faced the barn, her back to Frank. The message was clear. "Come on, Grace. Take the shot. Maybe you'll hit me. Or maybe you'll end up paralyzing another colleague."

"Shoot him, Michelle!" Kendra cried wildly. "Shoot this fucker!"

Another smack of cold steel slammed her face. "Shut up, bitch!"

Frank's stomach churned. If he could, he'd drop the weapon and use his own hands to pound the hell out of this smug little bastard. He remembered the promise he made about bringing Elijah in alive. Alive, not unwounded.

The standoff was taking too damned long. The element of surprise was gone…if they ever had one at all. Elijah's confidence was increasing. Frank straightened. He wore a bulletproof vest. An impact would hurt and leave him stunned, dazed. But it would not be fatal. He hoped Elijah would aim for largest mass—his chest and not his unprotected head or legs. He stole a glance at Michelle. She shook her head. She didn't like it, but Frank's intent was clear.

Frank would draw Elijah's fire and take a bullet to the Kevlar. If Leach took the bait and fired on Frank, Michelle could use the opportunity to incapacitate him. Frank didn't like the odds but they'd passed the point of no return. He just hoped the bullets weren't Teflon coated and laced with polytetrafluorethylene, the same cop killers that tore apart his home.

"You think I'm gonna fall for that? I shoot you. *She* shoots me. You think I'm an idiot?" Elijah hooted.

Frank took a step toward the domestic terrorist. "No, I don't think you're an idiot. I think you're chicken shit." He attempted to draw Leach into an illogical rage. He mocked Elijah's goofy grin with one of his own. "You think you're a real man, Leach. Let's see. Put the gun down. You and me. Mano a mano."

"You're fuckin' nuts!"

Frank strode closer. "My partner kicked your ass. And she's a *girl*, for Christ's sake. I'm sure Xavier gave you shit about that. Here's your chance. Drop the weapon, let Kendra go, and let's see who the real man is."

Leach chortled like a madman. "You really expect to provoke me like that? You think that'll work? Asshole."

"I know it won't work." Frank inched closer, now only ten feet away. "I know it won't work 'cause deep down inside you're a pussy!"

"Fuck you!" Leach shouted, his voice echoing through the early morning.

"Pussy!"

Elijah's jaw tightened. "I should've killed your wife when I had the chance. I knew it shouldn't be a warning shot."

That gave Frank pause, but only for a flash. "You want to hurt my wife? Make her a widow. Let's see what you got, tough guy."

Off to the side, Michelle breathed tenuously, "Frank, no." Her finger coiled around the trigger, her palms moistened. A gentle breeze kicked up hindering her vision.

"Fuck you, Grace!"

"Shoot him," Kendra screamed. "For the love of God, Michelle, shoot him!"

"Pussy!"

The taunting became too much. A raucous scream and

Leach extended his arm, took aim on Frank, and fired.

Frank darted right then reversed left and somersaulted.

In that instant, Michelle stepped right and planted her feet. She slipped slightly on the moist grass, not getting the footing she needed. She assumed a lopsided combat stance and squeezed off two quick rounds.

Kendra instinctively hit the ground.

The first sound was a chinking-pinging sound as the bullet sent Leaches weapon spiraling through the air. The second sound was Elijah squealing in agony. He dropped to his knees, screeching and trembling. His left hand clutched his right where two fingers had been blown off.

"He's down!" Michelle shouted as she approached.

Kendra blindly crab walked away from her captor, feeling her way along the grass. "Michelle? Michelle?"

Michelle grabbed hold of Kendra's upper arm and heaved her friend to safety. Her nose twitched at the reek of body odor. Kendra hadn't bathed in over a week.

Frank moved on Leach. He mouthed 'Good work' to his partner who simply nodded once. He then refocused on Leach. "Lay down, arms out!"

"You fuckin' shot me!" Leach howled in something between shock and tears. "I'm gonna fuckin' sue your ass, Grace!"

"I thought you're anti-establishment. On your chest, arms above your head. *Now*!"

On his knees, still clutching his hand, a geyser of blood spurted from where his thumb and index finger had been severed. Leach was turning ashen.

Seeing the crimson stream, Frank remembered he'd left his latex gloves in the car. "On your chest! Keep your hands—and your eight fingers—where I can see them."

"Fuck you!"

The powerful kick to his upper chest, courtesy of Frank's shoe, laid-him out.

He continued moaning, screaming incoherently, defaming Frank's mother. "You're gonna pay for this. You hear me." In spite of losing blood, two fingers, and teetering on the edge of shock, Leach snickered. "You're gonna *so* fuckin' pay. I should've killed her, Grace. Your wife. I shoulda."

Frank drove his knee into Leach's kidneys. "You have the right to remain silent. I suggest you exercise it."

Keeping his knee pressed into Leach's spine, Frank continued Mirandizing him. He pulled Leach's arm with such force Frank wondered if he'd dislocated the left shoulder. *Screw 'em.*

Cuffed, Leach was yanked upright. He drew his head back and snorted. The spittle landed on Frank's cheek. Leach laughed.

Frank raised his arm to wipe it away, *accidentally* elbowing Leach in the face. "Oops." To Michelle, he called out, "I'm putting shithead here in the car. Or maybe the trunk."

Michelle nodded affirmatively. Frank turned his prisoner and began marching him into custody. The perp walk stopped when Kendra Nichols stepped in front of them. During his time in law enforcement, Frank had seen *the look*. Victims hell bent on revenge, thinking illogically, and ignoring the consequences of irrational actions. He now observed that same fury in Kendra's eyes. He angled so she couldn't grab his weapon and go from prisoner to prey. "Take a breath, Detective." Her title, not her name.

Oblivious to Frank, Kendra shoved her hand into Elijah's crotch. He rose to his tiptoes.

"I should rip off your balls and hang 'em from my rear view mirror."

No wonder she and Michelle are friends.

"Go for it, bitch!"

Frank pulled Leach away. He'd promised Whitefield and Chief Kent he'd bring him in alive. That oath, however, didn't extend to Kendra. "He'll most likely be at the old Parker Center, MDC downtown. Just a little FYI for you."

Kendra struggled to draw her venomous icy glare away

from her tormenter long enough to say "Thanks." She leaned closer, nose to nose with Leach. "I may just have to pay you a visit."

He blew her a kiss. "Looking forward to it."

Frank pushed-shoved the terrorist away from the barn, around the home, and toward the rental car. "You must have a death-wish. Hell hath no fury like—"

Frank was cut off by a deafening blast that echoed through the fields. He recoiled, noticed a rising puff of smoke in the thicket to his left. He drew his weapon quickly and returned fire.

Gone.

He then felt something moist and gooey on his face. He lifted his hand, touched it. Brain matter.

Frank's promise would not be kept.

Elijah Leach was down, the top of his head blown off by a high-caliber rifle. His eyes stared into nothingness, the goofy grin frozen for eternity.

Chapter 22

Light surrendered to darkness. Twelve hours had passed since the arrest and subsequent assassination of Elijah Leach. The throng of news choppers and journalists arrived as quickly as local police, FBI, JTTF, and the rest of the alphabet agencies. Cable news networks were gearing their wall-to-wall coverage covering what transpired, spending almost as much time refuting earlier *facts* as they did reporting accurate information. Getting it first had, as always, superseded getting it correct.

Federal Agent Georgia Stephens, who'd been spearheading the investigation from day one while Frank and Michelle were still recuperating from the initial attack, was fit to be tied. Having two country bumpkins go rogue and try to play hero caused her ulcer to burn and her blood pressure to soar. It was *her* investigation, *her* case, *her* chance to make a name for herself. And two dimwits named Grace and Santana had fucked it up—both for her and for her country.

Frank and Michelle were grilled—interrogated—as if they were criminals. Nevertheless, there were positives. Detective Kendra Nichols, the Honorable Earl Sherman, and a high-class escort named Hiromi Komatsu, the latter whose abduction had not even been reported by anyone, were all rescued. The renegade cops from Hollywood Homicide had saved their lives. The ensuing media circus, however, glossed over the success and highlighted the failure.

Elijah Leach had been killed, murdered, while in the custody of, all people, the infamous Frank Grace. Four years earlier the same detective's actions were called into question. Riots followed. The LAPD had become the poster organization for everything unjust with the American legal system. Once again, it was that same irresponsible cop acting irrationally and finding himself in a firestorm.

Everyone from the LAPD to the FBI were releasing details piecemeal. Bloggers and conspiracy nuts had already taken to the Internet in droves and wasted no time in filling in the gaps. Considering the tarnished history of Detective Grace, it was obvious he played the role of assassin, a personal vendetta since he himself had been injured in the West Hollywood blast. While some initially applauded his action for slaying a terrorist, the long-range impact was dire.

Elijah's brother, Xavier, was out there—somewhere. There were no leads to his whereabouts since the West Hollywood bombing.

Hard drives were lifted and removed from the Paso Robles residence to be analyzed and picked apart. Authorities were actively searching for a clue on who or what the next target was. There were enough explosives, detonative contrivances, and incendiary devices on the premises to exact a catastrophic death toll. Elijah was dead and could not be questioned. Xavier, the more methodical and less rash of the two, was walking the streets. And although this procurement in a Paso Robles vineyard garnered beneficial results and quite possibly saved thousands of lives, the public remained on edge.

Was something else in the works? Where? If only Leach had not been *killed* by Detective Grace, he could've come clean. All a weary city could do now was hold its collective breath and wait for the next round of bloodshed.

Initially, Frank and Michelle took part in working the crime scene. However, when Stephens took the reins, they were promptly removed from the investigation. They spent the bulk of the day in what amounted to a time-out, tossed aside while the federal agent tried to figure out what the hell to do with them.

Frank and Michelle's story was in synch and fully corroborated by Kendra Nichols, the only witness. But Nichols was LAPD. She was one of *them.* Of course, she'd cover their asses.

Stephens instituted a gag order be placed on the freed hostages. This was still an ongoing investigation in the manhunt for Xavier. One seemingly harmless statement could hinder the chance to apprehend the lone terrorist roaming free.

Ironically, it was Judge Sherman who shone a positive light. Negating the gag order, unable to resist an opportunity for a quick sound bite, he boasted to the multitude of reporters about the bravery and courage that saved his life. "Detectives Grace and Santana acted appropriately and professionally." The fact that the department's most outspoken nemesis and harshest critic praised their work was one small victory.

Sherman, along with Nichols and Komatsu, were whisked away to an undisclosed location to be debriefed.

As the property was scrubbed for clues and torn apart, Frank reported in. He related events in detail to Police Chief Kent. To his surprise, the always-volatile chief listened and said nothing. When Frank concluded his narrative, Kent finally spoke. "You gave me your word you wouldn't fuck up." The line went dead. Frank wondered if that was an omen for his future with the LAPD. *Dead.*

Be it out of spite or maybe Kent was simply washing his hands of the mission he *knew nothing about*, he left no breadcrumbs behind. After hanging up he contacted his director friend. The Gulfstream was flown back to Los Angeles empty, compelling the detectives to return home on their own.

Frank drove while Michelle stared expressionlessly at the verdant hills rolling by. The distance between them an unending abyss. The first part of three-hour drive back was spent in silence. Individually, they each considered the botched takedown, questioning their own actions and ruminating over what was likely the end of their careers.

Frank chewed his bottom lip as guilt sliced his soul. For four years he'd been on borrowed time with the LAPD. Criticized, scrutinized, and second-guessed, every facet of his work picked apart. He'd become numb to it and knew eventually the hammer would fall. But he always hoped Michelle wouldn't be brought down with him. Her loyalty to Frank would now result in her own undoing. And just days shy of caring for her niece.

At the very least, they'd be suspended: At the most, terminated and ultimately shamed out of law enforcement. Frank wondered—yearned—since this was Santana's first infraction perhaps Kent or the powers-that-be would cut her some slack. Maybe she could avoid termination and not spend her career under the microscope, just like the petri dish Frank had been living in.

Ballistics would ultimately prove Elijah had not been murdered by Frank's Beretta. A different weapon entirely. Still, the public would never believe the truth. The LAPD was yet again protecting one of their own. Frank's words to Colby Ferrell just yesterday came back to him: *The only court that matters is the court of public opinion.*

"You know what I don't get?" he asked, but didn't wait for an answer. "Elijah came out of that outbuilding with the gun already pointed at Kendra's head."

Silence.

Frank continued. "Maybe you were right, Detective. Maybe we *were* set up. Maybe someone did tip him off we were coming."

She lowered her head but couldn't look at Frank. "Or maybe he just heard us."

Frank disagreed. "I don't think so. When he came out, there wasn't even a flicker of surprise to see us. I looked in his eyes. I think…I think he walked into that shed with the purpose of getting a hostage."

"Then who shot him, Frank?" Michelle clipped.

Her tone caught Frank off-guard. He took his eyes off the road longer than he should have. Michelle now faced him for the first time in an hour and the skeptical expression caused Frank to become rigid. Michelle had gone into the barn to free the remaining hostages. She didn't see what happened. Was his own partner doubting his story? Was his most ardent ally jumping ship? Or was Frank reading into something not there.

He chose not to travel down that road and reached for the radio.

Michelle had switched it on within seconds of departing Paso Robles. Background noise. A blatant sign she didn't want to talk. "Is it okay?"

Michelle shot a glance between the radio and her partner then grinned at the irony. Freddie Mercury was crooning "I Want to Break Free." At this moment, Michelle, too, wanted to break free.

"I know it's Queen and you like them, but—"

Michelle appeared astonished. "You know Queen?"

It was the first step in the long road back to a working relationship. "Cute."

She relented. "Go ahead."

"Thanks." He switched off the radio and repeated his earlier statement. "Who took out Elijah? That's the question."

Michelle scratched her forehead. Traffic was heavy and a red ribbon of brake lights snaked through the canyons. Her detective mind was taking a back seat to her personal mind. "No idea."

"None?"

She thought another moment. "Xavier?"

"Can't see it. Killed his brother? Nah."

"If Gordon Whitefield is willing to sell-out his family, why wouldn't Xavier murder his brother? Maybe it's in the genes."

Frank pretended to ponder that possibility, simply for his partner's sake.

Michelle shifted. "If something else is in the works, something big going down, eliminating his brother would be the best way to prevent him from talking."

"Don't think so," Frank claimed. "These guys aren't religious fundamentalists. They're not willing to sacrifice themselves. Or to sacrifice a sibling for their bogus cause."

"Whitefield?" she asked hesitantly.

"Can't see that either. He gave up his nephew, or *nephews*, to get the reward."

"I don't believe the reward stipulated they had to be brought in alive," Michelle said. "Five million leading to the *arrest* of Elijah and Xavier. If he gave the information and it was us who fucked up, does he still get the bounty? And with Colby Ferrell as his attorney, I'd have to say, yes."

Frank hadn't thought of that angle. "You think Whitefield is playing both sides?"

"Maybe."

They drove a while longer deep in thought. Frank ended the quietness. "Jack Ruby."

Michelle twisted her lips. "Nope, not him either. He's been dead since the sixties, Frank. Ya' know, the sixties— where all that music you listen to comes from."

"Oswald kills Kennedy. That is, if you buy the company line. Then Ruby kills Oswald. People say it was part of a cover-up. To use an expression from my high school chess days, sacrificing the pawn. Others feel that Ruby, who admired President Kennedy, was playing vigilante and took the law into his own hands."

"So you're saying that *someone* was pissed at the Leaches and wanted to play vigilante like Ruby did? How would they know where? They'd have to have followed us." She paused, considered it, but with more determination, insisted, "Nope. Plus, think of this."

"Go on," Frank said as he moved into the left lane to pass a slow-moving motor home.

"You didn't use your directional," Michelle pointed out. "Ruby was three feet away from Oswald and aimed for body mass. Elijah was right next to you, Frank. Whoever took that shot from…what?…forty or fifty yards, knows how to handle a weapon. Guy knew enough to leave no cartridges and no footprints. A real pro."

Frank scoffed. "You're saying someone hired a professional hit man?"

"It's no more unbelievable than any other theory." She paused then added, "Or maybe something else to consider."

"Okay?"

"Maybe the shooter was aiming at you and not Elijah."

Chapter 23

Christmas?

Who the hell names their kid Christmas? Celebrating your birthday on December twenty-fifth meant getting gypped out of presents. Her parents claimed they doubled her gifts but Christmas knew it wasn't true. She'd been told she was born on that day because she was a gift from God.

What a crock.

When Christmas was a child, her mom mentioned the due date was December twenty-ninth, but she delivered early. Christmas often wondered if labor was induced. "I was going to name you Christmas, no matter what day in December you arrived."

For most of her life, Christmas detested her name. By third grade, tiring of the ridicule, she tried out nicknames: Christy, Kristy with a *K,* Chrissy. She eventually settled upon *Krissy.* The name stuck, especially since she was told she looked like a Krissy.

As a teenager, her rebellion kicked into overdrive. Since her parents burdened her with such an outrageous name, she'd get them back. She smoked, she snorted, she drank. Tops became lower, skirts became shorter. Her mom was out of her life by this time but rebelling against her father's new wife was *sweet.*

Krissy still chuckled when remembering her father's reaction to meeting her prom date. He was twenty-three, covered in tattoos. And African-American. When she returned home the following morning, she had only vague recollections of the previous night. Her credo was simple: *If you remember last night, you didn't drink enough.*

It was her father's influence and not her grades that got her into a respectable university. Krissy had dreamed of traveling around Europe after high school. She envisioned a modeling career and what better place to launch one than Paris. But she was, for the most part, *forced* to go to college. She conceded. Why not? If her workaholic father and his materialistic wife were willing to foot the bill for her entire education, it meant more time to party.

It was just after eight in the morning when Krissy drove onto the grounds of her off-campus apartment in Costa Mesa. She staggered out of her new red sports car—she *was* Daddy's little girl after all—took two steps before steadying herself. The complex was spinning, a result of too much imbibing. She smiled remembering last evening with Vince. Much of it was a blur which validated her credo. With no classes until the afternoon she had ample time to sober up.

Making her way to her unit that faced what the leasing agent called a "tropical-themed pool," Krissy fumbled with her keys, unlocked her door, and entered.

Her two-bedroom was quaint, but better furnished than most of her classmates. Her stepmom helped decorate the place. No, *she* decorated it herself. Krissy had no input. Still, standing in the doorway, something didn't seem quite right. The TV was on but muted. A pizza box lay on the kitchen table. Two sofa cushions were on the floor.

The sound coming from one of the bedrooms caused gooseflesh to coat her arms.

Her father had insisted she keep a firearm on hand, registered of course. Costa Mesa was safer than most communities but Krissy was an attractive twenty-year-old girl living alone. He suggested a .44 caliber Ruger Redhawk, praising its reliability and light weight. And to aim for body mass.

"You shoot to kill, not wound," he advised her. "Wounding someone, even if you're in the right, only leads to lawsuits."

Her stomach churned, her knees weakened. The revolver was stored in her closet. She'd have to bypass the bedroom where the disturbance originated from. Krissy debated leaving and calling the police, but she didn't want to overreact. It would lead to her short-tempered father insisting she move home. There was no way in hell she was ready to surrender her independence.

She lowered her purse and cautiously slithered down the hall. The closed bedroom was ten feet away.

Five feet away.

Directly outside.

Krissy screamed and fell against the wall as someone flew out of the room at her.

"Damn!" shouted Nathan. "You scared the shit out of me, girl!"

Krissy slapped his well-defined—and yes, damn sexy—shoulder. "Asshole. What are you doing here?" She only now noticed he was naked. Her eyes instinctively dropped for an instant.

Nathan feigned a bashful smile, placed his fingers to his lips. "Shh." He stepped aside and allowed Krissy a peek. Intertwined amongst the tossed sheets were two sleeping girls, one recognizable by the python tattoo snaking her exposed calf. "Paige McCann?"

Nathan closed the door, the shit-eating grin plastered on his face. "*And* Mikayla Boyle."

"You're too much," Krissy commented sheepishly.

"Damn right, I'm too much. They're exhausted."

Krissy brooded over the best way to handle this delicate situation. She and Paige had been friends since their freshman days two years earlier. Paige moved in and for a time it was fun. But their idiosyncrasies began grating on each other. Krissy was prepared to ask her roommate to leave but Paige beat her to it, announcing she was moving into the dorm. Despite vacating last semester, she still had not returned the key. Coming home from class, the library, and her waitress job to find Paige in bed with whoever she felt like screwing that particular day was getting tiresome.

Nathan flashed his A-smile at Krissy and moved closer, violating her space. "Where you coming back from lookin' all tasty?"

Krissy rolled her eyes. Nathan was unquestionably a good-looking guy, hard to resist. She had given into his charms on three different occasions but the wrapping was better than the gift. He was pushing thirty and, after twelve years in college, wasn't even half way to graduating. The professional student was the self-proclaimed campus stud.

"I'm going for a shower. I want you gone by the time I'm out. All three of you." She started to walk away, her eyes inadvertently lowering for a final look.

It didn't go unnoticed. Nathan extended his arm, effectively blocking her. "A shower, huh? Need someone to wash your back?"

"I got it. Thanks."

Nathan detected alcohol on Krissy's breath. They'd hooked up previously and each time it was mind-blowing. He'd been astounded how much passion and lust was contained in a petite five-one frame. "I should shower, too. I'm dirty."

"You've got Paige and Mikayla."

"California's in a drought. If not for me, baby girl, think of it as saving the planet."

Krissy grinned and slipped beneath his barrier arm. "Twenty minutes. I want you gone."

"Christmas doesn't have to only *come* once a year."

"Like I've never heard that before."

Krissy opened the bathroom door twenty minutes later and perked her ears. No sound. Good. Surely if Nathan saw her draped in a towel it would obviously mean she wanted him. After all, didn't every girl want him?

Confident she was alone she bounced into her bedroom. Before dressing, she picked up her phone and sent two texts.

The first was to Paige: *We need 2 talk.* The second was to Vince: *Had fun last nite. C U again?*

Waiting for a reply, Krissy crossed the room to her closet. Before she could decide what to sleep in, her phone pinged. It was not a response but rather an incoming message. The note was typed properly, no *text-ese*. She read the missive three times, pursed her lips and wondered why Dr. Cranborne wanted to meet with her immediately.

∽◌∾

The university was established in the mid-sixties. And Dr. Marjorie Cranborne was considered a relic even back then. She was cultured and intellectual but also snooty, and patronizing to her students. She quoted Longfellow, Alcott, Milton, and Dickens as if it was the word of God. It was obvious she'd been compelled into teaching this particular class. *The Evolution of the Vampire in Twentieth Century Literature* was something Dr. Cranborne would never stoop to. But she was not able to retire and the University Regents believed courses needed to be more appealing to a younger generation. As she gazed over the top of her half-moon eyeglasses and saw students more enraptured in blood-sucking dead people than Holden Caulfield and Atticus Finch, Dr. Cranborne knew without a doubt paradise was truly lost. Her lack of enthusiasm, overly strict grading, and general disinterest she took in the lectures resulted in her moniker: *Count Bitchula.*

Krissy rapped her knuckles on the closed office door. No answer. She knocked a second time. Same result. A dry erase board displayed the professor's office hours. A poor representation of Cranborne with a stake through her heart had been doodled alongside. According to the display, the professor had no office hours until tonight. Krissy withdrew her phone and reread the text. She mulled over the likelihood of a dinosaur like Cranborne lowering herself to texting a student. Then again, if she'd been forced to teach a class beneath her, the university could easily encourage her to rely on texting.

Hearing tapping on a keyboard a few offices away, Krissy strode down the hall and inquired of this other instructor if he knew where Dr. Cranborne was.

"She doesn't have office hours until tonight," confirmed the professor, who looked to be in his late twenties.

"Yes, I see that. But she sent me a—thank you, anyway." Krissy left the building and purchased a Cinnamon Dolce Latte from a vendor just across the Quad. Sitting cross-legged on the grass and enjoying her drink, she grew irritated at the interruption of her schedule. She'd hoped to sleep off the hangover and feel refreshed in time for this afternoon's Political Science class. Being summoned only to be stood up would ruin her rejuvenating nap.

One unidentifiable student waved. "Merry Christmas!"

"Hey, you."

Finishing the coffee, she tried Cranborne's office once more. The final attempt yielded the same result. Krissy was pissed. She started texting Cranborne but thought better of it. She'd respond later, after calming down.

Krissy traversed the student parking lot with deliberate steps, muttering under her breath. Beeping her car unlocked, she dropped behind the wheel and slid her iPod from the console. She scrolled through listings, searching for something befitting her incensed state.

An arm darted forward from the back seat. A powerful hand clenched tightly around her throat. She felt steel against the rear of her skull.

"Drive."

"Please—please don't hurt me," Krissy begged.

"Drive," he repeated through gritted teeth.

In the rear view, she saw eyes filled with anger and fury. As she slowly drove off campus, she wondered how Xavier Leach had gotten into her car.

Chapter 24

After returning home last evening Frank stood at the threshold of his children's rooms and watched them breathe. Jake gently snored. Ashley clutched her I-thingy to her chest. Frank longed for their innocence. In his bedroom, he emptied his pockets, locked his Beretta in the gun safe, and got undressed. Stepping into the shower, he turned the pressure on full force and let hot water pound his naked body. When finished, he felt no more cleansed. He threw on a T-shirt and shorts, got into bed, and spooned his wife.

"Oh, good, you're home," Abby breathed through the veil of sleep. She automatically angled her arm back and patted her husband's face to make sure she wasn't dreaming. "Everything okay?"

Rather than replying, he clung to her tightly, his security blanket saving him from the dangers of a cold, cruel world.

For two hours Frank watched the ceiling fan rotate but what he saw was the void of an uncertain future. "Idiot," he told himself. He tried to do what was right. However, he not only failed, he made a dangerous situation worse. It was impractical to even consider the field bordering the vineyard becoming a sniper's nest. Anyone in the ten thousand LAPD could have lost Elijah. But it wasn't any of them. It was, as always, Frank Grace, screwing up yet again.

Who could the assassin have been? Was it some wanna-be hero, a vigilante? Would Xavier have murdered his own brother simply to silence him? And if so, what was the next target? When would LA get hit again? Would the shrewder brother exact even greater revenge, striking a more devastating blow with higher casualties? Would Frank be the cause for more carnage, just like in Azusa?

Four years earlier, the name Frank Grace was a punchline, an easy target for late night comics. His likeness had made the rounds on Facebook as a meme. He was a piñata for politicians trying to get votes, a target for talk shows attempting to score higher ratings. Ashley was in third grade and Jake in kindergarten when the principal summoned Frank and Abby to her office and expressed, in no uncertain terms, her desire to have them transferred to a different school. "It's really for their own safety."

Frank was eventually found innocent of any wrongdoing. But the damage to him, his reputation, and, worst of all, his family, had been done. Time passed and eventually his name faded away.

But now he was again back in the spotlight.

It was a sign, perhaps, or maybe an omen, when Abby sleepily moved over and turned her back on her husband. He wondered if they should again consider moving out of LA. But where could they go?

As if hurting his family yet again wasn't bad enough this time he took his partner down with him.

As Frank's eyes grew heavy, he realized his career was over. The life he knew, the life he created for himself and his loved ones would be gone. From this moment forward, everything would be different.

❧❧❧

The exhaust fumes from the gridlocked Hollywood Freeway were wreaking havoc with Frank's already churning stomach. He was emotionally drained, physically beat and mentally sapped. His head pounded as if he'd been flung airborne into a brick wall. He was ten minutes away from West Bureau where he'd face the music, a swan song, when his phone chirped.

"Detective Grace," he answered, knowing this could be the last time he ever answered a call that way.

"Grace, where are you?" Chief Kent yelled.

"I'm on way in to West Bureau, sir."

The commissioner took a prolonged drag on a cigarette. "Santana with you?"

"No, sir."

"Well, where the fuck is she?"

Frank tramped the brake, nearly rear-ending a mini-van. "Not sure, sir. I'm assuming she's already at The Barn." He paused and, in an attempt to praise her work ethic, added, "She always arrives early."

"I want the whole team here by the top of the hour."

"Here?"

"My house, Grace!"

Frank was tangled in a vehicular sandwich and wasn't sure of his partner's whereabouts. "Can you give me a little more time, sir?"

Another pause, another inhale, another smirk. "Just get your asses here, pronto."

"Yes, sir," Frank replied into a now dead phone.

He knew this was the end. Terminating an officer was a lengthy process. Reports had to be filed, the Police Union needed to review. Even when the individual in question was not fighting the injunction, it still dragged on. However, Kent was the chief of police. In the past, Frank admired his no nonsense approach at cutting through red tape. Now, his propensity to move quickly would solidify the speedy culmination to Frank's career. And apparently, Michelle's as well.

Frank eased his loaner onto the shoulder and punched in Michelle's number. Her desk phone went to voicemail. He started to leave a message but opted for her personal cell.

On the fourth ring, a scratchy voice grumbled, "Hello."

"Michelle?"

"Yes. Who's this?"

She'd been sleeping. Frank frowned at the dashboard clock unable to recall the last time his gung-ho partner didn't arrive to the Barn before him. "It's Frank."

A noncommittal "Oh."

"You're not going in today?"

"Took the day off."

The only event more inconceivable than his partner coming in after him was his partner not coming in at all. "Kent just called. He wants to meet with us. *Pronto.*" The sustained silence prompted Frank to ask, "You there?"

"Yup."

"I'll be there in fifteen minutes."

"I need to get dressed. Make it twenty."

"Okay."

Michelle sighed defeated. "I guess this is it."

Guilt cutting his soul for destroying Michelle's career, he could only mutter a, "See you in twenty."

When he'd dressed this morning, Frank put on one his better suits but chose to forego a tie and go open collared. He wanted to at least look the part of a detective on his final day as one. Professional Frank. He also threw three empty boxes into the trunk in preparation of clearing out his cubicle.

His partner was the antithesis. In spite of meeting with the city's top cop she wore no make-up, a non-descript T-shirt, running shorts, and her hair tucked under a cap. Casual Michelle.

The drive from Sherman Oaks to Kent's mansion in posh Calabasas was filled with stone-like silence. Both detectives independently mulled over past career missteps while entering an uncertain future. Communication was non-existent. There was nothing left to say.

Frank gave their names to the man in the guard shack and entered Kent's palatial home. The chief clearly made good money, but Frank believed such a lavish manor only served to put greater distance between the constantly disparaged PD and the citizens of the city they served.

Michelle did not react to the affluence of the stunning home, the pristine lawns or the luxury vehicles parked atop the circular cobblestone driveway. Instead, she fell in step with Frank, clearly detached from her coming termination.

Charlotte Kent stepped from the home before the bell was wrung. She wore a sheer white top that accentuated full breasts, a necklace that drew attention to her cleavage, and formfitting jeans that hugged her shapely legs.

"Good morning, Mrs. Kent." Unlike the previous visit, Frank was not invited to use her first name. An awkward silence ensued before he added, "This is my partner, Detective Santana."

Michelle forced a grin but didn't offer a hand. Instead, she underwent a supercilious scan of her body by the tall former dancer.

The condescending mien on Charlotte's face indicated she disapproved with this detective's choice of attire for meeting the Police Chief of Los Angeles. "This way," she stated evenly.

Frank and Michelle followed like puppy dogs. During the stroll around the perimeter Michelle leaned into Frank, whispered, "She really doesn't have the ass to wear jeans that tight."

Charlotte's gait altered slightly. She peered over her shoulder and, with eyes on Michelle, asked matter-of-factly, "I always assumed the LAPD had some sort of height requirement."

"Fear not," Michelle countered. "I can handle myself."

Charlotte eyed Frank. *You actually work with this little bitch?*

Frank and Michelle were taken around to the rear of the property where Weldon Kent would hold court and hand down his sentence. He was poised at a wicker table below an umbrella, his voice carrying across the expanse. The person on the other end of the call getting a profanity-laced earful.

"Sit." Charlotte's statement was a command, not an invitation.

"Should I give you a paw also?" Michelle snickered.

Charlotte opened her mouth, closed it. After her husband stubbed out a cigarette and immediately lit another one, she moved her hand toward the overflowing ashtray. Thinking better of it, she picked up a cell, called her home, and advised the maid the ashtray needed to be emptied.

Frank and Michelle took two of the four empty chairs and waited uneasily for Kent to finish ripping someone a new asshole. The housekeeper appeared, a small-boned Latina. In broken English, she asked the guests, "Something drink?"

Charlotte jumped in. "My husband and I will take two fingers of Merlot." She turned to the detectives as an afterthought. "Water or something?"

"I'm fine, thanks," Frank replied.

"I'll have two fingers of Merlot as well," Michelle announced in a mock British accent.

"Merlot comes from Napa, Detective Sanchez, not England."

"Santana."

Charlotte rolled her eyes. "I would've taken you for a beer girl."

"This doesn't strike me as a beer home."

"And thank heavens for that."

Women. Frank kicked his partner under the table. Michelle flashed him the evil eye. Before an all-out catfight erupted, Kent ended the call and waved his arms frantically. "Where the hell is my damn ash tray?"

"Faustina's getting a fresh one."

Kent flicked his ashes onto the ground and got to the point. "Grace, you weren't followed here, were you?"

"No, sir."

"Good. Tell me what the hell went wrong up there. How did everything turn to shit?"

Frank breathed deep and prepared to relate details of the same story he told Kent on the phone from Paso Robles. Surprisingly, Charlotte lowered herself into one of the two unoccupied chairs. Although he was relieved to see no members of the union or any *brassholes*, the fact that the police chief's wife included herself was unexpected.

"Go ahead, Detective." Charlotte sat in an angled position facing Frank, her shoulder blocking Michelle from her sightline.

Frank spent fifteen minutes recounting the particulars. He underscored the successful rescue of three hostages, touting his partner's role in securing their freedom, while glossing over the slaying of Elijah Leach. He reminded the chief his partner was not around when Leach was eliminated.

Kent wasn't buying it. "How the hell did you lose a collar, Grace? You had the fuckin' guy in custody."

In his periphery, Frank noticed Michelle appeared uninterested, even bored. Although it was Frank's bust—and she knew it was clean—she was at a point where she just wanted this over. Her career was in the shitter. She yearned to move forward and waste no more time looking back.

With his partner offering no support, Frank realized Kent was angrily tapping cigarette ash into the ashtray. What stunned Frank was seeing abrasive and brusque Charlotte Kent wiping away a tear.

Temporarily sidetracked, Frank shook his head. "Anyone could've lost Leach," he proffered half-heartedly. His goal was to fall on the sword for his partner. At least Michelle could hopefully keep her badge.

After he concluded, Kent and his wife exchanged a drawn-out gaze, speaking without speaking. The chief slid his fingers through his closely cropped hair. "You fucked up, Grace. Again. That much is obvious."

"Sir, with all due respect, I—"

Kent cut him off. "This isn't the first time." He threw his chin at the cell atop a closed binder. "That was Colby Ferrell on the phone. He gave me the heads-up that he'll be filing suit against the city on behalf of Elijah Leach's uncle for wrongful death. If this…shit, if this goes to trial, that shyster's gonna royally screw us. I'm talking tens of millions and shitloads of negative press."

Frank wanted to rebuff but held his tongue. A fleeting look at his partner who was stifling a yawn.

"After your Azusa fuck-up, you cost the city millions in lawsuits, decreased tourism, and set the department's reputation back decades. Four years later, here we are again. Same damn thing." Kent clucked his tongue. "Frank fucking Grace."

Frank swallowed hard.

"You act impulsively at times. You're a rogue cop—reckless, hasty, and irresponsible. But as I told you the other day, you remind me of me years ago."

"Sir?"

Kent dragged on his cigarette and blew smoke into Frank's face. "I'm giving you one last chance."

Frank knitted his brows and looked at Charlotte for affirmation. She was still dabbing at her eyes for some reason. To his right, Michelle straightened, no longer apathetic. "Thank you, sir. I want you to know I won't let you down. I—"

Kent dismissed it. "Yeah, yeah, I know. But here's the thing, Grace. You have one final opportunity for redemption. Take it!" Kent threw a finger in his direction. "You do whatever you have to. I don't give a rat's ass about the law, about the Colby Ferrell's of the world, about rights and wrongs."

Frank curbed his astonishment, aghast the police chief was essentially directing him to disregard legal procedures. He momentarily wondered if he was being set up. But the brasshole was offering a brass ring and he better damn well reach for it. "Sir, you have my word I will find Xavier Leach."

Kent eyed his wife as if seeking her permission to continue. Charlotte nodded once. Kent pushed the manila folder across the table toward the detectives. "I'm not talking about finding Xavier." He withdrew several photos and spread them out for his guests to see. "I'm talking about finding my daughter. Krissy was abducted this morning."

Michelle leaned in and repositioned the photos for a better angle. They studied the images for a moment, looked at each other, and then nodded affirmatively at Kent. Charlotte's gentle sobbing now made sense. Her own children lived back east but Krissy was her stepdaughter, her husband's child. The tears were for her.

Kent's eyes misted over, then he quickly shook it off and resumed his role as chief of police and not parent. Taking on his traditional business tone he divulged the specifics of Krissy's kidnapping. A surveillance camera atop the Chemistry Building caught a man breaking into her car. Before campus police could arrive on scene, Krissy had returned. There was a momentary delay before she drove off. The car was picked up by CHP cameras who tracked the sporty Mitsubishi southbound on the San Diego Freeway, en route possibly to Mexico. Per Kent, the facial recognition program he'd already had experts utilize determined a ninety-eight-percent match that it was Xavier Leach who abducted his little girl.

Michelle, now engaged, became part of the conversation. "Why would Xavier go after your daughter?"

Frank answered for Kent. "For the same reason they went after my wife. It's personal to them." He immediately regretted his words. His wife. The chief's daughter. And shortly, Michelle's niece would be her responsibility. Things were hitting close to home.

"They've declared war on the LAPD," Kent spat. "It's high time we go on the offensive and take the fight to them." Someone in the distance diverted his attention. He signaled for the man to come over and pointed to the lone unoccupied chair. Frank and Michelle pivoted, simultaneously dropped their jaws and in unison cried out. "Wadkins?"

The pretentious detective smiled broadly and joined their little soiree.

"I—I don't understand," Frank stammered.

Kent said, "When I called you before, Grace, I said I wanted to assemble the entire team. *Team.* What? You think you're the only one I assigned to finding the Leaches?"

"Actually, yes, I did."

Wadkins popped an Altoid. "Don't feel bad, Frank. The chief wanted his best people working on the Leaches so he assigned me."

"How many others are in on this?" Michelle asked.

"That's not your concern, Detective Santana," Kent rebuked.

Frank faced Wadkins and grumbled, "So you've been working on this all along?"

"Yes."

"I would've liked to have known."

Kent jumped in. "I wanted everyone acting independently. The general consensus nowadays is for agencies and everyone to work together, but I've never believed that teamwork bullshit. With people operating autonomously, the chances increase tenfold for a successful outcome. The more lines you throw into the water the better chance you'll have of catching something."

Wadkins winked at Frank, then faced the chief's wife and asked with genuine concern, "How are *you* holding up, Charlotte?"

"As good as could be expected, thank you."

Why didn't I ask that? Frank wondered.

"Weldon?"

"She's my daughter, Troy. I want her back and safe."

"You have my word."

Frank looked around, half-expecting to see Rod Serling.

Charlotte? Troy? Weldon? Wadkins was on a first name basis with the chief of police and his wife. Had he wandered into the Twilight Zone? *Golden Boy indeed.* "Jimmy Stoner in on this, too?"

Wadkins arched a brow. "Stoner's a good kid, but I didn't need my partner's help." He winked at Frank's partner then pulled Krissy's photos closer. "Any beads on this Xavier shit bag?"

Wadkins had been apprised of Krissy Kent's kidnapping prior to arriving, whereas Frank and Michelle knew nothing until setting foot in the home. It was abundantly clear the police chief was playing favorites.

As Kent brought Wadkins up to speed, Frank and Michelle, hearing it for the second time, did a slow burn. When finished, Kent urged his people, "Bring my girl home."

"Are we supposed to work together this time?" Frank inquired, civility absent in his tone.

"You three can work that out." Kent adjourned the meeting. He stood, took one final puff, and headed into his castle. Charlotte began following but then backpedaled. "I want you to find my husband's daughter. I hate to think what Weldon would become if something…something unspeakable happened to Krissy." She fixated on Wadkins, not Grace or Santana.

The three detectives made their way from Kent's sprawling backyard around front. Wadkins, perhaps euphemistically, was in the lead. "Nice ride," he chided Frank while moving to his BMW.

"Hold up, Wadkins," Frank called. Face to face, he said, "I wish you would've come clean with me. You knew I was working on a link. Hell, I was the one who handed off Eddie Evanovich to you."

"Who?"

"Eddie Evanovich, the homeless man who seemed unimportant until his name came up in that video."

"Oh, yeah, that was beautiful, Grace. Pawning off some

bogus crap just to give me busy work and get me out of the way. Then it becomes integral to the investigation." Wadkins laughed. "Good job, *Detective.*"

"As detestable as this is to say, I feel we should work together from this point forward," Michelle opined.

"You do, do you?"

"Yes, a girl's life is at stake."

"And if her last name wasn't Kent, would you feel that way?"

"Hell, yes," Michelle snapped.

Wadkins egotistical smile widened. "I'll make you both a deal. You step aside, let me do my job. And when I'm up on stage getting a commendation—Chief Kent on one side and his daughter on the other—I'll maybe mention your names. Maybe."

Frank stepped closer. "Were you born a prick or is it something that developed over time?"

Wadkins cackled acerbically. "Those are good people. Charlotte's a good woman. Weldon's good for the city and good for the department. Yet, his legacy is in doubt cause of you. People look at the LAPD and, instead of seeing Weldon Kent, they see Frank Grace. You're bad news, Grace. Bad for the department, bad for the city, and bad for the police chief."

"You done?"

Wadkins cupped Frank's shoulder. "When I'm done, you'll know."

Frank twisted from Wadkins's touch. "Next time you put your hand on me, be ready to get knocked on your ass."

Wadkins waggled his finger "Tsk, tsk, no more doughnuts for you." With that, he slid behind the wheel of his Beemer, flipped Frank the bird, and substantiated his macho status by burning rubber.

Frank and Michelle got into the loaner but he didn't immediately start up the Chrysler-something. Staring vacantly through the window, Frank declared, "I'll do whatever's necessary to find Krissy. Not just 'cause she's Kent's kid but because it's the right thing to do. And I want to see the look on that smug bastard's face when I bring her in. First."

"When *we* bring her in."

Frank smiled. "You heard what Kent said. Whatever it takes."

"I just hope we're not being set up for another failure. Kent has us, Wadkins, and who knows how many others assigned to this. But it's clear he's pulling for Golden Boy."

"Then it'll be that much sweeter when I bring Krissy Kent home."

"We, Frank. When *we* bring her home."

Frank sighed. "You could've lost your career in there, Michelle. You're already on thin ice working with me. You dodged a big time bullet by Paso Robles turning to shit. I don't know what's next. I don't want to see you go down with me if it doesn't work."

Michelle narrowed her eyes. "Need I remind you, Detective Grace, we go down, we go down together. Now start the car and let's find Krissy."

Chapter 25

T he icy stares Frank weathered upon arriving in West Bureau-Hollywood conjured memories of four years ago.

When his suspension following the Azusa bloodbath ended, he was treated as an outcast, a leper. Fellow officers scorned Frank, both publically and privately. It took time to earn back their trust.

Some never relented. Now, after mucking up the Elijah Leach takedown—out of his jurisdiction—he was again on the receiving end of contemptuous glares. Michelle, however, was met with expressions closer to pity for being partnered with such a has-been.

Before Frank could make his way through the frosty squad room, his forearm was seized by Heather Craft. In a pained voice, she said, "I'm so sorry, Frank, so sorry. Anyone could've lost Leach, anyone. You weren't injured, right? You're okay?"

"Never better, Detective Craft."

"I can't imagine what you're going through. If you want to talk or need a shoulder, call me. You do have my number, right?"

"Umm, sure."

"Just in case you don't, here it is again." Craft tore a piece of paper from a nearby desk, jotted her number, and handed it to Frank, sandwiching his hand between hers.

Frank thanked her and trudged off to his cubicle where he unfolded Heather's note. Below her home phone, cell phone, office phone, email address, and Twitter handle, she drew a smiley face along with Xs and Os.

Michelle entered their shared workstation. "I'll take stalkers for two hundred, Alex."

"What can I say, Detective? Some guys have that animal magnetism, some guys don't."

Michelle winked. "When you find a guy like that, let me know."

An instant later, Wadkins appeared with palms extended. "I come in peace."

"What do you want?"

"Believe it or not," Wadkins began, "I want to apologize. I acted improperly before. I shouldn't have bitten your heads off." He turned, slid a chair from an empty desk, and rolled into their space, doing a double-take at Michelle's toned legs. "You know how Kent is. He gets people riled up. After that meeting, I'd walk through hell to find his daughter. Caught up in the moment. But I believe we *should* pool our resources."

"Funny that you feel that way now," Frank replied. "Before you had no desire to come clean and tell me you were working for Kent."

"Neither did you," Wadkins countered.

Good point. Frank backed down. "It's water under the bridge."

"Things've obviously taken a turn for the worse. Unless we nail Leach—and soon—who knows what's around the corner? Whaddaya say?"

Frank and Michelle stole a glance, seeking consent from the other. "Fine," Frank said. "But we need to be honest and open."

Wadkins whipped off a mock salute. "Definitely. Detective Santana?"

Michelle was less willing to climb aboard, but she agreed with an unremarkable nod.

Wadkins flashed his toothpaste commercial smile. "Maybe I'll even tack my name on at the end. Grantanawad?"

"Don't push it," Michelle quipped.

The three detectives locked themselves in an unused conference room. The LAPD had recently been slapped with a frivolous lawsuit, claiming interrogation rooms were adverse to perps being questioned. Station by station across the city, IRs were being upgraded to *user-friendly* décor and now it was West Bureau's turn. The room was filled with layers of sawdust. Damaged chairs and old hard drives were stacked in the corner. Wires dangled from the ceiling. A plastic covering was draped over the recently removed one-way mirror.

Two hours were spent discussing the best way to proceed. Frank couldn't help but wonder if Kent had assigned anyone else to find the Leaches prior and Krissy now. He asked Wadkins but the detective claimed ignorance.

As the brainstorming progressed, Wadkins somehow donned the role of lead investigator. This did not sit well with Grace or Santana. But since Golden Boy was on first name terms with *Weldon* and *Charlotte*, they let it slide. That, combined with the fact Wadkins had more leeway, played into Frank's decision to follow orders. He longed to knock the smug SOB down a few notches and find Kent's daughter first. But he'd let Wadkins take control…for now.

The triad agreed that Wadkins would ask Colby Ferrell to quash the litigation. "I'll schmooze him over," Wadkins claimed but he said *smooze*.

Michelle was assigned to contact Vernon Wayne/Gordon Whitefield. "You're a woman," Wadkins stated. "You'll come off more concerned about the loss of his nephew. Play the sympathy card, Santana. While expressing condolences for Elijah, see if you can get a bead on Xavier's whereabouts."

Michelle was never one for taking orders, a trait she picked up from her partner. But being micromanaged by

Wadkins, an equal who appointed himself lead, appalled her. Frank was tasked with contacting CHP and neighboring law enforcement agencies to track the location of Krissy's Mitsubishi.

Wadkins headed off to Century City after verifying Ferrell would be out of court for the remainder of the afternoon. Michelle's calls to Whitefield proved fruitless as she reached only voicemails. She decided to, hopefully, catch him at his last-known address. Before leaving, Frank asked in a whisper, "Wadkins?"

Michelle shook her head once. "I still don't trust him."

"Me neither. Glad we're on the same page, Detective."

"Always." And she left.

Minutes later, the desk sergeant phoned Frank advising him he had a visitor. Standing, he threw his suit jacket on and traipsed into the waiting area. The lone occupant was perusing flyers pinned to the bulletin board. A glance between Frank and Sergeant Lindstrom confirmed she was the one. "You asked to speak with me? I'm Detective Grace."

The woman turned. "Hello, Frank."

Frank blinked. Dressed in skinny black jeans, and a mint green V-neck sweater, she had her blonde hair in a ponytail. Her eyes looked weary, her skin gaunt.

"Sorry, Detective Nichols. I didn't recognize you."

"Kendra. You and Michelle saved my life. I think we can dispense with the formalities."

"Kendra," Frank said with a smile. "What can I do for you?"

She looked around and shuddered as if cold. "Can you spare me a few?"

"Sure. Let me find an unoccupied IR."

As he pivoted, Kendra reached for his arm and gave him a sideways glance. Her eyes appeared distant. "Can we speak outside? With what I've been through, the fresh air would be a welcomed change."

"Lead the way."

Kendra found a suitable location in the far corner of the

employee parking lot where there was no shade. After being held captive in darkness for so long, she savored sunlight.

Frank stood silently, waiting for her to open up. Finally, she did and her comment caught him flatfooted. "I want to apologize."

"*Apologize*? For what?"

"Michelle and I go way back. We were in the academy together." Kendra paused before continuing as if searching for the right words. "We kinda lost touch after a while. That happens, ya' know."

Frank nodded.

"Two years ago when Michelle told me she was going to be your partner, I…well, I pushed for her to ask to be reassigned."

"Understandable."

"Everyone in the department, hell, everyone in the city is familiar with the exploits of Frank Grace." She forced a smile. "But as her friend, I didn't want to see her career derailed. So I pushed. I pushed hard for her to find *anyone* else."

"I'm glad you were unsuccessful. Detective Santana's the best partner I've had the privilege of working with."

"That's why I feel a need to apologize. I said a lot of unkind things about you."

Frank waved it away. "No problem. You weren't the only one. But I do appreciate your honesty."

"You don't smoke, do you?"

"Not any more. I quit years ago."

"Me too. Seven years. But I lit up ten minutes after I was freed." She circumvented Frank and scooped up a twig from the pavement so she'd have something to do with her hands. After more internal debate, she locked eyes on Frank. "I understand now where you're coming from."

"Sorry?"

"Azusa. I didn't understand your actions back then. You took out four scumbags but gave chase to a fifth, even though he fled the scene."

Frank listened, unsure why Kendra was recapping.

"At the time, I, like everyone else, judged you. How could you go after them? How could you take out a guy as he was running away? Why did you act so irrationally and unethically?" She paused. "But now, after what I've been through, I understand."

Frank remained tightlipped.

"It's difficult to—"

"Hello?"

The person materialized out of thin air and sidled up beside Frank while appraising Kendra with an inspecting eye.

"Kendra, this is Detective Craft, " Frank said. "Detective Craft, Kendra." He skipped giving her last name.

Kendra nodded a greeting. Craft scanned Kendra from head to toe before addressing Frank. "I'm on way home. You have my number, right?"

Frank pointed to his head. "Committed to memory."

"Don't be a stranger." She departed but not before shooting the blonde an accusatory scowl. *Don't make a move on my man.*

"What was *that* all about?" Kendra laughed seconds later.

"Don't ask."

"Must be tough being the division stud."

Kendra and Michelle were alike. No wonder they'd been friends. "That title actually belongs to a Detective Wadkins." Redirecting the conversation away from himself, Frank asked, "You were saying?"

Kendra started to speak but not before Heather Craft tooted her horn while driving away, waved to Frank, and simulated a phone with her hand.

"It's difficult to separate it all," Kendra said when Craft had gone. "We're cops, detectives. Yet, somehow, in spite of what we encounter on a daily basis, we're supposed to…I don't know…disconnect. I never doubted my ability to do that. But now? Now, I understand."

Frank shook his head. "I'm not sure *I* understand."

"Payback. Retribution. I realize now why you chased that son of a bitch into an alley four years ago. You wanted blood. You—you saved my life. I'm talking as a friend, Frank, okay?"

"Please do."

"Had Elijah Leach not been shot, I would have done it myself. That was not some idle threat I made in the vineyard. I really was going to kill him. When you told me where he'd be booked, I—I believe you wanted me to take him out, didn't you?"

Frank mulled that over. Why had he told her? Was it a Freudian slip? Did he subconsciously covet having Kendra murder Leach? Frank had given his word that Elijah would be brought in alive. Was he secretly wanting Kendra to do his dirty work, do what he promised not to? "It was just something to say," he finally said.

"Sure. Sure it was." She smiled. "Again, I just wanted to say thanks for saving me. I know that sounds hackneyed but I mean it."

Frank was surprised when Kendra embraced him, holding him in a way that exhibited her immense gratitude. As he patted her back, he was thankful Heather Craft had driven away. He'd hate to have his stalker see this scene. When they separated, Frank asked, "Do you know when you'll be coming back?"

"To work?"

"Yes."

She clucked her tongue. "Not sure when. Or if. I really don't know if I can do it anymore."

"Take some time, Detective. From what I've heard, you're good at what you do." It was a lie. Frank only knew of her through the occasional namedropping via Michelle. But he plainly could see Kendra Nichols was adrift. She was at a crossroads and he hoped she'd choose the correct path.

"I'm off to get hold of Lori Edens."

"Oh?"

"Phil's wife. Or widow, I should say. I need to apologize for letting things happen between her husband and me."

"Good luck," Frank said, unsure how else to respond.

"Again, I'm sorry for what I said all those years back."

"Forget it."

"I won't, Frank. I can't forget."

He enjoyed the fresh air a moment longer. As Kendra drove out of the parking lot, she tapped her horn and mimicked Detective Craft's earlier act by making a phone with her hand.

The conversation was invigorating. All too often cases were just that: cases, file numbers, crimes to be solved. Even though she was a colleague, a fellow detective, Kendra Nichols had been up until a while ago just one more dossier. It was fulfilling to put a face with the name, a real person to a crime.

The sun was sinking nearer the horizon as another day was ending. Another day and still no closer to Xavier Leach. Frank decided he'd make a few calls, see if there were any breaks on Krissy Kent's twenty, and touch base with Michelle. Before he reached the entrance, Sergeant Lindstrom came racing from the building. "Grace! Where the hell you been, man?"

"I was speaking with…someone." He and Lindstrom moved closer to each other. "What's up?"

"You're still up in Toluca Lake, right?"

"Yep."

Over the top of his eyeglasses, Lindstrom recited an address he'd scribbled on a piece of paper.

Frank's heart skipped a beat. "That's my home."

"I thought so," Lindstrom gulped. "Just got a call. Gunshots, one person down."

Frank looked at his watch. Abby was off today, Ashley and Jake were already home from school. His entire family was there. *One person down?*

Chapter 26

He was unfamiliar with the loaner but Frank didn't give a damn. He raced home, rocketing along the shoulder, and creating his own lanes as he squeezed between other vehicles. He took the freeway off-ramp at sixty. Traffic was thick as tourists concluded their day at Universal Studios, Frank's driving resembling something out of a Hollywood action flick. His hand stayed on the horn and his foot tramped on the gas as he tore through numerous intersections. In his wake were cars spinning out of control and a torrent of obscenities. Squealing rubber was ear splitting, tread marks like breadcrumbs delineated his trail.

Frank yanked the wheel left, the vehicle fishtailing. Nearly losing control and then almost overcorrecting, he righted the Chrysler and floored it. In the distance, he saw a cavalcade of activity outside his house. Half a dozen police cruisers, three ambulances, a pair of news vans. And one midnight-black vehicle with *county coroner* emblazoned on the side. Unmindful to his neighbors who stared and pointed, their mundane afternoon now filled with excitement, Frank jammed the brake. Nose angling down, the car skidded to a haphazard stop in the middle of the street.

He leapt from the car, darted across his lawn toward the yellow crime scene tape that fluttered in the breeze. Out of nowhere, he was bear-hugged.

"Easy, Mack. Where do you think—"

Frank ignored the cop and began worming free.

The patrolman held steadfast, planted his legs firmly, and started moving Frank's wrist behind his back. "You want the bracelets, asshole?"

Frank pulled his arm free from the overzealous cop. "Abby! Kids!"

The cop reached for his weapon.

"That's Frank Grace," cried an authoritative voice from off to the side. "His house, let 'em through."

Throwing himself below the yellow crime scene tape, Frank collided with the upraised palms of a behemoth in his front yard. The detective gave his name. Frank didn't hear it. He was a good six inches shorter but built like an NFL linebacker.

Frank heard his heartbeat in his ears, his chest pounded. His legs hadn't trembled like this since the Northridge quake in '94. His eyes swept left and right. Crime scene tape. His house. His yard. No sign of his wife or children. "Where—where's my family?"

"Calm down, Detective Grace."

"Where's my fucking family?"

"Relax, Detective. Relax! And I'll take you around back."

Frank cocked his head. The backyard. *Is that where it happened, whatever the it is?*

More times than he could remember, Frank had been working a crime scene when a hysterical loved one happened upon the area. He was sensitive to their rage, their loss of common sense, the wildness in their eyes. Sensitive, but never understanding it—until now. "Okay." He breathed deep to avoid passing out. "Okay, Detective…"

"Schleffler."

"Schaeffer?"

"No, Schleffler. Can't blame my ex for going back to her maiden name. Follow me."

Tunnel vision. Everything around him was a cloud of

nothingness. As hectic as the scene was out front, his back-yard was chockfull of plainclothes cops and investigators. Two teams from Forensics were already on hand. Frank hadn't realized how many people could fit into what he always considered a small yard.

"Frank!"

Abby ran forward, launched herself against her husband. Their bodies intertwined, coming together like pieces of a jigsaw puzzle. They held one another tighter than they had in years. Her shoulders began rising and lowering as she buried her face into Frank's chest. Sobbing, she clung to him, muttering his name over and over.

He was surrounded by colleagues from law enforcement, mostly men with high levels of testosterone. But Frank didn't care as tears or relief trickled down his cheeks. "The kids?"

"They're okay, sweetie, they're all right, thank God." Abby clasped the crucifix hanging from her neck and found the strength to compose herself. "Jake's at his tutor and Ash—"

"Daddy!"

Ashley was lanky but she slammed against her dad with meteoric force. Frank nearly lost his balance and toppled to the ground in comedic style. It surely would've gotten a chuckle from the cops on the scene.

He cradled the back of his daughter's head. "You okay, Ash?"

Her nod lacked confidence.

"You sure?"

The second bow of her head displayed more poise. "Yeah, Dad" She embraced her father tighter. "I am now." After a lengthy hug, she commented, "Wait till I post this on Facebook."

Kids.

Frank laughed.

"Oh, c'mon dad. Even *you've* heard of Facebook."

Abby chuckled and, after wiping away another tear,

pulled her daughter to her chest, closer to her heart.

Reality hit him. Knowing his family was safe, he now used the guise of scratching his nose to block the tears. "So, what happened?"

"It was all so fast. Ash and I were starting to prepare dinner. We're at the kitchen counter. I turned to open that one cabinet above the fridge and that's when I saw him. He was just standing there. On our back deck. Looking in. God, Frank. I don't even know how long he'd been watching us for." Abby folded in on herself, chilled to the bone, shivering. She whispered, "He had a gun,"

Frank closed his eyes, took several deep breaths. His wife was the spiritual one but he found himself saying a silent prayer of thanks. When he opened his eyes, he noticed something he hadn't seen before.

Across the yard, handcuffed and down on his knees, a man in a simple white T-shirt and frayed blue jeans faced the rear cinder block wall of the yard, his back to the bustling activity.

"He pointed the gun right at Ashley, Frank. I froze." Abby's crying had subsided but now intensified, her weeping more pained. "I couldn't do—anything. I just became paralyzed. He was pointing a gun at our child. At our Ashley. And I—didn't—couldn't move. Why didn't I? Why did I freeze?"

Frank kissed his wife and daughter, said, "You're both okay," then turned and, in three long strides, pounced on the handcuffed man. Evading the sea of outstretched arms, he shouted, "You son of a bitch!" and grabbed the man by his shirt collar, tearing it in the process.

"Detective Grace!" warned a distant voice.

Frank spun the intruder with such strength the man nearly stumbled over his own shackled ankles. Frank cocked his arm. The man cowered, tucked his head down like a turtle retreating into its shell.

Seconds before shattering this piece of shit's skull, Frank blinked twice. Two officers he didn't know subdued him, thereby saving the man's head. One of them said, "This guy says he knows you."

It was as if Frank had just woken, dangling between a hazy dream and a vivid reality. "I do. Name's Santiago Mendes."

"Sandy, please."

"What—what the hell is going on?"

At his side, Abby wrapped her arm around Frank's waist. "No, sweetie, it wasn't him."

Frank now noticed splotches of blood intermingled with grass stains on Mendes's clothes.

Abby took hold of Mendes's shoulder, an indebted smile crossing her face. "He's the one who saved us."

It all clicked. Santiago Mendes, father of Josefina, had visited Frank a week earlier at West Bureau. He was thanking the detective for trying to help his daughter get back on the proper path. He'd given Frank his card—Sandy's Tree Trimming. Since Frank loathed landscaping and yard work, he contacted Mendes to utilize his services.

Still processing, Frank asked, "Is that true?"

"Si, Senor Grace. I was adjusting one of your sprinkler heads. Those azaleas are dying. I looked up and saw the hombre in your door. I—I didn't think. I just acted."

Frank gulped, deeply moved by the courageous act. Santiago Mendes acted bravely, putting his life at risk to save a family he didn't know, to save strangers. Frank recalled something else Mendes mentioned during their previous meeting. He firmly shook the hero's hand and nodded. "You would've made a helluva fine police officer."

Mendes's eyes softened. He dropped his head. Like Frank, he was clearly uncomfortable receiving praise. "Gracias," he whispered softly.

"Release him and get him checked out," Frank ordered to anyone within earshot. He then stole a glance at Abby who now leaned into Santiago and, in spite of his dirty attire, hugged the man gratefully. When she pulled away, Frank asked his wife, "Was it Xavier Leach?"

Abby nodded twice, trembled once. "Yeah."

Frank looked around, taking it all in. This was the second time the Leaches brought violence to his home and to his family. There wouldn't a third.

He turned to see his daughter awkwardly cornered by a police psychiatrist who just arrived. Jake was safe—well, safe as anyone could be with arithmetic—Mendes was a hero and, with the exception of a few bruises, uninjured. Leach escaped. But Sergeant Lindstrom claimed one person was down. *Who?*

Frank kissed his wife, tousled his daughter's hair, and strolled to the front lawn. Coming around, he sidestepped the active scene and the questions shouted at him from reporters now gathering across the street. His legs stopped moving. He became stock-still, staring at what he saw.

A paramedic made a futile attempt. A final series of chest compressions. Then he stopped and gently lowered the victim's eyelids with his palm. Wiping away perspiration, and weak from efforts to save the individual, he rose slowly and shook his head at his partner. Frank moved closer to the corpse. Hair was matted, mouth agape, the left side of his head obliterated from a high caliber bullet.

"Excuse us," said someone from the coroner's office as they wheeled a gurney past Frank and collapsed the legs. The sound of a body bag being zipped was unique and something Frank never liked hearing. He stepped back and watched somberly as Officer Newsted's corpse was placed in the rear of the morgue van. Just days ago Frank invited the young officer to join them in a family basketball game. Now he was dead.

"Damn shame," remarked someone Frank didn't know. "Wife's due with their first kid next month."

Frank couldn't respond. There were no words.

Chapter 27

"Thank you, Sheila."

Blake Finch's synthetic sneer morphed into a tight-jawed countenance as he peered into the camera. The green screen beyond his shoulder displayed an over-the-top caricature of the reporter with his mouth wide open. *Blake's Take* appeared below. Finch had been in broadcasting long enough to realize his viewers—and Americans in general—had short attention spans. To seize their interest, he needed a powerful opener. Tonight's editorial was no exception.

"Frank Grace, my friends. What exactly does this *detective* have on our police chief? Why is he allowed to remain part of those who protect and defend us, while his track record with the LAPD is a blood-soaked trail of miscues, missteps, and monumental mistakes?"

Finch's accusatory tone was now a voice-over as images of Il Vittorios, both before and after the Azusa bloodbath, appeared. Footage revealed a now empty lot—the restaurant having since been razed. Pictures scrolled as Finch chastised Frank. Grieving parents of the thugs Frank gunned down was shown, videotape of Frank avoiding reporters' questions years earlier, hiding his face behind his hand, scenes from funerals of those murdered in the West Hollywood explosion were sandwiched with file photos of wineries, wanted posters of the Leach brothers, and generic videos of police brutality—the brutality clips were not related to the LAPD. A minor infraction really—Finch's powerful message trumped journalistic integrity.

"I've spoken out against the LAPD repeatedly, as you are all aware. Many of you have written and accused me of biased reporting. I appreciate the criticisms. I actually welcome said criticism. I will admit, for the record, that the police do an admirable job of keeping us safe. I applaud their efforts and tip my cap." Finch mockingly doffed an imaginary hat. "But for all of the positives our policemen and policewomen achieve, it's consistently undermined by one unpredictable and unstable individual, the reckless and feckless Frank Grace."

Finch paused theatrically and bore his gaze into the camera now that the slideshow ended. "Our fine and beautiful Los Angeles recently joined the union of other cities struck by terrorism. Two men were wanted for questioning. One young man, Elijah Leach, was located to the north in a Paso Robles winery. Yet, somehow—and think about this my friends—a known and wanted terrorist handcuffed, in custody, and already detained, about to be placed into our justice system so he could receive a fair trial, somehow got assassinated. Hmm. Consider that. Arrested, detained, handcuffed, defenseless. And somehow, *somehow*, Mr. Leach gets executed. And again, Detective Grace's fingerprints are at the murder scene. Just before we came on air this evening, he is *yet again* embroiled in controversy. Details will be forthcoming in this rapidly developing story. What we can confirm is there was a shooting at the detective's residence. Perhaps his spouse burned dinner? Maybe a neighbor's dog relieved itself in his front yard. Nothing is out of the realm of possibility when it comes to a trigger-happy officer with a checkered past."

Finch let that linger in the air before wrapping up. "I approve of the work of our police force. I definitely appreciate anyone putting themselves in harm's way, risking their own life and their own safety, for the general public. But they are people, not superheroes. They are fallible. They certainly are human. And as such, they make mistakes. But this reporter believes Detective Grace has far surpassed his chances of allowable miscues. One mistake is acceptable. Numerous blunders exhibit a pattern of ineptitude. I therefore implore Police Chief Weldon Kent to terminate this so-called detective at once. Frank Grace claims to protect *us*. But who is protecting *us* from *him*? And that's Blake's Take. Sheila."

"Thank you, Blake. Jim?"

"Thank you, Sheila," Jim said, taking the handoff. "Remember to tune in at eleven. We'll have the latest on the salmonella outbreak at two local amusement parks, an update on the Ontario middle school teacher arrested in a hotel room with one of her students, a string of violent home invasions in Chino. And our own Hank Sugars tries out for the upcoming season of *The Nut House*. Thanks for watching. Good evening."

As the studio lights dulled, Jim unclipped the mike from his lapel. "Pretty tough op-ed piece, Blake. Grace piss in your corn flakes?"

Blake sneered. He was well on his way to replacing the archaic *Jim-asaurus* behind the anchor desk. "It's all about ratings, Jimbo."

Blake trudged to his offset workspace and quickly signed online to gage the response to his verbal flogging. It was about sixty-forty in support with more tweets, Facebook posts, and comments on the station's website coming in.

He called his wife. Thank God she wasn't picking up. The whiny screech on her voicemail grated on his nerves like fingers on a chalkboard. He advised her he'd be home late. As an afterthought, he added, "Give the kids a hug." He then dialed another number where he was greeted by a sensuous sultry tone on voicemail, the antithesis of his wife's vexing backwoods drawl.

Just hearing the inflection in Desiree's tone caused a stirring. She probably couldn't get to the phone because her husband was close by. Finch expressed his desire to see her this evening and offered a few options where they could rendezvous.

In his heart, Finch knew a hayseed from Bumfuck, Idaho like himself would never bed a hot piece like Desiree. It was mutual. She liked the excitement of having an affair with a big time reporter.

Watching Blake on TV with her husband at her side added to the kinkiness.

"Call me, Des. I've got a few things in mind for tonight." He ended the call, stretched, and again checked feedback online. When his phone clanged he lifted it quickly, anticipating the sexy voice that went with that killer rack. "Blake Finch."

No reply.

"Blake Finch. Hello."

"*The* Blake Finch?"

"The one and only."

"*The* Blake Finch whose got a hard-on for bringing down the LAPD?"

Finch checked the caller ID. *Restricted.* "*The* Blake Finch who has the veracity to question the PD when they act irresponsibly, yes. Who is this?"

"You're a credit to the profession."

"Thank you. I didn't get your name."

"Idaho to Los Angeles. Still wanting more?"

A bit uneasy, Finch moved in his seat. He considered the possibility he was speaking with Desiree's husband, whatever the fool's name was. "How can I help you?"

"Want to move up? Want the mother of all exclusives?"

"I'm listening."

"Woodward. Bernstein. Novak. Murrow. Cronkite. Finch."

Finch's laugh was not based in humor. "I must say you have my attention."

"Got something to write with?"

"Yes," Finch replied slowly. He jotted down an address, circled *midnight* several times.

"You come alone tonight, Finch, and this time next year you'll have a Pulitzer on your mantel."

ↁↁↁ

Since moving to Los Angeles, Finch had made five trips across the desert for weekend getaways to Vegas. One with his wife, four with Desiree. In spite of several road trips, he never noticed the abandoned water park until now.

Newberry Springs was a one-exit unincorporated town at the halfway point between Sin City and the City of Angels. In the late-fifties, Lake Dolores Waterpark first appeared, billed as "The Fun Spot in the Desert." In 1990, the park was sold to a group of investors who refurbished the grounds, decided on a retro theme, and rechristened it Rock-A-Hoola Waterpark. Music from a bygone era emanated through speakers across the desert oasis. Eventually, tourists stopped coming, too rushed to reach either LA or Vegas. Time, unrelenting heat of the Mojave Desert, and vandals with spray cans left the one time tourist attraction in ruins.

Exiting his Infiniti, Finch glimpsed his watch. Just after midnight. He hoped his contact had not left. He saw no other vehicles. The only sound on the desert floor was cars whizzing along I-15 and defiant rustling of fronds from dying palm trees losing their battle against the elements.

The once thriving waterpark had been mostly erased from the landscape. The few remaining structures were covered in doodles. Finch stepped away from his car and moved closer to where the park entrance once stood. He looked back, pursing his lips at the dead bugs that coated the grill of his precious ride.

Thwack. Thwack.

Finch whirled and gazed into the sinister night that blanketed the area. "Hello?"

No response. A second louder cry garnered the same stillness. Ears perked, he observed the thwacking was coming from a dangling slice of plastic scraping against the ground.

He began slogging into the forsaken parcel. His steps were light as if softer steps would protect his high-end Berluti loafers.

He didn't hear the man, didn't see him approaching through the obscurity. But he heard the breathing in his ear and felt something sharp pressed to his carotid artery.

"You come alone?"

Too terrified to speak, Finch barely nodded, but that only resulted in the blade pushing deeper into his neck. Mouth as dry as the desert he was part of, he managed a simple, "Uh huh."

The man held on a bit longer before releasing his grip. It took Finch a moment to realize he was free and he stepped forward. Spinning, he rubbed his neck, checking for punctures. He struggled to breathe while sizing up the furtive figure. There was no glow from the stars, no lights in the derelict park. But Finch felt his knees go weak, his legs becoming spaghetti. He'd been summoned to a long-since-forgotten spot in the middle of the desert by a killer. "What..." Finch gulped, tried to find the words, "What do you want, Mr. Leach."

"*Mr.* Leach? Nice touch." Xavier Leach was outfitted in head-to-toe black. Strips of light from headlights splintered his face, offering a hint of a fat lip and a purple shiner. The only bright object was the sheen of a menacingly sharp blade. "Take off your clothes."

"Pardon?"

Leach used the threatening stiletto as a pointer. "Take off your clothes. I need to verify you're not wired."

"I give you my word as a respected journalist and highly esteemed reporter I am not wired."

Leach arched a mocking brow.

Finch began undressing.

Down to his boxers, he was told, "Enough."

Finch remained motionless as the domestic terrorist

skulked around him. Not since that one night in college when he drank too much had he had another male stalk his frame in this method. He knew this time was different, confident he wouldn't wake up in the morning alongside another man wondering what the hell happened.

Satisfied the reporter was not bugged Leach took an at-ease position. He was far enough away to allow Finch a feeling of safety but close enough to swiftly cut him. "Are you a sellout?"

"Excuse me," Finch replied.

"I asked if you're a sellout."

"I don't understand."

"You clearly have an ax to grind with the LAPD. In that respect, Finch, we are very similar. You also have this borderline infatuation with bringing down the department. Again, we share a common purpose."

Finch tasted bile in the back of his throat. Being told—and correctly so—that he, a prized member of the media, had commonality with a cold blooded fanatic caused his stomach to flop.

"Perhaps we can help one another," Leach suggested. "Interested?"

Finch went for humor. "You have a pretty big blade there, Mr. Leach. Of course, I'll listen."

Leach didn't find it funny. Finch wondered when, if ever, the man last smiled.

"You obviously want to keep your career on an upward path. Idaho to LA. CNN or the *New York Times* next on your agenda?"

Finch flashed an awkward grin, confused but intrigued.

"I help you. You help me," Leach declared.

"What—what would you like?"

"I've got one hell of a story to tell, a stop-the-presses as they used to say. I share your hatred and distrust for the LAPD. Yours, however, is unfounded. Mine is grounded in realism."

Finch remained silent.

"I will turn myself in. Tomorrow. Noon. At your TV station. You'll get the exclusive. I want you to report it live. You're my insurance to make sure I don't get executed before I can tell the truth." Leach used his knife hand to scratch the back of his head. In that instant he seemed worn. "It's a win-win. You get the story of a lifetime and a one way ticket to book tours and TV appearances. And I get to come clean. The people have a right to know."

"Right to know what?"

"The truth."

Finch chewed on his lips, his fear giving way to visions of Jimmy Fallon and Oprah. As an added bonus, his newfound celebrity status would seal the deal on a future with Desiree and her double-Ds. In the short-term, he'd get *Jimasarus* out from behind the anchor desk, *his* anchor desk. He considered the logistics. Breaking in for a live update would normally be problematic. But with wanted fugitive Xavier Leach turning himself in at KLAG studios with Blake Finch playing liaison, it would be a ratings bonanza and a one way ticket to the top. Finch raised his hand like a schoolboy. "Two points I'd like to be candid about, if that's okay?"

"Yes?"

"Am I correct in assuming that you'll use the opportunity to…well, preach your anti-establishment rhetoric from a soapbox?" Realizing he may have come on too strong, Finch walked it back. "I have nothing personal against you. As a journalist, I'm obliged to report both sides of a story, no matter how unpopular or extreme they may be. I just can't help but wonder if I'm being used as a pawn."

"What's your other question?"

Leach's refusal to answer was a non-confirmation confirmation. Finch realized he was possibly being played for a fool. He could worry about spinning that later. If not him, there were plenty of other news outlets in LA. "May I be blunt?"

Leach nodded.

"It's somewhat short-sighted. If you're worried about living long enough to share your story, the trial won't happen for months, a year maybe. Just 'cause you don't meet your demise tomorrow when arrested doesn't mean something unforeseen won't happen next week or next month."

"That's why I took out an insurance policy. Krissy Kent."

Finch's jaw dropped. "You're the one who kidnapped the police chief's daughter?"

"If something happens to me, she dies. If I don't live to see a courtroom, she dies."

"You really expect to keep her secreted away until your trial date sometime in the future?"

Leach's expression said it all. *Don't doubt me.* "I wanted to increase my coverage by taking the daughter of Detective Grace, but some beaner landscaper cold-cocked me." He pointed to his injuries.

"*You're* the one who murdered Officer Newsted?"

"The *police* murdered my brother."

Finch seemed vindicated. "Frank Grace did it? Frank Grace killed your brother? I knew it all along."

Leach ignored the question. "Speaking of, there's a catch."

"Oh—kay," Finch said.

"I'm turning myself into the custody of one man and one man only. Frank Grace."

Finch knitted his brows. "Why him?"

"It's flawlessly symmetrical. You detest Grace. Grace abhors me. And all three of us share a mutual suspicion about the LAPD. See you tomorrow morning."

And, with that, Xavier Leach turned and became swallowed by darkness.

Finch took one step toward his vehicle before stumbling face first onto the desert floor. He'd forgotten his pants were around his ankles.

As he dressed, he was perplexed about Leach's insistence on involving Grace. Then it dawned on him. Grace had killed Elijah. Perhaps not directly but he was involved to some degree.

Xavier's decision to turn himself in to only Frank Grace was indeed symmetrical. Xavier planned to exact revenge on Grace for killing Elijah. Frank Grace was getting summoned to his own execution, and it would all be caught on live TV.

Whoo boy, the ratings will be tremendous!

Chapter 28

The trio of baroque chandeliers suspended from the high ceiling was more for ambiance than practicality. Two sets of leather sofas sat on opposite ends of the sprawling lobby, a frail man waxed the Rosa Aurora marble tile. Mail boxes situated in a glass-enclosed foyer where a bulky suited man stood sentry. Faux fountains, marble statues, and what looked like expensive paintings rounded out the décor.

The concierge with a mannequin-like complexion advised the guests "I need to call ahead. Our residents are to be advised when they have a visitor."

"Make an exception this time," Frank advocated.

"Sir, I'm forbidden."

"Why don't you get some coffee?" Michelle suggested.

The man acknowledged a security camera bolted above. "Can't do it." He reached for the intercom phone.

Frank stealthily slid the corner of a fifty dollar bill from behind his badge. "You'll get this on our way out."

Mannequin-man surreptitiously nodded and granted them passage. In the elevator, with placid music melodiously filling the car, Michelle commented "A fifty?"

Frank grinned, reached behind his badge, and pulled out the corner. And nothing more. There was no bill.

As the door pinged open on the twenty-fourth floor Frank and Michelle stepped from the elevator into a serene environment. The hallway was lined with thick carpeting, ersatz lanterns, and different yet equally tranquil melodies. "You're probably digging these tunes, huh?" Michelle chided.

"I refuse to even dignify that with a response."

She turned left then right, upon verifying the unit numbers. "This way." Approaching the residence, Michelle found herself talking in a whisper, not wanting to disturb the peacefulness. "I think I'm in the wrong line of work. This place is…wow."

"But you love what you do, Detective."

"True. But you wouldn't think *entertaining* could get you a high rise condo overlooking the Pacific."

"She must be good," Frank remarked as he knuckled the door and took position in plain view of a high-tech peephole.

Hearing a sound indicating they were being observed, Frank smiled. "It's Detectives Grace and Santana."

Hiromi Komatsu opened the door with a flourish and presented a sincere smile. "What a pleasant surprise." She wore a teal sports bra over full breasts that looked a touch too buxom for her five-three frame. A white headband, tight-fitting black cargo pants, and pink Nikes rounded out her outfit.

"Can we have a few minutes of your time?" Frank asked. His mouth had gone dry.

"You saved my life, Detectives. Of course you can. I was just about to start my routine."

Hiromi's condo was sparsely furnished but what she possessed were high-end items, primarily white and immaculate. She motioned for the detectives to follow. Michelle did a double take through the bay window that offered a spectacular ocean view. Frank, on the other hand, labored to draw his gaze away from Hiromi's taut body.

"You can stop holding in your gut," Michelle whispered.

The workout room was a combination office/fitness center: treadmill, stationary bike, mats, free-weights and a row-ing machine. Hiromi stepped onto the Nordic Track, adjusted some settings, and began jogging. "Do you work out?" she asked, looking at vigorous Michelle, not paunchy Frank.

"Not as much as I should."

"Really? You look buff, Detective Santana."

"Good genes, I guess."

"I'd say," Hiromi winked bewitchingly. "'Fitness—if it came in a bottle, everyone would have a great body.'"

"Shaun Thompson?" Michelle asked.

"No, Cher."

As Hiromi began her regimen, eyes staring at the muted TV, she started reaching for her iPod before remembering she had guests. "You wanted to talk?"

Cotton mouthed, Frank was distracted by the quasi-erotic gyrations of the molded goddess running in place. Noticing her partners' inability to suppress adolescent thoughts, Michelle took control. "How are you managing?"

"Considering what I went through, pretty well. I wasn't a prisoner as long as the other two. I've always been able to compartmentalize. It happened. It's done. No sense dwelling on it. Time to move forward." She modified some settings. The belt moved faster and she picked up the pace. Sweat beaded her neck. "You can cheat on your partner, but not on your workout."

Idle banter was exchanged for a few moments, mostly between Michelle and Hiromi. Frank threw in the occasional *uh-huh* just to appear involved. Watching the spirited Hiromi move in pseudo-sexual style made Frank forget why they were here.

Men. "My partner and I were wondering about something," Michelle said.

Looking at the TV, Hiromi didn't catch Frank being elbowed by his partner. Coming here was Frank's idea and it was time he stepped up. "Detective?" Michelle quipped, trying to remind him he was a police officer.

"Oh, uh, yes...Ms. Komatsu—"

"Hiromi."

"Hiromi. That's a lovely name by the way."

"It means widespread beauty."

"I'm not surprised."

Hiromi hadn't paid much attention to Santana's partner until now. He wasn't the kind of guy worthy of a second look. A slight pot belly, a touch of gray around his temples and posture not the best. But there was something semi-intriguing about him. Hiromi was blessed with the innate ability to read people, physically and financially, and then discuss brass tacks. She noticed a wedding ring and pegged him to be early-forties, probably a couple kids, quaint home, and a conservative sedan. A good man, doing good things. He'd be the type to pay for good dinner conversation, not services rendered. "Frank. What's *your* name mean?"

"'I'm American, honey. Our names don't mean shit.' Bruce Willis, *Pulp Fiction*."

"Oh, I *love* that film!" Hiromi shrieked.

"Me too!" He rocked on the balls of his feet, puffed out his chest and gave Michelle a look. *See, we do have something in common.*

Michelle rolled her eyes. "My partner was a bit confused about something."

"He was?" Hiromi asked, now looking at Frank.

"Yes," Michelle said. "Detective, why don't you explain?"

There was a pause before he refocused. "There were three individuals kidnapped by the Leach brothers. A detective, a judge, and yourself. They also made an attempt on my life, my family. Twice now. And broke into my partner's home as well."

Hiromi appeared concerned. "Is everyone okay?"

"Yes, thanks for asking. All victims are connected to law enforcement. Except for yourself."

"And your point is?"

"I'm wondering if you have any idea, Hiromi, why you'd be targeted. You're the exception." Frank was hoping Hiromi would validate the theory he'd formulated.

"Because of how I earn my living?"

"Well…yes."

"'Cause I'm not, oh, a pillar of society?"

Frank waited.

A smile of both confidence and innocence crossed her face. Hiromi drew her eyes away, as if the proper words would appear onscreen. As Racheal Ray whipped up a helping of chicken and ham rolls, she explained. "I have an exclusive clientele I cater to. I offer more than a service. I provide good dialogue, confidential encounters, enjoyable evenings. I'm a paramour, not a high-class prostitute. I've never rolled anyone or left anyone unsatisfied. You get what you pay for. Class, elegance, and a wondrous evening."

"I see," Frank replied. And he did.

"I don't simply spread for bread. It's a GFE."

"GFE?" Michelle inquired.

"Girlfriend experience. Kissing—on the lips. Not a fuck."

Frank raised his palms. "I'm not casting aspersions, Hiromi. But why do you think you'd be linked with the others?"

Hiromi kicked that around. She wasn't Heidi Fleiss. She'd never blackmail her clients, many of whom *were* pillars of society. Discretion was her *second* greatest gift. But after the abduction, she felt confident he'd never call her again. "If you're asking have I ever spent evenings and, yes, weekends out of town with the honorable Earl Sherman, the answer is yes."

"Thank you, Hiromi." Frank eyed Michelle, his belief now confirmed. Sherman's philandering was well known. When Frank first proposed his outlandish idea, his partner blew him off. Hiromi's admission of a relationship with Judge Sherman slid one more piece of the puzzle into place. Before Frank could follow-up, his phone chirped. "Excuse me a moment."

"Sure."

Frank moved into the hallway and answered the *un-*

known number. Moments later, he returned. Hiromi, now off the treadmill, had a towel draped over her thin but well-developed shoulders and moved to the pads where she extended her toned legs. Fire in his eyes, he stated, "Detective Santana, we need to go. Thank you very much for your time, Hiromi. We'll be in touch."

Hiromi's expression was one of surprise with a splash of disappointment. She uncoiled herself and promenaded to Frank. A friendly grin appeared on her high cheekbones and perfectly rounded features. "Give me a call sometime, Frank. Maybe we can grab dinner or something."

"Uh…"

Michelle jumped in, announcing they'd let themselves out. In the hallway, she remarked, "Did you remember to pick your tongue up off the floor?"

Frank ignored her. "Xavier Leach is turning himself in."

Chapter 29

I don't like it," Michelle asserted after Frank informed her about his call from Blake Finch.

He moved into the left lane on the eastbound leg of the Ventura Freeway, stepped on the gas, and sped toward KLAG's studios in Burbank.

"I don't either but he *is* turning himself in."

Michelle checked the magazine in her Glock. "The guy's been on the lam. We've got no good leads. What about Kent's daughter? Krissy with him?"

"Finch didn't say."

"If Xavier thinks you murdered his brother, we could be walking into an ambush."

Frank shook his head. "He's in a TV studio. There are plenty of people around. Per Finch, Leach wants his arrest videoed. I guess that's his way of making a statement on live TV about not trusting the police. And society as a whole."

"I wonder if he's wired with explosives."

Frank smirked.

"It would make an even *bigger* statement to blow himself up on live TV and take out dozens with him."

Frank considered that before dismissing it. "The Leaches are anarchists, not terrorists willing to martyr themselves. They'll only go to a certain point for their cause."

"Hope you're right." She stared through the window in

silence, her thoughts drifting to her niece. She wanted this to end—now. In forty-eight hours, Sophia would be her responsibility. Having Leach in custody would make her feel less like a potential target. "If this truly ends today, it flies in the face of that crazy theory you concocted."

Frank cocked his head. "Trust me, I sure as hell hope I am wrong. If I'm right, then…" He couldn't finish.

Michelle took a deep breath. "Yup, I know." She glanced at the dashboard clock. "Golden Boy?"

"Wadkins says he's meeting us there." Frank sensed apprehension and explained his decision. "Call it a CYA. Paso Robles turned ugly. I doubt it will happen again, but if it does, I want Wadkins with me. He's got Kent's ear—for some reason—and, though I hate to admit it, I may need him to cover for me if things turn south again."

"I don't trust him."

"Agreed. But like they say, keep your friends close, right?"

Michelle twisted her lips before redirecting the conversation. "I wish we'd given Kent a heads-up. It'd be nice having extra hardware when we arrive. Last time we tried this without the feds, it didn't turn out well."

"Leach insisted it be this way."

"He's cornered in a studio. If the FBI, JTTF, Agent Stephens, and all her men show up, Leach can't run. He'll be cornered."

"Unless you're right, Michelle, and he is wired with explosives."

"Now I'm the one hoping I'm wrong."

"A studio full of hostages would turn bloody." He considered before concluding, "It'll be a clean and easy collar."

Michelle eyed her partner.

"Hopefully."

Shortly thereafter, Frank pulled to the guard shack. "Detective Grace to see Blake Finch." Assuming the rent-a-cop was unaware the most wanted man in America was on the premises, Frank chose to downplay the visit. The portly man flipped pages on a clipboard before raising the gate without a word.

Frank was pleased that the front of KLAG faced the main thoroughfare of Glen Oaks Blvd and was shielded by thick shrubbery. If Leach, for some reason, made a break for freedom, there'd be obstacles hindering his escape.

"Let's roll," Frank breathed after backing into a spot and exiting the car.

Wadkins was waiting. He moved closer, greeted them, and threw his thumb toward the studio. "He's here."

"You've seen him?" Michelle asked.

"No. But Finch confirmed he's on property."

"Unarmed?"

"I didn't ask a reporter to pat-down a fugitive, Santana."

"Well, I'm not thrilled about a possible set-up, Wadkins."

"Well, Santana, you can sit your pretty little buns right here and let me handle this."

"*We* called *you*," Michelle snapped.

Frank played peacemaker. "We're all here. Leach is inside. Let's not get in a pissing contest and screw up now, okay?"

Santana and Wadkins hesitated then nodded.

"Good." Frank took one step toward the entrance but was stopped by Wadkins.

"I have to call Finch."

"Huh?"

"They're going live once you both showed up. They want to film everything, starting when we first walk in."

Michelle seethed. "Jesus Christ!"

"Times we live in," Frank said. "This is the twenty first century's white Bronco."

☙❧

Weldon Kent was often accused of harboring a Napoleon

Complex. But as he sat in the conference room, he hated being made to feel small. He glowered at the expensive suits and Ivy League-educated feds. This was his city, his domain, his territory. Damn, it was even *his* conference room. Yet, he was downgraded like some rookie cop.

Scowling, he eyed the snooty interlopers who reduced him to insignificance. This was Los Angeles, for Christ's sake. He oversaw the third largest police force in the whole damn country. Yet, thirty minutes into today's bullshit brainstorming, he had yet to be acknowledged.

Agent Georgia Stephens sat, as expected, at the head of the enormous conference table worthy of a zip code. The fed went through the motions of asking for input, but Kent knew it was for naught. Stephens, who Kent was sure got the job due to the fact she was a woman, was a dictatorial tyrant. Kent could sense it. He chewed the hell out of Nicorette while shooting condescending looks at DC's best and brightest. He could wait. His day would come— eventually. His thoughts shifted to Charlotte and those statuesque legs. Say what you will about these DC public servants, none of them would be going home to a flexible former dancer.

Stephens lowered her reading glasses and opened a file containing the latest profile of Xavier Leach, when a harried looking pencil pusher scurried into the room. Stephens's expression of annoyance at the interruption changed into a look of confusion. "Are you sure?" she asked of her assistant.

The man nodded.

"What station?"

"All stations, Agent Stephens."

Stephens rubbed the bridge of her nose. "I've just been informed that Xavier Leach is turning himself in." Murmurs of confusion and disbelief filled the room. "Chief Kent?"

Kent sat up straighter. "Yes?" he asked enthusiastically.

Stephens pointed to the remote. "Kindly make yourself useful and turn on the TV."

Kent grunted. "Of course, your excellency."

ოჯო

Wearing his finest suit, Finch combed his hair one final time as the cameraman counted down. "Four, three, two…"

"Thank you, Jim. Ladies and gentlemen, residents of Los Angeles, citizens across southern California. I'm Blake Finch, broadcasting live with a KLAG exclusive. Here with me, outside our Burbank studio, are three officers of the first-rate Los Angeles Police Department."

The camera panned the trio.

"Detectives Troy Wadkins, Michelle Santana, and Frank Grace."

Frank remained stoic. Michelle pushed her tongue into her cheek. Wadkins flashed a smile that said *I'm ready for my close-up, Mr. Demille.*

"You heard me correct. Frank Grace, the officer who I've been quite critical of in my numerous editorials, is here as well."

Frank's gut tightened as Finch and his cameraman approached. "I'm sorry to hear about the shooting at your home yesterday, Detective Grace."

Frank nodded but said nothing.

"Is everyone okay?"

"Yes. Thanks for your concern," Frank said sardonically.

"We clearly view the role of law enforcement through different prisms, Detective Grace. I do applaud your fortitude to let bygones be bygones for the greater good of our citizens." Playing for the cameras, going for the Pulitzer and ultimately the national spotlight, Finch proffered his hand. Frank swallowed his disgust, accepted the olive branch.

Finch and his cameraman panned right. "Detective Santana."

Michelle stole a look at Frank. *Get me out of this.*

"In a matter of moments, you, along with these other fine

officers, will enter the KLAG studios and bring the most wanted man in America into custody."

If Michelle had her druthers, she'd bop Finch in his nose and get this dog-and-pony show over with. She detested journalistic sensationalism. Being unwittingly thrust into this luridness caused blood to course through her body like a raging fire. Returning the comment with equal cynicism, she announced, "That's quite correct, Blake. This is a huge day in the history of Los Angeles, as evidenced by the new wardrobe you purchased for this special occasion."

Ignoring the sleight, Finch asked, "Do you feel that your role in the apprehension of one Mr. Leach will advance the opportunities for women in law enforcement across our nation?"

She feigned thoughtfulness. "I haven't considered that, Blake. But now that you mention it…well, I think I'll take this opportunity to announce my candidacy for senator from the great state of California."

The cameraman couldn't help but laugh. Wadkins also chuckled. Frank smiled broadly. *That's my partner.* Undeterred, Finch looked into the lens. "And there you have it. Yet another KLAG exclusive courtesy of me, Blake Finch."

The three ring circus now centered on Wadkins as he downed an Altoid nanoseconds before his big moment. If anyone appeared to be seeking political office, it was he. With poise, professionalism, and moxie, Wadkins thanked everyone on the planet. It came off more like an acceptance speech at the Academy Awards than a *pre-game show* arresting a wanted killer. He gave a shout-out to every federal agency involved, making sure to point out that, although it was the LAPD physically bringing Leach into custody, it was a team effort. He thanked the public for their vigilance and standing proud in the face of horrific brutality, Chief Weldon Kent being his role model, and of course the grit of Blake Finch and KLAG as a whole. He also thanked his wife, Melina, a former Laker girl, for making him a better man and giving him beautiful children. Finch pulled the mike back but Wadkins added as an afterthought, "And also, I'd like to thank Detectives Grace and Santana for backing me up."

Frank and Michelle eyed each other. The purpose was to arrest Xavier Leach without incident. And allow the city to return to pre-terrorism calmness. It didn't matter which organization—local or federal—achieved this. It perturbed them that Wadkins had reduced them to a support role. On the other hand, by assuming the principal role, if things somehow turned to shit, the focus would be on Wadkins, not Frank.

With Blake Finch in front and the cameraman bringing up the rear, the trio of detectives—Wadkins leading—were filmed marching through the halls. It was obvious to Frank that they were guided in a circuitous path through the labyrinth of corridors. The reason was simple: drag it out as long as possible for better ratings.

Standing outside a nondescript paneled door, Finch spoke some final words to his viewers. He pushed open the door then rapidly stepped aside, granting access for the cops. There was no way in hell he'd walk into a room with a killer.

The room had been stripped of all furniture. The walls barren except for prominently displayed KLAG banners. This was a moment in TV history like no other, and the station would be affiliated with it for all eternity.

Wadkins, Grace, and Santana spread out. Leach turned from the window he'd been daydreaming through. He wore a black denim jacket over a white T-shirt, jeans, and sneakers. Plain. His face exhibited self-assurance.

"Xavier Leach," Frank announced. "You're under arrest."

Leach nodded once and began moving his hands toward his jacket.

"Slow, Leach! Keep your hands in sight!" Wadkins commanded, coming up on Leach's six, opposite Frank.

Michelle was on point by the doorway. Hand at her side,

fingers twitching close to her Glock, she moved only her eyes. If Leach made one false move, it'd be her task to take him down.

The arrest was textbook. Frank Mirandized him. Wadkins cuffed him and handled him gentler than he wanted, due to the glare of the camera. It would make the police chief proud and left no gray areas for anti-cop bloggers. The perp-walk through the hall was recorded by the backpedaling cameraman. Leach, his smile somewhat goofy and reminiscent of his brother, was sandwiched between Wadkins and Grace with Santana trailing behind and Finch safely in the rear.

Once outside, the lunchtime air was sliced by the rotor wash of two news choppers overhead. KLAG may have the exclusive, but following the procession downtown was open season. Frank glanced up. *White Bronco indeed.*

As the trio of detectives guided Leach across the lot, the cameraman stood steadfast at the entrance. The position afforded him a prominent view of a terrorist being arrested with KLAG banners draped from lampposts in the backdrop. Like Finch, he too was determined to win a Pulitzer.

Frank hustled forward and opened the rear door to his Chrysler-something. Wadkins steered Leach around him and went toward his Beemer.

"Um, Detective Wadkins?"

Wadkins turned and sighed. "Yes?"

"The perp insisted on turning himself in to me."

Wadkins rolled his eyes. "And he did. But I'll bring him in myself."

"Troy—"

Wadkins stepped closer, keeping Leach at his side and said in a hushed tone, "Look, Grace, let's cut the shit, all right. We both know how Chief Kent feels about me. And how he feels about you. You were the opening act but this is my show. I'm the star." He threw his chin toward the cameraman forty yards away. "Don't cause a scene."

Frank knew it'd be a media circus downtown. National

networks, local affiliates, reporters and bloggers every-where. And Detective Wadkins would be the one bringing in the man who had terrorized a city. Then again, as long as Xavier Leach was brought into custody, it really didn't matter which detective did it.

Frank had had enough of the spotlight four years ago. "Fine."

Wadkins sneered. "I really don't care if you're fine with it or not. Now, do a good job and bring up my rear." He jostled Leach toward his vehicle.

Leach, however, stood his ground and scowled at Frank. "Too bad my brother missed putting a bullet through your wife's pretty head. Maybe some other time, Herr Grace."

Frank took the bait. "That's one thing you don't have too many of. Tomorrows. I can't *wait* to see you fry, shithead."

Unfazed, Leach turned the verbal assault on Michelle. "Still got that duplex in Sherman Oaks, bitch?"

"Where's Krissy Kent?" Michelle clipped.

"Not until I get my day in court."

"You're a fool, Leach," Wadkins interjected. "You honestly think we won't find her? We have ways to get information out of you. And if not us, how's the F-B-fucking-I sound?"

"Typical dumb cop. Missing the big picture."

"What's that mean?" Wadkins snorted.

"You'll see. You'll all see. I am but one spoke in a large wheel."

Michelle looked at her partner, the color drained from her face. *Maybe you're right after all.*

"No," Wadkins said. "You are but a piece of trash, soon to be in a very small cell for a very long time."

"Speaking of long, I've got something long for your Laker wife."

Leach was handcuffed, helpless, and outmanned three-to-one. Yet, he maintained the upper hand.

"In the car, dickwad," Wadkins ordered.

Unconcerned with the camera crew, Kent's Golden Boy

belligerently tossed his prisoner in the rear seat. Frank and Michelle scooted to his Chrysler. By the time the pair of automobiles exited KLAG, a third and fourth chopper joined the aerial patrol. Pulling onto Glen Oaks Blvd, Frank drew close to Wadkins's rear bumper. From his vantage point, he could see Leach's head bobbing in antagonistic fashion, clearly taunting Wadkins. Frank chuckled, relieved it was Wadkins taking him in. Perhaps Leach would bring down the smug detective a few rungs.

With relief in her voice, Michelle called in. "Ten-fifteen, prisoner in custody. I say again, prisoner in custody."

Her transmission was confirmed, along with, "Nice work detective."

"Ten-four." Michelle inhaled, blew it out slowly, and looked cautiously at Frank.

"Wadkins is taking the Five downtown."

Reading her partner's thoughts, Michelle communicated an eleven-fifty-one, police escort. America's most wanted terrorist was fifteen minutes shy of being booked before ultimately handed over to the feds. Frank didn't want the arrest of another Leach screwed up.

Wadkins turned left at the intersection of Olive and First Streets and headed south. The freeway entrance ramp was one block away. Frank followed.

Wadkins' BMW moved to the right lane. The directional came on.

And then he shot through the intersection, leaving Frank's Chrysler in a cloud of burned rubber.

"What the—"

Frank tramped the gas and tore through the intersection. In his periphery, the enormous front grill of a city bus bore down on his side of the vehicle. He jerked the wheel, the car fishtailed.

Behind them the sound of twisted metal was heard.

Michelle looked back. The bus rear-ended a pick-up, shoving an F-150 into a second sedan.

A full block ahead Frank saw cars swerving, everyone

trying to avoid the out of control BMW rocketing down the street. One car veered into oncoming traffic, colliding head-on into a small Hybrid. A full-size Chevy leapt the curb and plowed into a bus stop, sending people diving for safety. The Beemer zigged and zagged between slow-moving vehicles. Cars had stopped every which way in the middle of the street. Motorists getting out and already on their phones, either calling nine-one-one, their insurance company, or, more likely, filming the event in the hope it would go viral.

Frank tugged the wheel left, crossed the double line, and floored it, speeding directly into oncoming traffic and channeling his inner Popeye Doyle in *The French Connection.*

Horns blared. Tires squealed. Profanities screamed. Middle fingers went up. Frank's foot tap-danced between the gas and brake.

He cut the distance in half, crossed back with the flow of traffic, and advanced closer to Wadkins and Leach. He heard Michelle call it in, heard her say something. But it was white noise. Frank was on the BMW's tail, mere feet between the two speeding cars, zig-zagging wildly like on a slalom course. He saw a struggle going on. Leach leaning over the front seat fighting to gain control of the car, Wadkins attempting to fight him off while maintaining control of the speeding vehicle and not injuring any pedestrians.

Wadkins's car swung hard right, swerved left, overcorrected. Motorists attempted to steer clear of the erratic driver. The Beemer lurched right, became a thirty-five hundred pound projectile as it jumped the curb, obliterating a mail box in the process, hurtling across a parking lot and rocketing through the lobby of a Residence Inn.

"Shit, shit, shit." Frank followed Wadkins's trail of destruction and screeched to a halt. Dazed hotel guests staggered from the destruction, stepping through a gaping hole where the hotel's entrance had been obliterated. They were shaking shards of glass from their hair and clothes. A valet rolled around in pain, screaming and clutching his leg. A guest squatted over him urging him to stay calm.

Grace and Santana lunged from the loaner, drew their weapons, and approached.

"Wadkins!" Frank shouted.

The sweet odor of leaking gasoline swathed the hotel lobby. A thunderous blast knocked Michelle onto her backside and Frank to one knee. The Beemer's rear window exploded, raining a thirty yard area in a deluge of glass. Flames burst forth from the engine. The stench of burned rubber choked the air.

Shielding his face with one hand, Beretta clutched in his other, Frank advanced on the demolished vehicle that plowed halfway through the lobby before coming to a stop at a fountain.

Wadkins toppled out. Bent over, coughing up a lung, he staggered toward Frank. As Michelle ushered guests and employees to safety, Frank yanked hard to open the jammed rear door.

"Bastard broke free. He leaned over and went for my gun, Grace."

The door yielded. Frank lifted the handle and with heat mounting, fearing a greater explosion, flames engulfing the front seat, the air became heavy. Hard to breathe.

"I didn't have a choice. He grabbed my piece."

Leach was sprawled across the backseat and nonresponsive. Frank holstered his weapon, grabbed hold of Leach's shins, and wrenched him free. He heaved the terrorist over his shoulder and carried him away from the demolished vehicle.

"He went for my piece!" Wadkins claimed again.

Outside, lungs searing, Frank dropped to his haunches. He lowered Leach onto the asphalt.

"Stay clear," Michelle ordered the hysterical crowd and then approached her colleagues. "Eleven-forty-one?" *Ambulance needed.*

Frank placed his ear to Xavier's chest. Then, he looked at Michelle and shook his head once. "Eleven-forty-four." *Coroner requested.*

During the frenzied scene and chaotic rescue, Frank hadn't noticed it until now. Blood was congealing at an entry wound between Leach's eyes. Frank looked at Wadkins.

"He went for my piece, Grace. I had no choice."

Krissy Kent was buried five days later.

Chapter 30

Nearly twelve hundred mourners attended the service for Chief Kent's daughter, not including the throng of media prohibited from entering Forest Lawn.

Capitalizing on humanity's morbid curiosity, a news chopper circled before being escorted away by a second helicopter, this one operated by the LAPD. The two extremists who terrorized the city were dead. All of the fatalities from the initial West Hollywood attack had been interred. Kendra Nichols, Earl Sherman, and Hiromi Komatsu were freed. Krissy's funeral was the exclamation point on two weeks that paralyzed a city. After today, attention would be shifted elsewhere.

Many in attendance never met the girl and knew nothing of her, other than who her father was. Street cops arrived in uniform to pay their respects. Detectives and higher-ups from across Southern California dressed in black. The only item more gut-wrenching than laying one of their own to rest was saying goodbye to a child of one of their own. Christmas Jewel Kent had been a pawn, sacrificed and ensnared in something not of her doing. She paid the ultimate price.

Michelle, in a black dress that hung below her knees, black shoes, black stockings, and a black shawl, stood with her partner. Frank, sporting a charcoal suit, black tie, white shirt, and polished shoes, was grim, somber. Once more, he'd been wedged in controversy. Although it was Wadkins who lost a Leach this time, Frank was again close by.

Where is Wadkins anyway?

The minister blathered on. His rote words, hindered by the Santa Ana winds, were muffled through speakers set up to accommodate the teeming crowd.

In spite of an immense joint effort by local and federal authorities to locate Krissy after Xavier's death, it was a group of high school kids who stumbled upon her. Armed with cases of beer and marijuana, the teenagers were scouring an isolated section of Griffith Park. Seeking privacy, they entered a long forgotten shotgun shack. Inside, they discovered her corpse.

Upon the priest's final words, Kent immediately lit up. Smoking was prohibited on the grounds, but being police chief had its perks. Some funeral-goers gradually departed while others formed a line to express condolences. Kent wore an open collared shirt, suit jacket, black slacks, and an expression of heartache. Charlotte's dress, Frank thought, was too snug to her hips, the mid-thigh length too short.

Frank took his place at the end of the procession. Michelle stood for a moment before skulking away. "You're not coming?"

Forlornly, Michelle gazed down the knoll toward Covenant Way. Unlike the immaculate hillside with well-maintained headstones, the section she now viewed was filled with simple markers tightly cluttered. "It's been too long. I'm gonna go see my brother."

Kent was on auto-pilot. The endless sea of handshakes and tired clichés about Krissy being in a better place flowed in an endless stream of ambiguity. When the chief noticed Frank near the rear of the line, he summoned him forward.

Frank hesitated at first, unsure if Kent was signaling him. He confirmed and walked over. Shaking the commissioner's hand, he wanted to say something less generic. But all he heard himself utter was, "I'm sorry."

Kent spoke mechanically, his typical gruff hoarseness

now a weak outbreath. "She loved those *Fast and Furious* movies. Me? Never got into 'em." A tear trickled down his cheek but he quickly dabbed it away. The police chief was not supposed to have feelings. "She tried to get me to watch them but…" He shrugged. "I always had something else to do. I was always too busy, too damn busy. I always thought there'd be time."

Frank lowered his head.

Kent threw his chin forward. "That Paul Walker fella? He's buried right over there. Hope Krissy appreciates it."

"I'm sure she would, sir."

Kent eyed the casket. "That's—that's my little girl in that—that box."

Frank swallowed hard, refusing to acknowledge the bronze coffin laced with angels and a representation of Jesus on top. He recalled the afternoon Xavier Leach visited his home and pointed a gun at Ashley, *his* little girl. "If there's anything you need, sir, or you, Mrs. Kent, please."

"You've done enough," Kent replied.

Frank didn't know what to make of that.

Charlotte's embrace caught Frank off guard. Despite the fact she just buried her husband's only child, the abundance of perfume seemed inappropriate. "Thank you for trying, Detective Grace. Weldon and I appreciate your efforts. We won't forget."

જેન્જ

"You okay?" Frank asked as they sat in traffic on the southbound 405.

Finally answering, Michelle mumbled in a sullen voice, "Fifteen. Diego was just fifteen. So long ago yet it seems like yesterday." She patted her red-rimmed eyes with a balled-up tissue. "I've forgotten so much about him. I don't even recall what his voice was like. Weird how time does that, huh?"

"Yep."

"I remember his handwriting." She sighed. "Man, it was dreadful. Mama always got on him for that. Strange. Strange what we remember and what we forget." She choked back tears. "I wouldn't recognize his voice but I remember his sloppy handwriting." Another long pause. "So…"

He touched her knee. "We don't need to discuss this now. Your head's elsewhere."

"I need my head in the present, not the past."

Frank waited a beat before wading into dangerous waters. "The good news is I'm right. The bad news is I wish I wasn't."

"It's not one hundred percent."

"No, but it's pretty close." Disappointingly, traffic was too heavy for Frank to remove his grip from the wheel and wring his hands as he put things together. "You know what I don't understand?"

"Why someone is *in* a movie but *on* a TV show?"

"That, too," he replied after some consideration. "Xavier kidnapped Krissy for nothing more than leverage, a bargaining chip. He wanted to use his arrest as…as a platform. When we were taking him in, he said we were missing the big picture. One spoke in a large wheel, remember?"

"Yes."

"Krissy was found in a torture box, a sweatbox, with one minuscule hole providing oxygen. The shack was chockfull of heating lamps, power supplied by a generator. The temperature in that cabin was what, one twenty two? And higher in the sweatbox."

"She dehydrated to death. Painful." Michelle shuddered. Recollections from Afghanistan flitted across her mind. "I've seen a lot, but that's not a pleasant way to go."

Frank exited the freeway and was grateful for the red light. He kneaded his hands. "Leach wouldn't face trial for eight months minimum, probably longer. He didn't want his bargaining chip dead. If Krissy *was* found dead, then his worst fears about being murdered while in custody would come to fruition.

He needed her alive, but since he turned himself in, someone else had to be involved to check on her. Food and what not."

"And while a lot of Griffith Park is uninhabited, it's still in the heart of the city," Michelle threw in. "Not some remote cabin up in the hills."

"Someone else is involved, like I've thought for a while."

"How do you want to move forward from here?"

Frank weighed that for a moment. "Slowly. I just need to confirm one or two more things."

"One step at a time," Michelle said.

"Like a mine field."

∽∽∽

The jet engines yanked Michelle back to attentiveness of her surroundings. "Why are we here anyway?"

"Something I remembered during the funeral." Frank pulled his car into a parking space facing the unremarkable brick building.

Michelle eyeballed the structure. "Bomb Detection K9 Unit?"

Frank climbed from the vehicle. Michelle followed and started toward the entrance.

"Not going in," Frank declared.

Michelle sidled alongside her partner and followed his line of sight at...*what?* She frowned at the insignia on the exterior wall. "Is this some Art Deco thing I'm missing?"

Frank squinted at the building. "I guess some effects of the concussion are still lingering. But during Krissy's funeral, I remembered where else I'd seen that same symbol." He pointed to a logo on the side of the building.

"Where?"

"In the back seat of the Leach's car, just before the explosion."

Chapter 31

Frank jerked awake with a start as a shadow moved across the living room.

"Did I startle you?"

He blinked away sleep and rose to embrace his wife. He glanced at the TV. *Everybody Loves Raymond* had given way to *Golden Girls.* "You startle me every day."

They held each other longer than usual, the remnants of the unsuccessful attack on their home still haunting the family. Frank's kiss was heartfelt, not programmed.

Abby smiled. "Did you do something I don't know about?"

"What, I can't compliment my better half?"

"I just finished a twelve-hour shift at the hospital, my hair's a mess, I'm beat, and I smell." She paused. "So, either you're hiding something or you're drunk."

"Drunk on love."

Abby playfully slapped his chest, slid achy feet from her sneakers, and plodded into the kitchen.

"Jake conked out before nine. Ash said she was going to be twittering."

Abby chuckled. "Tweeting."

"You say tomato, I say tom-ah-to. There's some left over pizza you can heat up."

"Frank!"

"Abby!"

"Pizza *again*? We talked about eating healthier."

Frank pointed up. "Don't blame me."

"God told you to order a pizza?"

"No, the kids did."

"Baby, I don't want them thinking they always get to eat crap when I'm not home."

"One of the toppings was pineapple. Pineapples are healthy, right?"

Abby yawned, slid the box from the fridge, lifted two slices, and put them on a paper towel. "What am I going to do with you?"

Frank slinked behind his wife and nuzzled her neck. "I can think of a few things."

Abby giggled as her knees weakened. "Jake's asleep?"

"Uh huh."

"You always know how to get me," she cooed, turning to face him.

"What can I say? I have a nurse fetish."

"Now, you tell me? *After* I bought that cheerleader ensemble for our anniversary?"

After making love, Frank lay in bed minding the ceiling fan spinning as quickly as his thoughts. He was oblivious to the Dodge Ram parked in the shadows outside his home.

⁊✺⁊

Wadkins sat meditatively in the gloom of his Simi Valley residence. A fixture from the hallway fragmented a beam of light across three items situated before him. With trembling fingers, he lifted the framed photograph of himself and Melina from their wedding day.

He hearkened back to happier times when their dreams seemed attainable and their innocence was still intact. He lowered it, placing it alongside the family Christmas photo from five months ago. They all seemed so happy, so cheerful, so perfect.

He noted the third object on the table, his fully loaded firearm.

His eyes unexpectedly welled up. Blinking away tears and analyzing the photos, he couldn't help but wonder how everything so wonderful had turned to shit.

There were two Troy Wadkins: One was brash, arrogant, and damn cocky. The other was an insecure confounded soul.

His swagger allowed him to get into bed with any female he chose. He'd been propositioned more times he could re-call. Yet, he never had caved. In spite of infinite offers, he remained faithful.

Melina, however, played by different rules.

Wadkins lifted his eyes when hearing a car in the street. When the vehicle passed, he swigged his beer, did a double-take at the gun, and stared at the clock over the sink. *Almost midnight.*

Somewhere, sometime, somehow, he lost his way. Many marriages ended in divorce. In others, infidelity was almost accepted. Couples dealt with betrayal and moved forward. A marital speed bump.

The first time he learned of Melina's infidelity, he sur-prisingly was not stunned. She, like him, was one of the beautiful people. She, like him, had individuals approaching her. Whereas he resisted the temptation, Melina did not. She radiated sex without trying to. Promiscuity and seductive-ness oozed from the pores of her goddess-like form. Twist-ed as it might be, he was initially aroused, knowing some-one else was banging his wife. In a perverted way, it stroked his ego, more proof that others envied him and coveted what he had.

Then one instance of recklessness became two, then a third. One-nighters attributed to an overabundance of alco-hol became weekend getaways and ongoing affairs. The titillating wore off. Melina would return home and curl up beside him in bed with residue of her other lovers.

It went from being a warped turn on to an acceptable

norm. They had two children together, a decent nest-egg, a moderate-sized home, and newer cars. So what if she was fucking other men? He'd still get his ration—now and then. Sharing Melina with faceless lovers was better than not having her at all.

He eyed the clock again, wondered who it was tonight. Would she be home soon? Would she return before dawn? Perhaps he'd again lie in bed with only memories of what his marriage had once been and what an ultimately screwed-up existence he had now.

Wadkins scooped his Beretta from the table, studied the family portrait. His children were asleep upstairs. Caressing the gun, stroking it affectionately, he regretted not having his kids spend the night with his parents. He shut his eyes and released the safety.

Thinking, thinking…

഑ഌ഑ഌ

He ignored the chiming, assuming it was part of his dream. When it was followed by a thundering knock that shattered the stillness, Wadkins straightened. Shaking away cobwebs, he stood and shuffled to the front door. Glancing over his shoulder, he realized his weapon had fallen from his grasp as he slept.

"Detective Wadkins?" asked one of the two officers from the portico.

He nodded.

"Troy?" asked the thinner of the two beat cops.

He didn't recognize this rookie, but the newbie obviously recognized him. Although he was not alert, Wadkins automatically flaunted his million-dollar smile.

"Sir," the first officer said. "A body was discovered earlier this evening matching…"

The officer continued speaking, but Wadkins paid no attention. Making a positive ID, gathering up belongings, and the rest of the routine was something Detective Wadkins knew all too well.

For the first time, he was on the receiving end of bad news. He listened mindlessly, looked at his wristwatch, and ached to turn back the hands of time.

Chapter 32

West Bureau Hollywood, like all precincts across Southern California, was covered in a blanket of lament. After Elijah and Xavier Leach were eliminated, and with the feds now back in DC where they belonged, the LAPD yearned for a much-needed lull. Granted, there'd always be crime, but a brief respite would be welcome.

The kidnapping of Detective Nichols, the murder of Chief Kent's daughter, the failed abduction of Frank Grace's daughter and possibly wife. Violence was hitting close to home. And now, Melina Wadkins, the wife of a well-known detective, was found dead. Family members of the LAPD had been targeted. And, as Frank glanced at Michelle, her anguish was blatant. Her niece was now in her care and living under her roof.

Two unidentified men who'd been caught on video surveillance in a swank nightclub with Melina were wanted for questioning. They were the last two individuals to see her alive before her body washed up.

"Mornin' Grantana," bellowed the perpetually upbeat Lorne Woolley. Woolley, Frank had heard, was quite the detective in his day. The man was pushing seventy, long since retired. But he enjoyed doing odds and ends around the Barn. His belly entered a room before the rest of him. He downed unhealthy food high in fat and cholesterol.

However, he was an avid churchgoer, free of vices, and had a childlike exuberance for pranks. Physically, the fact a man like this made it past forty was perplexing. His worry-free life and easygoing demeanor, not his diet, was what got him to an advanced age.

He was collecting donations. Despite Wadkins restricting Melina's funeral to close friends and family, Woolley was organizing a benefit. A barbeque, sack race, and bounce house was scheduled for the following weekend. "Who doesn't love a bounce house? It'll be a celebration of life."

Michelle arched a brow, first at Woolley then Frank. The corpulent "activities director" was a faithful servant to the Lord. "Death," he once said, "is a return home, something to be welcomed, a temporary good-bye." It was a charming notion, Michelle admitted, but she wasn't in any particular hurry. She removed a fifty and handed it over. Noticing the denomination, Frank matched it.

"Thanks, Grantana," Woolley said and lumbered away.

"There's fifty pissed away," Frank griped.

His outlandish presumption was hard to believe when Michelle first heard it. The murder of Melina Wadkins seemingly slammed the door on her partner's theory. Although he was not yet conceding, Michelle found it daunting to stand by him. They'd been a team two years and she never wavered in support for her partner. But this time, it was extreme. "The guy lost his wife. Cut him some slack."

Frank would've liked more support from his colleague, but he understood her skepticism. His head told him he was on to something but his heart hoped he was wrong. If he was correct, the whole thing stunk to high heaven. "I'm going to see Johnny."

"Frank." Michelle grasped his hand as he sauntered away. "Think of the ramifications. Once you open that door, are you willing to walk through?"

He departed without answering.

As usual *Cyberopolis* was an intimidating sea of technology beyond Frank's mental capacity.

"Johnny?" he said safely from the doorway.

"Frank, c'mon in. How's it hangin'?"

Frank entered Johnny's world. "If I'm wrong, I'll be the one hanging. Did you find it?"

From his wheelchair, Johnny snickered. "You doubt me?" He rustled papers and handed a couple of documents over. Before Frank could speak, Johnny raised his palms. "I don't want to know. I have no problems doing what I do, but hacking into one of our own?" He shook his head. "You're risking everything this time, aren't you?"

"Yup."

Frank walked out, where he was met by Michelle. She seized the papers from his hand. A drawn-out breath followed. "Let's go."

Always taken aback at how quickly her short legs moved, Frank caught up with her. "You don't have to put your ass on the line, Detective."

Marching toward the exit, Michelle said as much for herself as for her partner, "Yes, Frank, I do."

❧❦❧

The detectives sat outside the entrance to Bennie's Salvage Yard for over one hour. Five minutes before closing, knowing the staff would be eager to go home, they entered, feeling as if they stepped through a time machine. A MAC computer was the only hint of anything post-1950. The ruddy-faced man behind the counter dropped his shoulders and pointed to a wall-mounted clock with a classic T-Bird backdrop. "Jesus H. Christ on a cracker, could ya have possibly waited any longer?"

Frank made a show of looking at his watch. "Yes, three minutes. Want us to come back in two?"

The man who had *Bennie* stitched to his work shirt cursed under his breath. Red-faced, with a shock of bedraggled white hair, and blue workman clothes, he looked like an

American flag with a bad disposition. He folded his arms across his plump chest.

"You've got a car we need to get into," Michelle said.

"Now!" the man howled. "Now? Mahatma Gandhi on a popsicle stick, are you yankin' my chain?"

The stoic detectives remained silent.

"Abe Lincoln in a stovepipe hat, fine." The man angrily pulled a cumbersome flipchart with reports taken off an antiquated IBM.

Michelle leaned into her partner and aimed her chin at the antediluvian green and white reams of paper. "Right up your alley, isn't it, Detective Grace?"

Ignoring her quip, Frank placed his hands on the grungy countertop. "Blue BMW brought in six days ago. Registered owner is Troy Wadkins. Insurance company deemed it a total loss earlier today. We need to see it." This was the final piece of information Frank had gleamed from Johnny.

Bennie twisted the bulky flipchart one way then another, adjusted his reading glasses, and snorted when a receptionist announced, "It's five, I'm gone." He scribbled down the vehicle's location, pulled a crude map of the premises, and irritably circled the location of the auto in question in red six times. "Make it snappy. I ain't got all night."

Ten minutes later, Michelle leaned into the shell of what remained of Wadkins's singed BMW. The front and rear windshields had been blown out, coils present where upholstery had been, heat had morphed the dashboard into a tapestry of melted plastic.

"Moses in matzo ball soup, c'mon already!" shouted an exasperated Bennie, hustling over.

Frank ignored him and asked of his partner, "Got it?"

Seconds later, she nodded. "Got it."

By the time Bennie trudged over, the detectives had what they came for. Frank snickered. "Thanks for your hospitality."

"Yeah, whatever."

In the front seat of Michelle's Honda, she and Frank

huddled close. Johnny had educated Michelle how to upload data from the damaged GPS of a wrecked car. She had successfully downloaded the most recent thirty travel destinations from the GPS history onto her phone. She scrolled through each one meticulously. After reviewing all the addresses, Michelle was deflated. "It's not here."

"It's gotta be!"

"Frank, it's not."

He stared through the window, losing himself in his thoughts and doing a slow burn. He slammed his fist into the console.

"Hey, watch it! This is my car."

"Michelle, I'm not wrong this time. I can feel it."

She waited before doing a second run-through. The results were the same. "They're pretty much all local. Wadkins hasn't left the city recently."

"Unless he used his wife's car."

"Frank—Oh, never mind."

"What?"

"The Leaches are dead. Xavier tried to harm your family. Elijah broke into my home. But there's nothing here. It's a dead end."

Frank ignored his partner. "I've got one last place to look."

"I can't help you tonight." Michelle smiled sweetly. "Sophia and I are watching *Toy Story.*"

"Again?"

Michelle nodded sheepishly. "Lucky me, huh?"

"You love it, don't you?"

Michelle deliberated for a moment. "Yeah, I actually do."

"Good. That's nice."

"You've got Abby and the kids so it's old hat for you. For me, it's new. I like it. I like knowing someone depends on me, that someone needs me besides you and Lieutenant Gallardo. No offense."

"None taken. I understand."

A passing silence ended when Michelle clutched her partner's shoulder. "The Leaches of the world come and go. Families stay."

He exhaled. "You're right."

Michelle returned to West Hollywood, dropped Frank off at his loaner. He waved goodbye as his partner drove home to spend the evening with her niece. Frank called Abby. When he advised his wife he'd be working late, she was not happy.

☙❦❧

Hours after the sun was swallowed by the Pacific, Wadkins pulled the car into his driveway. He killed the engine but didn't immediately get out. Melina's perfume still lingered. He detected a hint of her shampoo on the headrest, an extra pair of her sunglasses hung from the visor. He had reluctantly adjusted the front seat, loath to make any changes. She was gone—murdered—but he felt even subtle changes would erase traces of her.

The insurance company deemed his BMW a total. Getting back his wife's Audi from forensics, he was glad to have any transportation. It felt comforting yet distressing, pleasing yet disagreeable, to be driving her car.

Wadkins enjoyed the finer things as indicated by his tailored suits, Italian shoes, luxurious automobiles, and oft polished teeth. The money bequeathed to him from Melina's life insurance policy could buy him a lot. But it wouldn't be used for material things. Instead, it would be the foundation for which he would build a new life, a chance to start over.

He ambled toward his front door, stopped, peered around the tranquil tree-lined hamlet. Maybe it was his cop gut. Maybe it was his growing paranoia. But Wadkins felt eyes in the night. He scanned the neighborhood, shrugged at the absurdity of his suspicions, and walked in. The grill of a

Chrysler shaded beyond a hedgerow one street over went unnoticed.

⌁⌁⌁

Shielded by shrubbery, Frank checked his wristwatch and continued surveillance. Thirteen years on the force. But this was his first stake-out of a fellow officer.

The porch light switched on after Wadkins entered. A sliver of light fractured through the living room verticals. Moments later, it went out and a light from the second-story came on. Frank surreptitiously slinked down when he noticed Wadkins looking out. Frank saw the detective peruse the street before drawing the drapes.

In a conversation that seemed trivial at the time, nothing more than idle banter, Wadkins once casually revealed, "The first thing I do when I get home is shower and wash the scum off me." Frank would now take advantage of that seemingly insignificant statement.

Wearing everyday trousers, a jeans jacket over a non-descript T-shirt, and a baseball cap—all items he stored in a locker at the Barn and had changed into—Frank nonchalantly strolled over as if he belonged here.

Michelle was far better than Frank with the hardware, always kicking his butt on the firing range. But he offset that shortcoming with his aptitude in picking locks. Without altering his confident gait, he turned left and sauntered up the driveway. Melina's Audi was parked in plain sight of passing motorists and nosey neighbors.

The fact that Wadkins left the auto unlocked indicated one of two things: Either he apparently felt safe in the affluent suburb or he wouldn't be staying long. Frank had to move quickly.

When it came to technology, he and the others at West Bureau were on different planets. Hell, different universes. What took Frank nearly ten minutes to accomplish, his partner or the master of *Cyberopolis* could've accomplished in seconds. Frank wasn't sure how to download the destinations and coordinates from the GPS log. He would simply scroll through and jot down anything confirming his theory. He inspected the directory while keeping a vigilant eye on the home.

After a gut-wrenching seven minutes that felt like seven hours, Frank's eyes opened wide. "Shit," he mumbled to nobody. His preposterous, absurd, and ludicrous theory had now been substantiated. Never in his life had he regretted being correct.

His moment of elation/remorse did not last. A hint of light cracked the downstairs verticals. The porch light dimmed. Wadkins was coming out.

There'd be no time to leap from the car, scamper across the lawn, and haul-ass to his vehicle without being discovered. Frank only had one option. Exiting the vehicle, he approached the front door.

"Grace?"

Frank manufactured surprise. "Oh, hey, Troy."

"Grace, what're you doing here?" Wadkins asked warily.

"I was tying up coupla loose ends with Roscoe Woods," Frank lied.

"Who?"

"Woods, the fella who rented his property in Pasadena to the Leaches' uncle, Gordon Whitefield." Part of being a good detective also required good acting. Frank delivered his lines with conviction.

"I see." Wadkins took a prolonged gaze at the Audi. Like Frank, he also knew being a good thespian was a requirement of carrying a badge. "Again, why are you *here*?"

Frank squared his shoulders and contrived awkwardness. "You haven't been in. Just wanted to see how you were holding up."

Wadkins smirked. "Since when do *you* give a shit about *me?*"

Frank extended his palms. "Granted, you and I aren't exactly tight, Troy. But we're both members of the same brotherhood. Something happens to one of us, it happens to all of us."

"Mm hmm."

"And, well, I could've lost Abby. That scumbag Xavier broke into my home. Elijah broke into my partner's."

"But the Leaches are dead, remember?"

"And thank goodness for that."

"Where's your car, anyway?" Wadkins queried, checking the area.

"Over there," Frank pointed. "I didn't know if Kent had someone stationed outside your home and didn't want to just drive right up." Frank added a smile for affect. Tom Hanks he wasn't.

Wadkins narrowed his eyes at Frank before overtly pointing to his wrist. "I'd love to stay and shoot the shit, Grace, but I need to pick up my kids."

Frank made a show of stepping back. "My bad. Don't let me keep you."

"See ya around." Wadkins slid behind the wheel of his wife's Audi, appeared to study the interior for signs of any disturbance.

"Later." Frank about-faced, his casual stroll transforming to a sprint after Wadkins drove away. As he ran to his Chrysler, he called his partner. Four rings, voicemail, Sophia, *Toy Story.* "Michelle, it's me," he barked into the phone. He instinctively waited for her to pick up before remembering it wasn't an answering machine. "I'm tailing Wadkins." He started the car. "Just like I suspected, Wadkins *was* in Paso Robles last week. He took Melina's car. *He's* the one who shot Elijah from the woods!"

Chapter 33

Frank disliked following Wadkins solo. More effective tails consisted of various vehicles alternating on point to prevent detection. Still, he had no choice but to go it alone.

He doubted Wadkins's claim that he was picking up his children and within fifteen minutes his suspicion was confirmed. Wadkins was heading into the city.

Eastbound on the Ronald Reagan Freeway, the Audi maintained a consistent speed. Brakes were tapped as they approached the Five. From several car lengths back, with a semi used for blocking, Frank watched Wadkins veer right at the last minute for the off-ramp. He had no other option but to do the same, hoping his abrupt move would not be seen. Frank cut into merging traffic, a move that resulted in being flashed by high-beams of the motorist behind him who apparently owned this portion of the freeway.

A few miles later, now southbound on the Five, the Audi took the off-ramp. When no other cars exited, Frank realized he'd need to divert. Wadkins stopped at the intersection at the bottom of the hill. Even though the light was green, he waited to see if anyone was following. Frank had no choice but to continue southbound on the freeway. He slowed and with another car bearing down on him, maneuvered onto the shoulder.

He got out, his clothes flapping in the backwash of vehicles whizzing by. Fisting the guardrail, Frank peered through the trees bracketing the freeway. It took him a beat to locate the white Audi. Wadkins was parked in front of a McDonalds. Facing the street, he waited and watched automobiles exit the highway.

Frank would do the same if he suspected a tail.

After an interminable ten minutes, Wadkins, confident no one was following him, exited the parking lot. Frank would have to abandon the hunt if Wadkins chose surface streets. Luckily, he didn't. Wadkins made two rights and was speeding up the entrance ramp. Frank scooted around, waited for a lull that allowed him to open the door. He threw himself behind the wheel, slammed the loaner into gear, and mashed the accelerator.

Passing through Toluca Lake, Frank glimpsed the time. He wondered if Abby was still angry with his working late. He thought about what his children were doing. Then he refocused on Wadkins.

Wadkins approached the same exit Frank took when making the commute from home. *Is he heading to the Barn?* Frank contemplated briefly before Wadkins headed elsewhere.

Now westbound on Sunset Blvd., traveling away from West Bureau-Hollywood, Frank lost him twice before picking him up again. Bottlenecking was atypically heavy for a weeknight. Frank's gut tightened when his quarry drew nearer the location of the initial West Hollywood bombing. *Returning to the scene of the crime, asshole?*

Pursuing from a less than desirable distance, Frank doubted Wadkins believed his cockamamie story about stopping by his house to see how he was holding up. Running into him *accidentally* again would blow Frank's cover.

Sunset Blvd. bent left. Wadkins turned right and entered the historic landmark.

The Chateau Marmont was one of the city's most prestigious addresses. Everyone from Errol Flynn, Clark Gable, and Marilyn Monroe to Dustin Hoffman, Spike Lee, and

Leonardo DiCaprio had secluded themselves away at the exclusive elite hotel. James Dean and Natalie Wood rehearsed for their roles in *Rebel without a Cause* here. John Belushi died of a cocaine overdose in one of the bungalows. Now, Wadkins added his name to the guest list.

Unable to follow Wadkins, Frank continued along Sunset before hastily U-turning. He pulled into a vacant lot of an upscale pet groomer that afforded him an unimpeded view of the hotel's entrance. Through verdant shrubbery Frank watched Wadkins exit the lobby, hand the keys to a valet, and head toward the poolside cottages. The confident swagger Wadkins perpetually exhibited was less pronounced. Frank waited twenty minutes before coming out of the shadows.

The front desk clerk was decked out in a costume more befitting a guard at Buckingham Palace. "Can I help you?" His face was stretched so tight from Botox Frank wondered if it hurt to speak.

He flashed his badge wallet in a blur. "Gang and Narcotics Division, Jim Stark." The name of the character James Dean played in *Rebel without a Cause*.

Botox stiffened. Luckily, no guests of the swanky hotel were within earshot. "Wha—wha—what can I do for you?"

Confident that Wadkins used an alias Frank gave a description. "You have a guest who just checked in. My age, though he probably appears mid to late thirties. Black hair, brown eyes, six three."

"Yes?"

"I need to know what room he's in."

"Sir, I'm unable to disclose that information. We here at the Chateau Marmont pride ourselves on granting privacy to our guests." The clerk arched a skeptical brow at this detective's casual appearance.

"We're working a stake-out. That's why I look this way," Frank claimed. "My task force has had this individual under surveillance for six months. Listen up—" Frank read the name from Botox's lanyard. "—Colton, I'm getting hemorrhoids from sitting on my ass too long. I stink from too much coffee and my partner smokes more than a '72 Pinto. I'd like to end this tonight so I can get home to my family before my wife files for divorce and my kids graduate high school."

"I'm sorry. I'd like to help but—"

"Your manager around?"

"Not at this hour. He leaves at five."

Frank reached over the counter and yanked the antiquated-looking handset. "Call him."

"Sir!" Colton bristled. "I'm prohibited from contacting him unless there's an emergency."

Frank chewed his lip, feigned thoughtfulness. "Have it your way, Colton." He then placed one finger to his ear and spoke into the lapel of his jeans jacket to no one. "Trojan Horse, this is Lone Wolf." Frank nodded as if someone replied. "Trojan Horse, we've got a code green, repeat, code green. Advance with armed incursion on all poolside bungalows on my command. Suspect armed and dangerous. Proceed with caution. Repeat, proceed with caution. Innocents on premises. On my go." He eyed Colton. "Keep your head down, son." Frank pivoted on his heels. As expected, he didn't get far.

"N—number s—six," stammered the clerk, shaking like a sheet on a clothesline in an afternoon breeze. "He's in number six."

"Thanks, Colton. Tell your boss you deserve a raise."

The zigzagging walkway wound below impenetrable overhanging branches. Sunlight had not reached the ground in decades. The air was humid and hung heavy like a rainforest. A young couple strolled in the opposite direction, too busy ogling each other to notice Frank.

Exiting the faux forest into the clearing, Frank studied the row of single story cottages on the pool's far side. Ballistics on the bullet extracted from Elijah Leach's obliterated brain had been "inconclusive." But Frank knew, beyond a reasonable doubt, based on the GPS log, Wadkins *was* in

Paso Robles when Leach was assassinated from a snipers nest. He also knew Wadkins was tight with Kent. All it would take was one call from the chief to deem the tests inconclusive. And really, would anyone care about details? A domestic terrorist was dead. More power to the one who killed him.

Frank intended to confront Wadkins. Not only had Wadkins murdered Xavier using the guise of the terrorist reaching for his gun, but now Frank had proof placing him at the scene of Elijah's assassination. He didn't know if it would stand up in court but, short term, that was secondary. Frank had learned eons ago not to assume anything when it came to the judicial system.

Remaining in the canopy of the trees, Frank called Michelle. "Damn," he muttered reaching her voice-mail again. "It's me. I followed Wadkins to the Chateau Marmont." He recited the make, model, license, and approximate year. "I need you to get hold of a judge and obtain a warrant on the Audi. We need it in our hands before Wadkins deletes the coordinates. Or maybe get hold of Johnny and see if he can do his hacking thing. I'm about to confront Wadkins, possibly bust him. Don't call back. I'm going dark."

Frank powered down his cell, flipped off the safety on his Beretta, re-holstered it, and emerged from the shadows. He approached the room with an iron will, icy stare, and knotted stomach.

He studied the perimeter. The hotel's desire to create a romantic ambiance, in turn, produced numerous pockets of obscurity where someone could hide. Advantage: Wadkins.

Frank circumvented the deserted pool and advanced on the bungalow. As he walked nearer, he moved his right arm across his chest, fingers close to his sidearm—just in case. He had the element of surprise. Advantage: Frank.

He raised his arm to knock on the door.

"Detective Grace?"

Alarmed, heart nearly catapulting from his chest, Frank

spun. The figure seemed equally startled. She was holding an overflowing ice bucket, returning from the vending area.

"Mrs. K—Kent?" he stuttered.

"Please, Charlotte."

He cocked his head. "What—what are you doing here?"

Hair as big as ever, jeans as tight as ever, cleavage pronounced as ever, the police chief's wife smiled like she was still a dancer on stage. "I could ask you the same thing." She floated closer with the elegance of a slow moving layer of fine smoke. Acknowledging room number six with her chin, she claimed, "I'm here with Weldon."

"Weldon Kent?"

Charlotte tittered. "How many Weldon's do you know?"

Frank's head spun in a whirlwind of bewilderment. Feeling his knees would liquefy, he swallowed hard. "I saw Detective Wadkins enter."

"Of course you did. Weldon and I needed to escape for a few days. Krissy's…accident…is obviously taking a toll on him. I have my own children. You also do, correct?"

"Two."

"My husband invited Detective Wadkins to join us for a late night cocktail. Both men feel guilty: my husband for dragging the detective into it and the detective for letting my husband down." Charlotte paused. "He was going to meet with you in the next day or two."

"Wadkins is meeting with your husband?"

"Yes, in here." She took on a sorrowful look. "I know how men are. I grew up with three brothers. Fragile ego's and all that, especially in a macho field like law enforcement. I apologize for my husband not meeting with you first."

"No big deal."

"You're here now, so is my husband and Detective Wadkins. Might as well kill two birds with one stone. Can you hold this?" She handed the ice bucket to Frank before he could refuse. Charlotte slithered between him and the door, her well-rounded backside brushing close to Frank's crotch. Reaching into her skintight jeans to remove the key card, she accidentally grinded against him. "Woops."

The light flicked green. Charlotte opened. "Weldon" she called into the room. "Weldon, you'll never guess who I ran into. Detective Grace is with me." She stepped right. Frank followed her in.

The suite was quaint. The décor created to replicate hotel rooms from a bygone era, circa 1920s. It was costly to look inexpensive. A doorway across the living quarters lead to what Frank assumed was the bedrooms and bathrooms. He assumed that because he'd never stayed here, the price tag well beyond his paycheck.

"Weldon, honey?" Charlotte had trepidation in her voice. "I hope he's okay," she whispered to Frank. "Detective Wadkins?"

Frank slipped past Charlotte. He saw the door across the room start to open.

Then his body convulsed.

He crumbled instantly, the result of fifty thousand volts. The bucket thrown forward showering the room in a spray of ice cubes. Seizing, writhing in agony, Frank was experiencing unimaginable pain like he'd never known.

Charlotte dropped to a knee and again pressed the Taser against Frank's kidneys.

He grunted like a dying animal. His body jerked and jolted, roiling from the unrelenting torture. His muscles useless, his nervous system pulverized with electricity. Instinctively, in the midst of flopping about, he attempted to reach for his Beretta but the electroshocks that coursed through his body prohibited use of his arms and legs.

He glared up at Charlotte with both venomous hatred and pleading eyes.

Wadkins materialized alongside Charlotte, and gave Frank a sideways look. "Wrong place, wrong time, Grace. Again."

Frank had never been shot, though he'd been grazed several times. That was a piece of cake compared to this. Charlotte Kent and Troy Wadkins stole a glance at each other, then studied Frank as if he was their lab rat. He struggled to breathe, his tongue wilting between his lips as if he was epileptic.

Wadkins mocked him. "Cat got your tongue?"

Deprived of control over his body, Frank battled to roll onto his side. He feared swallowing his tongue and choking to death. He struggled to move his elbow, excruciating inch by excruciating inch, until he slightly lifted himself. "Tr—Troy—c'mere, ple—please."

Wadkins crouched lower, face inches from Frank.

Frank fought to stay alert, to stay conscious, to stay alive. His vision was fading, fading fast, darkening on the fringe. Breathing and speaking took a herculean effort. "I'm—I'm—gonna fucking kill you."

Wadkins laughed. "You're gonna kill me? It's the other way around, Grace." Wadkins reached for a nearby pillow and placed it over Frank's head to muffle the screams. He grabbed the Taser from Charlotte, pressed the weapon against Frank's neck, and discharged the device again, sending electricity surging through Frank's weakening agony-riddled body.

His legs kicked out. His arms flailed as if controlled by an invisible puppeteer. His screams went nowhere, stifled in his own throat. He prayed for the torture, the pain to end. He saw Abby and Ashley and Jake.

Then he saw nothing.

Chapter 34

Impenetrable blackness enveloped Frank so completely he couldn't see his hands in front of his face. He was hogtied with what felt like flexi-cuffs. His mouth was not gagged.

The effects of the Tasering lingered. Stiffness in his legs, a result of restricted movement for a prolonged period caused numbness. At least he wasn't dead. Yet.

Frank heard traffic beyond his pitch-black world. His body bounced and jarred. One swift thud slammed his head against something solid. He was in the trunk of a car. But for how long? And where was he being taken?

The confining space and tangled position afforded him little mobility but he managed to roll sideways. Pressing his left hip against the trunk liner he realized his Beretta and his cell had been taken.

The vehicle stopped. Two doors slammed. The lid lifted and he was greeted by the face of his captors. Charlotte Kent commented flatly, "Hey, tiger."

Wadkins heaved Frank from the trunk and tossed him face first on the ground. Laughter. Then Frank was yanked to his feet.

Shifting a glance between the chief's wife and the chief's golden boy, Frank confessed, "I sure didn't see this coming."

Wadkins's pompous grin had always grated on Frank's

nerves. In these present circumstances, it pissed him off.

"Of course you didn't see it coming. That's why you'll always be a pissant detective. You'll never be me."

"Thank goodness for that."

Wadkins launched a powerful jab into Frank's gut that doubled him over. "Betcha didn't see that coming either."

"C'mon, let's get this over with," Charlotte insisted while nervously glancing around.

Wadkins followed the order. He placed his hand around Frank's cuffed wrists and navigated him away from the vehicle.

A half-moon hung high, illuminating the gentle breaking waters of the Pacific. Frank tasted the salt of the sea on his lips. With Charlotte a few paces behind, Frank was directed across the isolated field closer to the edge of a high cliff. "Where are we?"

"Point Dume," Wadkins stated. "The same Point Dume where they found my wife. Right down there, Grace. Right down on that rocky shoreline seventy feet below."

As he was marched closer to the edge, Frank attempted to wriggle his wrists free. But Wadkins, like himself, was well trained. He knew how to bind a prisoner. "You're some piece of work, Wadkins. Your children must be so proud."

"Melina was a whore. She was good for three things: opening her legs, opening her mouth, and having life insurance. My kids will miss her for a while but three quarter of a million tends to help the grieving process."

Frank had been right all along. Wadkins *was* involved— up to a point. But Frank never envisioned Charlotte Kent's participation. "So, this is all about money?"

"Isn't it always?"

"You're one of us, Troy, a goddamn detective. You took an oath."

"I may very well be damned but you fail to see the big picture. You never have, never will."

"Enlighten me."

"Pussy and money, my man. Pussy and money make the

world go 'round. *That's* what it's all about."

"You'll never get away with this."

"As usual, you're too late. We already have."

"Let's just get this over with already," snapped a jittery Charlotte.

Frank turned. "I see who wears the pants in this operation. Tell me, Wadkins, does she keep your balls next to her Taser?"

Wadkins drew closer. "It's what's *in* those pants, Grace. Speaking of, maybe I'll go pay a visit to your wife after you're dead."

"You go near Abby, I'll—"

Wadkins drove a violent right jab into Frank's kidneys, so crushing d he nearly pissed himself. As Frank dissolved to a knee, Wadkins gripped his shirt collar and wrenched him vertical. "You'll what? Come back from the dead and haunt me?" He pretended thoughtfulness. "Now that I think of it, if time allows, maybe your daughter would be a nice little bonus."

"She's twelve!"

"Old enough." Wadkins looked back, winked at his cohort. *Just screwing with him.*

Charlotte rolled her eyes.

"My partner will track you down, both of you. Santana's a pit-bull. Once she sinks her teeth into something she won't let go."

"She's got her niece. You think she's going to risk her career *now*? The Santana you knew is gone."

Frank faced Charlotte grasping at straws. "You're in bed with a killer, lady. He's got the money. He doesn't need you. He already killed his wife. You honestly believe he won't put a bullet in your brain first chance he gets? You're meaningless to him."

Wadkins pressed an imaginary buzzer. "Wrong again, Grace. I didn't kill Melina." He tilted his head. "She did."

"Shut up, Troy!" Charlotte snapped.

It was all coming together, the puzzle pieces fitting perfectly in Frank's mind. Regrettably, he'd be taking it to his grave.

Moving quickly, Wadkins pressed the barrel of his .38 to Frank's temple. Charlotte approached and with precision, quickly unbound the flexi-cuffs from his wrists and ankles. They were sore, tender. But Frank wouldn't give his abductors the satisfaction of rubbing the sensation back.

Frank was prodded forward to within five feet of the precipice and a seventy-foot plunge to a rocky coastline below. Wadkins stood at Frank's ten o'clock, Charlotte at his two, both keeping Frank in their sights. Behind him, a sheer drop where death awaited.

"Now what? You expect me to make a run for it?"

"Au contraire." Wadkins raised and lowered his eyebrows in a maniacal expression. "I expect you to turn and walk right off the ledge."

Frank sneered. "You're joking, right?"

Wadkins thumbed the hammer, dropped one into the chamber. "No, Grace, I'm not."

Frank looked at Charlotte. Her stance, her grip, and the way she held the weapon indicated she was adept and acquainted with a gun. No novice. He wondered if Wadkins taught her. Or maybe Chief Kent himself.

Frank glimpsed over his shoulder. The foreboding darkness lurked like gates of hell with open arms. The drop was too high, the fall too steep. He'd never survive. He didn't have enough room to get a running start and attempt a swan dive into the Pacific. The coastline extended too far. And even if he could reach the water, he was no cliff diver. Crashing into the ocean from this height was tantamount to crashing onto cement. Frank realized there was no way out. "You expect me to just walk off this cliff and kill myself?" He paused. "You're fucking insane!"

"You can go out on your own terms, control your own destiny, and all that." Wadkins shrugged. "Honestly, I don't give a shit either way."

"You shoot me, dumbass, and when they find my body—"

"If." Wadkins interrupted. "*If* they find your body. High tide tonight, Frankie boy. You'll probably wash out to sea. Maybe in a few weeks a shoe might wash up." He smiled into the night. "Poor Abby Grace, standing over an empty coffin, never really knowing if her husband is alive or dead."

"As I was saying, dumbass, *when* they find me, they'll match ballistics to the weapon. They'll know it was your gun." Frank turned to Charlotte. "Or yours. Ex-cops are popular in jail. But a police chief's wife? Whoo boy, Charlotte, you'll be in for some good times."

"I'm hoping they *do* match ballistics," Wadkins claimed.

Frank frowned.

Wadkins snickered, eyed the Beretta in his hand. "This is your gun, Frank."

Frank made a face. "Why would I kill myself?" He made air-quotes over the last two words.

"Guilt."

"Guilt?" Frank asked incredulously. "Guilt over what?" His detective mind kicked in, the pieces coming together. He answered his own question. "You're going to pin this, all of this, this last two weeks, on me?"

Like some guy working a carnival, Wadkins said, "We have a winner."

Frank swallowed.

"Now turn and walk forward," Wadkins demanded.

So, this is how it ends. If Frank somehow reached the water, there'd be a chance, albeit a small one, he'd wash up. His family would have closure, a headstone with his name and a coffin with his remains. If he failed to reach the ocean, he'd pinwheel through the air, free-falling against a jagged rock face. The casket would have to be closed.

Frank had heard those stories about people who somehow cheated death, surviving after falling from great heights. A miracle. But Frank had never been that lucky.

And, if it was a *miracle,* while he admired Johnny, Frank would not—could not—live his life in a wheelchair.

"I always kinda liked him," Charlotte commented to Wadkins.

"Not me. I always thought he was a prick."

Liked. Thought. They were already talking about him in past tense.

"Turn around and walk, Frank," Wadkins breathed. "Now!"

Charlotte cocked the hammer on her firearm.

Although she was at ease, comfortable holding the weapon, Wadkins was better trained. Frank could leap at Charlotte, hopefully disarm her, and, in the ensuing chaos, possibly survive. Possible—not likely. She was ten feet away and Frank knew he'd never make it without being shredded by gunfire.

Wadkins stepped closer, took aim on Frank's head.

"You don't have the balls, Troy," Frank asserted, surprised at his own tenacity.

Wadkins narrowed his eyes. "Good-bye, Frank Grace."

Two lights out of darkness. The area immediately bathed in a beam of powerful halogen headlights. The eerie stillness ripped apart by the roar of a powerful engine. Pebbles and rocks kicked up in the wake of the charging vehicle.

"What the—"Wadkins shouted as he spun around.

Charlotte glanced at the onrushing vehicle for a split-second. But that was all Frank needed. He pounced like a cheetah.

Charlotte fell hard. Frank on top of her. He turned her sideways, putting her between himself and Wadkins. If Wadkins fired, he'd hit the police chief's wife.

Gunfire erupted, tearing through the tranquil night. Wadkins lay flat out, pressing himself into the ground of the open field. Dirt and gravel exploded all around him, bullets missing by inches.

The Dodge Ram fishtailed, swerved, and screeched to a stop forty yards north. The driver pushed out from the far side, took cover behind the expansive engine block, and exchanged salvoes with Wadkins.

Frank, wondering how Michelle found him and why she was driving a Dodge and not her Honda, was still weak from the Taser. Charlotte was strong, fit, tougher than he expected. She straddled him. He gripped her wrist tightly but she refused to surrender her gun. She brought the weapon around to Frank's face.

As Wadkins exchanged volleys of gunfire, he reverse-belly-crawled to aid Charlotte in her fight. Frank was having trouble holding her off. Two against one would seal Frank's fate.

Frank drew in his chin, thrust his head up, and drove his forehead into Charlotte's nose. In spite of the artillery barrage that blanketed the area, Frank heard cartilage snap like a twig. Charlotte didn't release the weapon but she did bring her hands to her nose. Blood squirted like a geyser between her well-manicured fingers. She released a torrent of vulgarity.

"That's not very ladylike." Frank skidded from below Charlotte's resilient dancer legs, thrust his foot into her hip, and sent her rolling into Wadkins. Twenty or so yards south, he noticed a boulder he could use for cover. If he could get to it, Wadkins and Charlotte would be in the open and vulnerable between him and Michelle.

He reached for his weapon. *Shit.* They'd stripped him of his Beretta. He turned to see Wadkins and Charlotte tangled like Ashley and Jake roughhousing. Charlotte's panicked screams about her nose being broken bordered on comical. Her anxiety would be her undoing. Frank needed her weapon. Either he'd grab her piece and retreat to the boulder or he'd put the gun to her head and see if Wadkins truly cared for her. *Pussy and money, right, Troy?*

Wadkins unraveled from Charlotte, bucking her away. He raised his weapon and took aim directly at Frank.

Frank observed the *tell* in Wadkins's gaze, the cold death stare of someone about to take a life. What Frank didn't see was Charlotte extending her muscular leg. The boot slamming into his groin caused Frank to double-over. A second sweeping kick boomed against his skull and sent him stumbling toward the edge of the cliff now just three feet away.

Frank bent at the waist, hands in his crotch as if that would magically stop the pain and return his testicles to their original location. Wadkins provided cover fire, releasing a barrage of salvoes at the Dodge. Charlotte sprang to her feet with agility that surprised Frank. He didn't have time to brace himself for another forceful kick that nearly dislodged his skull. He spun like a top, pirouetting nearer to the brink. He heard the crashing waves seventy feet below.

"You broke my nose!" Charlotte howled.

She lifted her leg again, preparing one final strike that would launch Frank over the edge.

Charlotte's lack of training worked to his advantage. Frank knew, as did Wadkins and every member of the LAPD, when engaged in hand-to-hand, or in this case foot-to-head, you altered your attack. When Charlotte pitched out her leg to send him plummeting to his death, he was ready. He dropped, grabbed her ankle, turned his wrists, and flung her.

She screamed, stumbled, lost her footing. Frank watched as he sent the police chief's wife over the edge and into the darkness.

He hobbled over and peered down. Charlotte was clinging onto a tangle of tree roots outspreading from the overhang. She was terrified, crying, and begging for help, her legs frantically kicking at nothing. Her feet searching for purchase that wasn't there.

Déjà vu. Azusa. Four years ago, Frank made a snap decision that he still wondered about. And always would. Six thugs brought terror to a restaurant. A gunfight ensued and four lay dead, killed by his own gun. Two fled into the night. Frank gave chase, pursued one down a dark alley, and released three rounds. One caught the fleeing suspect in the leg. He bled out en route to the hospital.

Had Frank gone too far?

Had he exceeded his authority?

Had he acted irrationally?

The DA said no. But Frank still wondered.

Frank Grace was a human being. Emotions, anger, retribution.

Now, as he watched Charlotte Kent clutching to vines for her life, he again needed to make a decision. He was not judge, jury, and executioner. He was a detective. On the other hand, this woman had tried to kill him. According to Wadkins, she had also killed Melina. And, somehow, was part of something bigger.

The decision, however, was made for him.

"Pull her up, Grace!" Wadkins pressed his gun against the back of Frank's head. "Now!"

Frank exhaled. "Okay."

Facing the Dodge while maintaining his weapon on Frank, Wadkins screamed, "I'll blow your partner's head off, Santana."

Frank lay flat-out on the ground. "Give me your hand, Charlotte."

The woman was panicking.

"Focus, Charlotte, focus. Give me your hand."

"You're gonna drop me. You're gonna throw me over! Help. Somebody, please help!"

"I'd like to, believe me. But you need to pay for what you did. So give me your hand."

With blood dripping from the nostrils of her now crooked nose, she asked pleadingly, "You promise?"

"You have my word."

"C'mon, Grace, pull her up!"

With trepidation in her soul, she had no choice but to put trust in a man she was trying to kill seconds earlier. She released her grip from the interwoven roots and slapped her hand into Frank's reassuring grip. "Please, don't let me fall."

"Use your legs for leverage. Push up."

Frank's muscles were taut, aching. He thought it would be ironic if she slipped free, a result of his deflated physical state from the Tasering she herself doled out. He did consider an *accident* for a fleeting instant. Then, he pulled her to safety.

Charlotte was on her hands and knees gasping, Frank on his haunches. Wadkins, standing upright, had not removed the gun from Frank's head. In the distance, sirens began penetrating the stillness.

"Get up, Grace," Wadkins commanded.

Frank's courageous act apparently carried no weight with Wadkins. He pulled Frank to his feet and moved behind him. He locked Frank's neck in the crook of his right arm, pressing the Beretta's barrel into his temple, and began backpedaling toward the car, the same vehicle that had transported them here.

"Toss the weapon where I can see it and put your hands up, Santana!" Wadkins shouted.

No reaction. The sirens grew louder.

"Now, goddammit. Now!"

A gun was tossed into the clearing. A pair of upraised arms appeared on the far side of the Dodge.

"Get your ass in the car, Charlotte," Wadkins yelled.

The chief's wife vacillated. She shifted glances between her accomplice and the man who, yes, broke her nose, but also saved her life. "Troy—"

"Get in the fucking car!" he screamed.

In too deep, Charlotte obeyed and scooted to the passenger's side.

Wadkins coldcocked Frank, slammed the handle of his weapon into his head, and sent Frank crumbling onto his knees. He blew out the tires of the Ram, eliminating any possibility of being followed.

The Tasering, a lengthy period cuffed in a trunk, and a physical altercation on the side of a cliff left Frank drained. As Wadkins jumped behind the wheel, Frank rolled away to avoid being run over.

As the Audi skipped across the barren space and disappeared into the night, Frank heard harried footsteps approaching. "Thanks, Michelle."

She dropped to her haunches, held his face tenderly and looked into his eyes. "Frank, are you okay? Are you hurt?"

He did a double take, blinked repeatedly. It was *not* his partner. In fact, he wasn't sure what to think.

Chapter 35

"What—what are you doing here?"

Detective Craft ignored the question. With frightened eyes and a quaking voice, she asked, "How bad are you hurt? What do you need? How can I help?"

He hadn't trusted Wadkins for a while. He'd been blind-sided by Charlotte Kent's involvement. Now, Heather Craft unexpectedly appeared out of the shadows. At this moment, Frank didn't know who in the entire LAPD he could trust—except one person. "Gimme your cell. I need to get hold of my partner." He started to stand but the world spun.

She caringly snaked her arm around his lower back to steady him. "Easy, Frank, take it easy, please."

"Heather, give me your cell!"

She pouted. "In my truck."

The wailing sirens had since passed into the night on their way to another call.

Aided by the detective with the schoolgirl infatuation, Frank was assisted to her Dodge Ram. His mind was baffled by her arrival. He'd ask later. First he needed to reach Michelle.

Craft leaned into the truck in such a way it'd be impossible for Frank not to view her backside. She retrieved her cell. "Here ya go." She held the phone so Frank had to brush her fingers to take possession.

"Thanks." It wasn't his phone so he couldn't simply push two on speed dial. He dithered, trying to recall Michelle's number, and cursed technology in the process. After initially waking a female and getting cursed out in Spanish, he reached her.

"Frank? I've been trying to call back but you didn't answer."

"They took my phone."

"*They*? They who?"

"I'll explain later. Listen, I'm on the way to Kent's home."

"Now?" Michelle yipped. "It's almost four a.m."

"It's going down. They're going to kill him."

"Who?"

"There's no time. Meet me and I'll explain it."

Silence

"Michelle?"

"Let's call it in. We—"

"I'm not positive."

"You just said—"

"I know what I said!" Frank snapped then apologized. "But it's not one hundred percent. If I'm wrong, if I call in a 207A or a 417 to the police chief's home without due cause, I'm finished. He won't look the other way. Not again."

"Where are you now?"

"Point Dume. How quickly can you get to Kent's?"

"Point Dume?"

"I'll explain later. Just—get over to Kent's but wait outside, got it?"

"I'm on the way."

Frank ended the call and was greeted by a befuddled expression on Craft's face. He'd forgotten she was nearby. "The police chief? Someone's going to kill Chief Kent?"

Frank returned the phone and cupped her shoulder, an act that sent shivers along her spine and increased her body temperature tenfold. "I'm not certain," he confessed.

She scrunched her face. "It sorta looked like Detective

Wadkins, but I couldn't get a positive ID on him." Craft furrowed her brow as if recalling something. "Was that Chief Kent's wife with him? Charlotte, right?"

Frank nodded.

"Good Lord, Frank. What have you gotten into?"

Noticing the two punctured tires Wadkins had blown out, Frank sighed. "I need to get to Calabasas. You know anyone around here who can give us a ride?"

Craft was daydreaming. A potential assassination of the police chief, his wife and one of her fellow detectives involved? And just weeks ago, Frank himself was almost killed in an explosion. "I'm worried about you."

The tender touch of her hand against his cheek startled him. Light was limited but Frank thought he detected her eyes welling up. Michelle teased him mercilessly about Craft's obsession, infatuation. Her hand gently holding his face, skin on skin, a frightened look in her eyes and sincere concern for his safety indicated his partner was correct. For Craft this was more than a crush. For Frank, it was downright creepy. He removed her hand from his face. "Detective Craft, do you know anyone close by who you can call?"

"Marty." Her voice lacked enthusiasm.

"Marty?"

"Marty Cope, my partner when I worked out of Foothills Division."

"No cops."

"Good." She sighed. "His wife hates when I call."

Frank let that go. He regarded the night. "Did you notice anything on your way here? A convenience store, perhaps?"

"I was so scared for you, Frank. When I saw that gun at your head—"

Frank clasped her shoulders. "Detective Craft! Focus," he roared.

She stared into his eyes. For an instant, Frank thought his greatest admirer would plant a kiss on his lips. "I—I did pass a gas station down the road."

Relying on two flat tires would take too long to drive to

Calabasas thirty miles away. This would have to suffice. "Let's go."

Craft slipped behind the wheel, flashed a pleasing, yet awkward, grin at Frank. She finally had him next to her. Her heart skipped a beat.

It would not take a detective with thirteen years' experience to conclude Craft was moving in slow motion. She leisurely turned the ignition, casually fastened her seat belt, fiddled with the mirrors, checked her appearance in the rear view. She even went as far as to turn on her hazards. At a snail's pace, she crawled away from the overlook and crept along the winding road. Being alone with Frank Grace was a moment she'd dreamt of for years. There was no way in hell she'd rush it.

"I'm sorry," he breathed a moment later, suppressing his exasperation with her not bettering ten MPH.

She didn't know what he was apologizing for but she dismissed it anyway. He was her dream guy so she'd cut him plenty of slack.

He sighed. "I snapped back there. And I'm sorry."

Frank was adept at interrogating suspects. He was well versed in courtroom testimony. He'd spoken to the press during the Azusa Bloodbath. He'd been interrogated by Internal Affairs, raised two children, had a wife. But confronting someone enchanted with him was unchartered waters. Unsure how to phrase it, he simply asked, "Why were you there?"

She said nothing, pretending to intently focus on the desolate road as they clip-clopped along on two tires and two rims.

Frank didn't think she was linked in any way to Wadkins or the Kents, but he needed confirmation. "I have to know why you were there."

Her lips shuddered and her chin trembled. She reached for Frank's shoulder then pulled her arm back. She winced as if eavesdropping on a debate within her mind. "I—I can't."

"Can't what?"

She giggled nervously. "We work together, Frank. You'll never look at me the same. You'll laugh at me."

"You saved my life. I'd *never* laugh at you."

"You *really* don't want to know."

"Heather, I need to."

She wavered but when she broke she held nothing back. "You don't want to know that I renewed my gym membership 'cause of you. You don't want to know I asked Lieutenant Gallardo to assign me a workstation close to you. Do you think me sitting next to you in department briefings is just coincidence? You want to know I dress up nicer when I know we're on the same watch? The reason I have issues with every partner I'm assigned to is 'cause none of them hold a candle to you. I'm not religious, Frank, but I…well, sometimes pray at night. I pray for something to happen to your partner."

"Heather?" Frank mumbled in disbelief.

"Nothing bad. I like Santana. She seems like an okay detective…I guess. But just something to—I don't know—give *us* an opportunity to be, you know, a team."

Frank was speechless. He got the impression when she said *team* she was insinuating not just on-duty. "I appreciate you opening up to me. I do." *Oops.* Realizing how lovesick she was, Frank wished he wouldn't have said those last two words. *I do.* He chuckled. "You should talk to my wife. She'll tell you I'm about as far from perfect as someone can be."

She said nothing, swallowed hard, sniffled.

"That still doesn't explain why you showed up."

"I followed you."

"Pardon?"

Craft bowed her head self-consciously, similar to the way Ashley did when Frank caught her doing something. "I saw you leave the Barn and followed you. First to the stakeout, which I'm guessing was Detective Wadkins's home, then to the Chateau Marmont. And finally here."

"You followed me?"

"Yes. Please don't be angry with me, Frank. I couldn't handle it if you were angry with me."

Frank emitted a nervous laugh because he didn't know what else to do. "I don't understand. You followed me?"

"It's not the first time."

"*What?*"

"No, it's not. I spend many nights parked outside your home. I see you have a good life. You've got two wonderful children. And I'm…envious."

Frank felt violated. And disappointed: Violated knowing his home had been under surveillance, disappointed with himself for having no idea he was being tailed while he tailed Wadkins. His skills were waning. His skin crawled at this disturbing revelation but he put on his psychiatrist hat. "You'll meet someone one day, probably when you least expect it."

"I have met someone. But unfortunately he's married with two wonderful children."

They spoke no more for the duration of their painfully sluggish excursion to a convenience store.

Gas-n-Go.

Frank wasn't sure if that referred to the pumps outside or the snack bar inside.

He'd been caught off guard by Craft's admission of feelings toward him. What she did now was even more bizarre. She lifted her cell and called roadside assistance. Frank was about to ask the obvious: *why didn't you call them before? It would've saved time.* He answered it himself. She wanted to use the opportunity of finally being alone with him to open her heart. It was her come-to-Jesus moment.

A delivery truck drove up. Frank waited, watched, and then, as the driver got out of the truck, he again thanked Craft, though it felt stroppy. The fact she didn't offer to accompany him to Kent's home indicated she'd gone as far as she was going with Frank.

"See you around," she whispered.

A question? A statement? Frank didn't know. He pursed his lips. "Yep."

He met the deliveryman coming out of the store. "I need your van."

The man lifted his eyes from an I-thingy. "Like hell you do, dipshit."

"It's not open for discussion, pal. Give me the keys."

As Frank stepped into the light, the man's shoulders sagged. "Hey, you're that cop, Frank Grace. The one from Azusa."

"In the flesh."

With trembling fingers, the man handed over the keys. "Take it, go 'head."

Frank stepped into the panel truck, brought the engine to life, and tore out of the parking lot. After four years, one positive had finally come from Azusa.

As he took the meandering county road as fast as the bulky vehicle would travel, heading toward the 101, Frank inhaled deeply. The odor from the rear was satirically familiar. *Doughnuts.*

Chapter 36

By the time Frank arrived in Calabasas a new day was dawning. That unique time of day when light and dark merged into one. Sort of like this entire case. Spotting Michelle's Honda one block down from Kent's home, Frank pulled alongside.

"Nice van."

"Cops and doughnuts, right?" Frank angled his body and peered into the back seat. Sophia was asleep.

"Hard to find a babysitter at five in the morning."

Frank nodded. "You ready?"

"What'd you find out?"

"No time now. You'll hear it as I tell Chief Kent."

The sentry in the guardhouse eyed Frank suspiciously. The visitor was not dressed like a detective—no ID, bedraggled, and drove a doughnut van. The guard indicated he'd need to call ahead and get an okay.

"Fine."

Minutes later, they were amongst the lavish furnishings of Kent's palatial home. The décor was more apropos to an A-list movie star than a police chief.

When first entering, Frank and Michelle were uneasy about their shoddy appearance. Frank wore muddy trousers, a nondescript T-shirt, muffed hair, and a two-day beard. He hadn't showered in twenty-four hours. Michelle, roused from sleep and summoned quickly, wore brown cargo pants, sneakers, an older tank-top, no makeup, and had her hair hanging loosely to her shoulders. Their concern about attire was quickly put to rest when they saw the head of the LAPD sitting in a winged back chair wearing black socks, blue boxers, and a wife beater T-shirt.

"What's going on?" he hissed while lighting a cigarette.

"Thanks for seeing us—" Frank began.

As always, the harried chief had no time for bullshit pleasantries. "Cut to the chase."

Standing a few feet in front of his boss, Michelle dutifully alongside, Frank asked, "Sir, is your wife here?"

Kent arched a skeptical brow. "Charlotte? No. No, she isn't. She needed to get away and is spending a few days at Big Bear." He sized up his visitors, adding, "Not that that's your concern."

"I have some information that will trouble you, information that won't sit well."

"All I ever hear anymore is bad news. Spill it."

"We need you to come with us. Somewhere safe."

Kent snickered then laughed in Frank's face at the absurdity.

Frank decided to go for broke. "I have reason to believe your life is in danger."

Kent blew smoke, raised his mug from an adjacent table, sipped his coffee. "That's why you've come barging in?"

"Yes, sir."

"This city is shot to hell, detectives. We're losing the fight." He acknowledged a family photograph on the mantel to his right, a photograph including his deceased daughter. "Everyone's life is in danger. No one is safe."

"*Immediate* danger."

Kent looked at Frank's partner. Santana nodded but also appeared to be learning this information firsthand along with him. "Three decades I've been part of the LAPD. Three long decades, Detective Grace. My life's been in *immediate* danger for thirty years. I've been shot, stabbed, assaulted, thrown off a fire escape. And I'm still here."

"This time is different."

"I have a state of the art security system and former United States Marines working as guards. I'm well-protected."

Michelle spoke for the first time. "Just allow my partner to explain. I was hesitant to buy what Detective Grace was selling. And he's *my* partner."

Kent sordidly shook his head. "The riots back in '92. OJ, Detective Lazarus sentenced to twenty-eight years for murder, Officer Mercano accepting sexual favors in exchange for not arresting a woman, Christopher Dorner, the widespread corruption exposed in the Rampart Scandal. Now domestic terrorism. All in our city and all during my time on the force. So, tell me, Detective, tell me *how* it's different this time." By the time Kent concluded, he was red faced and raising his voice.

"Detective Troy Wadkins is a murderer."

That gave Kent pause. He glared at Grace then Santana. He stubbed out a cigarette and immediately lit another. Leaning forward, he mumbled impassively, "Troy Wadkins is a murderer?"

"Yes, sir."

"Any why, pray tell, is he a murderer?"

Frank inhaled and glimpsed at Michelle. She nodded once.

Here goes everything. "I accessed the GPS in his wife's Audi, Melina. The history log places Troy Wadkins in Paso Robles at the time I lost Elijah Leach. I've never lost a detainee before and never in that fashion. Leach was right next to me and was taken out from a sniper's nest in the distance. It was breezy, the sun wasn't up. And yet it was a perfectly executed kill shot. Leach was murdered by someone who *knew* what they were doing."

"Ballistics was inconclusive."

Frank didn't address that. "The morning of the explosion in West Hollywood, I stood alongside the Nissan. Elijah was behind the wheel. Xavier came up to me from behind."

Frank pantomimed Xavier's approach. "He was coming from the direction of Ground Zero. He picked up his cell and called in a code to detonate the bomb."

"So how does that tie in to *Wadkins* being a killer?"

"In the rear seat of the Nissan I observed a bomb blanket. It's a device used to shield the bomb squad boys in a controlled blast. They use them all the time."

"I'm well aware what a bomb blanket is, detective. Don't waste my time."

"Yes, sir." Frank paused, regrouped. "The insignia on the bomb blanket matches the squad's insignia."

Standing silently, Michelle knew where Frank was heading. The afternoon at the K9 Bomb Squad when he studied the building's exterior and the emblem outside now made sense.

"You're saying they—the Leaches—stole the explosive coverlet from the bomb squad?"

"No, sir, I'm saying someone supplied it to them."

"And that someone is Detective Wadkins?"

"I believe so."

"You *believe* so or you *know* so?"

Frank took a leap of faith. "I know so."

Kent sprang to his feet. "And why in God's green earth would Detective Wadkins do this?"

"I'm not yet one hundred percent positive on his reasoning. But the proof is irrefutable."

Kent released a loud belly laugh, ashes falling to the floor in the process. He was the shortest in the room. Yet, despite his attire and pasty bony legs, he remained the most authoritative presence. He pushed out his cheek with his tongue. "Anything else?" He was obviously unimpressed.

Michelle, watching her friend throw away his career, came to Frank's aid. "He also murdered Xavier Leach."

"And how exactly did he do that, Detective Santana? Educate me."

Michelle explained. "It was Wadkins—"

Kent interrupted. "Treat the man with respect. He's not a convicted felon. It's *Detective* Wadkins."

"Yes, sir. When Detective Wadkins took the collar on Xavier at KLAG, he placed him in his vehicle. Why would he do that? There were two of us. Yet, Detective Wadkins chose to bring in Leach solo. And then, it just so happens that somehow Leach manages to break free of the handcuffs, attempts to gain control of the vehicle, and, in the process, winds up shot dead. It's all conveniently neat." She stopped, added, "Sir."

"Also seems coincidental that, after all these years, Detective Wadkins fails to properly secure a prisoner—" Frank added. "—a prisoner wanted for domestic terrorism."

"Perhaps he made a mistake."

Frank snickered. "A mistake? With the eyes of the entire nation on our department, it's a bad time to get careless."

Kent enumerated on his fingers, his cigarette bobbing between his lips. "First of all, Detective Grace, I don't appreciate your tone. Secondly, I don't appreciate your unfounded allegation. You're accusing a brother, indicting a fellow detective of a very serious offense. Murder by some gangbanger is one thing. A killing by one of our own would pulverize this city like never before. The department's reputation would take decades to recover, if ever. And thirdly, you of all people should watch where you throw stones."

"Meaning?"

"Meaning you've made your share of mistakes also. Azusa ring any bells?"

Frank's neck warmed. He realized the last thing the chief needed on his plate was dealing with a psychopath cop on his payroll. Was the chief really going to sweep this under the rug and never let it see the light of day? Would Wadkins' punishment for homicide be a slap on the wrists and a simple reprimand?

Kent broke the silence and when he did, it baffled Grace and Santana. "If anything, Detective Wadkins deserves your gratitude, not these outlandish allegations."

"Gratitude? What the fuck for?"

Kent squared his shoulders. "Watch your tone, Grace. You're on thin ice and it's cracking fast."

Playing mediator, Michelle put her palm on Frank's chest in a calming manner. "Why do we owe the detective our gratitude?"

"It's evident your career is under the microscope, Grace," Kent said, "Has been since Azusa. Yours as well, Detective Santana, by drawing the short straw and being partnered with him."

"If I may say so, sir," Michelle interjected, "being teamed with Detective Grace is the best thing to happen to my career."

Frank stifled a smile.

"Be that as it may, keeping in mind Azusa as well as having Elijah Leach assassinated while in your custody, you were being scrutinized more than ever. One more fuck-up and you'd be done. Detective Wadkins took it upon himself to bring in Xavier Leach from KLAG. He put his life at stake by redirecting the spotlight from you. *That's* why he deserves your gratitude."

Frank shut his eyes, shook his head in revulsion. For some reason, his mind drifted to the monthly poker games he and buddies from West Bureau enjoyed. Frank would usually close the evening with more in his pocket than at the outset. He wasn't a gifted card player, but he knew how and when to bluff. "I received an encrypted email that provided me the name of Eddie Evanovich. I utilized my sources and though it took a while, I traced the origin of that email."

"And?"

"It was sent from Troy Wadkins's IP address."

Michelle knew her partner was winging it but she remained pokerfaced.

Kent pulled on his chin, angled over and stubbed out his cigarette. "That's bullshit."

Frank doubled-down on his own falsehood. "It's not, sir."

Kent wouldn't accept there was a killer on the LAPD. Or maybe couldn't. "The man deserves your gratitude."

"Gratitude, my ass."

"I warned you once, Grace. Watch your tone." Kent paused long enough to light up a third cigarette. After a moment of retrospection, he added, "Let's say, just for shits and giggles, you're correct. Wadkins did murder Xavier in his car. Wadkins acted like Jack-fucking-Ruby and killed Elijah in Paso Robles. A vigilante. So what?"

"So what?" Frank barked.

"The man's a hero."

"A hero? Sir, with all due—no, you know what? Screw that *with all due respect* crap."

"Frank—" Michelle cautioned, trying to calm her partner.

"No, I want to know why he's a hero to you. I'd love to know, 'cause I sure don't see it."

Kent threw his finger at Frank. "Those bastards fucked with me. With my city. They cost us millions in damage and tourism. On my watch! The FB-fucking-I, the JTT-fucking-F, Homeland-fucking-Security. The entire United States fucking government couldn't find a pair of shit-for-brains anarchists. But you know what? Troy Wadkins did. One of *mine* found them."

"I found Elijah," Frank quantified, immediately regretting the one-upmanship.

"And Wadkins eliminated them, *both* of them." Kent took a drag and amended his statement. "Both of them, if you're correct." He pointed to the window. "If you're right, there's not one resident of my city, not one American, who wouldn't have taken out those pricks if they had a chance to. Wadkins deserves a fucking statue!"

"Sir," Michelle said, shocked at the chief's irate logic. "That's not how it's supposed to work. We have laws for a reason."

"We do indeed, Santana. There's black, there's white and then there's gray. I'm not validating these ludicrous accusations but if you are correct, and Wadkins did execute those two fuck heads, more power to him. I say the man's a hero."

"The man's a hero," Frank mimicked in disgust.

"To me, to this city, and to millions across this country, yes he is. What our city lost monetarily we saved in not having to put on a dog and pony trial that would have cost taxpayers more."

"A hero," Frank mirrored. He couldn't believe it.

"*If* he acted in the manner you claim, a claim with no evidence admissible in a court of law, I might add."

Michelle feared this day coming since the formation of the Santana/Grace partnership. She'd been fully cognizant their careers were on divergent trajectories. Now, two years later, after she and Frank had built trust, reliance, and friendship, she was witnessing personally the culmination of his career. The curtain was coming down on Frank Grace and Michelle had a front row seat. What her partner said next would solidify the end result.

"Your wife's got great legs."

Kent glared at Frank as if he was dog shit encrusted in the sole of his shoe. His body stiffened, his fists clenched. "Are. You. That. Stupid?"

"Charlotte used those legs and kicked my ass tonight."

Kent stepped closer. "She won't be the only one, Grace."

Michelle placed herself between her partner and her boss. She looked wide-eyed at Frank. *What are you talking about?*

"I saw your wife tonight."

"You son-of-a-bitch!" Kent roared. He jumped at Frank in blind rage. Michelle used her training and subdued the police chief.

Dispensing with the *detective* title, Frank declared, "I tailed Wadkins last night to the Chateau Marmont. And that's where he met Charlotte."

"She's in Big Bear."

"No, she's not. She used a drive-stun Taser on me, subdued me. Then she and Wadkins placed me in the trunk and drove me out to Point Dume." Frank explained the rest, omitting the creepy part about Detective Craft.

Kent's fists unclenched, his shoulders dropped along with his head. Weakly, "She's in Big Bear."

Frank allowed the magnitude of Charlotte's infidelity to sink in.

Kent turned away, waggling his head, and shambled toward the mantel where framed photographs lined the shelf. He held the brick edifice to balance himself.

Frank brought down the other shoe—gently. "She admitted murdering Melina Wadkins." He paused, amended his statement. "Wadkins claimed she did, but Charlotte didn't deny it."

Kent lifted his hooded eyes. The photos before him presented a pictorial history of his years with the department, from his cadet status to graduation from the academy and ultimately his ascension to police chief of Los Angeles. There were images of Krissy as well as Charlotte's children from her first marriage. Hardened, rigid, tough, stoic, Weldon Kent began sobbing.

Seeing this, Frank felt a pang of guilt for opening Kent's eyes to his wife's infidelity.

Michelle, shocked by this revelation, resisted the temptation to walk over and console the chief. She remained at her partner's side.

Kent, still facing away, mumbled something inaudible.

"Pardon me, sir?"

"She killed Melina Wadkins?"

"Afraid so."

"And Krissy."

Frank and Michelle stared at Kent's defeated posture and then at each other. *Did you hear that, too?*

"I'm sorry, sir," Michelle said, "Did you say—"

"Yes. Yes, goddammit, yes."

Kent raised his arm and drove his fist into the brick with enough fury to break his hand. He lifted a family Christmas photo and stared at it. "She murdered my baby, my Krissy."

"I don't—understand," Frank stammered.

Kent's hand trembled, the framed family photo slipping free. He squatted to pick it up.

Michelle stepped over and helped Kent stand on rickety legs.

The chief traced Krissy's face with shaky fingers. Her smile was flawless, innocent with a smattering of mischief. He made no effort to hide the tears. It'd only been days, yet it seemed an eternity. His child was gone. "Krissy," he breathed, followed by a stern, "Charlotte." Kent was bearing his soul, speaking with his heart and not his head.

Frank wished he was wired. He doubted Kent would implicate his wife once he gained control of his emotions. "Your wife murdered your daughter?"

"Her stepdaughter. This was…" His words trailed off.

Michelle hesitated before taking the chief's hand in her own. "Sir—Chief Kent. Detective Grace and I work for you. You can tell us."

Kent struggled with the enormity. He began patting himself down. Realizing the chief was craving a cigarette, Frank ambled to the table. He lifted the pack, tapped one out. He started handing it over filter first. Then he froze.

His insides churned, his brain pulsed within his confining skull.

The filter.

Kent smoked an uncommon brand. The filter dotted with drawings of diamonds. Frank, a smoker in his youth, knew those addicted never paid attention to the filter. But now his fingers shook.

He'd seen this filter design only twice: a stubbed out cigarette in an ash tray at the Mar Vista home the Leaches rented from their uncle and again at the Paso Robles winery. Neither Xavier nor Elijah Leach smoked.

And now Frank was seeing it a third time.

As Kent took the cigarette, Frank wondered why the man who commanded a police force large enough to rival the army of a small nation had been in the home of domestic terrorists.

Chapter 37

Kent inhaled deeply and remained lost in the family portrait of happier days gone by before being pulled back to the present by Detective Santana. "Your wife, sir?"

Unable to meet their eyes, he spoke to the framed picture instead, confessing sins to his deceased child. "It was Charlotte's idea. Originally. My wife's from back east, both her kids from her first marriage live there now. I fought hard for Krissy to stay here with us. But she insisted on her own place." Kent swallowed, still gazing mournfully at his daughter's image. "My little girl wanted her independence, her freedom. I knew with my child gone and Charlotte's three thousand miles away, the house would feel…empty." He lifted his head, eyed Frank. "You plan on sending yours to college?"

"Hopefully. Not sure if Abby and I can swing it." For an instant they were just two guys chatting about their children's future.

Kent resumed speaking to Krissy. "Charlotte longed to be close to her children. But how could I give this up? This is my home, my city. Being a cop is all my grandfather knew, all my father knew, and all I know. Cop DNA since I was in the womb. Then Charlotte came up with a plan."

Frank and Michelle knew they'd need to let it come naturally, not force it. The same approach they utilized when questioning a suspect they now put into action with the chief of police.

"An attack here in LA," Kent said steadily. "It would put me in the national spotlight. Apprehending terrorists could do wonders for one's career. And, yes, political aspirations."

Michelle swallowed hard. "Sir, I don't…How?"

"Think Nine/Eleven. Mayor Giuliani used his newfound fame from that hellacious day to run for president seven years later. He seized the opportunity. You didn't see the mayor of DC throwing his hat in the ring. Or the mayor of Shanskville…if they even have a mayor."

"You wanted to be president?" Frank sneered.

"I don't know squat about politics, I *play* politics. But I prefer accomplishing things, not engaging in bi-partisan doublespeak. I know the law. My ambitions were lower than the mayor's. Lower, more attainable."

"Attorney general," Frank quantified.

"Attorney general," Kent confirmed. "There's an election soon, a new administration. Using my status after nabbing two terrorists would make me the clear-cut choice." He paused. "That's how Charlotte saw it, and damned if I could shoot any holes in it. We'd be back east, she'd be close to her children, and I'd have a cleaner job."

"But, sir, the bomb attack in West Hollywood?" Michelle said.

Kent looked at her. "You served in the military, correct?"

"Two tours, yes, sir."

"A false flag operation to use military lingo. A set-up. Think about it: An abandoned building where the bulk of damage would be in dollars, not blood, on a stretch of Sunset that tourists avoid and locals know better than to wander into. Coupla' bums, drug dealers, and hookers."

"A few tourists and locals were killed *also*."

Kent shrugged. "The misfortune of bad timing."

Frank didn't know if he should laugh or cry, arrest the

man or choke the daylights out of him. He was the city's top cop who commanded a force of ten thousand strong.

Yet, he put all of this at stake—his career, his reputation, his legacy—because of his wife's harebrained scheme. Maybe Wadkins was correct, after all.

Pussy and money.

Michelle folded her arms across her chest. "How'd the Leaches get dragged in?"

"Pawns," Kent said frankly. "To pull this off, we needed to make it credible. Anti-establishment, anarchistic radical types. They had those predilections. Parents killed at Waco, no future, no hope, no commitments. They fit perfectly."

"So you made a pact with a couple of revolutionaries?" Michelle asked, thinking out loud. "Talk about a deal with the devil."

"Four million. They were promised four million apiece wired into an account of their choosing. They'd blow up a building, instill some panic, and leave the very country they loathed."

"Where would you come up with that kinda money?" asked Frank.

"If California was a country, we'd have the tenth biggest economy on the planet. Siphoning eight million is pocket change. But they'd never get to see one plum nickel."

"Didn't they realize they were being set-up?"

"Eight million's a lot of money, Detective Santana. They gambled. If not them, someone else would have been enlisted."

"But you said they were pawns, patsies," Frank said. "So you never intended to deliver the cash?"

Kent snickered. "Of course not, Detective Grace. What kind of man do you think I am?"

Frank had plenty of answers to that, all of which he kept to himself.

"The Leaches were tools. Right from the outset, I intended to double-cross them. I'd keep tabs on them, string 'em along as the media built fear to a crescendo. And then, when the time was right, I'd bring down the hammer. They'd be arrested. I'd look like a hero. Hello, Washington."

"They'd obviously never get to testify."

"Correct. That's the beauty of it." Kent met Frank's eyes with a prideful expression that one of his own had solved the riddle. "You *were* spot-on, Detective Grace. Detective Wadkins *did* murder Elijah and Xavier."

"So what'd you promise Wadkins?" Frank asked.

"Quarter of a million. Untraceable. And with *his* fame, he'd be the obvious choice to replace me as chief."

Frank held his pulsating head. "Why involve me? Your ducks were all in a row."

Kent had to look away. As hard as it was to come clean about what he'd already shared, this next bombshell would be greater. "I built upon the foundation my wife laid." He finished the cigarette, discarded it, and continued. "If I'm using a terrorist attack in LA as the jumping off point to launch my tenure as attorney general, I couldn't leave behind any unfinished business. Seeking confirmation from the United States Senate, I needed to make sure there were no loose ends."

Frank and Michelle exchanged a look, both confused.

Kent sighed, disappointed he needed to break it down so simplistically. "Loose ends like Detective Nichols, loose ends like the *honorable* Judge Sherman."

"You had the Leaches kidnap them?" Frank cried, aghast.

"Earl Sherman's the worst thing to happen to the LAPD since Rodney King. The worthless judge handcuffs us and then expects us to keep the city safe. Fuck him. It was payback." Kent faced Michelle. "I know you and Kendra Nichols were friends at one time, but admit it. The woman's a slut, a blight on the LAPD."

Taking umbrage with the malevolent statement, Michelle snorted. "Do you really believe Kendra's the only one in the entire department with a dubious past?"

"Of course not," Kent stated dismissively. "But she's the

only one who slept with the police chief." He waited a beat, allowing Grace and Santana to lift their chins. "She sealed her fate the summer before last. Too much alcohol, too much stress, and Charlotte and I were having issues. When Kendra Nichols, twenty years younger, threw herself at me…well, I may be police chief but I still have wants."

Frank nearly burst out laughing. Moments ago, Kent was visibly demoralized by his wife's adultery. Yet, he, too, had strayed. Frank had never felt so grateful for the bullshit-free marriage he had with Abby.

"If I'm to become attorney general, I can't risk having a Kendra Nichols in my past. I'm not Anthony Weiner or Gary Hart or Bill Clinton," Kent locked his eyes on Frank. "Or loose ends like you."

Frank's gut tightened. He should've seen this coming, but it was appalling nonetheless.

"The Azusa Bloodbath four years ago brought this department to its knees. And almost me down as well."

"I acted accordingly that night, sir." Frank found it interesting that in spite of everything presently surrounding him, he still defended an action from years earlier.

"Yes. No. Doesn't matter. Your blatant act set us back years, due to detrimental press. And as such, Detective, you and I will be forever linked. Does anyone see Mark Fuhrman and not think OJ?"

It all came together in Frank's mind—quickly. "You set me up too."

"Most definitely," Kent confirmed with nary a hesitation. "Right from the outset you were played. Do you honestly believe that being in West Hollywood at the precise moment a bomb detonated was just random? Or that Wadkins just happened to seek shelter in a liquor store under the guise of purchasing a six pack for his auto mechanic?"

Frank shoved his hands into his pockets, nostrils flared. He rocked on the balls of his feet. Knowing the chief purposely placed him in harm's way took a back seat to another fact. "So you're the one who had Elijah Leach take a shot at my wife that night."

"Of course," Kent claimed, matter-of-factly. "You were dragging your feet, and I believed you required a motivational kick in the ass. I needed you in the game, Grace. I brought you in to keep an eye on you. Keep your friends close and all that. Why the hell do you think I assigned you to track down the Leaches? I'm the puppet master and you are my marionette."

"Son of a bitch," Frank spat. "You could've killed my wife."

"Elijah's the one who shot at your house."

"That makes it okay?"

"You needed a kick in the ass, Grace," Kent repeated.

"So do you."

The two men glared, waiting for the other to make the next move. Michelle disrupted the testosterone-leaden competition and kept her focus on the end result. "What went wrong?"

"We underestimated our enemy."

Frank found it downright laughable. Kent was in bed with Xavier and Elijah. Yet, he talked as if he was an observer.

"The exhilaration over their big payday wore off," Kent continued. "They started getting antsy and questioning if they'd live to see one red cent of that money. When they deviated from our plan and kidnapped that hooker—"

"Hiromi Komatsu."

"Whatever. When they kidnapped her, it proved they had gone rogue and couldn't be trusted. That's when I realized I'd been double crossed. I *did* send Wadkins to Paso Robles to eliminate them. I knew *you* never would take them out. I was confident both brothers would be present. But with only Elijah removed and Xavier unaccounted for things went haywire. I lost control."

"*That's* why Xavier kidnapped Krissy," Michelle mused. "It was to get back at you. He knew he'd never be allowed to stand trial and he needed, as he said, a bargaining chip. One spoke in a very large wheel. As long as he had the chief's daughter stowed away, you'd make sure he'd see the inside of a courtroom."

"It was lose-lose, Detective Santana. Leach gets his day in court, and I'm destroyed. He gets killed, no one finds my daughter, and I'm destroyed."

Frank summed up while wringing his hands. "Your wife concocts an idea to relocate back east. You build on it, hoping to become the top cop in the country. You solicit a couple kids with antigovernment tendencies, join them at the hip, knowing all along they're pawns. They wise up, realize you'll betray them. You lose your daughter in the process. And in the cruelest twist of all, your beloved Charlotte, the one who hatches the whole scheme, ends up sleeping with the guy you recruited to silence the Leaches." Frank sneered. "It all evened out, didn't it?"

"What do you mean?"

"You fucked up," Frank barked. "Your flawlessly devised plot was anything but flawless. You ended up losing everything—your reputation, your child, your legacy, your wife." Frank took a step forward. "And now your freedom. Chief Kent, please turn around and place your hands behind your back." As soon as Frank announced his intention he realized he had no cuffs.

"You have nothing on me, Grace," Kent snarled. He'd run the full gamut of emotions and was now back to defiance. "What I just told you is hearsay. You have no proof of anything." He laughed sardonically. "And who do you think people will believe: a highly esteemed leader of law enforcement or a trigger happy burn-out with a checkered past?"

"Two against one. I'll testify under oath as well."

"Detective Santana, you sealed your fate when you were teamed with Frank Grace. He'll go down. You can step aside or go down with him."

"I'll take that chance. Frank Grace is my partner. And my friend."

"You've got nothing, not a single fucking thing on me. This was all Charlotte's doing."

"I knew my ears were burning for a reason."

The trio pivoted quickly. Charlotte Kent stood in the hallway, a suitcase in each hand for effect. She lowered the luggage and sashayed to her husband putting an extra lilt in her hips.

"What happened to your nose?" Kent asked.

"All those years on Broadway, choreographer for two different studios. Yet, I'm still a klutz." Charlotte chuckled. "I tripped getting out of the tub. Pretty funny if you think about it."

Frank's head-butt at Point Dume apparently never happened.

"You're home early," Kent pointed out.

"After breaking my nose, skiing didn't sound too appealing. And, what can I say? I've been worried about you, honey." She kissed him on the lips. He didn't turn away. Rotating, she asked, "Detectives Grace and Santana, why are you here at this ungodly hour?"

Charlotte had changed her clothes, cleaned herself up, and bandaged her nose. All remnants of the earlier altercation had been removed.

"Taser anyone lately, Mrs. Kent?" Frank asked. *Mrs. Kent?* In spite of everything, he still treated the police chief's wife with respect.

Charlotte scrunched her face. "Taser anyone?"

Weldon Kent had two loves in his life. One was the department he directed. The other was at his side, smelling delightful and exuding sexuality. He'd implicated his wife as well as incriminated himself. However, there was no record of his admission. As the Kents faced the detectives, side by side, a united front, he realized he and his wife could still come out unscathed. One simple call would ruin Grace and Santana. They wouldn't even land gigs as bank guards.

However, Charlotte *had* lied, deviated from their perfect plan—*her* perfect plan. Her plot went up in flames and his little girl was now dead. Rubbing salt in the wound was the fact she ended up screwing their co-conspirator.

"You see Troy lately?" he questioned rigidly.

"Troy? Troy Wadkins? No, I haven't. Why?" Charlotte presented an expression of bafflement. Shifting glances between the detectives and her husband, she asked, "What's going on here?"

"Detective Grace," Kent explained, "claims he saw you at Chateau Marmont with Wadkins."

Charlotte chuckled uproariously. "Rooms there are a fortune. And why—why would I see Troy?"

"You tell me."

Charlotte feigned pensiveness, the weight of the world pushing down on her shoulders. She shot a fretful peek at Frank and Michelle before speaking softly. "Maybe we should discuss this in private?"

"No. I want to know. Did you meet Wadkins?"

Shocked, Charlotte said nothing.

"They know," Kent declared. "I told them."

Impassive, Charlotte contemplated her next play. Finally, "Yes, I met him. We needed to discuss some things—"

"*What things?*" Kent screamed.

Frank eyed Michelle. Nothing went south quicker than a domestic disturbance call. The fact it involved the chief of police was immaterial.

"I think we should discuss this in private, honey."

"Goddammit, no!" Kent stepped away, not wanting his thoughts swayed by being in close proximity to her. "Are you *fucking* Wadkins?"

Charlotte's perplexed look transformed into one of hurt and distress. If her shapely killer legs wouldn't soften her husband's anger, tears would. She began weeping.

Michelle rolled her eyes.

"Honey, you're my husband. You're the one I love. We have a history, and we will have a future. Is Troy good looking? Yes. But I would never throw away the best part of my life for one night with him."

Kent started reaching for a cigarette.

"Now we should discuss some things—alone." Charlotte pointed her chin. "This is a family matter, Detectives. I'm not about to air our dirty laundry in public. My husband will help me upstairs with my luggage. I take it you can see yourselves out." She wiggled her fingers. "C'mon, honey."

Kent dawdled. He narrowed his gaze on the detectives, regret about confessing written on his face. Maybe Grace lied, concocted the whole story about his wife's infidelity to secure a heartfelt confession. "I agree. It's best you leave."

He didn't take Charlotte's hand but did fall in step, following her across the living room, passing in front of a window fronting the driveway.

The explosion sent shards of glass like spears shooting in all directions.

Chief Kent went down.

Frank and Michelle crouched, turned, and impulsively reached for weapons neither was carrying. The high-caliber bullets tore through the window, imbedding themselves in furnishings and walls and the mantel. The Kent Christmas photo was blown to a million pieces.

Charlotte stood stock-still, hands covering her gaping mouth. "Weldon?" she breathed.

Detective Wadkins appeared, his supercilious smile more pronounced than ever. Instantly, Frank comprehended. Charlotte had killed Wadkins's spouse, Wadkins would kill hers.

Michelle, however, hadn't put that together. Instead, her eyes widened and she felt a hollowness in her chest she'd never felt before. And hoped to never feel again. Wadkins had a hostage.

"Aunt Michelle!" Sophia cried.

Chapter 38

Minutes ago, Kent dubbed himself the puppet master. However, within seconds of having a bullet tear through his shoulder, it became evident Wadkins was pulling the strings.

Despite being shot and down on his knees and Wadkins taking aim on his head, Kent hurled unending profanities at the double-crossing backstabbing detective. Wadkins cocked the hammer.

Kent didn't ease up. Watching helplessly, Frank again pictured Tom Berenger in *Platoon:* The only one who could kill Barnes was Barnes. Weldon Kent was too tough to die.

Charlotte sauntered over and took hold of Wadkins wrist. Pressing her amble bosom against his shoulder, she shook her head once. "I'll call him."

Call who? Frank wondered.

Wadkins looked around, then zip-tied his boss, gagged his mouth, and herded him into a coat closet. "The more you try to break free, the more likely you'll bleed out." After locking the chief in darkness, he knotted one end of another zip-tie to the brass handle of the closet door before fastening the other end around the leg of a weighty armoire. Kent could not escape.

Frank and Michelle could do nothing but watch. Wadkins and Charlotte operated as a cohesive well-trained duo. There was constantly a weapon at Sophia's head.

Wearing pink jammies and a Tigger T-shirt, Sophia was resolute. She'd wept initially but now the nine-year-old showed bravery beyond her years. The same, however, could not be said for her aunt.

"You'll be okay, sweetheart," Michelle offered from across the room, voice quaking. "*We'll* be okay."

"Let the girl go," Frank avowed.

"She's my ticket outta here, Grace."

"She's got nothing to do with this!" Michelle shouted defiantly. In reality she was more upset with herself than Wadkins. Since agreeing to take custody of her niece, she'd been fearful. No, scared. Unlike her partner who was adept at disconnecting his work life from his professional life, Michelle had never before had to care for anyone but herself. Leaving Sophia asleep in the car was irresponsible, careless, idiotic. If this ended badly, how—oh, God—*how* would she explain it to Bianca? She faced Frank, wondering how the hell he managed. "Take me instead," she pleaded with Wadkins.

"Back up, bitch," Wadkins snapped.

"Don't call my aunt the B-word," Sophia said. "You're a bad man."

Michelle's lips trembled with both pride and trepidation.

Wadkins bent at the waist and whispered loud enough for all to hear. "And why am I bad man?"

"'Cause you are. You called my aunt a bad name, and you shot that man in the shoulder and you're holding a gun to my head. I'm a little kid. Grownups shouldn't do that."

"Don't you think your aunt has shot people?"

"Maybe—but they were probably bad and deserved it. Just like you."

Michelle's eyes welled. Her tone altered from boldness to helplessness. "Just let her go, Troy. I'm asking you as a favor."

Wadkins stood. "Fear not, Santana. Do what I say and you'll get her back. Try anything and you'll have another family member to visit at Forest Lawn."

"He's here," Charlotte announced peering through the curtains moments later.

"Showtime boys and girls. Move."

જ્એજ્

Frank's last time in a stretch limo was on his ten-year wedding anniversary when, normally frugal, for that occasion he pulled out all the stops.

As they sipped Dom Perignon Rose, the chauffeur drove him and Abby to LAX where they boarded a flight for a romantic weekend at the Fairmont on San Francisco's Nob Hill.

This time, however, there was no six hundred dollar bottle of wine, no Abby in a little black dress highlighting her blonde hair and dazzling cobalt eyes, no Frank wearing his Armani. Instead, he and Michelle sat side by side, the barrel of a .38 aimed at his chest. Sophia sat across the spacious compartment sandwiched between Wadkins and Charlotte. The opaque windows reminded Frank of the two-ways back at West Bureau.

When initially shepherded into the limo, he assumed they'd head into the city. Now westbound on the 101, Frank wondered what the destination was. A return to the winery in Paso Robles was possible but unlikely. Observing Charlotte who seemed lost watching the countryside roll by, Frank asked, "Who's Lyman?"

Charlotte drew her gaze back from the fertile foothills.

"Lyman." Frank angled his chin indicating the driver beyond the soundproof barrier.

"He works for Marv Friedman, the movie director. He and Weldon are good friends. He often allows us use of his private jet and, in this case, one of his limos."

Wadkins cast a wary eye on Charlotte before addressing Frank. "Ironic, isn't it?"

"What is?"

"The same Gulfstream you chartered to Paso Robles will also be my vehicle of escape."

"Ours," Charlotte reminded him.

"Yes, ours."

"You may be bright, Wadkins," Frank remarked, "but you're not shrewd."

"I've got a gun pointed at you, so tell me who's not shrewd."

"You really think Kent won't find you? You're a pariah, a scourge. You've been a cop long enough to know we come down harder on our own. You'll spend the rest of your days looking over your shoulder. You too, Charlotte."

"Hawaii, the Marshall Islands, Manila, and lastly Brunei where's there no extradition," Wadkins announced. "Seven hundred thousand from Melina's life insurance goes a long way in Brunei."

Frank shifted his glance between them. First, he smiled, then chuckled, and finally burst out laughing.

"Something funny?"

"Funny? It's absolutely his-fucking-sterical." Noticing Sophia, he apologized for using the F-word.

"We've all had a rough morning and can use a laugh, Grace. Why don't you share?"

Frank spoke to Wadkins, as if Charlotte didn't exist, playing on what he perceived was doubt creeping in, as indicated by her vacant stare through the window. "*She* was born with a silver spoon in her mouth, *her* family comes from old money. New York aristocrat, a social climber if there ever was one. Broadway dancer, movie choreographer. I'm sure she'll be ecstatic living in…in…Brunei." Chuckling, Frank held his gut for affect.

"Brunei is modernized. Fifth richest nation in the world."

Frank looked at Michelle. "Brunei? You believe this guy?"

Silence filled the suddenly oppressive limo. Wadkins looked at Charlotte. Charlotte returned to contemplating the scenery.

Michelle, picking up on the seeds of doubt planted in Charlotte's mind, added to her partner's antagonism. "Seven hundred thousand, you said?"

"Yes."

Michelle snickered at Charlotte. "Lady, you must be one helluva piece of ass."

"Trust me, Santana, she is. More of a woman than *you'll* ever be."

"Three million more?"

"What?"

Michelle angled forward which caused Wadkins to tighten his grip on the gun. "Before you showed up and put a bullet in Kent's shoulder, he told us everything—*including* his intention of giving you three million." She held up three fingers.

"You're baiting me. He told me a quarter million."

Michelle continued lying. "If he was willing to pay the Leaches four million apiece, you really think you'd get only two hundred fifty thousand?" Michelle shook her head pitifully. "Two hundred fifty thousand *with* Charlotte, three million *without*." She faced Charlotte. "Hope you're worth it, lady." Michelle leaned back and relished the daggers of confusion expressed on their faces.

"She's lying, Troy," Charlotte maintained. "That's not true." Her words carried strength but didn't diminish Wadkins's suspicion.

Charlotte's jaw clenched, upset she had to defend herself against a boldfaced untruth. She couldn't risk it falling apart now. "Tell him the truth, you little bitch. Tell him you're lying."

Michelle guffawed, "Sure, okay, okay, I'm lying. Feel better?" As the co-conspirators cagily studied each other, Michelle mirrored her partner. "Brunei!"

The next ten minutes were spent in silence, everyone contemplating their own role, until Wadkins announced, "We're here."

The limo traversed the wetlands known as The Goleta

Slough and entered the grounds of Santa Barbara Municipal Airport. SBMA was nowhere close to air traffic when compared to LA's other airports. It was, however, beyond the immediate reach of Kent's police force.

Lyman parked fifteen yards from the Gulfstream V. He adjusted his chauffeur's cap, exited, dutifully opened the door for his passengers, and got a bullet in the gut for his trouble. When leaving Kent's home, they'd driven by the corpse of Kent's security guard. Lyman was the second innocent person Wadkins had shot in the last hour. Frank instinctively leaned forward but was held in check by a .38 to his forehead. "Tsk, tsk," Wadkins scoffed. He grabbed Sophia's clammy hand and yanked her out.

"You said you'd let her go!" Michelle cried.

"I certainly will," Wadkins responded. "*After* we get to Brunei."

"You son of a bitch!" Unconcerned for her own safety Michelle dove across the rear compartment, throwing herself at Wadkins. She felt something slam against her cheek and got knocked back against the seat. The powerful left cross by Charlotte stunned her. Michelle slid her hand across the laceration. She'd been slashed by, of all things, Charlotte's lustrous wedding ring.

Stepping over the writhing body of the driver, Charlotte exited wordlessly, grabbed Sophia, and started ushering her toward the waiting jet.

Wadkins stuck his head into the vehicle for a parting shot. "You said something about three million, didn't you?"

Frank and Michelle didn't respond.

The pompous smirk reappeared. "I could probably get that for Sophia. Nine years old, American? Be worth a fortune on the sex slave market."

Frank's jaw tightened, Michelle's rage boiled. But they were powerless with Wadkins holding the gun. In the distance, Charlotte struggled with an obstinate nine-year-old. Sophia threw her arms in all directions, hopelessly digging her heels into the stairs leading into the plane.

"Aunt Michelle, help!"

"I love you, Soph!" Michelle shouted through a veil of tears.

Her niece disappeared into the cabin.

"I should kill you both," Wadkins declared. "But I won't. Your penance will be to live tortured lives. You, Grace, are finished. Your career is kaput. You think I'll be looking over *my* shoulder? I can resurface and be at your front door whenever I damn well feel like it, whenever you least expect it. Think about that when you curl up with your wife every night or send your kids to school every day. And you, Santana? You'll never see your niece again, always wondering who she got sold to." He chuckled. "I'll send you a postcard."

"See you on the other side of the world," Michelle affirmed.

"I'll be waiting."

Wadkins backpedaled, hoisting the wounded driver to his feet. Lyman was in and out of consciousness. His head bobbed, his palm clutching the gaping wound in his belly. The limp chauffeur was dragged toward the extended stairs, his heels thumping against each step. At the top step Wadkins slammed the grip of the Beretta into the man's skull, sending him somersaulting down to the asphalt.

Frank and Michelle raced over to the victim. They eyed the wound, then each other. *Not good.*

The Gulfstream's turbine engines whistled to life. Clothes flapping in the tornadic gusts, Grace and Santana transferred the driver to the limo's rear compartment. Spitting up clumps of blood, foaming at the mouth, Lyman struggled to breathe, biting at the air. "My...my daughter..."

"What about her?" Frank gulped.

Lyman tried to sit up, couldn't. "Maddy."

"What about Maddy?"

"She's got—soccer at—one. I hafta be there. I— promised her—"

His body twitched, he coughed twice, his eyes became fixed.

Frank placed his hand over Lyman's face and lowered his lids.

Michelle looked away from the body and watched the jet containing her niece cross a median and taxi toward the top of the long runway.

It was a tick before seven a.m. The airport had not yet come to life.

Michelle interlocked her fingers atop her head. She couldn't breathe. "What am I—how do I tell my sister? How do I explain flying halfway around the planet to bring back Sophia? How will I even find her?"

Frank watched the Gulfstream approach the top of the airstrip. His partner was overcome with helplessness and drowning in despair. He'd never seen that look on her face. It tugged at his heart. If it was Ashley or Jake, he wouldn't just stand by. He and his partner did not share blood but Michelle was *family*. And that made Sophia family, too.

"I guess I'm going to Brunei," Michelle mumbled.

"Fuck Brunei. He's not getting off the ground."

Before Michelle could comprehend what was going on, Frank had thrown himself behind the wheel of the limo. She raced around and began riding shotgun. A flight controller in the tower had witnessed the shooting on the tarmac. Three security vehicles were advancing at a high rate of speed to apprehend Grace and Santana. In post Nine-Eleven America, airport security took no chances.

Viewing the onrushing patrol gave Frank pause. If someone observed the shooting of the limo driver that meant the Gulfstream would not be cleared for takeoff: Unless Wadkins breached the cockpit and held the pilot at gunpoint. Frank couldn't wait. He slammed the car into gear, told Michelle, "Buckle up," and pushed the pedal to the floor.

The elongated black Lincoln fishtailed then lunged, a trio of SUV's giving chase.

The limo rocketed forward adjacent to the runway. Sixty, seventy, then eighty miles per hour.

Michelle was fiddling with her phone. "I'm texting Sophia and telling her to stay down."

Frank knew it was pointless. Sophia wouldn't get the message. But Michelle had to try something, try *anything*. He turned a hard left and almost lost control. The enormous vehicle was twice the size and three times the weight of his own vehicle.

A muffled voice emanated through a bullhorn. The tinny words were unclear but Frank heard something along the lines of *stop* and *federal crime*. Michelle considered calling airport security, but there wouldn't be time. She screamed as she and Frank became coated with a shower of glass. The rear window had been shot out, obliterated, along with the partition separating the front and back seats. Airport security was shooting at them.

Frank wrenched the wheel left again.

The limo was at the west end of the runway and bulleting east. Six-thousand-fifty-two feet in front of them, the Gulfstream was positioned at the head of the airstrip. The pilot throttled, the mighty Rolls Royce engines roared to life, and the twenty-seven-ton jet containing five thousand gallons of jet fuel hurtled toward them.

With fear in her eyes and a quiver in her voice, Michelle patted Frank's knee. "Thank you." Her words were scarcely audible over the limo's growl.

"Just for the record," Frank said, while unbuckling his seat belt, "playing chicken with a small jet ain't exactly my favorite way to start the day."

The Lincoln sped east at ninety. The Gulfstream soared west at approximately the same velocity, approaching its takeoff speed.

Frank flinched and inadvertently tugged the wheel as another bullet from the pursuing security detail demolished the rear view mirror. He shouted a profanity and then righted the limo on a dead-ahead collision course.

Due to the speed of the two projectiles rushing toward each other, the distance between the jet and the car disappeared quickly. They were seconds away from a head-on impact.

∽∾∽

The Gulfstream was running out of room. The pilot needed more ground and more speed to lift the bird to the sky. But some lunatic had trespassed onto the strip, hindering his departure, and was now speeding in his direction, thwarting the takeoff.

"I can't make it!" the pilot screamed to the deranged man who'd pistol whipped the flight attendant, burst into the cockpit, and now held a gun to his head.

"Get us in the air!" the mad man shouted.

"I can't! We don't have the room."

"I said get us into the fucking air!" an unhinged Wadkins shouted.

"We'll come down after fifty feet," the frantic pilot yelled back. "I can't defy the laws of gravity."

Wadkins turned his wrist, sent the brains of the co-pilot splattering across the window, then turned the gun back on the pilot. "Figure it out!"

Captain Cahill glowered at the lunatic. Brain matter smeared along the window and skull fragments splaying his instrument panel. He'd flown dozens of sorties in Viet Nam, spent twenty five years working for United, and came out of retirement when moviemaker Marv Friedman offered him a lucrative salary. The money was good, but it wasn't worth not seeing his grandchildren grow up. "It's impossible!"

The distance between the limo and the Gulfstream dissolved swiftly. Frank and Michelle could see into the cockpit of the plane. The co-pilot was slumped over as if he'd been murdered. The pilot was pushed forward as Wadkins pressed his gun to the rear of the captain's skull.

Seconds before contact, Frank yanked the wheel left.

The pilot tap-danced on the rudders and pulled the yoke left also. The Gulfstream pitched, wobbled. The unnatural lurch knocked Wadkins into the co-pilot's corpse.

The Gulfstream and the limo were going too fast. *Too damn fast.* Captain Cahill realized early he'd run out of airstrip before lifting his plane. Now, his second fear was confirmed. A crash.

Michelle tried to throw herself onto the floor of the car, but her seat belt held her in place. She put her head between her knees as much as possible then felt Frank throw himself on top of her, shielding her body with his.

The limo spun, whirling like those spinning tea cups at Disneyland that Frank's children and Michelle's niece loved. It stopped perpendicular on the asphalt ribbon.

The pilot couldn't react in time.

The landing gear of the zooming Gulfstream was sheared off by the limo. Michelle screamed but it went nowhere, muted by the deafening, ear-splitting ground-shaking eruption of metal tearing metal. The top of the limo peeled back like tinfoil.

Frank uncoiled from his partner. Michelle straightened, gazed west down the runway. The fuselage had been torn free, separated from the landing gear, and scraped to a grinding halt a hundred or so yards down the runway. The vehicles that had been pursuing swerved to avoid the cascade of flying debris and deluge of engine parts.

"Oh my God, *No!*" Michelle screamed.

The fuselage containing Wadkins, Charlotte, and, more importantly, her niece, exploded and disappeared in a massive fireball.

Chapter 39

With an empty heart and heavy gait, Michelle got out of her car, trudged across the parking lot, and entered the facility. Her head hung low, shoulders slouched, she wondered if she'd ever again be able to look someone in the eye.

She crossed the lobby, oblivious to the anxious families in the waiting room and the antiseptic aroma that hung in the air. Turning right, she walked twenty feet and waited for the elevator. Something inside compelled her to glance left. Down the corridor and around the bend was the emergency room and a smaller waiting room. She knew that because it was there where she, her sister and her mother had once heard Something they'd never forget. Three words.

I'm very sorry.

Michelle's mom crumpled to her knees sobbing uncontrollably in Spanish. Bianca flew into a rage and started slapping the chest of the surgeon whose scrubs were coated in blood. Michelle, however, just stood there. Diego, her brother, gone? One minute they were in the front yard of their East LA home playing with their puppy. The next minute gunfire shredded the quiet morning.

She crawled over and held his face. He was scared, he was shaking, he was crying. He was trying to say something, to tell her something. But the words never left his throat.

She didn't know what was so important. And after hearing those three words, she never would.

The chime of the elevator pulled Michelle back to the present. She entered, pressed the button, rode up, and trekked down the hall. Standing at the entrance to the room, she wasn't sure if she had the resolve to cross the threshold. The bed looked enormous. Or maybe the person in it was simply that small. All she could view was a face with luxuriant black hair, the rest of the patient's body shrouded by blankets and tubes. Three IV poles stood sentry. Michelle steeled herself and entered. She tenderly touched the shoulder of the person sitting in the bedside chair and mumbled weakly, "How's she doing, Bianca?"

Bianca, like her sister, kept her head down, either also unable to look anyone in the eye or simply refusing to acknowledge her sister. She remained silent.

Though she had no idea what she was looking at, Michelle studied the IV bags, the numerous wires and tubes and hoses extending below the blanket and into her niece's little body. She watched the heart monitor for a moment, heard the cuff tightening and loosening on Sophia's arm. The girl's pulse was high, her blood pressure 160/100. She had a fever. A large incision like train tracks crisscrossed the right side of her face. Michelle winced but she knew full well not all scars were visible.

Sophia's eyes were closed but her jaw was taut. Michelle closed her own eyes, leaned over, and kissed her niece on the forehead. Bianca groaned. Turning, she exhaled. "I don't know what to say."

Bianca stared at her child. Nothing else in the world mattered.

"Is there anything I can do?"

"You've done enough."

"She's here—because of me."

Bianca nodded.

"If I could change places with her, I would."

"I wish you could too."

Michelle's chin quivered. "This is my fault. And I want you to know I'm sorry."

Bianca smirked, still refusing to acknowledge her sister's presence. Maybe that would never change.

Michelle went to the window and peeked through the blinds. From here the city actually looked beautiful. After some time she heard her sister say, "Let's talk outside."

In the hallway, Bianca looked beyond her sister's shoulder. A young father was sandwiched between two boys, maybe early teens, listening intently to a physician. Even from thirty feet away, Bianca could see the man deflate as if the life had just been sucked out of him, the future he planned for his family slipping away with each word the physician said. "It's funny," she remarked flatly.

"What is?"

"Just two weeks ago, I paid four hundred dollars to enroll Sophia in a tumbling class at the *Y*. Now, with her right arm amputated at the elbow that sure won't happen."

Michelle had no response. What could she say?

Bianca laughed mirthlessly. "If I bring in a note from the surgeon verifying my daughter had her arm cut off, they'll reimburse me. For half. *Half.* Funny, isn't it? Would someone really make that up?"

Michelle shrugged.

Bianca exhaled. And when she did, Michelle smelled alcohol on her sister's breath. So much for rehab. Her sister had started drinking again. Apparently heavily. She opened her mouth to say something then closed it. Who the hell was she to tell someone how to live their life?

"Was it worth it, Michelle?"

She squinted.

Bianca waved her arms. "All of this. Everything. Was it worth it?" Her voice grew steadily louder, magnified by the stillness of the hospital. "So you nab the bad guy, some crazy crooked cop. Wonderful. He'll spend the rest of his life in jail. And that Kent woman, Charlotte, right? I heard on the news she's claiming she was a pawn, claiming that

Wadkins blackmailed her family, threatening to go public about an affair the police chief had with some cop, Nichols. So, she walks away scot free. And Wadkins spends his life in prison. And Sophia? She's nine and will live the rest of *her* life with a prosthetic arm." Bianca shuddered, hugged herself. "Imagine when she gets to high school. You know how cruel kids can be."

Michelle tried to swallow but couldn't. Her throat had closed up.

"So, was it worth it?"

"That's the way the system works."

"Well, the system fucking sucks!"

Michelle couldn't disagree.

A timid nurse came over and asked them to keep their voices down, then walked away.

"You're part of the system, Michelle."

She couldn't disagree with that either. "What do you want me to do, Bianca?" she asked softly.

"Just stay away. From me, from my child. You're dead to me." She tightened her jaw and for the first time bore into her sister's eyes with such intensity, Michelle instinctively backpedaled. "I wish it'd been you all those years ago and not Diego."

And with that, Bianca hustled around her sister, forcefully brushing against her shoulder, entered the room, and dramatically closed the door, effectively keeping Michelle on the outside.

⌘

Twenty-four-year-old Luis Zamora took pride in the fact he never gave in to temptation. Be it when he was eight and his friend offered him a cigarette for the first time, eleven when the same friend offered him a joint or thirteen when a different friend slid a small bottle of Jack Daniels from his backpack in the schoolyard and handed it over, Luis always,

always, resisted. Even at his bachelor party when that stripper with the killer body who looked like Mila Kunis offered to take him in the back and blow his mind—literally and figuratively—Luis still resisted.

Now, however, he faced the toughest challenge yet.

Officer Zamora had been assigned to stand guard outside the hospital room of a terrorist, a colleague within the LAPD, who was apparently the mastermind behind bringing a city of ten million to its knees.

Zamora knew he was a cop, a public servant, not judge, jury, and executioner. But still…

A young male came out from the nurse's station. "You're Zamora, correct?"

"Yes, sir."

"There's a call for you. Someone from the police chief's office."

Chief Kent? Curling his lips and questioning why the chief would need to speak to him, Zamora automatically straightened his posture and started walking to the station.

The male nurse stopped him. "I'm sorry, you'll need to go outside or use a pay phone."

"Why?"

"We need to keep these lines clear."

Zamora pulled his cell but was stopped by the nurse who clearly believed Moses came down from Mt. Sinai with hospital policy. "Cellular phones can cause interference with our equipment."

Zamora vacillated.

"She said it was very urgent and insisted on speaking with you. *Pronto.*"

Knowing Chief Kent relished using that word and that it apparently filtered down to his staff, Zamora peeked into the room. Wadkins was drugged up on all sorts of painkillers. Zamora nodded to himself then scurried toward the elevator. He noticed a pay phone in an alcove but a woman was engaged in a heated conversation.

The elevator pinged. Zamora turned on his heels and

jumped in, wondering what Chief Kent wanted that was so urgent.

❧❧❧

Michelle heard the ping followed by harried footsteps. A quick glimpse over her shoulder showed the young cop hurrying into the elevator. "Yeah, you too," she said to the dial tone and hung up.

Wearing generic blue jeans and an unremarkable shirt that would be burned when she got home, she pulled the Dodgers cap low to conceal as much of her face as possible and verified her hair was tucked beneath the cap. She'd be unidentifiable by the cameras lining the hallway.

Passing the elevator, she knew she only had a few minutes until the cop returned. With a purposeful stride, she confidently marched down the hall. She knew exactly where she was going. She just was unclear what she'd do when getting there.

The hour was late, staff was limited. With patients sedated and surgeons and physicians only visiting during normal hours, nurses used this time to update their charts. The gentle sound of heart monitors and other devices wafted into the corridor.

Michelle entered the room undetected and stealthily closed the door behind her, then walked determinedly to the bed.

Wadkins's heartbeat was a textbook eighty beats per minute. Body temperature ninety-eight-point-six. His blood pressure one twenty over eighty. He had one small bandage on his cheek and not even close to the amount of IV's and tubes Sophia had. *Golden Boy, indeed.* Even asleep, the pompous grin remained etched across his face. He had one wrist handcuffed to each bedrail. Two wrists. Twice as many as Sophia.

"Wake up, shithead."

Wadkins didn't stir.

Michelle studied the few tubes entering his body and the lone bag on the IV pole. Thinking, thinking…

Weighing her next move.

Eyes sweeping the private room, Michelle noticed two chairs for visitors, a large foam pillow on one of them. She looked at the pillow, narrowed her eyes at Wadkins, then walked over, lifted the pillow, and returned to Wadkins' bedside.

Thinking, thinking…

"Wake up, shithead," she repeated, softer this time. When Wadkins still didn't respond, Michelle began tapping the pillow against her leg.

Thinking, thinking…

"Detective Santana?"

Michelle spun. "Mrs. Kent?"

"Charlotte, please." The police chief's wife reached back and turned the light out in the bathroom she'd just exited. She moved in such a way to keep whatever she was holding behind her back away from Michelle's sightline.

"What're you doing here?"

"What're *you* doing here?" Charlotte responded, moving the item further out of sight. But not before Michelle noticed it was the foam pillow from the second chair.

The two women stared at each other, stared *through* each other, waiting for the other to speak, trying to read each other's mind, each other's thoughts—each other's intention.

Chapter 40

"Grantana, you're up," Lieutenant Gallardo bellowed across the squad room.

Frank stood, put on his sport coat, and tapped his partner's shoulder. Michelle indicated she needed to finish her phone call.

Traipsing the maze of cubicles, Frank approached Gallardo's office. On the way, he knuckled Detective Craft's desk and tendered a pleasant grin.

Craft blushed then looked away like a shy schoolgirl caught eying a cute boy. She returned to organizing her new digs after requesting a workstation far away from Frank.

Since opening her heart to him, days earlier at Point Dume, she'd avoided him completely. Embarrassed. He'd always found her interest irritating, but now Frank realized he kind of missed it.

After ten minutes in the lieutenant's office, he returned to the shared workstation just as Michelle concluded her call. He jiggled his note pad. "Coupla' hikers found a body in Griffith Park."

Michelle nodded and stood. "Back to the grind."

The pair shuffled into the smoggy haze that filtered sunlight of a late Saturday morning. A gathering of detectives clustered at the entrance to West Bureau, sharing a smoke or biting into an early lunch. Crossing the parking lot on the way to picking up the vehicle they signed out, Michelle pointed to the employee lot. "I see you finally got your car back."

Frank's bland and stripped Malibu had spent time in the shop after being damaged in the West Hollywood explosion. Getting his Chevy back was the first step in a return to the pre-Leach days. Frank drove out of the lot and headed north. He had plenty of questions for his partner. He just wasn't sure if he wanted the answers.

Four days had passed since it all ended. It was hoped that, after firsthand witnessing the department's efficiency and having his life saved by one of their own, Earl Sherman would reinvent himself from outspoken adversary to ardent supporter. Instead, the judge chose to step down from the bench. After being kidnapped, beaten, and nearly killed, he'd seen enough violence for one lifetime. He appeared at peace, deciding to spend his remaining days playing golf and watching the Dodgers.

Sherman's decision to withdraw from the public was just the latest bad karma that befell the LAPD. Krissy Kent, the daughter of the police chief, was dead. Officer Newsted, the young patrolman who'd been given the simple mission of guarding the Grace home, was executed by Xavier Leach. The twenty-six-year-old was buried with honors. His wife, however, could not attend the service, having miscarried on her way to the funeral. Detective Grace's wife had nearly been shot. Detective Santana had her home broken into and then her niece taken hostage by, of all people, a highly respected detective, shortly after Wadkins's spouse herself was murdered. The entire department felt snake bit.

As if all of this wasn't enough, the most shocking incident happened yesterday.

Taking a side street to avoid gridlock on Sunset Blvd, Frank mused, "What do you make of Charlotte?"

Michelle hiked her shoulders. "They're saying it was an overdose."

"She'd been on sleeping pills for a decade. Seems unlikely she *accidentally* took too many."

"You think Kent killed his own wife?"

Frank's expression left no doubt. *Yes.*

"Maybe she really was distraught over everything," Michelle said.

"Maybe," Frank replied indifferently. After a moment, he borrowed the words of Chief Kent. "Loose ends."

The spin machine had operated on all cylinders and, when the smoke settled, Police Chief Weldon Kent came out the victim. The woman he cherished, his beloved Charlotte, had begun a torrid affair with a rogue, unstable Troy Wadkins. Anyone could see that Weldon and Charlotte were a strange-looking couple. Charlotte was sexual and provocative, and Wadkins was a good-looking guy. It made sense after all.

Charlotte had murdered Wadkins's wife and Wadkins planned to murder Charlotte's husband. The money from Melina Wadkins's life insurance policy would set them up nicely. Elijah and Xavier Leach were both viewed as domestic terrorists. Charlotte and Wadkins initially recruited the anarchists in an attempt to disgrace the police chief and ultimately have him resign in shame so they could be together.

Frank knew there were many unanswered questions still lingering. But no one would ask, and no one would push. Angelenos were happy to put all of this behind them. Charlotte Kent, Troy Wadkins, Elijah and Xavier Leach had been neatly packaged with a big bow and presented as a gift. The four individuals behind it all were now dead. Nice, neat, and no loose ends. Everyone could move forward.

Vernon Wayne/Gordon Whitefield, the uncle responsible for raising two revolutionaries, was forced to hightail it out of California. No one wanted the uncle of a terrorist in their neighborhood. Rumor had it he relocated to Vegas under another assumed name.

Hiromi Komatsu, the paramour of Earl Sherman and hostage of the Leaches, signed a book deal in the neighborhood of seven figures.

In spite of that, various TV appearances, and being cast in the upcoming season of *The Nut House*, she held steadfast to her principles. The name of the Honorable Judge Sherman never was made public.

Kendra Nichols was granted an extended leave. Michelle met her for dinner the night before last, two old friends catching up after losing touch. Kendra was undecided about returning. A cousin of hers was a small town sheriff up in South Dakota and, with his deputy retiring, there was a job available. "It might be a good time to start over," Kendra had hypothesized.

Start over. Michelle wondered if she'd ever be able to.

Chief Kent walked through a field of shit and emerged smelling like a rose, a victim of infidelity. In spite of being shot, locked in a closet, and left to bleed to death, the chief again proved too tough to die. The paramedics had been called to his home by Detective Grace.

Frank was hailed as a hero, though he didn't feel like one. He was largely credited, albeit not by the book, for stopping one of the Leaches in their tracks, saving the chief's life, and bringing to light the scheme hatched by a crooked cop and an adulterous woman. Perhaps the scales would finally be balanced against Azusa.

Stopping at a red light, Frank glanced at his partner. Michelle was noticeably preoccupied. The Sant-ace team was about to investigate a fresh homicide. He needed to know where her head was. Still, he couldn't find the right words so he asked instead, "How's Sophia holding up?"

"Kids are resilient," Michelle said softly. "Adults not so much."

"How're things between you and Bianca?"

Michelle rested her elbow on the door, held her chin in the palm of her hand, and gazed through the window. A heavily intoxicated man staggered down the street, two teenagers mocked the walk of a heavyset woman, and an elderly man pulled his wife closer as three gangbangers strutted in their direction. "I really hate this city."

"No you don't. You love it. You're the one who's determined to make it Utopian, remember?"

"Not any more. Everything's different. I'm different." After a moment, she added, "I don't know how you do it."

"Do what?" Frank glimpsed his partner whose eyes were misting over.

"Ashley, Jake, Abby. I—how do you manage?"

Frank could see the guilt in his partner's body language. "You need to ask Abby about it. I wonder that every day."

"Sophia—I left her in the car. I was sure she'd be okay. She was sleeping." She shook her head as if trying to dislodge her guilt. "Stupid, so fucking stupid."

"You couldn't have known Wadkins would show up. That just as easily could've been my kids in that car." Frank had his own remorse to deal with. "I was the one who called you, remember?"

Michelle ignored his attempt to lessen the guilt tearing apart her spirit. "She could've been killed, Frank. I almost got my own niece killed. It's funny the lies we tell ourselves, the justification, the…sacrifices we make."

Frank frowned.

"My niece, my nine-year old niece, had her right arm amputated at the elbow. And I'm happy about it because it's better than the alternative." Michelle chuckled without mirth. "Thank God, I don't have my own kids. Shit, I don't even have a dog."

As Frank drove north on Beachwood Drive, the landscape and thick shrubbery of Griffith Park on his right, he couldn't hold back. "Wadkins?"

Michelle remained silent.

"I need to know."

"Need to know what?"

"The hospital cameras showed Charlotte walking into his room at the same time Officer Chang left his post to be replaced by Officer Zamora. An hour later, they caught someone else entering the room also." Frank studied his partner.

Michelle kept her gaze forward, not meeting his eyes.

"Nondescript clothes, Dodgers cap pulled low, probably about five-four."

"Okay, and?"

"Any thoughts who that could be?" Frank's tone bordered on accusatory.

"None."

"So Charlotte smothered Troy Wadkins with a pillow."

"Is that a question or a statement, Detective Grace?"

Surprised by his partner using his title, he replied, "You tell me."

"Charlotte was pretty fit and Wadkins was injured and handcuffed."

Frank gave her a look. "How'd you know he was handcuffed?"

Michelle hesitated, her chin trembled. "I'm assuming. I mean, he was in custody, right? Why wouldn't he be?"

"Or it took one person to smother him and a second person to hold him down."

Michelle now did look at her partner. "Charlotte smothered him and now she's dead, likely killed by her husband. So I guess we'll never know."

"Is *that* a question or a statement, Detective?" Frank now said.

"Let it go, Frank."

"I need to know, Michelle. Were you there? Was that you in the room with Charlotte?"

As if she'd never before seen Griffith Park, Michelle seemed mesmerized by the landscape. "Does it matter? The son of a bitch had blood on his hands. Elijah Leach, Xavier Leach, Lyman the limo driver, and who knows how many others? And almost my niece."

"Did you murder Troy Wadkins, Michelle?"

"That fucker got what he deserved," Michelle growled.

Frank took his hands off the wheel, opened his palms. "We are partners. And friends. I need to know."

"Yes, we are. So, why does it matter?"

"I think I have a right to know."

Michelle pursed her lips as Frank maneuvered the car between numerous police cruisers, forensics vans, and a transport from the coroner's office. "We have a new case now. That's old news."

Frank knew her well. Partners needed to be in synch and share an unbreakable bond. He felt in his heart Michelle had been involved and knew in his soul she was the one in the room with Charlotte Kent. He just wanted to know *she* trusted *him* enough to come clean. Softly, he asked, "Are you guilty, Michelle?"

Sophia. "I'm guilty of a lot." Michelle exited the car, leaving Frank without an answer.

Frank watched her advance toward the crime scene. Michelle was correct. Either she was the one responsible for taking Wadkins's life or she stood by and watched Charlotte do it. Either way, she wasn't innocent. *But who really is?* Frank preferred black and white movies where the lines between good and evil were distinct, separate, and less blurred. He detested the gray areas. Yet, his entire world was a gray area. Life was a gray area.

Frank and Michelle presented their badges to a uniformed cop and signed their names into the logbook. They put on latex gloves, slipped booties around their shoes, and moved beneath the crime scene tape. Off to the side, an older man dressed in hiking attire was being questioned about finding the murdered victim. Frank and Michelle traipsed deeper into the thicket toward the corpse.

Forty yards farther, a quartet of officers hovered close to the body bag. Forensics was on the scene, closely analyzing one high-heeled shoe and a woman's pair of panties. A patrolman, looking about half Frank's age, read notes he'd scribbled on a pad.

Frank listened half-heartedly. At the outset of an investigation, he always became filled with emptiness. Bitterness, too. The snuffing out of a life over something trivial—rage, revenge, money, passion—was always pointless. As he squatted down, pangs of guilt coursed through his veins. In a way, he was glad this case would be less personal, not hitting close to home. He and his partner would investigate the murder of some unknown faceless person.

Frank leisurely unzipped the bag. When seeing the pale expressionless face and lifeless eyes focused on nothing, his shoulders dropped. So much for not hitting close to home. "Oh, God."

Noticing the change in her partner's body language, Michelle took a knee. "You know her?"

Before Frank could answer, a commotion erupted behind them. A man raced through the shrubbery, avoiding outstretched arms, crying and screaming. "Josefina! Josefina!"

Frank stood, wrapped Santiago Mendes in a bear hug, and whispered, "I'm sorry, Sandy."

Three words.

Sandy Mendes wrestled free, paying no attention and not recognizing the detective who'd held him. He couldn't pull his eyes from a black shroud that contained his little girl. He threw himself onto the ground and began rocking her rigid unresponsive small body. He screamed her name repeatedly, his words echoing through the woods as if, with enough fervor, he could bring her back. Santiago Mendes, the man who saved Frank's daughter, bawled like a dying animal holding the body of his own daughter.

As an officer chastised the frenzied father about contaminating the area and tried to pull him off, Frank lumbered away. He walked through heavy brush and came upon a clearing that afforded a spectacular view of the city in the valley below. From this vantage point, the city sparkled.

He didn't flinch at the familiar touch of his partner. "Josefina Mendes. I know her," he said. "She was...the morning of the bomb, I...she just wanted to fit in. Fourteen. She's just fourteen, Michelle. Two years older than Ashley."

Frank fished into his pocket, retrieved his cell, and began punching in his daughter's cell to...well, just to talk with her.

Michelle placed her hand over the phone. "It's Saturday. Be a dad, not a detective."

Frank gulped and looked at his partner with confusion. "Fourteen. Why? What's the point?"

Knowing there was no sensible answer and realizing she once again had nothing else in her life, Michelle said, "Go home, Frank. Spend time with your family. I've got your back."

Frank presented a small smile that displayed his appreciation. With the conversation they concluded moments earlier on the ride over still fresh, he said, "And I've got yours."

About the Author

From his earliest memories, Rob Silverman had two dreams. One was to play Right Field in the majors, the other was to become a published author. Well, he ended up batting .500.

His first foray into writing came in 2008 when he started blogging for a popular website. An avid reader, he spends his spare time yelling at the TV during the baseball season, listening to Bruce Springsteen and classic rock from the '80s, re-watching all six seasons of *LOST*, or waiting for one of his two spoiled dogs to get out of his favorite chair so he can sit down.

Feel free to check out his website:
http://www.robsilvermanbooks.com/

And to follow him on Facebook:
https://www.facebook.com/Rob-Silverman-author-377042895829631/

www.ingramcontent.com/pod-product-compliance
Lightning Source LLC
Chambersburg PA
CBHW070759120726
47910CB00001B/224